THAT
MAINWARING
AFFAIR

Maynard Barbour

That Mainwaring Affair

Maynard Barbour

© 1st World Library, 2006
PO Box 2211
Fairfield, IA 52556
www.1stworldlibrary.com
First Edition

LCCN: 2006938093

Softcover ISBN: 978-1-4218-3387-3
Hardcover ISBN: 978-1-4218-3287-6
eBook ISBN: 978-1-4218-3487-0

Purchase *"That Mainwaring Affair"*
as a traditional bound book at:
www.1stWorldLibrary.com/purchase.asp?ISBN=978-1-4218-3387-3

1st World Library is a literary, educational organization
dedicated to:

- Creating a free internet library of downloadable ebooks

- Hosting writing competitions and offering book
  publishing scholarships.

Interested in more 1st World Library books?
contact: literacy@1stworldlibrary.com
Check us out at: www.1stworldlibrary.com

1st World Library Literary Society

Giving Back to the World

"If you want to work on the core problem, it's early school literacy."

- James Barksdale, former CEO of Netscape

"No skill is more crucial to the future of a child, or to a democratic and prosperous society, than literacy."

-Los Angeles Times

Literacy... means far more than learning how to read and write... The aim is to transmit... knowledge and promote social participation."

- UNESCO

"Literacy is not a luxury, it is a right and a responsibility. If our world is to meet the challenges of the twenty-first century we must harness the energy and creativity of all our citizens."

- President Bill Clinton

"Parents should be encouraged to read to their children, and teachers should be equipped with all available techniques for teaching literacy, so the varying needs and capacities of individual kids can be taken into account."

- Hugh Mackay

CHAPTER I

THE MAINWARINGS

The fierce sunlight of a sultry afternoon in the early part of July forced its way through every crevice and cranny of the closely drawn shutters in the luxurious private offices of Mainwaring & Co., Stock Brokers, and slender shafts of light, darting here and there, lent a rich glow of color to the otherwise subdued tones of the elegant apartments.

A glance at the four occupants of one of these rooms, who had disposed themselves in various attitudes according to their individual inclinations, revealed the fact that three out of the four were Englishmen, while the fourth might have been denominated as a typical American from the professional class. Of rather slender form, with a face of rare sensitiveness and delicacy, and restless, penetrating eyes, his every movement indicated energy and alertness. On the present occasion he had little to say, but was engaged in listening attentively to the conversation of the others.

Beside a rosewood desk, whose belongings, arranged with mathematical precision, indicated the methodical business habits of its owner, sat Hugh Mainwaring, senior member of the firm of Mainwaring & Co., a man approaching his fiftieth birthday. His dress and manners, less pronouncedly English than those of the remaining two, betokened the polished man of the world as well as the shrewd financier. He wore an elegant business suit and his linen was immaculate; his hair, dark and slightly tinged with gray, was closely cut; his smoothly shaven face, less florid than those of his companions, was particularly noticeable on account of a pair of dark gray eyes, cold and calculating, and which had at times a steel-like glitter. Though an attractive face, it was not altogether pleasing; it was too sensuous, and indicated stubbornness and self-will rather than firmness or strength.

Half reclining upon a couch on the opposite side of the room, in an attitude more comfortable than graceful, leisurely smoking a fine Havana, was Ralph Mainwaring, of London, a cousin of the New York broker, who, at the invitation of the latter, was paying his first visit to the great western metropolis. Between the two cousins there were few points of resemblance. Both had the same cold, calculating gaze, which made one, subjected to its scrutiny, feel that he was being mentally weighed and measured and would, in all probability, be found lacking; but the Londoner possessed a more phlegmatic temperament. A year or two his cousin's junior, he looked considerably younger; as his hair and heavy English side whiskers were unmixed with gray and he was inclined to stoutness.

Seated near him, in an immense arm-chair which he filled admirably, was William Mainwaring Thornton, of London, also a guest of Hugh Mainwaring and distantly connected with the two cousins. He was the youngest of the three Englishmen and the embodiment of geniality. He was a blond of the purest type, and his beard, parted in the centre, was brushed back in two wavy, silken masses, while his clear blue eyes, beaming with kindliness and good-humor, had the frankness of a child's.

Hugh Mainwaring, the sole heir to the family estate, soon after the death of his father, some twenty-five years previous to this time, became weary of the monotony of his English homelife, and, resolved upon making his permanent home in one of the large eastern cities of the United States and embarking upon the uncertain and treacherous seas of speculation in the western world, had sold the estate which for a number of generations had been in the possession of the Mainwarings, and had come to America. In addition to his heavy capital, he had invested a large amount of keen business tact and ability; his venture had met with almost phenomenal success and he had acquired immense wealth besides his inherited fortune.

His more conservative cousin, Ralph Mainwaring, while never quite forgiving him for having disposed of the estate, had, nevertheless, with the shrewdness and foresight for which his family were noted, given to his only son the name of Hugh Mainwaring, confident that his American-English cousin would never marry, and hoping thereby to win back the old Mainwaring estate into his own line of the family. His bit of strategy had succeeded; and now, after more than twenty years, his foresight and worldly wisdom were about to be rewarded, for the occasion of this reunion between the long-separated cousins was the celebration of the rapidly approaching fiftieth birthday of Hugh Mainwaring, at which time Hugh Mainwaring, Jr., would attain his majority, and in recognition of that happy event the New York millionaire broker had announced his intention of making his will in favor of his namesake, and on that day formally declaring him his lawful heir.

This had been the object of the conference in the private office of Hugh Mainwaring, and now that it was over and all necessary arrangements had been made, that gentleman turned from his desk with a sigh of relief.

"I am heartily glad that this business is over," he said, addressing his guests; "it has been on my mind for some time, and I have consulted with Mr. Whitney about it," with a slight nod towards the fourth gentleman, who was his attorney and legal adviser. "We have both felt that it should have been attended to before this; and yet, as I considered this would be the most fitting time to make a final adjustment of affairs, I have on that account delayed longer than I otherwise would have done. Now everything is arranged in a manner satisfactory, I trust, to all parties immediately concerned, and nothing remains but to draw up and execute the papers, which will be done to-morrow."

"You are not then troubled with any unpleasant superstitions regarding the making of a will?" commented Mr. Thornton.

"No," replied the other, slowly. "I am not of the opinion that it will hasten my exit from this world; but even if it did, I would have the satisfaction of knowing that my own wishes would be carried out in the settlement of my estate, and that no one would derive any benefit from my demise excepting those whom I consider legally entitled thereto."

Ralph Mainwaring looked curiously at his cousin through half-closed eyes.

"I suppose," he remarked, very deliberately, "that even in case there were no will the property would revert to our branch of the family; we are the nearest of kin, you know."

"Yes, I know your family would be considered the lawful heirs," Hugh Mainwaring replied, while he and Mr. Whitney exchanged glances; "but this is not England; here any common adventurer might come forward with some pretended claim against the estate, and I prefer to see affairs definitely settled in my own way."

"Of course," responded the other, resuming his cigar. "Well, speaking for myself, I am more than willing to relinquish any share I might have had for the boy's sake, and I don't suppose, Thornton, that you have any objections to raise on Edith's account."

"Oh, no, no," replied that gentleman, with a pleasant laugh." I never considered Hugh a bad son-in-law to begin with, but I'll admit he is a little more attractive now than ever."

The little clock on the marble mantel chimed the hour of four, causing a general movement of surprise. "'Pon my soul! had no idea it was that late," exclaimed Mr. Thornton, taking out his watch, while Hugh Mainwaring, touching an electric button, replied,- "This business has detained us much longer than I anticipated. I will give some instructions to the head clerk, and we will leave at once."

He had scarcely finished speaking, when a door opened noiselessly and a middle-aged man appeared.

"Parsons," said Mr. Mainwaring, addressing him in quick, incisive tones, "I am going out to Fair Oaks, and probably shall not be at the office for two or three days, unless something of unusual importance should demand my presence. Refer all business callers to Mr. Elliott or Mr. Chittenden. Any personal calls, if specially important, just say that I can be found at Fair Oaks."

Parsons bowed gravely, and after a few further instructions retired.

"Now, Mr. Whitney," Hugh Mainwaring continued, at the same time touching another electric button, "you, of course, will be one of our party at Fair Oaks; my secretary will accompany us, and the papers will be drawn up to-morrow in my private library, after which you will do us the honor to join us in the pleasures of the following day."

"I am at your service, Mr. Mainwaring," responded the attorney; "but," he added, in low tones, intended only for Hugh Mainwaring's ear, but which were heard distinctly by the private secretary, now standing beside the desk, "would it not be better to draw up the will here, in your private office? My presence at the house on the present occasion might attract attention and arouse some suspicions as to your intentions."

"That makes no difference," replied Hugh Mainwaring, quickly, but also speaking in a low tone; "my private papers are all at the house, and I choose that this business shall be conducted there. I believe that I am master in my own house yet."

Mr. Whitney bowed in acquiescence, and Hugh Mainwaring turned to his secretary,-

"Mr. Scott, just close up everything in the office as quickly as possible and get ready to accompany me to Fair Oaks; I shall need you there for two or three days."

It was not the first time the private secretary had accompanied Mr. Mainwaring to his elegant suburban residence, and he understood perfectly what was expected of him, and immediately withdrew to make his preparations as expeditiously as possible.

For some reason, which Hugh Mainwaring had never stopped to explain even to himself, he always accorded to his private secretary much more respect and consideration than to any one of his other numerous employees.

Harry Scott was not only a young man of superior education and good breeding, but what particularly impressed his employer in his favor was a certain natural reserve which caused him to hold himself aloof from his associates in the offices of Mainwaring & Co., and an innate refinement and delicacy which kept him, under all circumstances, from any gaucherie on the one hand, or undue familiarity on the other; he was always respectful but never servile. He had been in the employ of Hugh Mainwaring for a little more than a year, and, having frequently accompanied him to Fair Oaks to remain for a day or two, was, consequently, quite familiar with the house and grounds.

As he re-entered the room, having exchanged his business suit for one more suitable to the occasion, there was not one present but what instinctively, though perhaps unconsciously, recognized in him a true gentleman and treated him as such. Tall, with a splendid physique, finely shaped head, dark hair, and eyes of peculiar beauty, he was far from being the least attractive member of the party which, a few moments later, entered the Mainwaring carriage, with its coat of arms, and rolled away in the direction of Fair Oaks.

CHAPTER II

FAIR OAKS

The home of Hugh Mainwaring was one of many palatial suburban residences situated on a beautiful avenue running in a northerly direction from the city, but it had not been for so many years in his possession without acquiring some of the characteristics of its owner, which gave it an individuality quite distinct from its elegant neighbors. It had originally belonged to one of the oldest and wealthiest families in the county, for a strictly modern house, without a vestige of antiqueness lingering in its halls and with no faint aroma of bygone days pervading its atmosphere, would have been entirely too plebeian to suit the tastes of Hugh Mainwaring.

From the street to the main entrance a broad driveway wound beneath the interlacing boughs of a double line of giant oaks, from which the place had derived its name. Beautiful grounds extended in every direction, and in the rear of the mansion sloped gently to the edge of a small lake. Facing the west was the main entrance to the house, which was nearly surrounded by a broad veranda, commanding a fine view, not only of the grounds and immediately surrounding country, but also of the Hudson River, not far distant.

The southwestern portion of the building contained the private rooms of Hugh Mainwaring, including what was known as the "tower," and had been added by him soon after he had taken possession of the place. This part of the house

Maynard Barbour

was as far removed as possible from the large reception-rooms, and the apartments on the second floor comprised the suite occupied by Mr. Mainwaring. The first of these rooms, semi-octagonal in form, constituted his private library, and its elegant furnishings and costly volumes, lining the walls from floor to ceiling, bespoke the wealth and taste of the owner. Across the southwestern side of this room heavy portieres partially concealed the entrance to what Mr. Mainwaring denominated his "sanctum sanctorum," the room in the tower. This was small, of circular form, and contained an immense desk, one or two revolving bookcases, and a large safe, which held his private papers and, it was rumored, the old Mainwaring jewels. Back of the library was a smoking-room, and in the rear of that Mr. Mainwaring's dressing-rooms and sleeping apartments.

This suite of rooms was connected with the remainder of the building by a long corridor extending from the main hall, but there was on the south side of the house an entrance and stairway leading directly to these rooms, the upper hall opening into the library and smoking-room. From this southern entrance a gravelled walk led between lines of shrubbery to a fine grove, which extended back and downward to the western shore of the small lake already mentioned.

But the especially distinguishing characteristic of Fair Oaks since coming into the possession of Hugh Mainwaring was the general air of exclusion pervading the entire place. The servants, with the exception of "Uncle Mose," the colored man having charge of the grounds, were imported,-the head cook being a Frenchman, the others either English or Irish, and, from butler to chambermaid, one and all seemed to have acquired the reserve which characterized their employer.

Comparatively few servants were employed and few were needed, for never, until the present occasion, had Fair Oaks been thrown open to guests. Occasionally Mr. Mainwaring brought out from the city two or three gentleman friends, whom he entertained in royal fashion. Sometimes these guests were accompanied by their wives, but such instances were extremely rare, as ladies were seldom seen at Fair Oaks.

In the entertainment of these occasional guests Mr. Mainwaring was frequently assisted by Mrs. LaGrange, known as his housekeeper, but in reality holding a position much more advanced than is usually implied by that term. Among those who had been personally entertained by Mrs. LaGrange, this fact, of itself, excited little comment; it being evident that she was as familiar with the fashionable world as was their host himself, but surrounding her was the same dim haze of mystery that seemed to envelop the entire place, impalpable, but thus far impenetrable.

She had come to Fair Oaks some fifteen years previous to this time, dressed in deep mourning, accompanied by her infant son, about three years of age, and it was generally understood that she was distantly related to Mr. Mainwaring. She was a strikingly handsome woman, with that type of physical beauty which commands admiration, rather than winning it; tall, with superb form and carriage, rich olive skin, large dark eyes, brilliant as diamonds and as cold, but which could become luminous with tenderness or fiery with passion, as occasion required. To those whom she sought to entertain she could be extremely charming, but to a few even of these, gifted with deeper insight than the others, it seemed that beneath that fascinating manner was a dangerous nature, a will that would brook no restraint, that never would be thwarted; and that this was, in reality, the power which dominated Fair Oaks.

After years of mysterious seclusion, however, the beautiful home of Hugh Mainwaring, while maintaining its usual reserve towards its neighbors, had thrown open its doors to guests from across the water; and on the particular afternoon of the conference in the private offices of Mainwaring & Co., there might have been seen on one of the upper balconies of the mansion at Fair Oaks a group of five English ladies, engaged in a discussion of their first impressions regarding their host and his American home. The group consisted of

Mrs. Ralph Mainwaring and her daughter Isabel; Miss Edith Thornton, the daughter of William Mainwaring Thornton and the fiancee of Hugh Mainwaring, Jr.; Miss Winifred Carleton, a cousin of Miss Thornton; and Mrs. Hogarth, the chaperone of the last named young ladies.

Understanding, as they did, the occasion of this their first visit to the western world, and being personally interested in the happy event so soon to be celebrated, they naturally felt great interest in their new surroundings. The young ladies were especially enthusiastic in their expressions of admiration of the house and grounds, while Mrs. Mainwaring, of even more phlegmatic temperament than her husband, remarked that it was a fine old place, really much finer than she expected to see, which was quite an admission on her part.

"It is just as lovely as it can be!" said Winifred Carleton, coming from the railing, where she had been watching the broad expanse of ocean visible in the distance, and seating herself on a divan beside her cousin. "I do think, Edith, you are the most fortunate girl in the world, and I congratulate you with all my heart."

"Thank you, Winnie," replied Miss Thornton, a pronounced blonde like her father, with large, childlike blue eyes; "but it will be yours to enjoy as much as mine, for you will always be with me; at least, till you are married, you know."

"That is a very reckless declaration on your part, for I am likely never to marry," responded Miss Carleton, lightly. She was an orphan and an heiress, but had a home in the family of William Mainwaring Thornton, who was her uncle and guardian.

Isabel Mainwaring, reclining in a hammock near Miss Thornton, smiled languidly. She was tall, with dark hair and the Mainwaring cold, gray eyes. "You seem to ignore the fact," she said, "that our cousin is likely to live in the exclusive enjoyment of his home for many years to come."

"You mercenary Wretch!" retorted Miss Carleton; "are you already counting the years before Mr. Mainwaring's death?"

"Isabel, I am shocked!" exclaimed Mrs. Mainwaring.

"I don't know why," replied that young lady, coolly. "I was only thinking, mamma; and one is not always accountable for one's thoughts, you know."

"But," said Miss Thornton, wonderingly, raising her large eyes, full of inquiry, to Mrs. Mainwaring, "after our cousin has announced his intention of making Hugh his heir, don't you think he will be likely to extend other invitations to visit Fair Oaks?"

"Undoubtedly, my dear," replied Mrs. Mainwaring, "there will probably be an exchange of courtesies between the two branches of the family from this time. Though I must say," she added, in a lower tone, and turning to Mrs. Hogarth, "I do not know that I, for one, will be particularly anxious to repeat my visit when this celebration is once over. So far as I can judge, there seems to be no society here. Wilson has learned from the servants that Mr. Mainwaring lives very quietly, in fact, receives no company whatever; and, I may be mistaken, but it certainly seems to me that this Mrs. LaGrange occupies rather an anomalous position. She is here as his housekeeper, a servant, yet she entertains his guests, and her manners are anything but those of a servant."

"Why shouldn't she, mamma?" inquired Isabel, rather abruptly."Cousin Hugh has never married,-which is a very good thing for us, by the way,-and who would help him entertain if his housekeeper did not?"

"It is not her position to which I object so much," remarked Mrs. Hogarth, quietly, "though I admit it seems rather peculiar, but there is something about her own personality that impresses me very unfavorably."

"In your opinion, then, she is not a proper person," said Mrs.Mainwaring, who was fond of jumping at conclusions; "well, I quite agree with you."

"No, " said Mrs. Hogarth, with a smile, "I have not yet formed so decided an opinion as that. I am not prepared to say that she is a bad woman, but I believe she is a very dangerous woman."

"Dear Mrs. Hogarth, how mercilessly you always scatter my fancies to the winds!" exclaimed Miss Thornton; "until this moment I admired Mrs. LaGrange very much."

"I did not," said Miss Carleton, quickly; "from my first glimpse of her she has seemed to me like a malign presence about the place, a veritable serpent in this beautiful Eden!"

"Well," said Isabel Mainwaring, with a slight shrug, "I see no reason for any concern regarding Mrs. LaGrange, whatever she may be. I don't suppose she will be entailed upon Hugh with the property; and I only hope that before long we can buy back the old Mainwaring estate into our own branch of the family."

"That is just What your father intends to have done whenever the property comes into Hugh's possession," replied Mrs. Mainwaring, and was about to say something further, when a musical whistle attracted the attention of the ladies, and, looking over the balcony railing, they saw Hugh Mainwaring, Jr., approaching the house, on his return from a day's fishing, accompanied by Walter LaGrange, a young sophomore, home on his vacation.

The former was a typical young Englishman, with a frank, pleasant countenance. The latter, while inheriting his mother's beauty and resembling her in a marked degree, yet betrayed in his face a weakness which indicated that, lacking ability to plan and execute for himself, he would become a ready tool to aid in carrying out the designs of others.

The ladies, having discovered the hour to be much later than they supposed, and knowing that the gentlemen would soon return from the city, speedily adjourned to their dressing-rooms to prepare for dinner.

CHAPTER III

THE LAST WILL AND TESTAMENT
OF HUGH MAINWARING

Immediately after breakfast the following morning, Hugh Mainwaring, having excused himself to his guests, retired to his private library, in company with his secretary and Mr. Whitney, his attorney. A number of fine saddle horses having been brought around from the stables, the young people cantered gayly down the oak-lined avenue, intent upon a morning ride, their voices echoing musically through the grounds. The elderly people, after a short chat, gradually dispersed. Mrs. Mainwaring retired to her room for her accustomed morning nap; Mrs. Hogarth sought the large library and was soon absorbed in the works of her favorite author, while Ralph Mainwaring and Mr. Thornton strolled up and down the gravelled walks, enjoying their cigars.

"This is a very good bit of property," remarked Mr. Mainwaring at length, running his eye with cold scrutiny over the mansion and grounds; "taking into consideration the stocks and bonds and various business interests that will go with it, it will make a fine windfall for the boy."

That it will, and Hugh certainly is a lucky dog!" responded Mr. Thornton; "but you seem to have some definite knowledge regarding our cousin's finances; has he given you any idea as to what he is really worth?"

"He? Not a word." Then noting an expression of surprise on his companion's face, Mr. Mainwaring continued. "I have a number of business acquaintances on this side the water, and you may rest assured I have kept myself well posted as to the way things were going all these years. I have had something of this kind in view all the time."

"I might have known it," replied Mr. Thornton, with an amused smile. "I never yet saw a Mainwaring who did not understand how to feather his own nest. Well, as you say, it is a fine piece of property; but, do you know, Mainwaring, it strikes me that the old boy seems a bit anxious to get it disposed of according to his own liking as quickly as possible."

"It does look that way," the other acknowledged.

"Well, now, doesn't that seem a little peculiar, when, with no direct heirs that we know of, the property would in any case revert to your family?"

Ralph Mainwaring puffed in silence for a few moments, then removing his cigar and slowing knocking off the ashes, he replied very deliberately,-

"It is my opinion that he and that attorney of his are aware of some possible claimants, of whom we know nothing."

"That is my idea exactly," said Mr. Thornton; "and, don't you know, it has occurred to me that possibly, unknown to us, Harold Mainwaring may have left a child, whose existence is known to Hugh."

"That would cut no figure in this case, " Mr. Mainwaring answered, quickly. "Even had there been a living child, - which there was not, - he could make no claim whatever, for Harold was disinherited by his father's will."

"Yes, I know the old gentleman disinherited Harold, but would his heirs have no claim?"

Maynard Barbour

"Not under that will. I was present when it was read, and I remember it debarred 'both him and his heirs, forever.'"

"Poor Harold!" said Mr. Thornton, after a moment's silence; "he was the elder son, was he not?"

"Yes, and his father's favorite. It broke the old man's heart to disinherit him. He failed rapidly after that occurred, and he never was the same towards Hugh. I always thought that accounted for Hugh's selling the old place as he did; it had too many unpleasant memories.

"Harold died soon after that unfortunate marriage, I believe."

"Yes; he learned too late the character of the woman he had married, and after the death of their only child, he left her, and a few years later was lost at sea."

"Well," continued Mr. Thornton, after a pause, "have you the remotest idea as to who these possible claimants against the property may be?"

"Only the merest suspicion, as yet too vague even to mention; but I think a day or two will probably enable me to determine whether I am correct or not."

At that moment, Harry Scott, the private secretary, appeared, with a message to the gentlemen from Hugh Mainwaring, to the effect that he would like to have them join himself and Mr. Whitney in his library.

As they passed around to the southern entrance with the secretary, they did not observe a closed carriage coming swiftly up the driveway, nor a tall, slender man, with cadaverous features and sharp, peering eyes, who alighted and hastily rang for admittance. But two hours later, as Mr. Thornton was descending the winding stairway in the main hall, he caught a glimpse of the strange caller, just taking his departure. The stranger, hearing footsteps, turned towards Mr. Thornton, and for an instant their eyes met. There was a mutual recognition; astonishment and scorn were written on Mr. Thornton's face, while the stranger cowed visibly and, with a fawning, cringing bow, made as speedy an exit as possible.

At luncheon that day both Hugh Mainwaring and a number of his guests seemed rather preoccupied, and the meal passed in unusual silence. Mrs. LaGrange exerted herself to be particularly entertaining to Mr. Whitney, but he, though courteously responding to her overtures, made no effort to continue the conversation. Even the genial Mr. Thornton was in so abstracted a mood that his daughter at last rallied him on his appearance, whereupon he turned somewhat abruptly to his host with the inquiry,-

"Are you personally acquainted with Richard Hobson?"

For an instant, Hugh Mainwaring seemed confused, and Mr. Whitney, always on the alert, noted a peculiar expression flash across the face of Mrs. LaGrange, and was also conscious of an almost imperceptible start on the part of the young secretary seated near him.

Mr. Mainwaring quickly recovered himself and replied, deliberately, "Richard Hobson, the attorney? I believe I met him once or twice, years ago, in London, but I cannot claim any acquaintance with him."

"Dick Hobson does not deserve the name of attorney," remarked Ralph Mainwaring; "he is a shyster and a scoundrel."

"He certainly bears a hard reputation," rejoined Mr. Thornton; "and I would not have mentioned his name, only that I met him here about half an hour since, and that caused me to make the inquiry I did."

Hugh Mainwaring paled visibly, though he remained calm. "Met him here, in my house? Impossible!" he exclaimed, at the same time glancing towards the butler, but the face of that functionary was as immobile as rock. "I did not suppose the man was in this country!"

"Oh, yes," replied Ralph Mainwaring; "he left England about two years ago; he played one too many of his dirty games there and took the first steamer for America, hoping, I suppose, to find a wider sphere of action in this country."

"Possibly I may have been mistaken," remarked Mr. Thornton, quietly, realizing that he had unconsciously touched an unpleasant chord, "but the resemblance was certainly striking."

An awkward silence followed, broken by young Scott, who excused himself on the plea of important work and returned to Mr. Mainwaring's library, where he was soon joined by all the gentlemen excepting young Mainwaring. In the hall, Hugh Mainwaring paused for a few words with the butler, and the attorney, passing at that moment, caught the man's reply, given in a low tone,-

"No, sir; Mrs. LaGrange."

A little later, the last will and testament of Hugh Mainwaring was signed by the testator, and duly attested by Ralph Mainwaring, William Mainwaring Thornton, and William H. Whitney. As the last signature was completed, Hugh Mainwaring drew a heavy sigh, saying in a low tone,-

"That is as I wished, my namesake is my heir;" then taking the document, he placed it in the hands of his secretary, adding, "Lay this for the present on my desk. To-morrow I wish it to be read in the presence of all the members of the family, after which, Mr. Whitney, I desire to have it put in your possession for safe keeping until it is needed; when that will be, no one can say; - it may be sooner than we think."

A marked change had come over his manner since luncheon, and his tones, even more than his words, made a deep impression on the mind of every one present. The shade of melancholy passed, however, and, ringing the bell, Hugh Mainwaring ordered carriages for himself and his guests for the afternoon and departed, leaving his secretary to attend to some private work in the library. Harry Scott's manner, upon finding himself alone within the private rooms of Hugh Mainwaring, betrayed intense excitement. He pushed his work impatiently from him and, rising, began to walk swiftly, though noiselessly, back and forth, the entire length of the two apartments. Twice he paused before the large desk, and taking therefrom the will, already familiar to him, read its contents with burning eyes while his face alternately flushed and paled. Then folding and replacing the document, he turned towards the safe, muttering,-"It is no use. I have searched there once before and could find nothing."

Suddenly he exclaimed, "No one knows what may happen; this may be my last opportunity! I will search once more and leave not a corner unexplored."

Having locked the library, he returned to the safe. He knew the combination, and soon the great doors swung open, revealing the contents arranged with the precision for which Mr. Mainwaring was noted in his business habits. Conscious that he had abundance of time for the work he had undertaken and that he was secure from interruption, he began a careful and methodical search through all the compartments. Various private documents were examined and then replaced in exactly their original position, but all seemed of no avail. He discovered no trace of that which he hoped to find.

At last he came to a metallic box, which he surmised, from its weight and general appearance, contained the old family jewels. Should he open that? A moment's thought decided the question; he would leave nothing unexplored. Further search revealed the key concealed in a tiny drawer. He applied it to the lock; the cover flew backward, and a dazzling light flashed into his face as a ray of sunlight fell across his shoulder upon the superb gems, gleaming and scintillating from the depths of their hiding-place. But he paid little heed to them, for, in a

Maynard Barbour

long and narrow receptacle within one side of the box, his keen eye had discovered a paper, yellow and musty with age, the sight of which thrilled him with hope. He quickly drew it forth, and a single glance at its title assured him it was indeed the object of his search. With a low cry of joy, he locked and replaced the metallic box, and, opening the ancient document, he eagerly scanned its contents, an expression of intense satisfaction overspreading his features.

He was still perusing the paper when he heard footsteps approaching the library through the long corridor, followed an instant later by a knock. Depositing the precious document safely within an inside pocket, he swung the doors of the safe together, turning the handle so as to lock it securely, and, crossing the library, unlocked and opened the door.

The butler was standing there, and, handing Scott a card, said, briefly,

"A gentleman on private business; must see Mr. Mainwaring or his secretary at once."

Scott glanced at the card: it bore the name of "J. Henry Carruthers," with a London address, and underneath had been hastily pencilled the word "Important."

"Show the gentleman up," he said. The butler bowed and was gone, and in an incredibly short time, while yet Scott's pulse throbbed wildly from his recent discovery, the stranger entered the room.

He was a little above the average height, with a somewhat commanding presence, rather pale face, dark moustache, and black curling hair. He wore dark glasses, and was dressed in a tweed suit, slightly travel-worn, but his manners were those of a gentleman.

"Mr. Scott, I believe," he said, addressing the secretary.

"That is my name, sir; please be seated. What can I do for you, Mr. Carruthers?"

"Will you inform me, Mr. Scott, of the earliest hour at which I can see Mr. Mainwaring? I called at his city office and was directed here; but the butler states that Mr. Mainwaring is away from home, and is unable to say when he will return, or how soon he would be at liberty to see me."

"Mr. Mainwaring will probably return about five o'clock; but it is rather difficult for me to state when you could see him, as he is entertaining a number of guests, and it is doubtful if he would care to attend to any business just at this time, unless it were of special importance."

"My business with Mr. Mainwaring is of special importance," replied the other; "and I would be very glad if he could give me a little time to-morrow."

"Perhaps, if you would give me some intimation of its nature," Scott suggested, "Mr. Mainwaring might consent to make an appointment for the following day. I hardly think he would see you sooner. To-morrow is his birthday, and, as it is to be celebrated by him and his guests, it is doubtful whether he would attend to any business on that day."

"Indeed!" said Mr. Carruthers, rising, while Scott was conscious of a peculiar scrutiny fixed upon himself from behind those dark glasses; "it had escaped my mind, but now I recall that Mr. Mainwaring is to celebrate his birthday by making his young English cousin and namesake his heir. I certainly would not intrude at a time so inopportune."

The secretary started. "I was not aware that Mr. Mainwaring's intentions were generally known," he remarked.

"Perhaps not," replied the other, in a peculiar tone. "I merely heard it mentioned, and all parties have my congratulations and best wishes. Kindly say to Mr. Mainwaring that when the happy event is over I hope he will give me his earliest consideration. My address for the present will be the Arlington House.. Do not take the trouble to ring, I can find my way."

"You will find this way much shorter, sir, " Scott replied, opening the door into the southern hall. Mr. Carruthers thanked him and, with a profound bow, took his departure.

As the hour was late, Scott found it necessary to devote himself at once to his work, and he had but just completed it when the sound of wheels was heard outside, and a few moments later his employer entered the room.

The latter studied Mr. Carruthers's card quite attentively, and frowned upon learning that his intentions regarding the making of his will had become known by outsiders, but he soon seemed to forget the occurrence. Soon all were gathered about the dinner-table, and the evening passed very pleasantly.

When, at a late hour, Hugh Mainwaring, in the dimly-lighted veranda, bade his guests good-night, he grasped the hand of his namesake and said, in a tone remarkably tender,-

"Hugh, my boy, the distance is long between the twenty-first and the fiftieth mile-stones on the journey of life. Heaven grant, when you shall have reached the latter, you may look back over a brighter pathway than I do to-night!"

Then, as the young man passed, he murmured to himself "If I could but have had just such a son as he!"

He did not see, though there was one who did, a woman's form glide away in the dim light, her eyes gleaming with malignant fire.

CHAPTER IV

A TERRIBLE AWAKENING

For some time after his guests had retired, Hugh Mainwaring remained outside, walking up and down in the starlight, apparently absorbed in thought. When at length he passed into the house, he met his secretary coming out for a solitary smoke.

"Come to my library, Mr. Scott, before you retire for the night," said Mr. Mainwaring.

"At once, sir, if you wish, " the secretary replied.

"No, there is no hurry; any time within an hour," and he passed up-stairs.

Half an hour later Harry Scott passed down the corridor towards the library, but paused on hearing an angry voice within, which he at once recognized as Mrs. LaGrange's.

"Where would you be to-night?" she cried, "where would you have been all these years, if I had but exposed your dishonesty and duplicity? You defrauded your only brother during his lifetime; you have persistently ignored your son, your own flesh and blood; and now you would rob him, not only of his father's name, but of his father's fortune, - cast him off with a mere pittance, - and put this stranger in the place which is rightfully his, and wish that you had been given such a son as he! You are in my power, and you know it only too well; and I will make you and your high-born, purse-proud family rue this day's work."

Hugh Mainwaring's reply to this tirade was inaudible, and Scott, feeling that he already had heard too much, withdrew, and continued walking up and down the halls until the library door opened and Mrs. LaGrange came out. She swept past him in a towering rage, seeming scarcely aware of his presence until, as he passed down the corridor and entered the library, he was suddenly conscious that she had turned and was watching him.

He found Mr. Mainwaring looking pale and fatigued.

"I will detain you but a moment, Mr. Scott," he said, speaking wearily; "I have a few instructions I would like you to carry out early in the morning; and I also want to say that I wish you to consider yourself as one of my guests to-morrow, and join with us in the festivities of the occasion."

Scott thanked his employer courteously, though there might have been detected a shade of reserve in his manner, and, after receiving brief directions for the following day, withdrew.

He went to his room, but not to sleep. His mind was too full of the events of the day just passed, as well as of the expected events of the morrow. His thoughts reverted to his discovery of the afternoon, and, taking the shabby document from his pocket, he read and re-read it carefully, his features betraying deep emotion. What should be done with it? Should he let his employer know at once of the proof which he now held against him? Or should he hold it for a few days and await developments?

It was nearly three o'clock when he was aroused from his abstraction by a slight sound, as of stealthy footsteps in the rear of the house. He listened intently for a moment, but hearing nothing further and discovering the lateness of the hour, he hastily extinguished the light and, too exhausted and weary to undress, threw himself as he was upon a couch and was soon sleeping heavily.

The sun was shining brightly into his room, when Harry Scott was awakened the next morning by a woman's scream, followed by cries and sobs and a confused sound of running to and fro. Almost before he could collect his thoughts, be heard steps approaching his room, and, rising, hastily exchanged the smoking-jacket in which he had slept for a coat. He had barely time to make the change when there was a loud knock, and some one called his name in quick, sharp tones.

Opening the door, he saw Mr. Whitney standing before him, while in the background servants were running in different directions, wringing their bands and moaning and crying hysterically.

"Mr. Scott," said the attorney, in tones trembling with excitement, "come to the tower-room at once Mr. Mainwaring bas been murdered!"

"Mr. Mainwaring murdered!" he exclaimed, reeling for an instant as if from a blow. "Great heavens! it cannot be possible!"

"It is terrible, but a fact, nevertheless," replied Mr. Whitney; "he was murdered last night in his private rooms."

"How and when was it discovered?" Scott inquired, his mind still dazed by the wild torrent of thought surging through his brain as he recalled the events of the previous night.

"Hardy, his valet, was the first to discover it this morning. We have telephoned for his physician and for the coroner; they will be out on the next train from the city."

Harry Scott shuddered as be entered the familiar room where he had taken leave of his employer but comparatively few hours before. Even amid the confusion, he noted that in the outer room everything appeared the same as when he last saw it, but the portieres at the farther side, pushed widely open, revealed a ghastly sight.

Upon the floor, about half-way between the desk and safe, his head resting in a small pool of blood,, lay Hugh Mainwaring. He was inclined slightly towards his right side, his arm partially extended, and on the floor, near his right hand, lay a revolver, while an ugly wound just above the right eye and near the temple showed where the weapon had done its deadly work. The closely cut hair about the temple was singed and his face was blackened, showing that the fatal shot had been fired at close range. There were no indications, however, of a struggle of any kind; the great revolving-chair, usually standing in front of the desk, had been pushed aside, but everything else was in its accustomed place, and the desk was closed and locked.

Ralph Mainwaring was already kneeling beside the body; Mr. Thornton and young Mainwaring, who had entered immediately after Scott and the attorney, stood speechless with horror. With what conflicting emotions the young secretary gazed upon the lifeless form of his employer, fortunately for him at that moment, no one knew; a s his mind cleared, he began to realize that his position was likely to prove a difficult and dangerous one, and that he must act with extreme caution.

The silence was first broken by Mr. Thornton, who exclaimed, -

"Terrible! Terrible! What do you think, Mainwaring? is this murder or suicide?"

"Time alone will tell," replied Mr. Mainwaring in a low tone; "but I am inclined to think it is murder."

"Murder without a doubt!" added Mr. Whitney.

"But who could have done such a deed?" groaned Mr. Thornton.

Hugh Mainwaring was attired, as when Scott had last seen him, in a rich dressing-gown; but as the secretary knelt beside the silent form and touched the left hand lying partially hidden in its folds, he gave a slight start, and, quickly passing his hand within the dressing-gown, announced in a low tone,-

"His diamond ring and his watch are both gone!"

"Robbery!" exclaimed young Mainwaring; "that must have been the object of the murderer!" While his father, glancing towards the safe, remarked, -

"We must ascertain whether anything else is missing."

"We will make a thorough examination of the room after the coroner's arrival," said Mr. Whitney, "but, for the present, everything must remain as it is."

"Should we not send for a detective at once?" Mr. Thornton inquired.

"I have already telephoned for one upon my own responsibility," replied the attorney.

"When were you last in these rooms, Mr. Scott?" asked Ralph Mainwaring of the secretary, who had risen to his feet and was making a careful survey of the room.

"About twelve o'clock last night, sir," was his reply; then noting a look of surprise on the faces about him, he added,-

"I came at Mr. Mainwaring's request, as he wished to give directions regarding some work to be done this morning."

"He was alone at that time?"

"Yes, sir."

"How did he appear?" inquired Mr. Thornton.

"The same as usual, except that he seemed very weary."

"Was he in this room?" asked Mr. Mainwaring.

"No, sir; he was seated in the library."

The sound of voices in the corridor attracted Mr. Mainwaring's attention, and he turned quickly to his son, -

"Hugh, I hear your mother's voice; go and meet her. The ladies must not be allowed to come in here."

Mr. Thornton turned to accompany young Mainwaring. Near the door he met his daughter and Miss Carleton, while a little farther down the corridor were Isabel Mainwaring and her mother. With terror-stricken faces they gathered about him, unable to believe the terrible report which they had learned from the servants. As best he could, he answered their numerous inquiries, and, having escorted them to another part of the house, left them in charge of young Mainwaring, while he returned to the library.

Meanwhile, the news of the murder had spread with lightning-like rapidity, and already crowds of people, drawn by that strange fascination which always exists for a certain class in scenes of this kind, were gathering on the grounds outside the house, forming in little groups, conversing with the servants, or gazing upward with awe-stricken glances at the closely-drawn shutters of the room in the tower. The invisible barriers which so long had excluded the public from Fair Oaks had been swept away by the hand of death, and rich and poor, capitalist and laborer, alike wandered unrestrained up and down the oak-lined avenue.

At the door of the library, Mr. Thornton found Ralph

Mainwaring and the attorney conversing together in low tones.

"Yes," Mr. Mainwaring was saying, "as you say, it is undoubtedly murder; but I confess I am at a loss to understand the motive for such a deed, unless it were robbery; and you do not seem to give that idea much credence?"

Mr. Whitney shook his head decidedly. "Unless we find very strong evidence in that direction, I cannot believe that this is any case of common robbery."

But to what other motive would you attribute it?" inquired Mr. Mainwaring.

"Until further facts have been developed which may throw light upon the subject, I do not feel prepared to say what the motive might have been."

"You evidently have your suspicions," remarked Mr. Mainwaring, while Mr. Thornton inquired,-

"Had our cousin any enemies that you know of?"

Mr. Whitney turned a keen, penetrating glance upon Mr. Thornton for an instant, and the latter continued, -

"I thought it possible that in his business relations he might have incurred the enmity of some one of whom you knew."

"No," the attorney answered, quickly, "I am not aware of anything of that nature. Mr. Mainwaring made few intimate friends, but he was universally respected by all who knew him. If he had any enemies," he added, very slowly, "they were within his own household."

Ralph Mainwaring looked sharply at the attorney, but Mr. Thornton exclaimed, -

"'Egad! sir, but you surely do not think this deed was

committed by any one of the inmates of this house?"

"As I have already said," replied Mr. Whitney, "I am not prepared to state what I do think without further knowledge of the facts in the case."

"Of course we understand that," rejoined Mr. Mainwaring; "but we desire to have the benefit of your opinions and judgment regarding this case so soon as you do feel justified in expressing them, and, since you are vastly more familiar with the circumstances surrounding it than we, we wish to rely on your suggestions in this matter,"

The attorney bowed. "My advice for the present would be to take care that no one leaves the premises, and that you also send for Mrs. LaGrange.; I wish to see her," he said briefly, and passed into the library.

Ralph Mainwaring beckoned to the butler; who was standing at a little distance, awaiting orders.

"Call the housekeeper at once, Mr. Whitney wishes to see her in the library; and send Wilson to me, and also the coachman."

With a silent acknowledgment of the order the butler withdrew, and a moment later, John Wilson, a middle-aged man and a servant of Ralph Mainwaring's who had accompanied him from London, appeared, followed by Brown, the coachman at Fair Oaks.

Mr. Mainwaring first addressed the latter. "Brown, for the next hour or so, I wish you to be stationed in the hall below. Keep back the crowd as much as possible; when the coroner and physician arrive show them up at once, but on no account allow any one else to come up-stairs."

Then turning to his own serving-man, as Brown departed to the duties assigned him, Mr. Mainwaring continued,

"For you, Wilson, I have a task which I cannot intrust to any one else, but which I know you will perform faithfully and discreetly; so far as you are able, keep a close watch upon every one within this house, without seeming to do so; pay close attention to all conversation which you hear, and if you hear or see anything unusual, or that seems to have any bearing on what has occurred, report to me at once. Above all, do not let any of the servants leave the premises without they have my permission."

"Very well, sir," Wilson replied; as he moved away the butler reappeared.

"The housekeeper has not yet left her room, sir," he said, addressing Mr. Mainwaring. "I gave the message by the chambermaid, and she sent word that she had been prostrated by the terrible news this morning, sir, but that she would see Mr. Whitney in a few moments."

As the man retreated, Mr. Thornton paused suddenly in his walk up and down the corridor, -

"'Pon my soul, Mainwaring! it strikes me-particularly since hearing that will read yesterday-that there must have been something with reference to that woman-well-rather peculiar, don't you know."

"It strikes me," replied Mr. Mainwaring with marked emphasis, "that there may be something rather 'peculiar,' as you call it, in that direction at present, and I believe Mr. Whitney is of the same opinion."

"How is that? You surely do not think it possible that in his mind she is in any way associated with this murder-if it is a murder?"

"He evidently suspects some one in this house, and for the present we can draw our own inferences. Regarding those provisions in the will to which you just now alluded, I can assure you I was not too well pleased; but I knew it was useless to raise any objections or questions; to my mind, however, they furnish a clue as to the possible claimants against the estate, which we were discussing yesterday, and perhaps a clue to this latest development, also."

"By my soul! it looks like it; but surely she could have no valid claim."

"Valid or not," replied Ralph Mainwaring, "there must have been a powerful claim of some kind. When a man of Hugh Mainwaring's type leaves a handsome annuity to his house-keeper, and an interest in his business worth fifty or seventy-five thousand to her son, it may be considered pretty strong evidence that-"

At a warning glance from Mr. Thornton, Ralph Mainwaring paused abruptly and, turning, saw Mrs. LaGrange coming noiselessly down the corridor. She was dressed with even more than usual care, with quantities of rich lace fastened loosely about her shapely neck and falling in profusion over her beautifully moulded wrists and hands. Her dark, handsome features bore no trace of recent prostration, but betrayed, instead, signs of intense excitement. She bowed silently and passed onward, entering the library so quietly that the attorney, absorbed in thought, was unaware of her presence until she stood before him. He started slightly, and for an instant neither spoke. Each was silently gauging the power of the other.

For some time, Mrs. LaGrange had been conscious that Mr. Whitney was one of the few whose penetration could not be blinded by her blandishments. In addition, the fact that he was the private solicitor and legal adviser of Hugh Mainwaring did not tend to inspire her with confidence regarding his attitude towards herself. Nevertheless, he was an eminent attorney and this was a critical moment; if she could gain his favor and his services in her behalf, it would be a brilliant stroke of policy. Her plans were well laid, and she was prepared to assume whatever role was necessary, so soon as his words or manner should give her the desired cue.

For this, she did not have long to wait; one searching glance, and she had read in the piercing scrutiny and cold scorn of his keen blue eye that, so far from winning favor from him, he would prove her most bitter opponent, and as quickly she determined upon her future course of action.

Mr. Whitney, on the other hand, though a frequent visitor at Fair Oaks, and familiar with the fascinating manner with which, when she chose, Mrs. LaGrange entertained the guests of Hugh Mainwaring, was now forced to acknowledge to himself that never had he seen this handsome woman so beautiful as at the present moment. The eyes looking into his with such depth of meaning,-the expression, the attitude,-all were utterly unlike anything which he had ever seen; but his face grew only the more stern, for the thought then and there occurred to him that perhaps here was the solution of the mysterious power which this woman had wielded over the man whose lifeless form was now lying in their presence.

He observed that the luminous eyes grew suddenly cold, while her head assumed its usual haughty poise;, the brief spell was over, and each understood the other.

After a few general directions, Mr. Whitney remarked, "This day's events will be far different from what we had anticipated."

"Yes," she replied, with a mocking smile, "in that it brings to the guests of this house, instead of future expectations, the immediate realization of their wishes!"

"It is not to be conceived for one moment that any of them take that view of what has occurred," he replied, in a tone of displeasure.

"Possibly not," she rejoined, "although the prospective long life of their host seemed to greatly detract, at least in the case of one of their number, from their enjoyment of the occasion which they had come to celebrate."

"To whom do you refer?" he inquired.

"It is unnecessary to give names," she answered, coldly; "but had the Mainwarings of London known the facts which I know, they would never have crossed the water to take part in the farce which was enacted here yesterday. There are Mainwarings with better right and title to this estate than they, as they will soon learn."

Neither by look nor gesture did she manifest the least consciousness of, or concern for, the inanimate form visible in the adjoining room. With sudden directness, and ignoring the implied threat in her last words, Mr. Whitney asked,-

"Mrs. LaGrange, at what hour did you last see Hugh Mainwaring?"

She was about to reply, when Scott entered from the tower-room. He had heard her last remark, and his dark, piercing eyes were fixed upon her face in keen scrutiny. She was quick to note the fact and hesitated an instant, while a change, inexplicable to the attorney, passed over her face,-surprise, a shade almost of fear, and haughty defiance were visible in quick succession; then, turning again towards Mr. Whitney, she answered, indifferently,-

"It was quite late last night; I do not recollect the hour."

As the attorney was about to speak, Mr. Thornton appeared at the door of the library.

"Beg pardon, Mr. Whitney, but I believe the coroner and others have arrived; as you know the gentlemen, will you kindly meet them?"

"Certainly. Mr. Scott, you will please remain here," and the attorney hastened out into the corridor.

Again Mrs. LaGrange and the secretary faced each other in silence, each apparently trying to read the other's thoughts and probe the depth of the other's knowledge; then, as the gentlemen were heard approaching, she withdrew, leaving him alone.

CHAPTER V

IMPORTANT DISCOVERIES

As the attorney, in response to the summons from Mr. Thornton, hastened from the corridor into the main hall, five gentlemen were slowly ascending the broad stairway, conversing together in subdued tones. One, younger than the others and evidently more familiar with the surroundings at Fair Oaks, stepped quickly in advance of the rest and extended his hand to Mr. Whitney in silent greeting. This was Dr. Hobart, Hugh Mainwaring's physician and one of his most intimate friends, although a number of years his junior. Following him were Mr. Elliott and Mr. Chittenden, of the firm of Mainwaring & Co., while bringing up the rear were the coroner and a gentleman, somewhat below medium size and of modest appearance, whom the attorney greeted very cordially and afterwards introduced to Mr. Thornton as Mr. Merrick. Proceeding at once to the library, they were joined a moment later by Ralph Mainwaring and his son. The necessary introductions followed, and Mr. Mainwaring having given the butler instructions to admit no one into the library, Mr. Whitney made a brief statement regarding the discovery of the murder, and all passed into the room in the tower.

Dr. Hobart at once bent over the prostrate form with genuine sorrow. The millionaire broker had been one of his earliest patrons, and their acquaintance had soon ripened into a mutual attachment, notwithstanding the disparity in their ages. After a long look at the face of his friend, he gave place to the coroner, who was also a physician. They partially lifted the body and both examined the wound, the small man who had accompanied the coroner looking on silently. It was found that the bullet had entered just above the right eye and had passed through the brain in a slightly downward direction, coming out near the base upon the same side. The most careful search failed to disclose the bullet, and attention was next directed to the revolver lying upon the floor near the right hand. It was a Smith & Wesson, thirty-two calibre, with but one empty chamber, that from which the fatal bullet had probably been discharged.

"Can any of you gentlemen tell me whether or not this belonged to the deceased?" inquired the coroner, holding up the revolver.

There was an instant's pause, and Mr. Whitney replied, "I know that Mr. Mainwaring owned a revolver, but, having never seen it, am unable to answer your inquiry. Perhaps his secretary could give you the desired information."

"I have often seen a revolver lying in Mr. Mainwaring's desk," said the secretary; "but I doubt whether I could identify it, as I never observed it closely. I should judge, however, that this was the same size and make."

"Would it not be well to see if it is still there?" suggested the attorney. "I suppose you have a key to the desk."

"I have, sir," he replied, at the same time producing it. Crossing the room, he unlocked and opened the desk. An instant later, he announced, as he closed the desk, "It is not here."

There was a subdued. murmur, and Mr. Thornton was heard to exclaim, "Suicide! That has been my impression all along."

Ralph Mainwaring glanced inquiringly at the attorney, who shook his head emphatically, while the coroner once more inspected the wound with an air of perplexity.

"Doctor," inquired Ralph Mainwaring, "in your opinion, how long has life been extinct?"

"I should judge about eight or nine hours," replied Dr. Hobart. "What would you say, Dr. Westlake?"

"That would be my judgment, also."

"You would say that death was instantaneous?" questioned the attorney.

"Without a doubt. It could not have been otherwise?" Ralph Mainwaring consulted his watch. "It is now half after nine; in your judgment, then, this must have occurred about one o'clock this morning?"

"About that time."

"At what hour was Mr. Mainwaring last seen by any one in this house?" asked the coroner.

"As nearly as we have ascertained thus far, at about twelve o'clock."

"Twelve? Indeed! By whom? and where?"

"By his private secretary, and in the library adjoining."

"Very well," said the coroner, after a pause, during which he had made a memorandum of certain details which he considered of special importance; "the undertaker can now be summoned as I believe he is waiting below, and we seem to have ascertained all the facts possible in this direction; and, Mr. Whitney, I will next see the valet, whom you say was the one to discover the situation this morning."

In the slight confusion and delay which ensued, Mr. Elliott

and Mr. Chittenden took their departure, with the usual expressions of condolence and regret, followed a few moments later by Dr. Hobart, who was accompanied downstairs by young Mainwaring.

Meanwhile, Mr. Merrick, having made a close scrutiny of the lifeless form, had been slowly walking back and forth in the tower-room and library, his hands in the pockets of his short sacque coat and his eyes apparently riveted on the floor. Several times in the library he paused and, bending downward, seemed to be intently studying the carpet; then, after two or three turns about the room, he sauntered towards the windows and doors, examining the fastenings of each in turn, and, on reaching the door opening into the southern hall, suddenly disappeared.

"A very mysterious case!" commented the coroner, when he had finished his interview with the valet. "Thus far nothing can be learned which throws much actual light on the subject one way or another, but if anybody can unravel the mystery, Merrick can."

"Merrick!" repeated Mr. Thornton, turning to Mr. Whitney in surprise. "Is Mr. Merrick a detective?"

"He is. I did not introduce him as such, for the reason that in a case of this kind he usually prefers to make his first visit incognito if possible."

"Very well; you have taken the responsibility in this matter. You understand, of course, Mr. Whitney, that we want no amateur work in a case like this."

"Mr. Merrick is no amateur," said the attorney, quietly; "he is one of the most trusted and one of the surest men on the force."

"Before we go any farther," interposed Ralph Mainwaring, "I suggest that we ascertain whether or not there has been a robbery. We can at least satisfy ourselves on that point."

"Acting on your suggestion, we will examine the safe," said Mr. Whitney; "though I, for one, am not inclined to think there has been any robbery. Without a knowledge of the combination, the safe could not be opened unless force were employed; and it certainly bears no evidence of having been tampered with."

"Proceed with your investigation, Mr. Whitney," said the quiet voice of the detective, who had entered unobserved from the smoking-room; "unless I am greatly mistaken, the person we are after is some one pretty familiar with various 'combinations' in these apartments."

There was a general expression of surprise, and all turned towards Mr. Merrick for an explanation, but a glance at his impassive face convinced them that questions would be useless.

With a few swift turns the secretary unlocked the safe and the ponderous doors swung open, showing books and papers in their accustomed places. Everything appeared in perfect order; but as the attorney began a rapid examination of the interior, he suddenly uttered a sharp exclamation, while, as he continued his search, his manner betrayed considerable excitement.

"Anything wrong, Mr. Whitney? anything missing?" queried Ralph Mainwaring.

"Everything is missing!" the other exclaimed, after a moment's pause, turning around with a pale face and holding in his hand an empty cash box; "there is absolutely nothing left but an old cheque-book, a few drafts, and some other papers of no value whatever except to Hugh Mainwaring himself!"

Half a score of questions were instantly raised: "Was there a large amount of money in the safe?" "Did it contain anything of great value?"

Scott, standing silently in the background, seemed to see again the brilliant gems flashing in the sunlight, as he had seen them in his search on the preceding day, but he said nothing.

"There was a considerable amount of cash," the attorney was saying. "Mr. Mainwaring deposited a large sum there when he last came out from the city, and," he added more slowly, "the old family jewels were kept in the safe."

"The Mainwaring jewels!" echoed both the Englishmen. "Impossible! incredible!" While Ralph Mainwaring exclaimed, "Why, they were worth a fortune several times over in themselves!"

"I am aware of that," answered the attorney. "I often remonstrated with Mr. Mainwaring, but to no purpose; for some reason which he never explained he always kept them there."

"I would never have believed him capable of such recklessness," said Mr. Thornton.

"Recklessness!" exclaimed Ralph Mainwaring; "it was the biggest piece of imbecility I ever heard of! What is your opinion now, Mr. Whitney, regarding a robbery in connection with this case?"

"That there has been a robbery I am forced to admit," the attorney replied, courteously but firmly; "but my opinion of the matter is still unchanged. I regard the robbery as only incident to the murder. I do not yet believe it to have led to the deeper crime."

"Do you know, Mr. Scott, whether any one beside yourself understood the combination of the safe?" Ralph Mainwaring inquired.

"I do not, sir," the secretary replied, conscious that all eyes had turned upon him at the inquiry and that the detective was observing him closely.

Meanwhile Ralph Mainwaring loudly lamented the missing jewels, until it was evident to all that their loss, for the time at least, had completely overshadowed all thought of the tragedy they were investigating.

"They must be recovered at all hazards and at any price," he said, addressing the detective. "There were single gems in that collection which cost a fortune and which have been heirlooms in the family for generations."

After further search which failed to disclose anything of importance, or any clue regarding either the murder or the robbery, arrangements were made for the inquest to be held at three o'clock that afternoon, and the party was about to leave the apartments, when Mr. Whitney paused.

"One moment, gentlemen; there is one more point I would like investigated. I maintain that we have not yet discovered the most essential clue to this case-something to throw light on the possible motive which prompted the murder of Hugh Mainwaring. I now wish to make a final trial. Mr. Scott, will you once more open Mr. Mainwaring's desk for us and take out the will that was deposited there yesterday?"

Ralph Mainwaring started. "The will? You surely do not think-"

"I think it might be safer in our own possession," said the attorney, with a peculiar smile.

"And right you are!" added Mr. Thornton, approvingly. "I wonder you had not thought of that yourself, Mainwaring."

Meanwhile, Scott, having opened the desk in compliance with the attorney's request, had looked for the will where he had last seen it on the preceding day, and, failing to find it, was searching through the numerous receptacles containing Mr. Mainwaring's private papers. The silence around him became oppressive, and suddenly looking up, he encountered the glance of both Mr. Whitney and the detective, the former with an expression of triumph in his keen eyes. Perplexed and bewildered, Scott exclaimed in a mechanical tone,-

"The will is gone; it is nowhere to be found!"

"I thought as much," said the attorney, quietly.

CHAPTER VI

THE INQUEST

The crowd, which early in the day had gathered about Fair Oaks, instead of diminishing, seemed rather to increase as the hours slipped away. Little by little the facts became known to outsiders,-the loss of the old family jewels, concerning whose existence and probable value vague rumors had been circulated in the past, the drawing up of the will on the preceding day and its strange disappearance in connection with the sudden and mysterious death of the testator, - all combined to arouse public interest and curiosity to an unusual degree; it seemed the culmination of the impenetrable mystery which for years had shrouded the place.

As the hour for the inquest approached, the crowd was augmented by each suburban train, until a throng of business men of all classes, interspersed with numerous reporters eager for the details of the affair, covered the grounds and even sought admittance to the house, for the millionaire broker, though a man of few intimate friendships, was widely known and honored in the financial and commercial world.

Shortly after the arrival of the 2.45 train from the city, the Mainwaring carriage came rapidly up the avenue, two or three other carriages following in the rear. As it stopped, Mr. Whitney alighted, followed by an elderly gentleman of fine appearance and two officers of the special police, who immediately began to force back the crowd, while the attorney and his companion hastily entered the house and were met by the butler, who, in response to a hurried inquiry, directed them up-stairs.

In the private library they found the detective who had been left there alone at his own request. There was a brief interview between the three, after which Mr. Whitney begged his companion to excuse him for a moment, and beckoning Mr. Merrick into the tower-room, asked eagerly, -

"Well, what success? Have you struck the trail?"

With an enigmatical smile, the detective replied, "The game has doubled back on the trail pretty adroitly, but I have made one or two little discoveries that may be of value later. What do you think of this?"

Opening a small note-book, he took therefrom several pieces of burnt paper, most of which were so blackened that the faint traces of writing which they bore were illegible. On a few pieces, however, words and parts of words could be distinctly read.

Mr. Whitney studied the bits of discolored paper for a moment, and then exclaimed in excited tones,

"Good heavens, man! it is the will! The will drawn up in these rooms yesterday! See, here is the date, 'this seventh day of July, in the year of our'-the rest is gone."

"Here is part of a name," said the detective, "'nor Houghton LaGra'-"

"Eleanor Houghton LaGrange!" exclaimed the attorney, "and below you can just trace the words, 'this amount of annuity to be'; and here are other bits, 'as to my estate and all property,' 'to hold the same forever, together with.' Well, I should say these were of value; where did you find them?"

For answer, Mr. Merrick pointed to a small fireplace behind the safe, near which a large screen was standing.

"Strange!" exclaimed the attorney. "I never noticed that before, much as I have been here."

"It escaped my observation for some time," replied the other." I searched the fireplace in the library, but this grate is very small and was concealed by that large screen, as well as by the safe. Evidently, it was seldom used, and was selected for that reason by whoever destroyed the will, as more likely to escape notice."

"Rather a bungling piece of work," commented the attorney, "leaving these partially burned scraps. I wonder that he or she, whoever it was, did not make sure that they were entirely consumed."

"The person may have heard some sound and, fearing detection, hastened away before the job was completed, "suggested the other.

"Well, it is past three, we must hasten; you found nothing more?"

"Nothing of special importance. I have learned one fact, however; the murder was never committed in this room, but in the library."

"The library! Why do you think that?"

"I do not think it, I know it, and was confident of it while we were making the examination this morning. Say nothing about it, however, for the present. We will go now, if you are ready."

Joining the gentleman still awaiting them in the library, they descended into the lower hall, where the detective suddenly disappeared.

Meanwhile, the coroner and members of the jury, after alighting from their carriages, marched gravely up the broad stairs and were conducted by a servant into one of the private apartments where lay the body of the murdered man. Under the direction of Dr. Westlake, the jury individually viewed the wounds, noting their location and character, and, after a brief visit to the room in the tower, all passed downstairs and were shown into the large library on the first floor.

The coroner occupied a large arm-chair at one end of a long writing-table in the centre of the room, the jury being seated together near his left, while on each side of the table chairs had been placed for the accommodation of a few of the more prominent reporters, the others, less favored, stationing themselves at the doorways and open windows.

In the room back of the library were the servants, the women grouped about the great arched doorway with white, frightened faces, the men standing a little farther in the rear, while in a dim corner, partially concealed by the heavy portieres and unseen by any one excepting the servants, was the detective.

When everything was in readiness, Mr. Whitney entered the room with the gentleman who had accompanied him out from the city and followed by the London guests. In the lead were Ralph Mainwaring and his son, the entrance of the latter causing a small stir of interest and excitement, as a score of pencils at once began to rapidly sketch the features of the young Englishman, the intended heir of Hugh Mainwaring. The young man's face wore an expression of unconcern, but his father's features were set and severe. To him, the loss of the will meant something more than the forfeiture of the exclusive ownership of a valuable estate; it meant the overthrow and demolition of one of his pet schemes, cherished for twenty-one years, just on the eve of its fulfilment; and those who knew Ralph Mainwaring knew that to thwart his plans was a dangerous undertaking.

Mr. Thornton followed, escorting Mrs. Mainwaring and her

daughter, the cold, gray eyes of Isabel Mainwaring flashing a look of haughty disdain on the faces about her. Bringing up the rear was Mrs. Hogarth with her two charges, Edith Thornton and Winifred Carleton, the face of the latter lighted with an intelligent, sympathetic interest in her surroundings.

Harry Scott next entered, pausing in the doorway for an instant, while just behind him appeared Mrs. LaGrange. The room was already crowded, and Miss Carleton, seated near the door, with a quick glance invited the young secretary to a vacant chair by her side, which he gracefully accepted, but not before a tiny note had been thrust into his hand, unseen by any one excepting the detective.

Pale, but with all her accustomed hauteur, Mrs. LaGrange, accompanied by her son, passed slowly around the group of reporters, ignoring the chair offered by the attorney, and seated herself in a position as remote as possible from the guests of the house and commanding a full view of the servants. Her gown was noticeable for its elegance, and her jewelled hands toyed daintily with a superb fan, from whose waving black plumes a perfume, subtle and exquisite, was wafted to every part of the room.

In the silence that followed, the coroner, with a few brief words, called for the first witness, George Hardy. A young man, with a frank face and quiet, unassuming manner, stepped forward from the group of servants. After the usual preliminaries, the coroner inquired,-

"How long have you been in the employ of Mr. Mainwaring?"

"Nearly four years, sir."

"During that time you have held the position of valet?"

"Yes, sir."

"At what time this morning did you discover what had occurred?"

"About seven o'clock, sir."

"You may state how you came to make this discovery, giving full particulars."

"I had gone as usual to the bath-room to prepare the bath for Mr. Mainwaring, and when everything was in readiness I knocked at his door to waken him. There was no answer, and, after knocking several times, I unlocked the door and looked in. I saw he had not occupied the room, but I didn't think much about that, and went on through the smoking-room into the library, and then I saw Mr. Mainwaring lying on the floor in the next room. At first I thought he was sick and went to him, but as I got nearer I saw that he was dead, and then I noticed the revolver lying beside him."

"What did you then do?"

"I was frightened, sir, and I went to call help as quick as I could."

"Who was the first person whom you met and told of your discovery?"

"Well, sir, I went first for Mr. Whitney, because he was a friend of Mr. Mainwaring's and a lawyer, and I thought he would know what to do; but on my way to his room I met Wilson, Mr. Ralph Mainwaring's valet, and I told him what had happened; then I called Mr. Whitney and told him Mr. Mainwaring had shot himself."

"Did you get the impression that Mr. Mainwaring bad shot himself from the fact that the revolver lay near his band, or had you any other reasons for that inference?"

"No, sir, that was the only reason."

"Can you state positively whether this revolver belonged to Mr. Mainwaring?" asked the coroner, at the same time passing the weapon to Hardy.

"Yes, sir," replied the latter, promptly, handing it back after a moment's inspection, "that is Mr. Mainwaring's revolver. I've cleaned it many a time, and there's little marks on it that I know sure."

"Very well. After summoning Mr. Whitney, did you call any other members of the household?"

"Mr. Whitney sent me to call Mr. Ralph Mainwaring; but I met Wilson again, and he said he had just told Mr. Mainwaring and Mr. Thornton, and was on his way to the room of young Mr. Mainwaring. Down the hall I met the butler and told him what had happened, and we both went into the library, and I stayed there till Mr. Whitney came."

"When did you last see Mr. Hugh Mainwaring?"

"Shortly after dinner last evening, between seven and eight o'clock, I should say, sir."

"Where was that?"

"In the main hall down-stairs, sir. He stopped me to say that he would not need me last evening, and that after locking up his rooms for the night I could have my time to myself."

"Was the locking of his rooms usually included among your duties at night?"

"Yes, sir; his private rooms and the hall on the south side."

"Did you have any stated time for doing this?"

"At nine o'clock, sir."

"You locked the rooms as usual last night?"

"Yes, sir; that is, I locked them all right, but it was later than usual."

"How was that?"

"About half an hour after Mr. Mainwaring spoke to me, the housekeeper came and asked me to keep the rooms open till about ten o'clock, as she was expecting callers and wanted to receive them by the south hall into her private parlor."

"At what time did you lock the rooms?"

"A few minutes after ten, sir. I felt kind of uneasy, because it was Mr. Mainwaring's orders that the rooms be shut at nine; so soon as 'twas ten o'clock I went around outside, and, seeing no light in her parlor, I went in and locked the hall and then went up-stairs to lock the rooms there."

"Did you see any strangers about the place at that time?"

"No, sir."

"You saw no one in any of Mr. Mainwaring's private rooms?"

"No strangers, you mean? No, sir."

"Was there any one in his rooms?"

"The housekeeper was in the library. She had gone up-stairs that way, she said, and had found the door into the main hall locked, and hearing me come, she waited for me to open it."

"Had you locked the door into the main hall?"

"No, sir; that door wasn't usually locked in the evening. I don't know who locked it, but I opened it for her and then locked it again."

"Are you positive there was no one else in those rooms at that time?"

"Yes, sir, pretty sure," replied Hardy, with a smile, "for I looked them over uncommon thorough last night. I thought at first that I smelled smoke, like something burning, but I looked around careful and everything was all right."

At this point Mr. Whitney held a whispered consultation with the coroner for a moment.

"You say," continued the latter, "you thought you smelled something burning; could you state what the material seemed to be?"

"Well, sir, I thought it was like paper burning; but I must have been mistaken, for the papers on the table was all right and there was nothing in the fireplace."

"Did you see or hear anything unusual about the place at any time last night?"

"No, sir."

For a moment the coroner was occupied with a slip of paper which had been passed to him through a number of hands; then he said,-

"Before you are dismissed, will you describe the locks used on the doors of Mr. Mainwaring's library and the south hall."

"They had the ordinary locks, sir; and then, in addition, a small, patent lock, that when a certain spring was turned the door locked of itself and could not be opened from either side unless one had the key and understood the working of the spring."

"Who had keys to fit these locks?"

"No one but Mr. Mainwaring. When he was home and wanted the doors unlocked, he hung the keys in a particular place in the library where I could find them, and when he went away he always took them with him."

"Did you unlock the library doors this morning?"

"Only the door into the main hall when I went to call Mr. Whitney,-that had nothing but an ordinary lock; but the other door, into the south hall, was unlocked and the keys gone when I first went into the library."

"One question more. Do you know whether any one else in the house had knowledge of or access to, these particular keys?"

"I don't know for certain, sir, but I think not."

The attorney was next called upon, and came forward, while Hardy resumed his former place among the servants.

"Mr. Whitney," said the coroner, after the witness had given the details of his arrival in the tower-room in response to the valet's summons, "will you please state when, and under what circumstances, you last saw Hugh Mainwaring living."

"At nearly eleven o'clock last night. Mr. Mainwaring had just bidden his guests good-night, and I believe they had all retired to their rooms, leaving him and myself together upon the veranda in front of the house. I remained with him about ten minutes, I should judge, talking over the events of the day which had been of unusual interest. I remember his remarking that he should not retire for an hour or so, as, to use his own expression, his thoughts would not let him sleep. We clasped hands with an exchange of good wishes. That was the last I ever saw him living or heard him speak."

Mr. Whitney's voice trembled slightly towards the close of his recital, but as he repeated Hugh Mainwaring's words a smile of scorn passed over the face of Mrs. LaGrange, who was seated directly opposite.

"Will you please state," said the coroner, "how Mr. Main-waring had been engaged during the day, yesterday."

"Until about half-past two his time was spent in the preparation, with the assistance of his secretary and myself, and the execution of his last will and testament. The remainder of the day was devoted to the entertainment of his guests."

"Will you give briefly and in general terms the conditions of the will."

"With the exception of an annuity to his housekeeper and a handsome bequest to her son, it conveyed everything to his cousin and namesake, Hugh Mainwaring, Jr., whom he intended to-day to formally declare his heir."

"Where was this document placed, Mr. Whitney?"

"It was, at Mr. Mainwaring's request, placed by his secretary on his desk in the tower-room."

"You can give no further information regarding this will, now missing?"

"Only this," replied Mr. Whitney, with marked emphasis, "that we now have positive proof that the will was burned."

There was a general movement of surprise, both among the members of the household and outsiders; and the attorney, closely observant of Mrs. LaGrange, saw her cheek, which but a moment before, at his mention of the annuity contained in the will, had flamed with anger, suddenly assume a strange pallor.

"Mr. Whitney, " continued the coroner, having consulted a small memorandum which he held, "do you know whether there were any strangers at Fair Oaks yesterday?"

"I have no personal knowledge on that subject. The secretary informs me that a stranger inquired for Mr. Mainwaring in the afternoon, and remarks were made at luncheon, that impressed me considerably, regarding some one who had called in the forenoon, whether to see Mr. Mainwaring I am not prepared to state."

"Will you state the nature of those remarks?"

"I should prefer to be excused until later in this examination. For the present, I will merely say that one of Mr. Mainwaring's guests incidentally met and recognized this caller; that the latter was evidently well and unfavorably known by both Mr. Mainwaring and his guests, and, if I am not mistaken, by the secretary also, and that the mention of the man's name seemed to affect Mr. Hugh Mainwaring very unpleasantly."

"In what respect, Mr. Whitney?"

"He grew very pale and appeared confused, if not alarmed, on learning that the man was in this country and had been seen at this house, and he seemed abstracted and very unlike himself for fully an hour after the occurrence."

"Will you state the name of this man?"

"He was spoken of as Richard Hobson, formerly an attorney, of London."

CHAPTER VII

A LITTLE ROYAL

"Harry Scorr, private secretary of Hugh Mainwaring," announced the coroner, when Mr. Whitney had resumed his chair.

As the young secretary walked deliberately through the crowded room, there were few who failed to remark his erect, athletic form, his splendid bearing, and especially the striking beauty of his dark face, with its olive tint, clear-cut features, indicative of firmness and strength, and large, piercing eyes, within whose depths, on the present occasion, there seemed to be, half hidden, half revealed, some smouldering fire. Instantly a half-dozen pencils were transferring to paper his form and features.

"Say, what are you 'doing' him for?" whispered one reporter to his neighbor. "He isn't anybody; only the old man's secretary."

"Can't help that," replied the other; "he's better looking than the English chap, anyhow; and, in my opinion, the old fellow would have shown better sense to have left him the 'stuff.'"

Meanwhile, young Scott, having answered a few preliminary interrogatories, turned slowly, facing Mrs. LaGrange, who was watching him with an intensity of manner and expression as though she would compel him to meet her gaze.

As his glance met hers, a look of inquiry flashed from her eyes to his, accompanied by an expression persuasive, almost appealing. But the only reply was an ominous flash from the dark eyes, as, with a gesture of proud disdain, he folded his arms and again faced his interlocutor, while, with eyes gleaming with revenge from under their heavily drooping lids and lips that curled from time to time in a smile of bitter malignity, she watched him, listening eagerly for his testimony, losing no word that he said.

The young secretary well understood the character of the enemy with whom he had thus declared war, though he was as yet in ignorance of the weapons she would use against him, but the honeyed words of the little note crushed within his pocket had no power to swerve him for an instant from the course upon which he had determined.

After a few general questions, the coroner said,

"Please state when and what was the first intimation received by you of any unusual occurrence."

"I was awakened this morning by a woman's scream and heard sounds of confused running in different directions. A few moments later Mr. Whitney came to my room and informed me of what had occurred, and I then went with him to the private rooms of Mr. Mainwaring."

"You were associated with Mr. Mainwaring yesterday during the greater part of the day and evening, were you not?"

"I was during the day, but I did not see him after dinner until late at night."

"Did you notice anything unusual in his appearance at any time yesterday?"

"He appeared rather depressed for about an hour after luncheon, during the execution of the will."

"Did you know any cause for such depression?"

"I attributed it, in my own mind, to the conversation at luncheon, to which Mr. Whitney has referred."

"Regarding one Richard Hobson?"

"Yes, sir."

"Do you know what, if any, relations existed between Mr. Mainwaring and this Hobson?"

The black plumes of Mrs. LaGrange's fan suddenly quivered, her cheek paled, and her breath came and went quickly, but these were the only signs of agitation which she betrayed, as Scott replied,-

"I have no knowledge as to what relations existed between them of late. I only know that Mr. Mainwaring had, years ago, some important private business with this man."

"Will you state the nature of this business?"

"Without giving exact details," Scott replied, speaking deliberately but with no hesitation, though conscious of the surprise and indignation depicted on some of the faces about him, "this man was employed as an attorney by Mr. Mainwaring before the latter came to this country, and has since, at various times, extorted money from him by threats of exposure regarding certain transactions."

The silence that followed this statement was of itself eloquent. The young secretary felt every eye fastened upon himself, and, though his own eyes were fixed on the coroner's face, he saw reflected even there the general expression of mingled astonishment, incredulity, and resentment. Unmoved, however, he awaited, coolly and impassively, the next words of the coroner.

"Mr. Scott," said Dr. Westlake, a touch of severity in his tone, "this is a serious assertion to make regarding a man so widely known as Mr. Mainwaring, and so universally considered above reproach in his business transactions."

"I am aware of that fact, sir," replied Scott, calmly, "but reference to the private letter-files of Mr. Mainwaring will prove the truth of my assertion. I made this statement simply because the time and place demanded it. You were endeavoring to ascertain the cause of Mr. Mainwaring's perturbation on learning yesterday of the arrival of Hobson. I have given what I consider the clue."

"How recently had this man Hobson extorted money from Mr. Mainwaring, and in what amount?"

"The last money sent him was about three years ago, a sum of five thousand dollars. Hobson wrote a most insolent letter of acknowledgment, stating that, as this money would set him on his feet for a time, he would not write again immediately, but assuring Mr. Mainwaring that he would never be able to elude him, as the writer would keep posted regarding his whereabouts, and might, some time in the future, call upon him in person."

"Can you describe this man's appearance?"

"I cannot, having never met him."

"Will you describe the stranger who is reported to have called in the afternoon."

"He was tall, quite pale, with dark hair and moustache. He was dressed in a tweed suit, somewhat travel-worn, and wore dark glasses."

"Did he state his errand?"

"Only that he wished to see Mr. Mainwaring on business of special importance. He at first seemed rather insistent, but, on

Maynard Barbour

learning that Mr. Mainwaring was out and that he would receive no business calls for a day or two, he readily consented to defer his interview until later."

"Did he leave his name or address?"

"His card bore the name of J. Henry Carruthers, of London. He gave his present address as the Arlington House."

"You noticed nothing unusual in his appearance?"

"The only thing that struck me as rather peculiar was that Mr. Carruthers seemed well informed regarding events expected to take place here, while his name was wholly unfamiliar to Mr. Mainwaring."

At this point a pencilled note was handed by the coroner to Mr. Whitney, who immediately summoned George Hardy and hastily despatched him on some errand.

"Mr. Scott," resumed the coroner, "were you in Mr. Mainwaring's private library at any time during last evening?"

"I was not. I spent the entire evening in my own room."

"When did you again see Mr. Mainwaring?"

"Not until after eleven o'clock. I had come down for a smoke in the grounds outside and met Mr. Mainwaring in the lower hall on the way to his rooms. He asked me to come to his library before retiring, as he wished to give some final directions for the next day. About half an hour later I went to the library door, but hearing loud and angry talk within, I waited in the hall some fifteen or twenty minutes until I knew Mr. Mainwaring was alone. I then entered, received his instructions, and went directly to my room for the night."

"Were you able to recognize the voices or hear any of theconversation?"

"I was. I recognized the voice of the housekeeper, Mrs. LaGrange; but feeling that I was hearing what was not intended for me, I walked back into the main hall and remained there until Mrs. LaGrange came out."

"You saw her leave the library?"

"Yes, sir; I passed her in the corridor."

"She saw you, of course?"

"She seemed scarcely conscious of my presence until we had passed; she then turned and watched me as I entered the library."

"What was the nature of the conversation which you heard?"

"I only heard what Mrs. LaGrange said. She evidently was very angry with Mr. Mainwaring."

"Can you repeat her words as you heard them?"

"Not entirely. She accused Mr. Mainwaring of dishonesty, saying that he had defrauded his only brother, and had ignored and robbed his own son to put a stranger in his place. The last words I heard were, 'You are in my power, and you know it only too well; and I will make you and your high-born, purse-proud family rue this day's work.'"

Harry Scott, with the proof of his employer's crimes in his possession, repeated these words with an indifference and impassiveness that seemed unnatural, while the smouldering fire in his eyes gleamed fitfully, as though he knew some secret of which the others little dreamed.

But, if spoken indifferently, the words were not received withindifference. The reporters bent to their task with renewed ardor, since it promised developments so rich and racy. Ralph Mainwaring's face was dark with suppressed wrath; Mr.

Thornton seemed hardly able to restrain himself; while the attorney grew pale with excitement and anger. Mrs. LaGrange alone remained unmoved, as much so as the witness himself, her eyes half closed and a cynical smile playing about her lips as she listened to the repetition of her own words.

"Did Mr. Mainwaring make no reply?" inquired the coroner.

"He did, but it was inaudible to me."

"You went into the library as soon as he was alone?"

"I did."

"At what hour was this?"

"A few minutes past twelve."

"Was that the last time you saw Mr. Mainwaring living?"

"It was."

"Can you state whether any one was in his rooms after you left?"

"I cannot."

"Mr. Scott, by your own statement, you must have been in Mr. Mainwaring's library within an hour preceding his death; consequently, I would like you to give every detail of that interview."

"I am perfectly willing, sir, but there are few to give. The interview occupied possibly ten minutes. Mr. Mainwaring appeared very weary, and, after giving directions regarding any personal mail or telegrams which might be received, stated that he wished me to consider myself his guest on the following day and join in the festivities of the occasion. I thanked him, and, wishing him good-night, withdrew."

"In which room were you?"

"We were both in the library. When I first entered, Mr. Mainwaring was walking back and forth, his hands folded behind him, as was usually his habit when thinking deeply, but he immediately seated himself and gave me my instructions. The tower-room was dimly lighted and the curtains were drawn quite closely together at the entrance."

"Did you hear any unusual sound after reaching your room?"

"Not at that time. I was aroused about three o'clock this morning by what I thought was a stealthy step in the grounds in the rear of the house, but I listened for a moment and heard nothing more."

"That will do for the present, Mr. Scott. You will probably be recalled later," said the coroner, watching the secretary rather curiously. Then he added, in a different tone,-

"The next witness is Mrs. LaGrange."

There was a perceptible stir throughout the crowd as, with a movement of inimitable grace, Mrs. LaGrange stepped forward, darting a swift glance of such venomous hatred towards Scott, as he again seated himself beside Miss Carleton, that the latter, with a woman's quick intuition, instantly grasped the situation and watched the proceedings with new interest and closer attention. As Mrs. LaGrange took her place and began answering the questions addressed to her, the eager listeners pressed still more closely in their efforts to catch every word, feeling instinctively that some startling developments would be forthcoming; but no one was prepared for the shock that followed when, in response to the request to state her full name, the reply came, in clear tones, with unequivocal distinctness, -

"Eleanor Houghton Mainwaring."

For an instant an almost painful silence ensued, until Dr. Westlake said,-

"Will you state your relation to the deceased?"

"I was the lawfully wedded, but unacknowledged, wife of Hugh Mainwaring," was the calm reply.

"Please state when and where your marriage took place," said the coroner, watching the witness narrowly.

"We were married privately in London, about three months before Mr. Mainwaring came to this country."

"How long ago was that?"

"A little more than twenty-three years."

"You say that you were privately married, and that in all these years Mr. Mainwaring never acknowledged you as his wife?"

"Yes. I was at that time a widow, and, owing to certain unpleasant circumstances attending the last months of my former husband's life, Mr. Mainwaring insisted that our marriage be strictly private. I acceded to his wishes, and we were married as quietly as possible. At the end of three months he deserted me, and for four years I did not even know where he had gone. During that time, however, I learned that my husband, who had been fearful of soiling his proud name by having it publicly joined with mine, was, in the sight of the law, a common criminal. I finally traced him to America, and five years after he deserted me I had the pleasure of confronting him with the facts which I had obtained. With passionate protestations of renewed love and fair promises of an honorable married life, he sought to purchase my silence, and, fool that I was! I yielded. He claimed that he could not at once acknowledge me as his wife, because he was already known as an unmarried man, but in the near future we would repeat the marriage ceremony and I should be the honored mistress of his heart and home. I believed him and waited. Meantime, our child was born, and then a new role had to be adopted. Had he not known that he was in my power, I would then have been thrust out homeless with my babe, but he dared not do that. Instead, I was brought to Fair Oaks dressed in widow's garb, as a distant relative of his who was to be his housekeeper. So, for my son's sake, hoping he would some day receive his rights, I have lived a double life, regarded as a servant where I should have been mistress, and holding that poor position only because it was within my power to put the master of the house in a felon's cell!"

"Can you produce the certificate of this marriage?" inquired the coroner, regarding the witness with a searching glance as she paused in her recital.

"Unfortunately, " she replied, in a tone ringing with scorn and defiance, "I cannot produce our marriage certificate, as my husband kept that in his possession, and frequently threatened to destroy it. If it is in existence, it will be found in his safe; but I can produce a witness who was present at our marriage, and who himself signed the certificate."

"State the name of this witness."

"Richard Hobson, of London."

"You are then acquainted with this Hobson?" the coroner inquired, at the same time making an entry in the memorandum he held.

"Naturally, as he was at one time my husband's attorney."

"He called at Fair Oaks yesterday, did he not?"

"He did."

"Do you know whether he called more than once?"

"He came a second time, in the evening, accompanied by his clerk."

"Was his object at either time to secure an interview with Mr. Mainwaring?"

"He called to see me on private business."

"Had he any intention of meeting Mr. Mainwaring later?"

"I know nothing regarding his intentions."

"Mrs. LaGrange," said the coroner, after a pause, "you were in Mr. Mainwaring's library between the hours of eleven and twelve last night, were you not?"

Her face darkened with anger at his form of address. "I was in my husband's library at that hour," she replied.

"How long were you there?"

"I cannot state exactly," she answered, indifferently; "perhaps half an hour."

"Did Mr. Scott repeat correctly your words to Mr. Mainwaring?"

"I have no doubt that he did. His memory on the subject is much better than mine."

"What was the meaning of your threat to Mr. Mainwaring, that you would make him and his friends regret the day's proceedings?"

"He understood my meaning. He knew that I could set aside the will, and could ruin him by exposing his duplicity and fraud."

"What reply did he make?"

"He answered me, as usual, with sneers; but I saw that he felt somewhat apprehensive. I wished to give him a little time to reflect upon a proposition I had made, and I left the library, intending to return later; but," she added, slowly and significantly, "I was superseded by another visitor."

"Explain your meaning," said the coroner, briefly.

"My husband's private secretary entered the library directly after I left. Some thirty minutes later I passed down the corridor towards the library, and was startled to hear Mr. Mainwaring, in loud and excited tones, denouncing some one as a liar and an impostor. The reply was low, in a voice trembling with rage, but I caught the words, 'You are a liar and a thief! If you had your deserts, you would be in a felon's cell to-night, or transported to the wilds of Australia!' There was much more in the same t one,but so low I could not distinguish the words, and, thinking Mr. Mainwaring was likely to be occupied for some time, I immediately retired to my room."

"Was the voice of the second speaker familiar to you?" inquired Dr. Westlake, in the breathless silence that followed this statement.

A half smile, both cunning and cruel, played around the lips of the witness, as she answered, with peculiar emphasis and with a ring of triumph in her tone,-

"The voice was somewhat disguised, but it was distinctly recognizable as that of Mr. Scott, the private secretary."

To Scott himself, these words came with stunning force, not so much for the accusation which they conveyed, as that her recital of those words spoken within the library seemed but the repetition of words which had rung in his brain the preceding night, as, alone in his room, he had, in imagination, confronted his employer with the proof of his guilt which that afternoon's search had brought to light. His fancy had vividly portrayed the scene in which he would arraign Hugh Mainwaring as a thief, and would himself, in turn, be denounced as an impostor until he should have established his claims by the indubitable evidence now in his possession. Such a scene bad in reality been enacted,-those very words had been spoken,-and, for an instant, it seemed to Scott as though he had been, unconsciously, one of the actors.

The general wonder and consternation with which he was now regarded by the crowd quickly recalled him, however, to the present situation, and awakened within him a sudden, fierce resentment, though he remained outwardly calm.

"At that time," continued the coroner, "were you of the opinion that it was Mr. Scott whom you heard thus addressing Mr. Mainwaring?"

"Yes, I had every reason to believe it was he, and I have now additional reasons for the same belief."

"Are these additional reasons founded on your own personal knowledge, or on the information of others?"

"Upon information received from various members of the household."

"Did you see Mr. Scott leave the library?"

"I did not."

"Can you state about what time you heard this conversation?"

"I went immediately to my room, and there found that it lacked only ten minutes of one."

"Did you hear any unusual sound afterwards?"

"I did not. I heard no one in the halls; and Mr. Mainwaring's apartments were so remote from the general sleeping-rooms that no sound from there, unless very loud, could have reached the other occupants of the house."

Further questions failed to develop any evidence of importance, and the witness was temporarily dismissed. Glancing at his watch, the coroner remarked,

"It is nearly time to adjourn, but if Mr. Hardy has returned we will first hear what he has to report."

As the valet again came forward, Dr. Westlake asked, "Were you able to learn anything concerning the strangers who were here yesterday?"

"Not very much, sir," was the reply. "I went to the Arlington first and inquired for Mr. J. Henry Carruthers, and they told me there was no such person registered there; but they said a man answering that description, tall and wearing dark glasses, came into the hotel last evening and took dinner and sat for an hour or so in the office reading the evening papers. He went out some time between seven and eight o'clock, and they had seen nothing more of him."

"Was Richard Hobson at the Arlington?"

"No, sir; but I went to the Riverside, and found R. Hobson registered there. They said he came in in the forenoon and ordered a carriage for Fair Oaks. He came back to lunch, but kept his room all the afternoon. He had a man with him in his room most of the afternoon, but he took no meals there. After dinner Hobson went out, and nobody knew when he came back; but he was there to breakfast, and took the first train to the city. I made some inquiries at the depot, and the agent said there was a tall man, in a gray ulster and with dark glasses, who took the 3.10 train this morning to the city, but he didn't notice him particularly. That was all I could learn."

As the hour was late, the inquest was then adjourned until ten o'clock the next morning. Every one connected with the household at Fair Oaks was expected to remain on the premises that night; and, dinner over, the gentlemen, including Mr. Whitney, locked themselves within the large library to discuss the inevitable contest that would arise over the estate and to devise how, with the least possible delay, to secure possession of the property.

Later in the evening Harry Scott came down from his room for a brief stroll through the grounds. A bitter smile crossed his face as he noticed the brightly illumined library and heard the eager, excited tones within, remembering the dimly-lighted room above with its silent occupant, unloved, unmourned, unthought of, in marked contrast to the preceding night, when Hugh Mainwaring lavished upon his guests such royal entertainment and was the recipient of their congratulations and their professions of esteem and regard.

As he paced slowly up and down the avenues, his thoughts were not of the present, but of the past and future. At the earliest opportunity that day he had returned to the city, ostensibly, to attend to some telegraphic despatches, but his main errand had been to consult with an eminent lawyer whom he knew by reputation, and in whom both Hugh Mainwaring and Mr. Whitney, in numerous legal contests, had found a powerful and bitter opponent. To him Scott had intrusted his own case, giving him the fullest details, and leaving in his possession for safe keeping the proofs which were soon to play so important a part; and Mr. Sutherland, the attorney retained by Scott, had been present at the inquest, apparently as a disinterested spectator, but, in reality, one of the most intensely interested of them all.

CHAPTER VIII

THE WEAVING OF THE WEB

Ten o'clock found an eager crowd assembled in and about the large library at Fair Oaks, drawn by reports of the sensational features developed on the preceding day. The members of the household occupied nearly the same positions as on the preceding afternoon, with the exception of the secretary, who had entered the room a little in advance of the others and had seated himself near the coroner.

Notwithstanding the glances of doubt and distrust which Scott encountered, and his own consciousness that suspicion against himself would deepen as all the facts in the case became known, he was as impassive as ever. Even Mr. Whitney was wholly at a loss to account for the change in the bearing of the secretary. He was no longer the employee, but carried himself with a proud independence, as though conscious of some mysterious vantage-ground.

On the other side of the coroner, but conveniently near Scott, was Mr. Sutherland, while in the rear, commanding a good view of both gentlemen, as well as of nearly every face in the room, sat Mr. Merrick, though to a stranger his manner would have implied the utmost indifference to the proceedings.

The first witness called for by the coroner was Johnson, the butler. For the first five or ten minutes his testimony was little more than a corroboration of that given by the valet on the preceding day, of the discovery of the death of Hugh Mainwaring.

"You say," said the coroner, "that at Mr. Whitney's request you remained in the upper hall, near the library and within call?"

"Yes, sir."

"Will you state how long a time you should think elapsed between the alarm given by Hardy and the appearance of the entire household, including both the guests and the servants?"

"Well, sir, Hardy gave the alarm a little after seven. The servants were already up and crowded around there imme-diately, and I should say that every one, including the ladies, was out within twenty minutes, or thirty at the latest, with the exception of Mrs. LaGrange and her son.

"At what time did the latter appear?"

"It must have been considerably after eight o'clock, sir, when she came to the library in response to a message from Mr. Whitney."

"And her son?"

"I did not see Mr. Walter LaGrange at all during the forenoon, sir."

"How was that?" inquired Dr. Westlake, rather quickly. "Was he not at Fair Oaks?"

"I cannot say, sir. I did not see him until luncheon."

"When did you last see Mr. Mainwaring?"

"A little after eleven o'clock night before last, - Wednesday night, sir. I was in the hall as he passed upstairs to his rooms, and I heard him ask Mr. Scott to come to his library."

"Did there seem to be any coldness or unpleasantness between them?"

"No, sir; they both appeared the same as usual."

"Did any strangers call at Fair Oaks Wednesday aside from those mentioned yesterday?"

"No, sir."

"Will you describe the strangers who were here, stating when they called and any particulars you are able to give?"

"The man giving his name as R. Hobson called between eleven and twelve, Wednesday morning. He was tall, with thin features, small, dark eyes, and a very soft voice. He came in a carriage, inquired for Mrs. LaGrange, and seemed in considerable haste. He stayed about an hour. The gentleman who called about four in the afternoon also came in a carriage and inquired for Mr. Mainwaring, saying he had been directed to Fair Oaks at the city offices of Mainwaring & Co. On learning that Mr. Mainwaring was out, he asked for the secretary; and I took his card to Mr. Scott, who gave directions to have him shown up into the library. I do not know when he left. He was tall, with black hair and moustache and dark glasses."

"Mr. Hobson's call occasioned considerable comment at luncheon, did it not?"

"Yes, sir."

"Did you observe that it had any effect on Mr. Mainwaring?"

"Well, sir, I thought he appeared considerably annoyed, and after luncheon he asked me whether Mr. Hobson had inquired for him."

"Did you admit Hobson when he called in the evening?"

"I did not, sir. I merely met him at the door and directed him to the south side entrance."

"At Mrs. LaGrange's request?"

"Yes, sir; in accordance with her instructions."

"Did she give any reason for such instructions?"

"Merely that his former call had caused so much remark she wished to receive him privately."

"Was he alone when he called the second time?"

"No, sir."

"Can you describe the person who accompanied him?"

"No, sir. The man stood so far in the shadow that I could only see the outlines of his form. I should say he was about the same height as Mr. Hobson, but considerably heavier."

"Do you know at what hour they left?"

"No, sir."

Further questions failing to elicit any facts bearing upon the situation, the butler was dismissed, and Brown, the coachman, took his place. The latter was far less taciturn than the butler, seeming rather eager to impart some piece of information which he evidently considered of special importance.

After a few preliminary questions, the coroner said,-

"At what time, and from whom, did you first hear of Mr. Mainwaring's death?"

"About half-past seven, yesterday morning, sir. I was a - taking care of the horses, sir, when Uncle Mose-he's the gardener, sir - he comes past the stable on his way to the tool-house, and he tells me that Mr. Mainwaring had been murdered in the night, right in his own rooms, and then he tells me-"

"How long had you been up and at work in the stables?"

"Before I heard of the murder? Well, about an hour, I should say. I generally gets up at six."

"Had you been to the house that morning?"

"No, sir; but I went right up there after seeing Uncle Mose, and I was in the kitchen telling what I had seen the night before, when the butler he comes down and said as how Mr. Ralph Mainwaring wanted me, and that I had better keep my mouth shut till I was asked to tell what I knew."

"Where were you last Wednesday night?" asked the coroner, rather abruptly.

Brown looked surprised, but answered readily, "I was out with some friends of mine. We all went down to the city together that night and stayed out pretty late, and it seems a mighty good thing we did, too."

"Why so?" asked the coroner.

"Well, sir," said Brown, deliberately, glad of an opportunity to tell his story and evidently determined to make the most of it, "as I said, we stayed out that night later than we meant to, and I didn't waste no time getting home after I left the depot. So, when I got to Fair Oaks, I thought I'd take the shortest cut, and so I come in by the south gate, off from the side street, and took the path around the lake to get to the stables."

"What lake do you mean?" interrupted the coroner.

"The small lake back of the grove in the south part of the grounds. Well, I was hurrying along through that grove, and all of a sudden I seen a man standing on the edge of the lake with his back towards me. He was very tall, and wore an ulster that came nearly to his feet, and he looked so queer that I stepped out of the path and behind some big trees to watch him. I hadn't no more than done so, when he stooped and picked up something, and come right up the path towards me. The moon was shining, had been up about two hours, I should say, but his back was to the light and I couldn't see his face, nor I didn't want him to see me. After he'd got by I stepped out to watch him and see if he went towards the house, but he didn't; he took the path I had just left and walked very fast to the south gate and went out onto the side street."

"In which direction did he then go?" asked the coroner.

"He went up onto the main avenue and turned towards the town."

"Can you describe his appearance?"

"Only that he was tall and had very black hair; but his face was in the shadow, so I couldn't tell how he looked."

"What did he pick up from the ground?"

"I couldn't see very plain, but it looked like a small, square box done up in paper."

"You did not try to call any one?"

"No, sir. The man didn't go near the house, and I didn't think much about it until Uncle Mose told me yesterday morning that the night before he seen-

"Never mind what he saw; we will let him tell his own story. Was that all you saw?"

"No, sir; it wasn't," replied Brown, with a quick side glance towards Mrs. LaGrange, who occupied the same position as on the preceding day. "I was going along towards the stables, thinking about that man, and all of a sudden I noticed there was a bright light in one of the rooms up-stairs. The curtains wasn't drawn, and I thought I'd see whose room it was, so I walked up towards the house carefully, and I saw Mr. Mainwaring's secretary. He looked awfully pale and haggard, and was walking up and down the room kind of excited like. Just then I happened to step on the gravelled walk and he heard me, for he started and looked kind of frightened and listened a moment, and then he stepped up quick and extinguished the light, and I was afraid he'd see me then from the window, so I hurried off. But I thought 'twas mighty queer-"

"Mr. Scott was dressed, was he?" interrupted the coroner.

"Yes, sir," Brown answered, sullenly.

"Did you go directly to your room?"

"Yes, sir."

"What time was this?"

"I heard the clock strike three just after I got in."

"You saw or heard nothing more?"

" No, sir."

"You knew nothing of what had occurred at the house until the gardener told you in the morning?"

"N-yes-no, sir," Brown stammered, with another glance towards Mrs. LaGrange, who was watching him closely.

"What did you say?" demanded the coroner.

"I said I didn't know what had happened till Uncle Mose told me," Brown answered, doggedly.

"That will do," said the coroner, watching the witness narrowly as he resumed his place among the servants.

During the latter part of Brown's testimony, quick, telegraphic glances had been exchanged between Scott and Mr. Sutherland, and one or two slips of paper, unobserved by any one but Merrick, had passed from one to the other.

Scott was well aware that the statements made by the coachman had deepened suspicion against himself. He paid little attention to the crowd, however, but noted particularly the faces of the guests at Fair Oaks. Ralph Mainwaring's, dark with anger; that of the genial Mr. Thornton coldly averted; young Mainwaring's supercilious stare, and his sister's expression of contemptuous disdain; and as he studied their features his own grew immobile as marble. Suddenly his glance encountered Miss Carleton's face and was held for a moment as though under a spell. There was no weak sentimentality there, no pity or sympathy,-he would have scorned either,-but the perfect confidence shining in her eyes called forth a quick response from his own, though not a muscle stirred about the sternly-set mouth. She saw and understood, and, as her eyes fell, a smile, inexplicable and mysterious, flashed for an instant across her face and was gone.

"John Wilson," announced the coroner, after a slight pause.

A middle-aged man, rather dull in appearance, except for a pair of keenly observant eyes, stepped forward with slow precision.

"You are Mr. Ralph Mainwaring's valet, I believe?" said the coroner.

"That I am, sir," was the reply.

"Have you been for some time in his employ?"

The man peered sharply at Dr. Westlake from under his heavy brows, and replied, with great deliberation, "Nigh onto thirty years, sir."

Then, noting the surprise in his interlocutor's face, he added, with dignity, "The Wilsons, sir, have served the Mainwarings for three generations. My father, sir, was valet to the father of the dead Hugh Mainwaring, the Honorable Ralph Maxwell Mainwaring, sir.

A smile played over the features of young Mainwaring at these words, but Scott started involuntarily, and, after studying Wilson's face intently for a moment, hastily pencilled a few words on a slip of paper which he handed to Mr. Sutherland, and both watched the witness with special interest.

His testimony differed little from that given by Hardy and by the butler. He stated, however, that, after accompanying Mr. Ralph Mainwaring to the scene of the murder, the latter sent him to summon Mr. Scott; but on his way to the young gentleman's room he saw Mr. Whitney in advance of him, who called the secretary and immediately returned with him to the library.

"Was Mr. Scott already up when Mr. Whitney called him?" the coroner inquired, quickly.

"He was up and dressed, sir," was the reply.

Wilson also corroborated the butler's statement that Walter LaGrange was not seen about the premises until luncheon, and stated, in addition, that the horse belonging to young LaGrange was missing from the stables until nearly noon. Having mingled very little with the servants at Fair Oaks, he had but slight knowledge concerning the occurrences of the day preceding the murder. His testimony was therefore very brief.

"Katie O'Brien, chambermaid," was next called; and in response a young Irish woman quietly took her place before the coroner. She answered the questions addressed her as briefly as possible, but with deliberation, as though each word had been carefully weighed.

"Did you have charge of the private rooms of Mr. Mainwaring?"

"Yes, sir."

"You took care of his rooms as usual Wednesday?"

"Yes, sir."

"Did you see Mr. Mainwaring during the day or evening?"

"I met him once or twice in the halls."

"When did you last see him?"

"About two o'clock Wednesday afternoon."

"State how you first heard of his death."

"I was working in the halls up-stairs about seven that morning and heard running back and forth, as if there was trouble. I went out into the front hall and met the butler, and he told me Mr. Mainwaring had been murdered."

"Did you go in to see him at that time?"

"Yes, sir, for a moment."

"Did you notice anything unusual in his rooms?"

"I didn't notice anything unusual in Mr. Mainwaring's rooms."

"Did you in any room?"

"Yes, sir."

"In what one?"

"In Mr. Scott's room, a little later."

"State what you observed."

"A few minutes after I left the library I saw Mr. Scott come out of his room and go away with Mr. Whitney, and I thought I would go in and do up the room. So I went in, but the bed was just as I had made it up the day before. It hadn't been slept in nor touched. Then things was strewn around considerable, and the top drawer of his dressing-case was kept locked all the forenoon until he went to the city."

"When did he go to the city?"

"About noon."

"Did you see Mr. Scott the day or evening preceding Mr. Mainwaring's death?"

"No, sir; but I know he was locked in Mr. Mainwaring's library all the afternoon, after the folks had gone out driving."

"How do you know the library was locked?"

"I was sweeping in the corridor, and I heard him unlock the door when the butler came up with some gentleman's card."

"Did you see the gentleman who came up-stairs later?"

"No, sir."

"Did you see Walter LaGrange at any time during yesterday forenoon?"

The witness colored slightly, but replied, "I think I met him once or twice; I don't remember just when."

"He was away from home part of the time, was he not?"

"I don't know where he was."

Nothing further of importance could be learned from the witness, and, as it was then past twelve, a short recess was taken until after lunch.

Scott took his place at the table with the guests, seemingly alike indifferent to cold aversion or angry frowns. He was conscious that Miss Carleton was watching him, her manner indicating the same frank friendliness she had shown him on the preceding day, and in response to a signal from her, as they rose from the table, he followed her into one of the drawing-rooms, joining her in a large alcove window, where she motioned him to a seat on a low divan by her side.

"You have made a bitter enemy in Mrs. LaGrange," she said, archly; "and she has marshalled her forces against you."

"Do you think so?" he asked, with an amused smile.

"Certainly. She displayed her tactics this morning. I am positive that much of the testimony was given in accordance with her orders."

"For the most part, however, the witnesses stated facts," Scott replied, watching her closely.

"Yes; but facts may be so misrepresented as to give an impression quite the reverse of the truth."

"That is so. And a misrepresentation having a foundation of truth is the hardest to fight. But," he added, in a lighter tone, "all this testimony against me does not seem to have produced the same impression upon you that it has upon the others.

Your suspicions do not seem, as yet, to have been very thoroughly aroused."

"Perhaps my suspicions are as dormant as your own apprehensions. I fail to detect the slightest anxiety on your part as to the outcome of this, one way or another."

"No," he replied, after a pause; "I feel no anxiety, only resentment that circumstances have conspired against me just at this time, and contempt for people who will be led by appearances rather than their own judgment."

"People sometimes use very little judgment where their own personal interests are concerned."

"In that case," said Scott, as they rose to return to the library, where the others had already preceded them, "I suppose the word of one unprincipled woman and of three or four ignorant servants will be allowed to outweigh mine."

They had reached the library and Miss Carleton made no reply, but Scott again saw the same inscrutable little smile play over her features, and wondered at its meaning.

CHAPTER IX

TANGLED THREADS

Upon resuming the examination, the first witness called for was Mary Catron, the second cook, a woman about thirty-five years of age, with an honest face, but one indicative of a fiery temper. Her testimony was brief, but given with a directness that was amusing. When questioned of the occurrences of the day preceding the murder, she replied,-

"I know nothing of what went on except from the gossip of the rest. My place was in the kitchen, and I had too much to do that day to be loitering round in the halls, leaning on a broom-handle, and listening at keyholes," and she cast a glance of scathing contempt in the direction of the chambermaid.

"Did this 'gossip' that you speak of have any bearing on what has since occurred?" the coroner inquired.

"Well, sir, it might and it mightn't. 'Twas mostly about the will that Mr. Mainwaring was making; and as how them that got little was angry that they didn't get more, and them as got much was growling at not getting the whole."

"How did the servants gain any knowledge of this will?"

"That's more than I can say, sir, except as I knows the nature of some folks."

Upon further questioning, the witness stated that on the night of the murder, between the hours of two and three, she was aroused by a sound like the closing of an outside door, but on going to one of the basement windows to listen, she heard nothing further and concluded she had been mistaken.

"Did you see the coachman at that time?" she was asked.

"A few minutes later I looked out again and I see him gaping and grinning at the house and jabbering to himself like an idiot, and I was minded to send him about his business if he hadn't a-took himself off when he did."

"He was perfectly sober, was he not?"

"Sober for aught that I know; but, to my thinking, he's that daft that he's noways responsible for aught that he says."

"Were you up-stairs soon after the alarm was given?" asked the coroner, when she had told of hearing from the butler the news of the murder.

"Yes, sir; I went up as soon as ever I heard what had happened."

"Who was in the library at that time?"

"Nobody but some of the servants, sir. I met Mr. Whitney just as I came out."

"Did you meet any one else?"

"I met no one, but I saw the housekeeper coming out of her son's room. She didn't see me; but she was telling him to get ready quick to go somewheres, and I heard her say to hurry, for every minute was precious.

Louis Picot, the head cook, could give no information whatever.

When the alarm was given, he had rushed, with the other servants, to the scene of the murder, and in his imperfect English, accompanied by expressive French gestures, he tried to convey his horror and grief at the situation, but that was all.

The two maids who attended the English ladies were next called upon; but their testimony was mainly corroborative of that given by the chambermaid, except that Sarah Whitely, Miss Carleton's maid, stated, in addition, that she had seen Mr. Walter LaGrange leave his mother's room in great haste and go down-stairs, and a little later, from one of the upper windows, saw him riding away from the stables in the direction of the south gate.

But one servant remained, "Uncle Mose," as he was familiarly called, the old colored man having charge of the grounds at Fair Oaks. His snow-white hair and bent form gave him a venerable appearance; but he was still active, and the shrewd old face showed both humor and pathos as he proceeded with his story. He had been a slave in his younger days, and still designated his late employer by the old term "mars'r." He was a well-known character to many present, including Dr. Westlake, who knew that in this instance questions would have to be abandoned and the witness allowed to tell his story in his own way.

"Well, Uncle Mose, you have been employed at Fair Oaks for a long time, haven't you?"

"Moah dan twenty yeahs, sah, I'se had charge ob dese y'er grounds; an' mars'r Mainwaring, he t'ought nobody but ole Mose cud take cyah ob 'em, sah."

"You were about the grounds as usual Wednesday, were you not?"

"I was 'bout de grounds all day, sah, 'case dere was a pow'ful lot to do a - gittin' ready for de big doins dere was goin' to be on mars'r's birfday."

"Did you see either of the strangers who called that day?"

"I'se a - comm' to dat d'rectly, sah. You see, sah, I wants to say right heah, befo' I goes any furder, dat I don' know noffin 'cept what tuk place under my own obserbation. I don' feel called upon to 'spress no 'pinions 'bout nobody. I jes' wants to state a few recurrences dat I noted at de time, speshally 'bout dem strangers as was heah in pertickeler. Well, sah, de fust man, he come heah in de mawnin'. De Inglish gentlemens, dey had been a - walkin' in de grounds and jes' done gone roun' de corner oh de house to go to mars'r Mainwaring's liberry, when dis man he comes up de av'nue in a kerridge, an' de fust ting I heah 'im a - cussin' de driver. Den he gets out and looks roun' kind o' quick, jes' like de possum in de kohn, as ef he was 'fraid somebody done see 'im. I was fixin' de roses on de front poach, an' I looked at 'im pow'ful sharp, an' when de dooh opened he jumped in quick, as ef he was glad to get out o' sight. Well, sah, I didn't like de 'pearance ob dat man, an' I jes' t'ought I'd get anoder look at 'im, but he stayed a mighty long time, sah, an' bime'by I had to go to de tool-house, an' when I gets hack the kerridge was gone."

"Could you describe the man, Uncle Mose?" the coroner asked.

"No, sah, I don' know as I could 'scribe 'im perzacly; but I'd know 'im, no matter where I sot eyes on 'im, and I know'd 'im the nex' time I see 'ira. Well, sah, dat aft'noon, mars'r Mainwaring an' de folks had gone out ridin', an' I was roun' kind o' permiscuous like, an' I see anoder kerridge way down de av'nue by de front gate, an' I waited, 'spectin' maybe I'd see dat man again. While I was waitin' by de front doob, all oh a sudden a man come roun' from de side, as ef he come from mars'r Mainwaring's liberry, but he was anoder man."

"Didn't he look at all like the first man?" inquired the coroner.

"No, sah; he looked altogedder diff'rent; but I don' know as I couldstate whar'in de differensiashun consisted, sah. Dis man was berry good lookin' 'ceptin' his eyes, an' dem yoh cudn' see, 'case he had on cull'ed glasses. Mebbe his eyes was pow'ful weak, er mebbe he didn't want nobody to see 'em; but I 'spicioned dem glasses d'rectly, sah, an' I watched 'im. He goes down to de kerridge an' takes out a coat an' says sump' in to de driver, an' de kerridge goes away tow'ds de town, an' he walks off de oder way. Bime'by I see 'im gwine back again on de oder side ob de street-"

"Was he alone?" interrupted the coroner.

"Yes, sah; an' I done kep' my eye on 'im, an' he didn' go on to de town, but tuhned down de fust side street. Well, sah, I didn' see no moah ob 'im den; but dat ebenin' I'd ben a - workin' roun' de house, sprinklin' de grass and gettin' ready foh de nex' day, when I happens to pass by de side dooh, an' I sees dem two men comm' out togedder."

"What time was this, Uncle Mose?" the coroner asked, quickly.

"Well, sah," said the old man, reflectively, "my mem'ry is a little derelictious on dat p'int, but I knows 'twas gettin' putty late."

"Are you sure these were the same two men you had seen earlier in the day?"

"Yes, sah; 'case I stepped in de bushes to watch 'em. Dey talked togedder berry low, an' den one man goes back into de house, an' I seen 'im plain in de hall light, an' he was de fust man; an' while I was a-watchin' 'im, de oder man he disappeahed an' I cudn' see 'im nowhar, but I know'd he was de man dat came in de aft'noon, 'case he look jes' like 'im, an' toted a coat on his arm. Well, sah, I t'inks it a berry cur'is sarcumstance, an' I was jes' comm' to de preclushun dat I'd mention it to some ob de fambly, when de fust man, he come to de dooh wid de housekeeper. I was in de shadder and dey didn' see me, but I heah 'im say, kind o' soft like, 'Remember, my deah lady, dis is a biz'ness contract; I does my part, an' I 'spects my pay.' An' she says, 'Oh, yes, yoh shall hab yohr money widout fail.' An' I says to myse'f, 'Mose, yoh ole fool, what you stan'in' heah foh? Dat ain't nuffin dat consarns yoh nohow,' an' I goes home, an' dat's all I know, sah. But I'se ben pow'ful sorry eber sence dat I didn' let mars'r Mainwaring know 'bout it, 'case I has my 'spicions," and the old darkey shook his head, while the tears coursed down his furrowed cheeks.

"How did you hear of Mr. Mainwaring's death?" asked the coroner.

"De coachman, he done tole me, sah."

"Why, the coachman stated that you told him what had occurred."

"No, sah; he done tole me; I'd come up to de place pow'ful ahly dat mawnin' 'case dere was to be such big doings dat day, an' I was gwine to de tool-house foh sump'in, an' I see mars'r Walter ridin' away from de stables pow' ful fas' on his hoss-"

"Do you mean Walter LaGrange?"

"Yes, sah; an' de coachman he came out an' I ax 'im whar de young man was gwine dat ahly, an' he say mars'r Mainwaring ben killed, an' mars'r Walter had to go to town as fas' as his hoss cud take 'im."

"Do you know when he returned?"

"He came back, sah, befo' berry long, an' den he went away agin and didn't come back till mos' noon."

When the old darkey had been dismissed the coachman was recalled.

"What did you mean by stating that you first heard of Mr. Mainwaring's death from the gardener, when the reverse was the truth?"

"I don't know," he replied, carelessly; "I s'pose I got mixed. I remember talking with him about it, and I thought he told me."

"You had forgotten the interview with Walter LaGrange, I presume."

Brown made no answer.

"Why did you not mention that?"

"I wasn't asked to," he replied in insolent tones; "you said nothing to me about Mr. LaGrange."

"You are expected to state in full every occurrence having any bearing on the situation. You may give the particulars of that interview now."

"There's nothing to tell more than Uncle Mose told. I was working in the stables as usual, and Mr. LaGrange came in in a big hurry and ordered me to saddle his horse as quick as I could, that Mr. Mainwaring had been murdered, and he'd got to go to town."

"At what time was this?"

"About half-past seven, I should say."

"Did he state his errand?"

"No, sir."

"When did he return?"

"I saw his horse standing in the yard outside the stables about half an hour after, and then 'twas gone, and I didn't see it again till noon."

Walter LaGrange was next called. He stated that he had spent the greater part of the day preceding the murder away from Fair Oaks; he had not been at home to luncheon or dinner, and consequently knew nothing of the strangers seen on the place that day. He had returned about half-past ten that evening, and remembered seeing Mr. Mainwaring and his guests seated on the veranda, but he had gone directly to his room without meeting any one. The first intimation which he had received of any unusual occurrence the next morning was when his mother entered his room and told him that Mr. Mainwaring had either been murdered or had committed suicide, no one knew which.

"Was that her only object in coming to your room?"

"No, sir; she wanted me to do an errand for her."

"Will you state the nature of this errand?"

"It was only to deliver a note."

"To whom?"

"To Mr. Hobson," the young man answered weakly, while his mother frowned, the first sign of emotion of any kind which she had betrayed that day.

"Did you deliver the note?"

"Yes, sir."

"Then, under your mother's orders, you went to the city on your second trip, did you not?"

"Y-yes, sir."

"Were you successful in finding Mr. Hobson there?"

"Yes, sir," the witness answered sullenly.

"You had other business in the city aside from meeting him, had you not?"

Between the coroner's persistence and his mother's visible signs of displeasure, Walter LaGrange was fast losing his temper.

"If you know so much about this business, I don't see the use of your questioning me," he retorted angrily. "It's no affair of mine anyway; I had nothing to do with it, nor I won't be mixed up in it; and if you want any information you'd better ask mother for it; it's her business and none of mine."

After a few more questions, which the witness answered sullenly and in monosyllables, he was dismissed.

"Mr. Higgenbotham," announced the coroner. The greatest surprise was manifested on every side as the senior member of a well-known firm of jewellers stepped forward; the same gentleman who had accompanied Mr. Whitney on his return from the city on the preceding day.

"Mr. Higgenbotham," said the coroner, "I believe you are able to furnish some testimony which will be pertinent at this time."

"Yes, Dr. Westlake," responded the other, in deep, musical tones, "I think possibly I can render you a little assistance in your investigations."

"Mr. Higgenbotham, do you recognize the young gentleman who has just given his testimony?"

"I do, sir," said the witness, adjusting a pair of eyeglasses and gazing steadily at Walter LaGrange. "I recall his features perfectly."

"You were personally acquainted with the late Hugh Mainwaring, I believe?"

"Yes, sir, intimately acquainted with him."

"You are, I believe, familiar with the Mainwaring jewels which are now missing?" continued the coroner.

Walter LaGrange looked uncomfortable and his mother's cheek paled.

"I am, sir; having had them repeatedly left in my possession for safe keeping during their owner's absence from home; and I have also a complete list of them, with a detailed description of every piece."

"Very well, Mr. Higgenbotham, will you now please state when, and under what circumstances, you saw this young gentleman?"

"I was seated in my private office yesterday morning, when my head clerk came in and asked me to step out into the salesrooms for a moment, as he said a young man was there trying to sell some very fine jewels, and, from his youth and his ignorance of their value, he feared something was wrong. I went out immediately and saw this young gentleman, who handed me for inspection a superb diamond brooch and an elegant necklace of diamonds and pearls. I instantly recognized the gems as pieces from the old Mainwaring collection of jewels. Simultaneously there occurred to my mind the report of the murder of Hugh Mainwaring, which I had heard but a short time before, although then I knew nothing of the robbery. Naturally, my suspicions were awakened. I questioned the young man closely, however, and he stated that his home was at Fair Oaks, and that his mother was a distant relative of Mr. Mainwaring's; that the jewels were hers, and she wished to dispose of them for ready cash to meet an emergency. His story was so plausible that I thought possibly my suspicions had been somewhat hasty and premature. Still, I declined to purchase the jewels; and when he left the store I ordered one of our private detectives to follow him and report to me. In the course of an hour the detective returned and reported that the young man had sold the jewels to a pawnbroker for less than one-fourth their actual value. About half an hour later I heard the news of the robbery at Fair Oaks, and that the family jewels were missing; and knowing that Mr. Whitney was here, I immediately telephoned to him the facts which I have just stated. He came in to the city at once, and we proceeded to the pawnshop, where he also identified the jewels."

Mr. Higgenbotham paused for a moment, producing a package from an inner pocket, which he proceeded to open.

"We secured a loan of the jewels for a few days," he continued, advancing towards the coroner. "Here they are, and here is a copy of the list of which I spoke. By comparing these gems with the description of those which I have checked on the list, you will see that they are identical."

He placed the open casket on the table. There was a moment's silence, broken by subdued exclamations of admiration as Dr. Westlake lifted the gems from their resting-place.

"You are correct," he said; "the description is complete. There is no doubt that these are a part of the collection. I see you have marked the value of these two items as seven thousand dollars."

"Yes; that is a moderate valuation. And were the prices of the other articles carried out, you would see that, with the exception of a few very small pieces, these have the least value of the entire lot. I believe I can be of no further service.

Mrs. LaGrange was next recalled.

"Have you anything to say in reference to the testimony just given?" the coroner inquired.

"I have this much to say," she replied, haughtily, "that I could have given you the history of those jewels, including, perhaps, some facts of which even Mr. Higgenbotham and Mr.

Whitney are in ignorance, and thus have spared you the infinite pains you have taken to make public the straits to which I was reduced, because of my position here, when in need of a little ready money. I could have informed you that they were originally a part of the old Mainwaring collection of gems, until they were given me by my husband."

"It hardly seems consistent that a man who treated his wife in the manner in which you claim to have been treated would bestow upon her gifts of such value as these," the coroner remarked with emphasis.

"They were of little value to him," she answered, with scorn; "as you have been informed, they were the poorest which he possessed. Besides, there were times when I could persuade him to almost anything, - anything but to acknowledge his lawful wife and his legitimate son."

"Was the money which you were forced to raise by the sale of these jewels to be paid to Hobson?"

"It was."

"In accordance with the terms of your contract with him, made a few hours preceding the death of Mr. Mainwaring?"

"Yes," she replied, defiantly. "And as you probably would ask the nature of that contract, I will save you the trouble. Knowing that my son and I were likely to be defrauded of our rights in the same manner in which Hugh Mainwaring had defrauded others, I engaged Mr. Hobson as my attorney, as he, better than any one else, knew the facts in the case. When I learned yesterday morning of my husband's death, I realized that I would have immediate need of his services, and accordingly sent him word to that effect. He demanded a large cash payment at once. The result of this demand v Mr. Higgenbotham has already told you."

"How was Hobson to secure for you your rights from

Hugh Mainwaring?"

"That was left entirely to his own discretion."

"Will you describe the appearance of Mr. Hobson's clerk?"

"Unfortunately, I am unable to do so. He was merely brought as a witness to our contract. I knew that he was present, but he remained in the shadow, and I took no notice of him whatever."

"Your contract, then, was a verbal one?"

"It was."

Upon being closely questioned, Mrs. LaGrange reiterated her assertions of the preceding day, laying particular stress upon the alleged interview between Hugh Mainwaring and his secretary, after which she was dismissed, and Harry Scott was recalled.

"Mr. Scott," said the coroner, "what were the relations existing between Mr. Mainwaring and yourself up to the time of his death?"

Scott flushed slightly as he replied, "Those ordinarily existing between employer and employed, except that I believe Mr. Mainwaring accorded me more than usual consideration, and I, while duly appreciative of his kindness, yet took especial pains never to exceed the bounds of an employee."

"Were there ever any unpleasant words passed between you?"

"None whatever."

"Was your last interview with Mr. Mainwaring of a friendly nature?"

"Entirely so."

"What have you to say in reference to the testimony given to the effect that your voice was heard and recognized in angry conversation with Mr. Mainwaring at nearly one o'clock?"

"I have to say that it is false, and without foundation."

"Do you mean to say that the statement of the witness was wholly without truth?"

"I do not deny that such an interview, as alleged by the witness, may have taken place, for that is something concerning which I have no knowledge whatever; but I do deny that she heard my voice, or that I was in the library at that time, or at any time after about twenty minutes past twelve."

"Was that the time at which you went to your room?"

"Very near that time, as my interview with Mr. Mainwaring could not have exceeded ten minutes."

"At what time did you retire?"

"I sat up very late that night, for my mind was so occupied with some personal matters that I felt no inclination for sleep. I lighted a cigar and became so absorbed in my own thoughts that I was totally unaware of the lapse of time, until I was aroused by what I thought was a stealthy step outside. I then became conscious, for the first time, that I was very weary, both physically and mentally, and I also discovered that it was nearly three o'clock. Astonished to find it so late, and exhausted by hours of protracted thought, I threw myself as I was upon a low couch, where I slept soundly until awakened in the morning.

Further questions failed to reveal any discrepancy in his statement, and he was dismissed.

The testimony of Ralph Mainwaring and of his son added nothing of interest or importance. Mr. Thornton testified to his incidental meeting with Hobson and to the reputation which the man had borne in London. When he had resumed his seat the coroner remarked,-

"As a matter of form, I will have to call upon the ladies, though it is not expected they will be able to furnish any information throwing light on this mysterious case."

It was, as he had said, little more than a ceremony and occupied but a few moments. Miss Carleton was the last one called upon. She stated that it was nearly eleven o'clock when she reached her room, but added that she did not retire immediately, as her cousin, Miss Thornton, had come in, and they had chatted together for more than an hour; that while so engaged, she heard Mr. Scott come up-stairs and enter his room, which adjoined hers, and lock the door for the night.

"At what hour was this?" inquired the coroner.

"It could not have been more than twenty minutes after twelve, as it was twenty-five minutes after twelve when my cousin went to her room, and this was about five minutes earlier."

"Can you state whether or not he left his room within the next half-hour?"

"I know that he did not," she replied. "I can testify that he remained in his room until after one o'clock. After my cousin left I discovered that the moon was just rising, and the view across the Hudson being extremely beautiful, as well as novel to me, I extinguished the light in my room and sat down by the open window to enjoy it. I heard Mr. Scott stepping quietly about his room for a few moments; then all was still. I sat for some time admiring the scenery, until I was aroused by hearing him pacing back and forth like a person in deep thought. I then found it was much later than I supposed, - nearly one o' clock, - and I immediately retired; but so long as I was awake I could hear him walking in his room."

As Miss Carleton finished her testimony it was evident that the tide of general opinion had turned somewhat in favor of the young secretary, but the latter quietly ignored the friendly glances cast in his direction.

It was generally supposed that all testimony in the case had now been heard. Considerable surprise was, therefore, manifested when the coroner nodded to Mr. Whitney, who, in turn, beckoned to some one in the hall. In response the butler appeared, ushering in a tall man, with cadaverous features and small, dark eyes, which peered restlessly about him.

"Richard Hobson," announced the coroner.

"At your service, sir," said the man, advancing with a cringing gait and fawning, apologetic smile.

"Mr. Hobson," said the coroner, after a few preliminaries, "I understand you were somewhat acquainted with the late Hugh Mainwaring."

"Well, yes, sir, somewhat," the other replied in soft, insinuating tones, but with peculiar emphasis on the word used by Dr. Westlake. "Indeed, I might say, without exaggeration, that I was probably better acquainted with that esti-mable gentleman than was any one in this country."

"When did you last see Mr. Mainwaring?"

"I have not seen him to speak with him for fully twenty-three years."

"You have corresponded with, him, however, in that time?"

The witness showed no surprise.

"We exchanged a few letters while I was in England. I have

neither heard from him nor written to him since coming to this country."

"When did you last see him, regardless of whether you spoke to him or not?"

"Probably within the last two or three weeks. I have occasionally met him on the street."

"Did Mr. Mainwaring see you at any of these times?"

"If he did, he did not recognize me."

"Did you see him when you called at Fair Oaks, Wednesday,-either morning or evening?"

"I did not."

"Mr. Hobson, will you describe the man who accompanied you when you called in the evening, Wednesday?"

"I could give you a general description. He was a large man, about my own height, but heavier, and rather good looking, on the whole. But I am not good on details, such as complexion, color of hair, and so on; and then, you know, those little things are very easily changed."

"What was his name?"

Mr. Hobson smiled blandly. "The name by which I know him is John Carroll, but I have no idea as to his real name. He is a very eccentric character, many-sided as it were, and I never know which side will, come uppermost."

"He is your clerk and in your employ, is he not?"

"Agent, I think, would be a preferable term. He is in my employ, he transacts certain business for me, but he does it in his own way, and comes and goes at his own discretion."

"Where is he at present?"

"I have no idea, sir."

"Did he leave for the city that night, or did he remain with you at the Riverside Hotel?"

"He was not with me at the hotel except for a few hours. I have not the slightest idea from whence he came to see me, when he went away, or in what direction he went. He was in haste to be excused as soon as our joint business was done, and I have not seen him since."

"Did he have on dark glasses that day?"

"Not when I saw him, but that was only in my room at the hotel, and for a few moments in this house; he would have no need for them at either place."

"Did he not accompany you from the hotel to Fair Oaks?"

"No, sir; we met here by prearrangement."

"When do you expect to see your agent again?"

"Whenever he has any business reports to make," Hobson replied, with an exasperating smile; "hut I have no idea when that will be. He has other commissions to execute; he is in the employ of others besides myself, and transacts some business on his own account also."

"I understand, Mr. Hobson, that you have repeatedly extorted money from Mr. Mainwaring by threatening to disclose facts in your possession regarding some questionable transaction."

"No, sir; my action could not be termed extortion or blackmail within the meaning of the law, though to any one conversant with Mr. Mainwaring's private correspondence it may have had that appearance. I was, however, merely making an effort to collect what was legally due me. Mr. Mainwaring, before leaving England, had voluntarily bound himself to pay me a certain sum upon the condition that I would not reveal certain transactions of considerably more than questionable character. I kept my part of the contract, but he failed in his. I wrote him, therefore, threatening, unless he fulfilled his share of the agreement, to institute proceedings against him, which would naturally involve a disclosure of his secret. He never paid me in full and the secret is still mine," he paused, then added slowly, "to keep or to sell, as will pay me best."

"Was Hugh Mainwaring ever married?" the coroner asked, abruptly.

"I believe he was not generally considered a married man, sir."

"Was there ever any private marriage?"

Hobson smiled enigmatically. "You already have the word of the lady herself, sir; that should he sufficient. I cannot reveal any of Hugh Mainwaring's secrets,-unless I am well paid for it!"

Hobson was dismissed without further questions, and the examination being now at an end, the coroner's jury retired to the room in the rear of the library. Very few left the house, for all felt that little time would be required for the finding of a verdict, and comment and opinion were freely exchanged.

"Well," said Mr. Sutherland, turning towards the secretary with a smile, "they did not learn one fact from that last witness, for I doubt whether one of the few statements he did make had an iota of truth in it. By the way, Mr. Scott, it's a very fortunate thing that you've got the proofs you have. It would be a risky piece of work to depend on that man's word for proof; he is as slippery as an eel. With those proofs, however, there is no doubt but that you've got a strong case."

"It will be hard to convince Ralph Mainwaring of that fact."

"Yes, he looks as though he would hold on to his opinions pretty tenaciously."

"Not so tenaciously as he would grasp any money coming within his reach!"

At a little distance, Mr. Whitney was engaged in conversation with the Englishmen.

"I never thought he could be in any way connected with it," he was saying. "In the first place, there was no motive, there could be none; then, again, I believe he is altogether above suspicion. I know that Mr. Mainwaring had the most implicit confidence in him."

"Well," said Mr. Thornton, "for my part, I'm heartily glad if there is nothing in it. I always liked the young fellow."

"That's just where I don't agree with you; I don't like him," Ralph Mainwaring replied in a surly tone. "He may be all right so far as this matter is concerned; I don't say yet that he is or isn't; but I do say that to defame a man's character after he's dead, in the manner he has, is simply outrageous, and, you may depend upon it, there's some personal spite back of it."

"Oh, well, as to Hugh's character, I don't think you or I are going to fret ourselves about that, "laughed Mr. Thornton. "He probably sowed his wild oats with the rest of us, and there may have been some reason for his leaving England as he did."

"I don't believe it," Ralph Mainwaring retorted, angrily; but before he could say more, the doors opened and the coroner's jury filed into the room. There was instant silence, and a moment later the verdict had been announced. It was what every one had expected, and yet there was not one but experienced a feeling of disappointment and dissatisfaction.

"We find that the deceased, Hugh Mainwaring, came to his death by the discharge of a revolver in the hands of some person or persons to us unknown."

CHAPTER X

BEHIND THE SCENES

The crowd dispersed rapidly, passing down the oak-lined avenue in twos and threes, engaged in animated discussion of the details of the inquest, while each one advanced some theory of his own regarding the murder. Mr. Sutherland had taken his departure after making an appointment with Scott for the following day, and the latter now stood in one of the deep bow-windows engrossed with his own thoughts. Suspicion had been partially diverted from himself, but only partially, as he well knew, to return like a tidal wave, deepened and intensified by personal animosity, whenever the facts he had thus far so carefully concealed should become known. He gave little thought to this, however, except as it influenced him in planning his course of action for the next few days.

He was aroused from his revery by the sound of approaching steps, and, turning, met Mr. Whitney.

"Ah, Mr. Scott, I was just looking for you. I thought possibly you had slipped back to the city with the crowd. I wanted to say, Mr. Scott, that, if it will be agreeable to you, I wish you would remain at Fair Oaks for the next few days, or weeks, as the case may be. Mr. Ralph Mainwaring has retained my services to aid in securing his title to the estate, and the will having been destroyed, complications are likely to arise, so that it may take some time to get matters adjusted. Much of the business will, of necessity, have to be transacted here, as all of

Mr. Mainwaring's private papers are here, and if you will stay and help us out I will see, of course, that your salary goes right on as usual."

An excuse fur remaining at Fair Oaks was what Scott particularly desired, but he replied indifferently, "If it will accommodate you, Mr. Whitney, I can remain for a few days."

"Very well. I cannot say just how long we may need you, though I anticipate a long contest."

"Against Mrs. LaGrange?"

"Yes; though she has, in my opinion, no legal right whatever, yet she will make a hard fight, and with that trickster Hobson to help her with his chicanery, it is liable to take some time to beat them"

"You expect to win in the end, however?"

"Certainly; there is no doubt but that Ralph Mainwaring will win the case. He will get the property either for his son or for himself. We are first going to try to have the will upheld in the courts. Failing in that, the property will, of course, be divided between the nearest heirs, Ralph Mainwaring and a younger bachelor brother; in which event, the whole thing will, in all probability, finally revert to his son Hugh."

"Mr. Whitney, what is your opinion of Mrs. LaGrange's story of a private marriage?"

The attorney shook his head decidedly. "One of her clever lies; but if she ever undertakes to tell that little romance in court, I'll tear it all to shreds. She never was married to Hugh Mainwaring; but," he added, slowly, "I may as well tell you that Walter was his son. Mr. Mainwaring the same as admitted that to me once; but I am certain that, aside from that fact, that woman had some terrible hold on him, though what I never knew. By the way, Mr. Scott, do you know anything of the particulars of that transaction to which those letters referred and to which Hobson alluded to-day?"

"Yes, sir."

Mr. Whitney looked keenly at the young man. "You obtained your knowledge originally from other sources than Mr. Mainwaring's correspondence, did you not?"

"Yes, sir."

"I thought so. Do you know, Mr. Scott, I would denounce the whole thing as a lie, a scheme of that adventuress, or that impostor, Hobson, or both, by which they hope to gain some hold on the heirs, were it not that, from your manner, I have been convinced that you have some personal knowledge of the facts in the case,-that you know far more than you have yet told."

Mr. Whitney paused, watching the young secretary closely, but there was no reply, and, with all his penetration, the attorney could read nothing in the immobile face before him. He continued,-

"Whatever that transaction may have been, I wish to know nothing about it. I was much attached to Mr. Mainwaring and respected him highly, and I want to respect his memory; and I will tell you frankly what I most dread in this coming contest. I expect nothing else but that either that woman or Hobson will drag the affair out from its hiding-place, and will hold it up for the public to gloat over, as it always does. I hate to see a man's reputation blackened in that way, especially when that man was my friend and his own lips are sealed in death."

"It is a pity," said Scott, slowly; "but if one wishes to leave behind him an untarnished reputation, he must back it up, while living, with an unblemished character."

"Well," said the attorney, tentatively, after another pause, "Mr.

Mainwaring's character, whatever it may have been before we were associated with him, certainly had no effect upon your life or mine, hence I feel that it is nothing with which we are directly concerned; and I believe, in fact I know, that it will be for your interest, Mr. Scott, if you say nothing regarding whatever knowledge you may have of the past."

Mr. Whitney, watching the effect of his words, suddenly saw an expression totally unlike anything he had ever seen on the face of the secretary, and yet strangely familiar.

Scott turned and faced him, with eyes cold and cynical and that seemed to pierce him through and through, remarking, in tones of quiet irony, "I am greatly obliged for your advice, Mr. Whitney, regarding my interests, but it is not needed. Furthermore, I think all your thought and attention will be required to look after the interests of Ralph Mainwaring," and without waiting for reply, he stepped through one of the low, old-fashioned windows opening upon the veranda and disappeared, leaving the attorney alone.

"By George, but that was cool!" ejaculated the latter. "And that look; where have I seen it? I believe that Ralph Mainwaring is more than half right after all, and there is something back of all this!"

So absorbed was he in his own reflections as to be wholly unaware of the presence of the detective in the hall, near the doorway, where he had paused long enough to witness the parting between Scott and the attorney, and who now passed quietly up-stairs, remarking to himself, "Whitney is pretty sharp, but he's more than got his match there. That young fellow is too deep for him or any of the rest of 'em, and he's likely to come out where they least expect to find him."

Half an hour later, Mr. Merrick, stepping from the private library into the upper southern hall, heard the sound of voices, which, from his familiarity with the rooms, he knew must proceed from Mrs. LaGrange's parlor. He cautiously descended the stairs to the lowest landing, in which was a deep window. The shutters were tightly closed, and, concealing himself behind the heavy curtains, he awaited developments. He was now directly opposite the door of the parlor, and through the partially open transom he could hear the imperious tones of Mrs. LaGrange and the soft, insinuating accents of Hobson. For a while he was unable to distinguish a word, but the variations in Hobson's tones indicated that he was not seated, but walking back and forth, while Mrs. LaGrange's voice betrayed intense excitement and gradually grew louder.

"You are not altogether invulnerable," Merrick heard her say, angrily. "You were an accessory in that affair, and you cannot deny it?"

Hobson evidently had paused near the door, as his reply was distinctly audible. "You have not an atom of proof; as you well know; and even if you had, our acquaintance, my dear madam, has been too long and of too intimate a nature for you to care to attempt any of your little tricks with me. You play a deep game, my lady, but I hold the winning hand yet."

"If you are dastardly enough to threaten me, I am not such a coward as to fear you. I have played my cards better than you know," she answered, defiantly.

"My dear lady," Hobson replied, and the door-knob turned slightly under his hand, "those little speeches sound very well, but we both understand each other perfectly. You want my services in this case; you must have them; and I am willing to render them; but it is useless for you to dictate terms to me. I will undertake the case in accordance with your wishes, but only upon the conditions mentioned."

The reply was inaudible, but was evidently satisfactory to Hobson, for, as he opened the door, there was a leer of triumph on his face. He glanced suspiciously about the hall, and, on reaching the door, turned to Mrs. LaGrange, who had accompanied him, saying, in his smoothest tones,-

"I shall be out again in two or three days. Should you wish to see me before that time, you can telephone to my office or send me word."

She bowed silently and he took his departure, but as she returned to her room, she exclaimed, fiercely, "Craven! Let me but once get my rights secured, and he will find whether I stand in fear of him!"

Having taken leave of Mrs. LaGrange, Hobson carefully avoided the front part of the house and grounds, taking instead the gravelled walk leading through the grove towards the lake in the rear and out upon the side street. As he was hurrying along this rather secluded avenue, he was suddenly confronted by Scott. Although strangers to each other, Hobson instantly conjectured that this must be the secretary who had betrayed such familiarity with the correspondence which had passed between himself and Hugh Mainwaring, and that it might be to his own interest to form the acquaintance of the young man.

Quick as thought he drew from his pocket a card, and, pausing suddenly in his rapid walk, said, with a profound bow,-

"I beg pardon; I cannot be mistaken; have I not the pleasure of addressing Mr. Scott?"

"That is my name," replied the secretary, coldly.

"I beg you will accept this card; and allow me to suggest that you may find it conducive to your interests to call upon me at the address named, if you will take the trouble to do so."

Scott glanced from the card to the speaker, regarding the latter with close scrutiny. "You seem very solicitous of the interests of a stranger, as it is not to be presumed that you have any ulterior motive in making this suggestion."

Hobson appeared to ignore the sarcasm. "It is barely possible," he continued, in his most ingratiating tones, "that I may be in possession of facts which it would be to your advantage to learn."

"In case you are, I suppose, of course, you would impart them to me simply out of pure disinterestedness, without a thought of pecuniary compensation?"

Hobson winced and glanced nervously about him. "I must hasten," he said; "I cannot stop for explanations; but you will find me in my office at two o'clock to-morrow, if you care to call. Meantime, my young friend, I am not perhaps as mercenary as you think, and I may be able to be of great assistance to you," and with a final bow, the man hastily disappeared around a turn of the winding walk.

Scott proceeded in the opposite direction in a deep study. "Is it possible," he soliloquized, "that that creature is on my track and has any proposition to make to me? Or, is he afraid that I know his secret, and that I may deprive him of his hold upon the Mainwarings? More likely it is the latter. A week ago I was looking for that man, and would probably have endeavored to make terms with him, though it would have involved an immense amount of risk, for a cast-iron contract wouldn't hold him, and his testimony would be worth little or nothing, one way or the other." Scott glanced again at the address on the card. "Not a very desirable locality! It probably suits him and his business, though: I believe, I will give the scoundrel a call and see what I can draw out of him."

Dinner was announced as Scott returned to the house, and a number of circumstances combined to render the meal far pleasanter and more social than any since the death of the master of Fair Oaks. Mr. Merrick was nowhere to be found, and the slight restraint imposed by his presence was removed. Mrs. LaGrange and her son were also absent, preferring to take their meals privately in an adjoining room which Hugh Mainwaring had often used as a breakfast-room. The silence and frigidity which had lately reigned at the table seemed to have given place to almost universal sociability, though Ralph Mainwaring's face still wore a sullen scowl.

As Mr. Whitney met the secretary, his sensitive face flushed at the remembrance of their late interview, and he watched the young man with evident curiosity. Scott was conscious, however, of an increased friendliness towards himself on the part of most of the guests, but feeling that it was likely to prove of short duration, he remained noncommittal and indifferent. As they left the table, Miss Carleton rallied him on his appearance.

"Mr. Scott, you are a mystery!"

"Why so, Miss Carleton, if you please?" he asked, quickly.

"Just now, when everybody's spirits are relaxing after that horrible inquest, you look more serious and glum than I have ever seen you. I threw myself into the breach this afternoon to rescue you from the enemy's grounds, whither you had been carried by the sensational statements of Mrs. LaGrange and the coachman and chambermaid, and I have not even seen you smile once since. Perhaps," she added, archly, "you didn't care to be rescued by a woman, but would have preferred to make your own way out."

"No," said Scott, smiling very brightly now; "I'll not be so ungrateful as to say that, though I believe I am generally able to fight my own battles; but I will confess I was somewhat disappointed this afternoon when you gave your testimony."

"How could that be?" she inquired, greatly surprised.

"Up to that time I had flattered myself that I had one friend who had faith in me, even though circumstances conspired against me. I discovered, then, that it was no confidence in me, but only a knowledge of some of the facts, that kept her from turning against me like the rest."

Scott spoke in serio-comic tones, and Miss Carleton looked keenly in his face to see if he were jesting.

"No; you are mistaken, Mr. Scott," she said, slowly, after a pause. "My confidence in you would have been just as strong if I had known nothing of the facts."

"Thank you; I am very glad to hear that," he answered. Then added, gently, "Would, it be strong enough to stand a far heavier strain than that, if it were necessary?"

His tones were serious now, and she regarded him inquiringly for a moment before speaking; then seeing young\ Mainwaring approaching with his sister and Miss Thornton, she replied, in low tones, -

"I have no idea to what you refer, Mr. Scott, and I begin to think you are indeed a 'mystery;' but you can be assured of this much: I would never, under any circumstances, believe you capable of anything false or dishonorable."

Scott's eyes expressed his gratification at these words, and he would then have withdrawn, but neither Miss Carleton nor young Mainwaring gave him an opportunity to do so without seeming discourteous. Both drew him into conversation and found him exceedingly entertaining, though reserved concerning himself. Isabel Mainwaring still held herself aloof and took little part in the conversation, but to make amends for this Miss Thornton bestowed some of her most winning smiles upon the handsome young secretary, her large, infantile blue eyes regarding him with wondering curiosity.

After a pleasant evening, Scott excused himself and retired to his room; but an hour or two later there was a knock at his door, and on opening it he saw young Mainwaring in smoking-cap and jacket.

"I say, Scott, won't you come out and have a smoke? I've got some fine cigars, and it's too pretty a night to stay in one's room; come out on my balcony and we'll have a bit of a talk and smoke."

Scott readily consented, and the two young men proceeded to the balcony upon which Mainwaring's room opened, where the latter had already placed two reclining chairs and a small table containing a box of his favorite Havanas.

For a few moments they puffed in silence, looking out into the starlit night with its beauty of dim outline and mysterious shadow. Mainwaring was the first to speak.

"I say, Scott, I'm awfully ashamed of the way that some of us, my family in particular, have treated you within the last day or two. It was confoundedly shabby, and I beg your pardon for my share in it, anyhow."

"Don't waste any regrets over that matter," Scott answered, indifferently; "I never gave it any thought, and it is not worth mentioning."

"I do regret it, though, more than I can tell, and I haven't any excuse for myself; only things did look so deucedly queer there for a while, don't you know?"

"Well," said Scott, pleasantly, "we are not out of the woods yet, and there is no telling what developments may arise. Things might 'look queer' again, you know."

"That's all right. I know a gentleman when I see him, unless I happen to lose my head, and that doesn't occur very often. Now it's different with the governor. He's got so confoundedly wrought up over that will, don't you know, that he can't think of anything else, and there's no reason in him."

"As I understand it," remarked Scott, "Mr. Mainwaring expects to win the property in any case, either for you or for himself."

"Yes; and naturally you might think that the loss of the will wouldn't amount to much, one way or the other; but it's like this: the governor and I are very different; I know we've got plenty of ducats, and that's enough for me, but not for him; he is ambitious. It has always galled him that we were not in the direct line of descent from the main branch of the Main-warings; and it has been his one great ambition since the death of old Ralph Mainwaring, Hugh's father, a few years before I was born, to win into his own family the old Mainwaring estate. He had an idea that Hugh would never marry, and gave me his name, hoping that I would be made his heir. Should the governor succeed in this scheme of his, he will immediately buy back the Mainwaring estate, although he knows I don't care a rap for the whole thing, and we will then have the honor, as he considers it, of perpetuating the old family line. On the other hand, if the property goes to the nearest heirs, it will be divided between him and his younger brother. Uncle Harold has no more ambition than I have, and though he is at present a bachelor, that is no guarantee that he will remain one; and, anyhow, it isn't likely that there will be much of his share left when he gets through with it. So you see how much importance the governor attached to that will."

"I understand," said Scott, as his companion paused. Then he added, musingly, "Your uncle's name seems to be rather unusual among the Mainwarings; I do not recall your having mentioned it before."

"What, Harold? On the contrary, it is the great name in our family, especially in the main line. I would have been given that name if the governor had not been looking out for Hugh Mainwaring's money. There was a direct line of Harolds down to my great-grandfather. He gave the name to his eldest son, but he died, and the next one, Ralph, Hugh's father, took up the line. Guy, my grandfather, was the youngest."

"One would almost have thought that Hugh Mainwaring would have borne the name of Harold," commented Scott.

Young Mainwaring smoked for a moment in silence, then said, in lower tones, "Old Uncle Ralph had a son by that name."

"Indeed! Had Hugh Mainwaring a brother?" Scott asked in surprise.

"Yes, there was a brother, but he died a great many years ago. There is quite a story connected with his name, but I don't know many of the particulars, for the governor seldom alludes to it. I know, however, that Harold was the elder son, but that Uncle Ralph disinherited him for marrying against his wishes, and afterwards died of grief over the affair, and soon after his father's death Harold was lost at sea."

"You say he married; did he leave any children?"

"No, I believe he had no children; but even if he had, they would have been disinherited also. Uncle Ralph was severe; he would not even allow Harold's name to be mentioned; and Hugh also must have turned against his brother, for I have heard that he never spoke of him or allowed any allusion to be made to him."

"Well," said Scott, after a pause, "I believe Hugh Mainwaring's life was far from happy."

"You are right there. I'll never forget the last words he ever spoke to me as I took leave of him that night. They were to the effect that he hoped when I should have reached his age, I would be able to look back over a happier past than his had been. It is my opinion, too, that that woman was the cause of his unhappiness, and I believe she is at the bottom of all this trouble."

Their conversation had drifted to the mystery then surrounding them, and for more than an hour they dwelt on that subject, advancing many surmises, some strangely improbable, but none of which seemed to bring them any nearer a solution of the problem.

"My first visit to this country has proved an eventful one," said young Mainwaring, as, at a late hour, they finally separated for the night, "and I don't know yet how it may terminate; but there's one thing I shall look back upon with pleasure, and that is my meeting with you; and I hope that from this time or we will be friends; and that this friendship, begun to-night, will be renewed in old England many a time."

"Are you not rather rash," Scott inquired, slowly, "considering how little we know of each other, the circumstances under which we have met, and the uncertainty of what the future may reveal?"

"No; I'm peculiar. When I like a fellow, I like him; and I've been studying you pretty closely. I don't think we need either of us be troubled about the future; but I'm your friend, Scott, and, whatever happens, I'll stand by you."

"So be it, then, Hugh," replied the secretary, clasping the hand of the young Englishman and, for the first time, calling him by name. "I thank you, and I hope you will never go back on that."

CHAPTER XI

SKIRMISHING

On the following morning the gentlemen at Fair Oaks were astir at an unusually early hour, and immediately after breakfast held a brief conference. It was decided to offer a heavy reward for the apprehension of the murderer of Hugh Mainwaring, while a lesser reward was to be offered for information leading to identification and arrest of the guilty party. Preparations were also to be made for the funeral, which would take place the next day, and which, in accordance with the wishes of Ralph Mainwaring, was to be strictly private.

Their conference at an end, Ralph Mainwaring ordered the carriage to take himself, Mr. Whitney, and the secretary to the depot.

"I believe I will ride down with you," said Mr. Merrick.

"Certainly; plenty of room. Going to the city?"

"Yes; but not with you gentlemen. We will part company at the depot and I will take another car."

"How are you getting on, Mr. Merrick?" inquired Mr. Thorton.

"As well as can be expected, all things considered," was the non-committal reply.

"Going to be a slow case, I'm afraid," commented Ralph Mainwaring, shaking his head in a doubtful way, while Mr. Thornton added jokingly, -

"We've got some mighty fine fellows over home there at the Yard; if you should want any help, Mr. Merrick, I'll cable for one of them."

"Thank you, sir," said the detective, with quiet dignity; "I don't anticipate that I shall want any assistance; and if I should, I will hardly need import it from Scotland Yard."

"Ha, ha! That all depends, you know, on what your man is. If the rascal happens to have any English blood in him, it will take a Scotland Yard chap to run him down."

"On the principle, I suppose, of 'set a rogue to catch a rogue,'" Merrick replied, smiling.

He bad scarcely finished speaking when Hardy suddenly entered the room.

"Beg pardon, sir," he said, addressing Ralph Mainwaring; "but the coachman is gone! We've looked everywhere for him, but he's nowhere about the place."

"When did he go?" asked Mr. Whitney, quickly.

"Nobody knows, sir. Joe, the stable-boy, says he hasn't been around at all this morning."

"Bring the boy here," said Mr. Mainwaring.

There was instantly recalled to every one present the memory of Brown's insolent manner at the inquest, together with his confused and false statements. In a few moments Hardy returned with the stable-boy, an unkempt, ignorant lad of about fourteen, but with a face old and shrewd beyond his years.

"Are you one of the servants here?" Mr. Mainwaring inquired.

"I works here, ef that's wot yer mean; but I don't call myself nobody's servant."

"How did it happen that you were not at the inquest?" he demanded.

"Didn't got no invite," was the reply, accompanied by a grin, while Hardy explained that the boy did not belong to the place, but had been hired by the coachman to come nights and mornings and attend to the stable work.

"What do you know about this Brown?" inquired Mr. Mainwaring, addressing the boy.

"Wal, I guess he's ben a - goin' it at a putty lively gait lately."

"You mean he was fast?"

"I guess that's about the size of it."

"When did you see him last?"

"Hain't seen nothin' of him sence las' night, an' then he was sorter crusty an' didn't say much. I come down this mornin' an' went to work, - he allus left the stable key where I could get it, - but I ham' t seen nor heard nothin' o' him. Me'n him," with an emphatic nod towards Hardy, "went up to his room, but he warn't there, nor hadn't ben there all night."

"Why do you think he was fast?"

"Wal, from all I've hearn about him I guess he's ben goin' with a kinder hard set lately. I've seen some putty tough-lookin' subs hangin' 'round the stables. There was a lot of 'em waitin' for him Wednesday night."

"Wednesday night!" ejaculated Mr. Whitney. "At what time?

and who were they?"

"I dunno who they was, but they was hangin' 'round about eight o'clock waitin' for him to go with 'em. An' then he's had lots of money lately."

"How do you know this?"

"I've hearn him a-jinglin' it in his room; an' night afore las' I clim' up-stairs and peeked in, an' he had a whole pile of gold pieces 'bout that high," measuring with his hands; "but he see me, an' he said he'd gimme a whalin' ef he catched me at it agin."

"Did you watch him last night?" asked Mr. Mainwaring.

"Yas; he acted so kinder queer that I waited 'round to see what he was goin' to do. After 'twas still an' he thought I'd gone, he come down an' started off towards the side street. Jes' fer fun I follered him; an' when he got to the lake he stopped and looked all 'round, as ef to make sure there warn't nobody to see him, an' then he takes somethin', I couldn't see what, out from under his coat an' chucks it quick into the lake, an' then he started on a run down towards the street."

"Couldn't you see what he threw?"

"No, I couldn't see what 'twas; but it struck the water awful heavy."

"Is that all you know about the affair?"

"Yas, that's all."

"Wait a moment," said Mr. Merrick, as the boy turned to leave the room. "Can you tell how many, or what kind of looking men were with Brown on Wednesday night?"

"There was three of 'em. One was a big feller with kinder

squint eyes, the other two was ornery lookin' fellers; one of 'em was dark like a furriner, an' t'other one had sorter yeller hair."

"How long were they there?"

"About half n hour, I guess. They was all gone 'fore nine o'clock."

"Did you hear anything that was said?"

"I hearn 'em talkin' somethin' about the boss."

"Mr. Mainwaring?"

"Yas. He'd made a kick about somethin' or 'nuther that afternoon, an' Brown he was cussin' mad, an' then when they went away I hearn one of 'em say somethin' about 'makin' a good job of it.'"

"How was this, Hardy?" inquired Mr. Whitney. "Had there been any words Wednesday between Mr. Mainwaring and the coachman?"

"Yes, sir; I had forgotten it; but now I remember that when he came back that afternoon, he found some fault with the coachman, and Brown was very insolent, and then Mr. Mainwaring threatened to discharge him."

"'Pon my soul! I should say here was something worth looking into," said Mr. Thornton, as the boy left the room, accompanied by Hardy.

"A great pity that we could not have had his testimony at the inquest," commented the attorney. "We might then have cornered Brown; but I was not aware that there was such a person employed on the place."

Meanwhile, a carriage ordered by telephone from the Arlington had already arrived at Fair Oaks.

"Well," said Ralph Mainwaring, "the carriage is waiting. We had better proceed to the depot; we can talk of this latest development on our way."

"You will excuse me, gentlemen," said Mr. Merrick, quietly, "I have changed my mind, and will postpone my trip to the city."

"Struck a new trail, eh?" queried Ralph Mainwaring, with a peculiar expression, as he paused to light a cigar.

"On the contrary, sir, only following up an old one," and, with a somewhat ambiguous smile, the detective withdrew.

The coachman's sudden disappearance, together with the facts learned from the stable-boy, formed the subject of discussion for the next half-hour between Ralph Mainwaring and the attorney, Scott listening with a thoughtful face, although taking little part in the conversation. Upon their arrival at the offices of Mainwaring & Co. they were given a cordial greeting by Mr. Elliott and Mr. Chittenden, after which they passed on to the elegant private offices of Hugh Mainwaring. Mr. Whitney was visibly affected as he entered the familiar rooms, and to each one was forcibly recalled the memory of their meeting a few days before. A brief silence followed, and then in subdued tones they began to discuss the business which had now brought them there.

At about two o'clock that afternoon, Scott found himself entering an ancient and dilapidated looking block in a rather disreputable part of the city. He had fulfilled his appointment with Mr. Sutherland, and after an hour's conversation both gentlemen appeared very sanguine regarding the case under consideration. As Scott was taking leave, he produced Hobson's card and related the particulars of their incidental meeting at Fair Oaks, and Hobson's urgent invitation to call upon him at his office.

Mr. Sutherland laughed. "About what I expected," he said. "It was evident from his remarks at the inquest that some one-probably Mrs. LaGrange-had posted him concerning you, and he is afraid you are onto his secret."

"I had questioned if it were that, or whether possibly he might be onto mine."

"Not at all probable," said the attorney, after a moment's reflection. "If he really understood your position, he would be far too cunning to allow you to get sight of him. You have the scoundrel completely in your power."

"Yes, as much as he is in anybody's power; but it is doubtful if any one can hold so slippery a rascal as he. I believe I will give him a call, however."

"It would do no harm, taking care, of course, that you give him no information."

"Oh, certainly," said Scott, with a smile, as he paused for an instant in the doorway; "my object will be to get, not give, information."

"His object will probably be the same," was Mr. Sutherland's parting shot, as he turned with a laugh to his desk.

Scott, having ascended a narrow, crooked stairway, found himself in a long, dark hall, poorly ventilated, and whose filthy condition was only too apparent even in the dim light. Far in the rear he saw a door bearing the words, "R. Hobson, Attorney." As he pushed open the door, a boy of about seventeen, who, with a cigarette in his mouth and his feet on a table, sat reading a novel, instantly assumed the perpendicular and, wheeling about, faced Scott with one of the most villainous countenances the latter had ever seen. Something in Scott's appearance seemed to surprise him, for he stared impudently without speaking. After silently studying the face before him for an instant, Scott inquired for Mr. Hobson.

"He is in, sir, but he is engaged at present with a client," said the boy, in tones which closely resembled Hobson's. "I will take in your card, sir."

The boy disappeared with the card into an adjoining room, returning a moment later with the most obsequious manners and the announcement that Mr. Hobson would be at liberty in a few moments. Scott rightly judged that this ceremony was merely enacted for effect, and contented himself with looking about the small, poorly furnished room, while the office boy opposite regarded him with an undisguised curiosity, which betrayed that this client-if such he could be regarded -differed greatly from the usual class. Young and untaught though he were, he had learned to read the faces about him, and that of his employer was to him as an open book, and the expression which flashed into Hobson's eyes as they fell upon Scott's card indicated plainly to the office boy that in this instance the usual conditions were reversed, and the attorney stood in fear of his visitor.

A few moments later the door of the next room opened noiselessly and Hobson, attired in a red dressing-gown and wearing his most ingratiating smile, silently beckoned Scott to enter. With a quick glance the latter took in every detail of the second apartment. It was somewhat larger than the first, but the furnishing was meagre and shabby in the extreme, and, with the exception of a small set of shelves containing a few dilapidated volumes, there were no visible signs of an attorney's office.

Hobson did not speak until he had carefully closed the door, then he said, in low tones,-

"As our conversation is likely to be of a confidential nature, you would perhaps desire greater privacy than can be secured here. Step this way."

He opened the door into a room so dark and so thick with stale tobacco smoke that at first Scott could discern nothing clearly.

"My den!" said Hobson, with a magnificent flourish, and Scott stepped within, feeling, he afterwards said, as though he were being ushered by Mephistopheles into the infernal regions, and this impression was not lessened by the first objects which he was able to distinguish,-a pair of skulls grinning at him through the smoky atmosphere. As his eyes became accustomed to the dim light he noted that the room was extremely small, with only one window, which opened upon the blank wall of an adjoining building, and with no furniture, save an enormous, high-top desk and two chairs. One of the latter Hobson placed near the window for his visitor, and then busied himself for a moment at the desk in hastily concealing what to Scott looked like some paraphernalia of the black arts. Upon the top of the desk were the two skulls which had first attracted Scott's attention, and which he now regarded rather curiously. Hobson, following his glance, said, by way of explanation,-

"Rather peculiar ornaments, I dare say, you consider those, Mr. Scott; but I am greatly interested in phrenology and devote much of my leisure time to its study. It is not only amusing, you know, but it is of great assistance in reading and understanding my fellow-men, and enables me to adapt myself to my clients, so to speak."

Having satisfactorily arranged his belongings, Hobson locked the door, and, seating himself behind his desk, appeared ready for business.

"Well, my young friend," he began, "I rather expected you, for I flatter myself that I understand enough of human nature to know that there are very few who will pass by an opportunity of learning something for the advancement of their own interests or the betterment of their own condition in life."

"That may be perfectly natural," Scott replied; "but you flatter yourself altogether too much if you think that I have come here with any expectation that you can advance my interests or better my condition."

"That remains to be seen. Much also depends upon yourself, for I take it that a young man of your calibre is not without ambition."

Hobson paused, regarding his visitor with sharp scrutiny, but receiving no reply, continued, "I might add, that to a young man with ambitious designs such as yours, I would probably be able to render great assistance."

"I am not aware of any unusual ambition on my part."

"Oh, no, nothing unusual. You simply had no intention of remaining Hugh Mainwaring's secretary any longer than was necessary. That was perfectly natural, perfectly laudable, my young friend, and I admire the shrewdness and foresight with which you set about to accomplish your designs. At the same time, I believe I am in a position to give you just the information and advice you need in order to insure your success."

Both men had the same object in view. Each wished to ascertain what the other knew concerning himself. Scott, unable to determine whether Hobson had spoken at random or with an inkling of the facts, answered, coldly, -

"I do not know to what you refer, or on what grounds you base the inference which you seem to have drawn."

"No? Then you will allow me to remark, Mr. Scott, that such familiarity as yours with a portion of Hugh Mainwaring's private correspondence, extending back over a period of fifteen or more years, taking into consideration the facts that you cannot be much more than twenty-five years of age, and have only been about two years in Mr. Mainwaring's employ, would indicate that you had sought to acquaint yourself with some facts connected with your employer's early life with the express purpose of using the same to your own advantage."

"You must see the inconsistency of such a supposition, when you consider that I have been in possession of these facts for some time-it is unnecessary to state how long-and have made no use of them whatever."

"Possibly," said Hobson, with emphasis, "your knowledge of the facts may not have been definite enough to warrant your use of them."

His voice and manner unconsciously betrayed the importance which he attached to Scott's reply. The latter detected this, and answered evasively, -

"It is sufficiently definite for any own personal satisfaction in any event."

Hobson shook his head. "It is useless to evade the point. You had an object in looking up that correspondence; you intended to make a good thing out of the facts you got hold of; and, if your information is sufficiently complete, you can make a good thing out of them yet."

"If I have not attempted anything of that kind in the past, would I be likely to try it at this late day?" Scott asked, with the air of one who is open to any available suggestion.

Hobson at once assumed a confidential manner, and, moving a little nearer his visitor, replied, in a low tone, -

"Look here, Mr. Scott, that's just why I wanted to meet you. You see I knew more about you than you think. I've taken an unusual interest in you, too; and, seeing the little game you were playing, and knowing that I held the trump card myself, I naturally would like to take a hand and help you out at the same time. Now, the point is just this, Mr. Scott: What do you really know concerning the transaction referred to in that correspondence? I suppose you are familiar with all the letters that passed on both sides?"

"Perfectly so."

"Certainly. But you will acknowledge, Mr. Scott, that those letters were expressed in very guarded terms, and, with the exception of possibly one or two, gave no hint of the nature of that transaction. Remember," he added, impressively, "I have an exact copy of the correspondence on both sides, and no one could ever assume any statement or admissions that were not there."

"I presumed that, of course," said Scott, calmly.

"Now, my young friend, let us get down to the actual knowledge which you have of the facts. You are, I suppose, aware that there was a missing will involved in the case?"

"I am; and that one or two of your letters purported to show that the missing will was destroyed by Hugh Mainwaring."

"Did I make any such allegation?"

"Not directly; but your allusions and references would be clear to any one having a knowledge of the English statutes."

Hobson started, and inquired quickly, "Are you familiar with English law?"

"I made myself familiar with your citations and references in this case."

"I see; you have indeed made a study of the case. Well, Mr. Scott, permit me to say that I accused Hugh Mainwaring of nothing which he had not previously confessed to me himself. Have you any knowledge concerning that will, - its terms or conditions, or the names of the testator or beneficiaries?"

"There was nothing in the correspondence to give any clue to those particulars. I could only gather that Hugh Mainwaring had defrauded others and enriched himself by destroying this will."

Hobson looked relieved. "Without doubt, he did; but allow me to call your attention to one point, Mr. Scott. You see how little actual knowledge you have of this affair. There are others- Mrs. LaGrange, for instance, and the mysterious individual whom she heard conversing with Mr. Mainwaring on the night of the murder, - all of whom know as much or more than you; and while this meagre knowledge of the case might perhaps have been sufficient to bring to bear upon Mainwaring himself, personally, it would have little or no weight with those with whom we would now have to deal. You know nothing of the terms of the will, or of the persons named as beneficiaries, whom, consequently, Hugh Mainwaring defrauded. You have no proof that he destroyed the will. In fact, my dear young friend, you could produce no proof that such a document ever existed at all!"

"Do I understand you, then, that those letters, Mr. Mainwaring's included, would not be regarded as proof?" Scott asked, with well-feigned surprise.

"Not of themselves with these people; I know them too well." Hobson shook his head decidedly, then continued, in oracular tones, "Remember, I am only speaking of your chances with them. Mainwaring's letters were very guarded, mine scarcely less so. They would have no weight whatever with men like Ralph Mainwaring or William Thornton. They might even charge you with forging the whole thing. The point is just this, Mr. Scott: in order to be able to get anything from these parties you must have complete data, absolute proof of every statement you are to make; and such data and proofs are in the possession of no one but myself. So you see I am the only one who can assist you in this matter."

"And what compensation would you demand for 'assisting' me?"

"We will not put it that way, Mr. Scott," Hobson replied, his small, malignant eyes gleaming with delight at the ease with which his prey was falling into his clutches. "It is like this:

Ralph Mainwaring and Thornton are prejudiced against me; I might not be able to work them as successfully as I could wish, but you and I could work together very smoothly. I could remain invisible, as it were, and give you the benefit of the information I possess and of my experience and advice, and you could then successfully manipulate the wires which would bring in the ducats for both of us. What do you say, my young friend?"

"Do you think that either Ralph Mainwaring or Mr. Thornton would care enough for any secrets you might be able to disclose to pay you hush money?"

"I object to the term of 'hush money.' I am merely trying to get what was due me from Hugh Mainwaring. As he never paid me in full, his heirs must. Yes, I could work them after they return to England and set up in style on the old Mainwaring estate. They would be rather sensitive about the family reputation then."

"Where are the beneficiaries of that will that was destroyed?" Scott suddenly inquired.

Hobson looked sharply at him. "Dead, long ago. Why do you ask?"

"I was thinking that if they or their heirs were living, it would be better to go to them with this information. They would probably pay a good price for it."

"You're right, they would," Hobson replied, approvingly; "but they are all dead."

"Were there no heirs left?"

"None whatever, more's the pity. However, I've got a good hold on these English chaps and will make them hand over the sovereigns yet."

The contempt which Scott had hitherto concealed as Hobson unfolded his plans was now plainly visible on his face as he rose from his chair.

"Don't hasten, my young friend," said Hobson, eagerly. "Sit down, sit down; we have not laid our plans yet."

"No, nor will we," was the reply. "If you think to make a cat's-paw of me in any of your dirty, contemptible pieces of work, you are mistaken. If you think that I came here with any intention of listening for one moment to any of your vile propositions, you are mistaken. I came here simply to satisfy myself on one point. My errand is accomplished, and I will remain no longer."

Hobson had sprung to his feet and now faced Scott, barring the way to the door, while fear, anger, defiance, and hate passed in rapid succession across his evil countenance, making his appearance more demon-like than ever.

"You lie!" he exclaimed, in a hoarse whisper. "I have not given you one word of information!"

"No," Scott interrupted, "you have given me no information, and you could give me none, for the reason that I know more concerning this whole affair than you do. I also have know-ledge of certain other matters regarding one Richard Hobson, alias Dick Carroll, and his London adventures."

Hobson's face had become a livid hue, and Scott detected a sudden movement of his right hand towards his desk.

"None of that!" he cried, warningly, at the same time springing quickly upon him with two well-aimed blows, one of which knocked a revolver from Hobson's hand, while the other deposited him in a heap upon the floor. While the latter was recovering from the effect of the stunning blow he had received, Scott picked up the revolver and, having examined it, slipped it into his pocket, saying,-

"I will keep this for a while as a souvenir of our interview. It may be needed as evidence later."

Hobson crawled to his feet and stood cowering abjectly before Scott, rage written on every lineament of his face, but not daring to give it expression.

"Who in the devil are you, anyway?" he growled.

"That is none of your business whatever," Scott replied, seizing him by the collar and dragging him to the door. "The only thing for you to do is to unlock that door as expeditiously as possible, asking no questions and making no comments."

With trembling fingers the wretch complied, and Scott, still retaining his hold upon his collar, reached the door of the outer room, where, with a final shake, he released him.

"Wait a moment," Hobson whispered, eagerly, half-paralyzed with fear, while his eyes gleamed with malign hatred. "You've got no hold on me by anything I've said, and you've no proof of that Carroll business, either."

Scott looked at him an instant with silent contempt. "You cowardly scoundrel! all I have to say to you at present is, be careful how you interfere with me! I'm only sorry I soiled my hands with you, but I'll do it again if necessary; and the next time you will fare worse!" and, opening the door, he passed quickly through the outer room, conscious of the amazed stare of the office boy, who had overheard his last words. Hobson did not attempt to follow him, but paced up and down his room, trembling with fear and rage combined, and vainly striving to imagine who his visitor might be. At last he sat down to his desk and began to write rapidly, muttering to himself, -

"I half believe-only that he's too young-that he is some hound over here trying to scent out the whole thing. But," he added, with an oath, "whoever he is, if he crosses my track he'll be likely to follow Hugh Mainwaring before long, that's all!"

CHAPTER XII

X-RAYS

On the morning following Scott's interview with Hobson, he awoke at an early hour, vaguely conscious of some disturbing influence, though unable to tell what had awakened him. He lay for a moment recalling the events of the preceding day, then suddenly remembered that this was the day fixed for the funeral of Hugh Mainwaring. None of the servants were astir about the house, but Scott soon became conscious of the sound of stealthy movements and subdued voices coming through the open window, and, rising, he looked out. At first he could see nothing unusual. It was just sunrise, and the river, at a little distance shimmering in the golden light, held him entranced by its beauty. Then a slight rustling in the shrubbery near the lake attracted his attention. The golden shafts of sunlight had not yet reached that small body of water, and it lay smooth and unbroken as the surface of a mirror, so clear at that hour that one could easily look into its depths. Suddenly a light boat shot out from the side nearest the grove, breaking the smooth surface into a thousand rippling waves of light. In the boat were two men, one of whom Scott instantly recognized as the detective; the other, who was rowing and had his back towards the house, seemed to be a stranger. Some one concealed in the shrubbery called to the boatmen, whereupon they rowed across in that direction, stopping a few yards from shore. Here they rested a few moments till the surface was again smooth, when, both men having carefully peered into the depths of the little lake, the detective proceeded to let

Maynard Barbour

down a drag into the water.

"By George!" Scott ejaculated, "the sly old fox is improving the opportunity, while every one is asleep, to drag the lake in search of whatever the coachman threw in there. All right, my dear sir, go ahead! But I'm somewhat interested in this affair myself, and I don't intend that you shall monopolize all the facts in the case."

Keeping an eye on the boat, he dressed quickly and, letting himself out at the front entrance, he hastened down the walk through the grove to the edge of the lake, keeping himself concealed among the trees. The boat was moving slowly back and forth, and was no win such a position that Scott could see the face of the man rowing, who proved to be, as he had thought, a stranger. On the other side, seated under the flowering shrubs and trees bordering the lake, was Joe, the stable-boy, watching proceedings with intense interest. With a smile, the young secretary followed his example, seating himself at the foot of an ancient elm whose branches drooped nearly to the ground.

"All right, Mr. Detective!" he said, "I can stay as long as you. If you fail to make a success of your work this morning no one will be the wiser, but in case you find anything I propose to know something about it myself."

The sun was now shining brightly, but the hour was yet so early that there was little danger of any one else appearing on the scene, especially as it was Sunday morning.

For nearly an hour Mr. Merrick and his companion rowed slowly back and forth in constantly widening circles, meeting with no success and saying little. Suddenly, while Scott was watching the face of the stranger, wondering who he might be, he heard a low exclamation and saw that the drag had fastened itself upon some object at the bottom of the lake. He watched eagerly as they drew it to the surface, and could scarcely restrain a cry of astonishment as he saw what it was, but before either of the men could secure it, it had slipped and fallen again into the water. With language more forcible than elegant, the drag was again lowered, and the boat once more began its slow trailing.

This time they had not so long to wait for success. The drag was brought to the surface, but carrying in its clutches an entirely different object, and one with which the young secretary was totally unfamiliar, - a somewhat rusty revolver.

Mr. Merrick's back was now towards Scott, but the latter saw him take something from his pocket which he seemed to compare with the revolver, at the same time remarking to the stranger, who was watching with an appearance of great interest,

"A pretty good find, Jim, pretty good! However, we'll have another try for that box, whatever it is. It may amount to something or it may not, but it will do no harm to make a trial."

Having let down the drag once more, he glanced at the house, then at his watch, saying, "No signs of any one astir; we're all right for another hour yet."

After a few more turns, Scott saw them suddenly pulling in the ropes, and once more the box appeared, rusty and covered with slime, but still familiar. He at once sprang to his feet and sauntered carelessly down the walk, humming a tune and watching the occupants of the boat with an air of mild curiosity. The stranger was the first to see him, and with an expression of evident disgust gave Merrick warning of his approach. If the detective felt any annoyance he did not betray it as be turned and nodded to Scott in the most nonchalant manner possible, as though dragging the lake were an every-day occurrence.

"You've been fishing, I see," said Scott, pleasantly. "How did you make out?"

"Well, I've made this find which you see here," answered Mr. Merrick, as the boat headed for shore. "I don't know yet what it is, but it has not lain long in the water, and it may be worth looking into."

Scott made no reply until the detective had sprung ashore; then, as the latter proceeded to examine the box, leaving his companion to take care of the boat and drag, he said, in a low tone, -

"That is likely to prove an important discovery, Mr. Merrick."

"You are familiar with it then?" queried the latter.

"I have seen it in Mr. Mainwaring's safe. That was the box in which he kept the old jewels that were stolen on the night of the murder."

Mr. Merrick whistled softly and studied the box anew. "Well, there are no jewels in it now, but we will open it. There is no one up yet to let us into the house, so suppose we go to the stables; we'll be safe there from intrusion."

They proceeded to the stables, and, arriving there, Scott was puzzled to see Merrick's companion at work and evidently perfectly at home.

"We are going to use your room a while, Matthews," said Merrick, carelessly. Then, noting the surprise on Scott's face, he added, "This is Matthews, the new coachman, Mr. Scott. I thought you knew of his coming."

"At your service, sir," said Matthews, respectfully lifting his cap in response to Scott's greeting, while the latter inquired, as he and the detective passed up-stairs together, -

"When did he come?"

"Yesterday afternoon. He applied for the position, and, as he happened to be an acquaintance of mine, Mr. Mainwaring hired him upon my recommendation. Now," as he locked the door of the room they had entered, "we will open this box as quickly as possible. I suppose there is no key to be found, and, if there were, the lock is too rusty to work."

With the aid of a file and chisel the box was soon opened. The satin linings were somewhat water-soaked and discolored, and the box appeared to be empty, but on opening an inner compartment there were exposed to view a pair of oddly shaped keys and a blood-stained handkerchief, the latter firmly knotted as though it had been used to bandage a wound of some kind.

"Ah!" said the detective, with peculiar emphasis, examining the handkerchief, which was of fine linen, with the initials "H. M." embroidered in one corner. "Did Mr. Mainwaring carry a handkerchief of that style?"

"Yes; he carried that, or one precisely like it, the last day of his life."

"Very good!" was the only reply, as the detective carefully folded and pocketed the article with an air that indicated that he wished to say no more about it. "And these keys, do you recognize them?"

"They were Mr. Mainwaring's private keys to his library and the southern hall."

"The ones the valet said were missing?"

"The same."

Mr. Merrick, after studying them curiously for a moment, consigned them to his pocket also, and then began a careful inspection of the interior of the box. Scott watched him in silence, thinking meanwhile of the old document which he had found hidden away in its depths, and inwardly rejoicing that it had not been left to be discovered by the detective. Nothing in Mr. Merrick's manner or expression betrayed the nature of his thoughts, and, so long as he chose to remain silent, Scott refrained from questioning him.

At length he closed the box, saying, indifferently, "Well, I don't know as there is any reason why I should detain you any longer, Mr. Scott. We have satisfied ourselves as to the contents of the box, and you have identified the articles. For the present, however, I would prefer that you say nothing of this."

"Certainly, Mr. Merrick. The discovery, whatever its import, is your secret, and I shall make no mention of it whatever."

"I don't know that it is of any special importance," said the detective, carelessly, as they prepared to descend the stairs; "but it only confirms the opinion that I have had all along."

"Don't you think that this tends to show that the murder and robbery were connected, notwithstanding Mr. Whitney's theories to the contrary?" Scott inquired, as they were about to separate.

"Possibly," replied the other, gravely. Then added, with a smile, "Mr. Whitney has his own preconceived ideas of the case and tries to adapt the circumstances to suit them, when, in reality, one must first ascertain whatever facts are available and adjust his theories accordingly."

They parted company at the door of the stables, but Scott had not reached the house when the detective, with a peculiar smile, returned to the room up-stairs, and once more opening the box, drew forth from underneath the satin linings a folded paper, yellow with age and covered with closely written lines; which he read with great interest, after which he remained absorbed in thought until aroused by the entrance of his friend, the coachman.

Several hours later Scott stood alone beside the casket of the murdered man. The head had been turned slightly to one side and a spray of white blossoms, dropped with seeming carelessness within the casket, concealed all traces of the ghastly wound, their snowy petals scarcely whiter than the marble features of the dead.

It lacked more than an hour of the time set for the funeral. None of the few invited friends would arrive for some time yet. The gentlemen of the house were still in the hands of their valets, and the ladies engrossed with the details of their elegant mourning costumes. Scott, knowing he would be secure from interruption, had chosen this opportunity to take his farewell look at the face of his employer, desiring to be alone with his own thoughts beside the dead.

With strangely commingled emotions he gazed upon the face, so familiar, and yet upon which the death angel had already traced many unfamiliar lines, and as he realized the utter loneliness of the rich man, both in life and in death, a wave of intense pity swept across heart and brain, well-nigh obliterating all sense of personal wrong and injury.

"Unhappy man!" he murmured. "Unloved in life, unmourned in death! Not one of those whom you sought to enrich will look upon you to-day with one-half the sorrow or the pity with which I do, whom you have wronged and defrauded from the day of my birth! But I forgive you the wrong you have done me. It was slight compared with the far greater wrong you did another, - your brother - your only brother! A wrong which no sums of money, however vast, could ever repair. What would I not give if I could once have stood by his side, even as I stand by yours to-day, and looked once upon his face, - the face of your brother and of the father whom, because of your guilt, I have never seen or known, of whom I have not even a memory! Living, I could never have forgiven you; but here, to-day, in pity for your loveless life and out of the great love I bear that father in his far - away ocean grave, - in his name and in my own, - I forgive you, his brother, even that wrong!"

As Scott left the room, he passed Mr. Whitney in the hall, who, seeing in his face traces of recent emotion, looked after him with great surprise.

"That young man is a mystery!" he soliloquized. "A mystery! I confess I cannot understand him."

A little later the master of Fair Oaks passed for the last time down the winding, oak-lined avenue, followed by the guests of the place and by a small concourse of friends, whose sorrow, though unexpressed by outward signs of mourning, was, in reality, the more sincere.

Mrs. LaGrange, who, as housekeeper, had remained at Fair Oaks, seemed, as the last carriage disappeared from view, to be on the verge of collapse from nervous prostration. No one knew the mental excitement or the terrible nervous strain which she had undergone during those last few days. Many at the funeral had noted her extreme pallor, but no one dreamed of the tremendous will power by which she had maintained her customary haughty bearing. When all had gone, she rose and attempted to go to her room, but in the hall she staggered helplessly and, with a low moan, sank unconscious to the floor. The screams of the chambermaid, who had seen her fall, summoned to her assistance the other servants, who carried her to her room, where she slowly regained consciousness, opening her eyes with an expression of terror, then closing them again with a shudder. Suddenly she seemed to recall her surroundings; with a great effort she rallied and dismissed the servants, with the exception the chambermaid, saying, "It was nothing, only a little faintness caused by the heat. The room was insufferably close. Say nothing of this to the others when they return."

With Katie's assistance, she exchanged her heavy dress for a light wrapper of creamy silk, and soon seemed herself again except for her unusual pallor.

"That will do, Katie; I shall not need you further. By the way, did Walter go with the others, or did he remain at home?"

"Mr. Walter is in his room, ma'am; and I heard Hardy say that he was packing up his clothes and things."

Mrs. LaGrange betrayed no surprise, no emotion of any kind. "Say to him that I would like to see him in my room at once."

The girl disappeared, leaving Mrs. LaGrange to her own reflections, which seemed anything but pleasant. The look of terror returned to her face; she clinched her hands until the jewels cut deeply into the white fingers; then, springing to her feet, she paced the room wildly until she heard the footsteps of her son approaching, when she instantly assumed her usual composure.

Walter LaGrange had left Fair Oaks immediately at the close of the inquest, and had not returned except to be present at the funeral, and even there his sullen appearance had caused general remark. Very little love had ever existed between mother and son, for neither had a nature capable of deep affection, but never until now had there been any open rupture between them. Though closely resembling each other, he lacked her ability to plan and execute, and had hitherto been content to follow her counsels. But, as he now entered his mother's room, a glance revealed to her that her authority and influence over him were past.

"You sent for me, I believe. What do you want?" he asked, as she looked at him without speaking.

"Do you consider your conduct becoming towards a mother who is risking everything for you and your interests?"

"Oh, my interests be hanged " he exclaimed, petulantly. "I don't see that you've accomplished much for my interests with all your scheming. A week ago I could hold up my head with any of the fellows. I was supposed to be a relative of Hugh

Mainwaring's, with good prospects, and that I would come in for a good round sum whenever the old fellow made his will, - just as I did. Now that's gone, and everything's gone; I haven't even a name left!"

"Walter LaGrange, what do you mean? Do you dare insinuate to your own mother-"

"Why don't you call me Walter Mainwaring?" he sneered. "As to insinuations, I have to hear plenty of 'em. Last night I was black-balled at one of the clubs where my name had been presented for membership, and a lot of the fellows have cut me dead."

"Walter, listen to me. You are Hugh Mainwaring's son and I was his wife. I will yet compel people to recognize us as such; but you must-"

"Tell me one thing," he demanded, interrupting her. If I was Hugh Mainwaring's son, why have I not borne his name? Why did he not recognize me as such? I'll claim no man for my father who would not acknowledge me as his son."

Then, before she could reply, he added, "If you were the wife of Hugh Mainwaring, what was the meaning of your proposal of marriage to him less than three months ago?"

She grew deathly pale; but he, seeming to enjoy the situation, repeated, sneeringly, "Less than three months ago, the night on which he gave you the necklace which you commissioned me to sell the other day! You urged your suit with a vengeance, too, I remember, for you threatened to ruin him if he did not come to your terms.

I only laughed then, for I thought 'twas another scheme of yours to get a tighter hold on the old man's purse-strings. It's nothing to me what your object was, but in view of the fact that I happened to overhear that little episode, it might be just as well not to try to tell me that I am Hugh Mainwaring's son.

You will naturally see that I am not likely to be interested vin helping carry out that little farce!"

Still controlling herself by a tremendous will power, the wretched woman made one more desperate effort. In low tones she replied, -

"You show your base ingratitude by thus insulting your mother and running the risk of betraying her to listening servants by your talk. Of course, this is all a farce, as you say, but it must be carried through. You and I were distantly related to Hugh Mainwaring, but what chance would we have against these people with no more of a claim than ours? I am compelled to assert that I was his wife and that you are his son in order to win any recognition in the eyes of the law."

For an instant her son regarded her with an expression of mingled surprise and incredulity, then the sneer returned, and, turning to leave the room, he answered, carelessly, -

"You can tell your little story to other people, and when you have won a fortune on it, why, I'll be around for my share, as, whatever my doubts in other directions, I have not the slightest doubt that you are my mother, and therefore bound to support me. But, for the present, if you please, I'll go by the old name of LaGrange. It's a name that suits me very well yet, even though," and a strange look flashed at her from his dark eyes, "even though it may be only a borrowed one," and the door closed, for the last time, between mother and son.

A low moan escaped from the lips of the unhappy woman. "My son - the only living being of my flesh and blood-even he has turned against me!" Too proud to recall him, however, she sank exhausted upon a couch, and, burying her face in her hands, wept bitterly for the first and only time in her remembrance.

Meanwhile, the guests of Fair Oaks, having returned from the funeral, had assembled in the large library below, and were engaged in animated discussion regarding the disposition to be made of the property. Ralph Mainwaring and Mr. Thornton, with pencils and paper, were computing stocks and bonds, and estimating how much of a margin would be left after the purchase of the old Mainwaring estate, which they had heard could be bought at a comparatively low figure, the present owner being somewhat embarrassed financially; while Mrs. Mainwaring was making a careful inventory of the furniture, paintings, and bric-a-brac at Fair Oaks, with a view of ascertaining whether there were any articles which she would care to retain for their future home.

Mr. Whitney, who, as a bachelor and an intimate friend of Hugh Mainwaring's, as well as his legal adviser, had perhaps more than any one else enjoyed the hospitality of his beautiful suburban home, found the conversation extremely distasteful, and, having furnished whatever information was desired, excused himself and left the room. As he sauntered out upon the broad veranda, he was surprised to see Miss Carleton, who had made her escape through one of the long windows, and who looked decidedly bored.

"It's perfectly beastly! Don't you think so?" she exclaimed, looking frankly into his face, as if sure of sympathy.

She had so nearly expressed his own feelings that he flushed slightly, as he replied, with a smile, "It looks rather peculiar to an outsider, but I suppose it is only natural."

"It is natural for them," she replied, with emphasis.

"I did not intend to be personal; I meant human nature generally."

"I have too much respect for human nature generally to believe it as selfish and as mercenary as that. I have learned one lesson, however. I will never leave my property to my friends, hoping by so doing to be held in loving remembrance. It would be the surest way to make them forget me."

"Has your experience of the last few days made you so cynical as that?" the attorney inquired, again smiling into the bright, fair face beside him.

"It is not cynicism, Mr. Whitney; it is the plain truth. I have always known that the Mainwarings as a family were mercenary; but I confess I had no idea, until within the last few days, that they were capable of such beastly ingratitude."

"Do you mean to say that it is a trait of the entire Mainwaring family, or only of this branch in particular?" he inquired, somewhat amused.

"All the Mainwarings are noted for their worship of the golden god," she replied, with a low musical laugh; "but Ralph Mainwaring's love of money is almost a monomania. He has planned and schemed to get that old piece of English property into his hands for years and years, in fact, ever since it was willed to Hugh Mainwaring at the time his brother was disinherited, and the name he gave to his son was the first stone laid to pave the way to this coveted fortune."

"I see. Pardon me, Miss Carleton; but you just now alluded to Hugh Mainwaring's brother. I remember some mention was made at the inquest of a brother, but I supposed it must be an error. Had he really a brother?"

"Ah, yes, an elder brother; and he must have been less avaricious than the rest of them, as he sacrificed a fortune for love. It was quite a little romance, you know. He and his brother Hugh were both in love with the same lady. The father did not approve, and gave his sons their choice between love without a fortune or a fortune without love. Hugh Mainwaring chose the latter, but Harold, the elder, was true to his lady, and was consequently disinherited."

"Poor Hugh Mainwaring!" commented the attorney; "he made his choice for life of a fortune without love, and a sad life it was, too!"

Miss Carleton glanced up with quick sympathy. "Yes, it seemed to me his life must have been rather lonely and sad."

There was a pause, and she added, "And did he never speak to you, his intimate friend, of his brother?"

"Never."

"Strange! Perhaps he was like the others, after all, and thought of nothing but money."

"No, I cannot believe that of Hugh Mainwaring," the attorney replied, loyally; then added, "What became of the brother, Miss Carleton?"

"He was lost at sea. He had started for Africa, to make a fortune for himself, but the boat was wrecked in a storm and every one on board was lost."

"And his family, what of them?" queried the attorney.

"He had no children, and no one ever knew what became of his wife. The Mainwarings are a very prosaic family; that is the only bit of romance in their history; but I always enjoyed that, except that it ended so sadly, and I always admired Harold Mainwaring. I would like to meet such a man as he."

"Why, I should say there was a romance in progress at present in the Mainwaring family," said Mr. Whitney, smiling.

"What! Hugh and Edith Thornton?" She laughed again, a wonderfully musical, rippling laugh, the attorney thought. "Oh, there is no more romance there than there is in that marble," and she pointed to a beautiful Cupid and Psyche embracing each other in the centre of a mass of brilliant geraniums and coleas. "They have been engaged ever since their days of long dresses and highchairs, - another of Ralph Mainwaring's schemes! You know Edith is Hugh's cousin, an only child, and her father is immensely rich! Oh, no; if I ever have a romance of my own, it must spring right up spontaneously, and grow in spite of all opposition. Not one of the sort that has been fostered in a hot-house until its life is nearly stifled out of it."

Mr. Whitney glanced in admiration at the fair English face beside him glowing with physical and intellectual beauty. Then a moment later, as they passed down the long hall in response to the summons to dinner, and he caught a glimpse, in one of the mirrors, of a tolerably good-looking, professional gentleman of nearly forty, he wondered why he suddenly felt so much older than ever before.

Miss Carleton was seated beside him at dinner, while nearly opposite was Harry Scott, conversing with young Mainwaring. He was quietly but elegantly dressed, and his fine physique and noble bearing, as well as the striking beauty of his dark face, seemed more marked than usual. Mr. Whitney watched the young secretary narrowly. Something in the play of his features seemed half familiar, and yet gave him a strange sense of pain, but why, he could not determine.

"Mr. Whitney," said Miss Carleton, in a low tone, "did you ever observe a resemblance at times between Mr. Scott and your friend, Mr. Hugh Mainwaring?"

The attorney looked up in surprise. "Why, no, Miss Carleton, I would not think a resemblance possible. Mr. Scott is much darker and his features are altogether different."

"Oh, I did not refer to any resemblance of feature or complexion, but his manner, and sometimes his expression, strikes me as very similar. I suppose because he was associated with him so much, you know."

Mr. Whitney's eyes again wandered to the face of the secretary. He started involuntarily. "By George!" he ejaculated, mentally, "Hugh Mainwaring, as sure as I live! Not a feature like him, but the same expression. What does it mean? Can it be simply from association?"

In a state of great bewilderment he endeavored still to entertain Miss Carleton, though it is to be feared she found him rather absent-minded. He was passing out of the dining-room in a brown study when some one touched his arm. He turned and saw Merrick.

"When you are at liberty, come out to the grove," the latter said, briefly, and was gone before the attorney could more than bow in reply.

CHAPTER XIII

THEORIES, WISE AND OTHERWISE

Half an hour later, having excused himself to Miss Carleton, Mr. Whitney hastened to the grove, where he found the detective sauntering up and down the winding walk, his hands behind him in a reflective mood, absorbed in thought and in the enjoyment of a fine cigar. He nodded pleasantly as the attorney approached.

"Going to be at liberty for some time?" he inquired, at the same time extending his cigar-case.

"Yes, for any length of time you please; it's a relief to get away from those egotists."

"H'm!" said Merrick, as he returned the cigar-case to his pocket after the attorney had helped himself; "I didn't think that you looked particularly anxious to be relieved of your company when I saw you. I really felt considerable delicacy about speaking as I did."

"Oh, to the deuce with your nonsense!" the attorney replied, his cheek flushing as he lighted his cigar. "If you had listened to the twaddle that I have all day, you would be glad to talk to almost any one for a change."

"In that event, perhaps you won't mind talking to me for a while. Well, suppose we go down to the stables, to the coachman's room; he is probably with his best girl by this time, and we will be safe from interruption or eavesdroppers."

"That suits me all right so long as Ralph Mainwaring doesn't think of looking for me there. That man makes me exceedingly weary!"

"Anxious to secure the property according to the terms of that will, I suppose."

"Anxious! He is perfectly insane on the subject; he can't talk of anything else, and he'll move heaven and earth to accomplish it, too, if necessary."

"Don't anticipate any difficulty, do you?"

"None whatever, unless from that woman; there's no knowing to what she may resort. It will only be necessary to prove that the will, if not in existence at the death of the testator, was fraudulently destroyed prior thereto, and I think we have a pretty clear case. By George, Merrick!" suddenly exclaimed the attorney in a different tone, as he paused on the way to the stables. "I hadn't thought of it before, but there's one thing ought to be done; we should have this lake dragged at once."

Merrick raised his eyebrows in mute inquiry.

"To find whatever Brown threw in there, you know; it might furnish us with an almighty important clue."

"H'm! might be a good idea," Merrick remarked, thoughtfully.

"Of course it would! I tell you, Merrick, I was cut out for a detective myself, and I'm pretty good for an amateur, now."

"Haven't a doubt of it," was the quiet response, and the pair resumed their walk. Both were soon comfortably seated in the coachman's room, their chairs tilted at just the right angle before a large double window, facing the sunset. Both smoked in silence for a few moments, each waiting for the other to speak.

"Well, my friend, what do you know?" inquired the detective, while he watched the delicate spirals of blue smoke as they diffused themselves in the golden haze of the sunlight.

"Just what I was about to ask you," said his companion.

"Oh, time enough for that later. You have been looking into this case, and, as you are a born detective, I naturally would like to compare notes with you."

Mr. Whitney glanced sharply at the detective, as though suspicious of some sarcasm lurking in those words, but the serious face of the latter reassured him, and he replied, -

"Well, I've not had much experience in that line, but I've made quite a study of character, and can tell pretty correctly what a person of such and such evident characteristics will do under such and such conditions. As I have already stated to you, I know, both from observation and from hints dropped by Hugh Mainwaring, that if ever a dangerous woman existed, - artful, designing, absolutely devoid of the first principles of truth, honor, or virtue, - that woman is Mrs. LaGrange. I know that Mainwaring stood in fear of her to a certain extent, and that she was constantly seeking, by threats, to compel him to either marry her or secure the property to her and her son and I also know that he was anxious to have the will drawn in favor of his namesake as quickly and as secretly as possible.

"Now, knowing all these circumstances, what is more reasonable than to suppose that she, learning in some way of his intentions, would resort to desperate measures to thwart them? Her first impulse would be to destroy the will; then to make one final effort to bring him, by threats, to her terms, and, failing in that, her fury would know no bounds. Now, what does she do? Sends for Hobson, the one man whom Hugh Mainwaring feared, who knew his secret and stood ready to betray it. Between them the plot was formed. They have another interview in the evening, to which Hobson brings one of his coadjutors, the two coming by different ways like the vile conspirators they were, and in all probability, when Hugh Mainwaring bade his guests good-night, every detail of his death was planned and ready to be carried into execution in the event of his refusing to comply with that woman's demands made by herself, personally, and later, through Hobson. We know, from the darkey's testimony, that Hobson and his companion appeared in the doorway together; that the man suddenly vanished-probably concealing himself in the shrubbery - as Hobson went back into the house; that a few moments later, the latter reappeared with Mrs. LaGrange; and the darkey tells me that he, supposing all was right, slunk away in the bushes and left them standing there. We know that the valet, going up stairs a while after, found Mrs. LaGrange in the private library, and at the same time detected the smell of burning paper. You found the burnt fragments of the will in the grate in the tower-room.

"Now, to my mind, it is perfectly clear that Mrs. LaGrange and Hobson proceeded together to the library and tower-room, where they first destroyed the will, and where she secreted him to await the result of her interview with Mainwaring, at the same time providing him with the private keys by which he could effect his escape, and with Hugh Mainwaring's own revolver with which the terrible deed was done. Later, finding that Mainwaring would not accede to her demands, I believe she left that room knowing to a certainty what his fate would be in case Hobson could not succeed in making terms with him, and I believe her object in coming down the corridor afterwards was simply to ascertain that her plans were being carried into execution. Now there is my theory of this whole affair; what do you think of it?"

"Very ingeniously put together! What about the jewels? Do you think Hobson took them?"

"No. I think Mrs. LaGrange got possession of them in some

way. She has no means of her own to hire that scoundrel, yet the darkey heard her promise to pay him liberally, and you see her very first attempt to pay him was by the sale of some of those jewels. I'll acknowledge I'm not prepared to say how or when she secured them."

"Could she open the safe?"

"That I cannot say. Mainwaring told me, some months ego, that he found her one day attempting to open it, and he immediately changed the combination. Whether she had discovered the new combination, I am unable to say; but she is a deep woman, and usually finds some way of accomplishing her designs."

"Brown, the coachman, seems to have no place in this theory of yours."

"Well, of course we none of us thought of him in connection with this affair until since his sudden disappearance yesterday, but I am inclined to think that he is to be regarded in the light of an accessory after the fact. I think it very probable that Mrs. LaGrange has employed him since the murder to assist her in concealing evidences of the crime, and that is why I suggested dragging the lake in search of what may be hidden there; but, according to his own story, he was in the city that night until some time after the murder was committed."

"Yes, according to his own story, but in reality he did not go to the city at all that night. More than that, he was seen in this vicinity about midnight with a couple of suspicious looking characters."

"By George! when did you learn that?"

"I knew it when Brown gave his testimony at the inquest."

"The deuce you did! and then let the rascal give you the slip, after all!"

"Don't give yourself any anxiety on that score; I can produce Brown any hour he's wanted. One of my subordinates has his eye on him day and night. At last reports, he and Brown were occupying the same room in a third-class lodging house; I'll wager they're having a game of cards together this evening."

"Well, well! you have stolen a march on us. But, if I may ask, why don't you bag your game?"

"I am using him as a decoy for larger game. Whatever Brown is mixed up in, he is only a tool in the hands of older and shrewder rascals."

Before the attorney could say anything further, Merrick rose abruptly and stepped to a table near by, returning with a package.

"What do you think of that?" he asked, removing the wrappings and holding up the rusty, metallic box.

"Great heavens!" ejaculated Mr. Whitney, springing forward excitedly. "Why, man alive, you don't mean to say that you have found the jewels!"

"No such good fortune as that yet," the detective answered quietly, "only the empty casket;" and having opened the box, he handed it to the attorney.

"Where did you find this?" the latter inquired.

"Fished it out of the lake."

"Ah-h! I should like to know when."

"While you were snoring this morning."

"Great Scott! They'll catch a weasel asleep when they find you napping! But, by George! this rather confirms my theory about that woman getting possession of the jewels and hiring Brown to help her, doesn't it?"

Without replying, Merrick handed over the revolver which had been brought to light that morning.

"Where did you get this rusty thing? Was it in the lake, also?"

The detective nodded affirmatively, and Mr. Whitney examined the weapon in some perplexity.

"Well, I must say," he remarked at length, "I don't see what connection this has with the case. The shooting was done with Hugh Mainwaring 's own revolver; that was settled at the inquest-"

"Pardon me! It was only 'settled' that the revolver found lying beside him was his own."

The attorney stared as Merrick continued, at the same time producing from his pocket the revolver in question, "This, as you are doubtless aware, is a Smith and Wesson, 32 calibre, while that," pointing to the rusty weapon in Mr. Whitney's hands, "is an old Colt's revolver, a 38. On the morning of the murder, after you and the coroner had gone, I found the bullet for which we had searched unsuccessfully, and from that hour to this I have known, what before I had suspected, that this dainty little weapon of Mr. Mainwaring's played no part in the shooting. Here is the bullet, you can see for yourself."

Mr. Whitney gazed in silent astonishment as the detective compared the bullet with the two weapons, showing conclusively that it could never have been discharged from the familiar 32-calibre revolver.

"Well, I'll be blessed if I can see what in the dickens that revolver of Mainwaring's had to do with the affair, anyway!"

"Very easily explained when you once take into consideration the fact that the whole thing was an elaborately arranged plan, on the part of the murderer, to give the affair an appearance of suicide. One glance at the murdered man convinced me that the wound had never been produced by the weapon lying at his side. That clue led to others, and when I left that room with you, to attend the inquest, I knew that Hugh Mainwaring had been shot with a 38-calibre revolver, in his library, near the centre of the room, and that the body had afterwards been so arranged in the tower-room as to give the appearance of his having deliberately shot himself beside his desk and with his own revolver."

"By George! I believe you're right," said the attorney; "and I recall now your statement that day, that the shooting had occurred in the library; I wondered then what reason you had for such an opinion."

"A small stain on the library carpet and the bullet told me that much. Another thing, which at first puzzled me, was the marked absence of blood-stains. There was a small pool of blood underneath the head, a slight stain on the carpet in the adjoining room, but none on the clothing or elsewhere. The solution to this I found on further investigation. The wound had been firmly and skillfully bandaged by an expert hand, the imprint of the bandage being plainly visible in the hair on the temples. Here is the proof that I was correct," and Merrick held up to the attorney's astonished view the stained and knotted handkerchief. "This, with the private keys belonging to Mr. Mainwaring's library, was in that box at the bottom of the lake. Do you consider Mrs. LaGrange or Hobson capable of planning and carrying out an affair so adroitly as that?"

"You've got me floored," the attorney answered, gazing at the proofs before him. "Hobson I know nothing about; but that woman I believe could scheme to beat the very devil himself; and yet, Merrick, when you think of it, it must have taken time-considerable time-to plan a thing like that."

"Or else," Merrick suggested, "it was the performance of an expert criminal; no bungling, no work of a green hand."

Mr. Whitney started slightly, but the detective continued. "Another point: Hobson, as you say, was the one man whom Hugh Mainwaring feared and who evidently had some hold upon him; would he then have dared denounce him as a liar and an impostor? Would not his use of such terms imply that he was addressing one whom he considered a stranger and unacquainted with the facts in the case?"

"I see," the attorney replied quickly; "you have in mind Hobson's accomplice, the tall man with dark glasses."

Merrick smiled. "You are then inclined to the opinion that J. Henry Carruthers, who called in the afternoon, is identical with the so-called Jack Carroll who accompanied Hobson in the evening?"

"Certainly that is a reasonable supposition. The descriptions of the two men agree remarkably, and the darkey was positive, both in his testimony at the inquest and in conversation with me, that they were one and the same person."

"Their general appearance seems to have been much the same, but their conduct and actions were totally unlike. Carruthers acted fearlessly, with no attempt at concealment; while, if you will stop to think of it, of all the witnesses who tried to give a description of Carroll, not one had seen his face. He always remained in the background, as much concealed as possible."

"I don't deny that you are correct," the attorney said musingly; "and they may have been two distinct individuals, Carroll evidently being the guilty party; but even in that event, in my opinion, he was only carrying out with a skillful hand the plans already arranged by that woman and Hobson."

"Whatever part Carroll took in the affair, he was undoubtedly Hobson's agent; and you will find that Hobson and Mrs. LaGrange have been more intimately associated and for a much longer time than you suspect," and Merrick repeated what he had overheard of the interview in Mrs. LaGrange's parlor, just after the close of the inquest.

Mr. Whitney listened with deep interest. "Well, well! And you heard her accuse him of being an accessory? Of course she referred to the murder. By George! I should have wanted them arrested on the spot!"

After a slight pause, he continued. "There's one thing, Merrick, in the conduct of Carruthers which I don't understand. Why, after telling the secretary that he would remain at the Arlington for the next two or three days, should he return to the city the next morning on the 3.10 train?"

"He seems to have been an impulsive man, who acted on the spur of the moment," Merrick answered; "but the strangest part of that is, that he did not return to the city at all. He bought a ticket for New York, but the conductor informs me there was no such man on board; while the north-bound train, which pulls out about five minutes later, had a passenger answering exactly to his description. The conductor on the latter train also informed me that, just as they were pulling out of the station, a man, tall and dark, rather good-looking, he should judge, though he could not see his face, and wearing a long, light overcoat, sprang aboard, decidedly winded, as though from running, and immediately steered for the darkest corner of the smoking-car, where he sat with his hat well drawn down over his face."

"Carroll again, by George!" exclaimed the attorney.

"Here is a problem for you to solve," Merrick continued, pointing to the revolver and box lying side by side. "You think Brown threw those in the lake. Who was the man that Brown saw standing beside the lake just before three o'clock in the morning, and what was he doing? He was tall and dark, and wore a long coat or ulster. Was that Carroll or Carruthers? Did he throw anything into the lake? And if so, what?"

Mr. Whitney gazed dubiously at the detective for a moment,

then began to whistle softly, while he slowly shook his head.

"No, Merrick; you've got me there! I never have had enough experience in this line that I could go into the detail work. I have to be guided by the main points in the case. Then, again, I gave Brown's testimony very little thought, as I considered him unreliable and irresponsible."

"Well, to come back to the 'main points,' then: what reasons have you for connecting Mrs. LaGrange and Hobson with this affair that might not apply equally well in the cases of certain other people?"

"What reason? Why, man alive! there is every reason to consider Mrs. LaGrange the instigator of the whole affair. In the first place, her one object and aim for the past seventeen or eighteen years has been to get hold of Hugh Mainwaring's property, to secure for herself and her son what she calls their 'rights'-"

"That is the point," Merrick interrupted. "You consider her guilty because she would be interested in securing a hold upon the property, although she, personally, has no claim whatever. Has it never occurred to you that there might be others more deeply interested than she, inasmuch as they have valid claims, being the rightful heirs?"

"I never thought of such a possibility," said the astonished attorney; "and I don't know that I understand now to whom you refer."

"I have learned from various reliable sources," the detective replied, "that Ralph Mainwaring has a younger brother, Harold, who is as much of a money-lover as himself, though too indolent to take the same measures for acquiring it. He is a reckless, unprincipled fellow, and having about run through his own property, I understand, he has had great expectations regarding this American estate, depending upon his share of the same to retrieve his wasted fortune. I learned yesterday, by cable, that since the departure of Ralph Mainwaring and his family for this country, his brother has been missing, and it is supposed, among his associates in London, that he took the next steamer for America, intending to assert his own claims."

"And you think-" the attorney interrupted, breathlessly; but Merrick shook his head and continued,-

"I have also, in the course of my investigations, incidentally discovered Hugh Mainwaring's secret, and, consequently, Hobson's secret, only that I know the real facts in the case, which Hobson does not know. You, as Mainwaring's friend, will not care to learn the details, and I shall not speak of them now, but I will say this much: there are probably in existence to-day, and perhaps not very far distant, heirs to this property, having a claim preceding not only that of Ralph Mainwaring or his son, but of Hugh Mainwaring himself."

There was silence for a few moments as the detective paused, Mr. Whitney's surprise rendering him speechless; at last he said, -

"Well, you are a truthful fellow, Merrick, and you never jump at conclusions, so I know your statements can be relied upon; but I'll be blessed if I understand how or when you have gathered all this information together. I suppose it would be useless to ask your deductions from all this, but I wish you would answer one or two questions. Do you think that this Harold Mainwaring, or those possible heirs you mention, would put in an appearance personally, or that they would work through agents and emissaries ?"

"Depends altogether upon circumstances. Harold Mainwaring would not be likely to appear on the scene unless he were pretty effectually disguised. As to the others,-if they were to assert their claim, -it would be difficult to say just what course they might take. I have made these statements merely to give you a hint of the possibilities involved in the case. It is now getting rather late, but I will give you one or two pointers to ruminate upon. Don't think that Hobson will run any risks or put himself to any personal inconvenience for Mrs. LaGrange. He is working first and foremost for Richard Hobson, after that for whoever will pay him best. Another thing, don't ever for a moment imagine that Hugh Main-waring's private secretary is looking for a job. It's my opinion he'll give you fellows one of the hardest jobs you ever tackled; and, unless I'm greatly mistaken, he's got brains enough and backing enough to carry through whatever he undertakes."

"Say! I don't know as I exactly catch your meaning; but that's one thing I wanted to ask you. What do you think of that young man, anyway? I can't make him out."

"I noticed that you had not assigned him any place in that theory of yours."

"No; he's been a mystery to me, a perfect mystery; but this evening a new idea has occurred to me, and I would like your judgment on it. Has he ever reminded you of any one? That is, can you recall any one whom he resembles?"

"Well, I should say there was a marked resemblance. I've often wondered where your eyes were that you had not seen it."

"You have noticed it, then? Well, so have I; but it has puzzled me, for, though the look was familiar, I was unable to recall whose it was until to-night. Now that I have recalled it, that, taken in connection with some other things I have observed, has led me to wonder whether it were possible that he is a son of Hugh Mainwaring's, of whose existence no one in this country has ever known."

"Hugh Mainwaring! I don't understand you."

"Why, you just acknowledged you had noticed the resemblance between them!"

"I beg your pardon; but you must recollect that I have never seen Hugh Mainwaring living, and have little idea how he looked."

"By George! that's a fact. Well, then, who in the dickens do you think he resembles?"

The coachman's step was heard at that instant on the stairs, and Merrick's reply was necessarily brief.

"Laying aside expression, take feature for feature, and you have the face of Mrs. LaGrange."

CHAPTER XIV

THE EXIT OF SCOTT, THE SECRETARY

One of the first duties which the secretary was called upon to perform, during his brief stay at Fair Oaks, was to make a copy of the lost will. He still retained in his possession the stenographic notes of the original document as it had been dictated by Hugh Mainwaring on that last morning of his life, and it was but the work of an hour or two to again transcribe them in his clear chirography.

Engaged in this work, he was seated at the large desk in the tower-room, which had that morning been opened for use for the first time since the death of its owner. He wrote rapidly, and the document was nearly completed when Mr. Whitney and Ralph Mainwaring together entered the adjoining room.

"Egad!" he heard the latter exclaim, angrily, "if that blasted scoundrel thinks he has any hold on me, or that he can keep me on the rack as he did Hugh, he'll find he has made the biggest mistake of his life. It is nothing but a blackmailing scheme, and I've more than half a mind to sift the whole matter to the bottom and land that beggarly impostor where he belongs."

"I hardly know just what to advise under the circumstances," Mr. Whitney answered, quietly, "for I, naturally, have some personal feeling in this matter, and I am forced to believe, Mr. Mainwaring, that there is something back of all this which

Maynard Barbour

neither you nor I would care to have given publicity. But, laying aside that consideration, I am of the opinion that it might not be to your interest to push this matter too closely."

"On what grounds, sir, do you base your opinion?" Mr. Mainwaring demanded.

The attorney's reply, however, was lost upon Scott, whose attention had been suddenly arrested by the imprint of a peculiar signature across one corner of the blotter upon which he was drying his work, now completed. Instantly, oblivious to everything else, he carefully examined the blotter. It was a large one, fastened to the top of the desk, and had been in use but a comparatively short time. It bore traces both of Hugh Mainwaring's writing and of his own, but this name, standing out boldly on one corner, was utterly unlike either. Nor did it resemble any of the signatures attached to the will on that memorable day when the desk with its paraphernalia had been last used.

Considerably perplexed, Scott suddenly recalled a small pocket mirror which he had seen in the desk. This he speedily found, and, having placed it at the right angle, leaned over to get a view of the name as it had been originally written. As he did so, he caught sight of some faint lines above the signature which he had not observed, but which were plainly visible in the mirror. It was well for the secretary that he was alone, for, as he read the signature with the words outlined above, he was spellbound. For a moment he seemed almost paralyzed, unable to move. His brain whirled, and, when he at last sank back in his chair, his face was blanched and he felt giddy and faint from the discovery which he had made. Gradually he became conscious of his surroundings. Again he heard, as in a dream, the conversation in the adjoining room. The attorney was speaking.

"I do not at present feel at liberty to give the source of my information, but I can assure you it is perfectly reliable, and my informant would never have made such an assertion unless he had ample authority to back it up."

"I don't care a rap for your information or its source," the other interrupted, impatiently. "The whole thing is simply preposterous. The estate descended regularly to Hugh Main-waring, and from him to our own family as next of kin. You can see for yourself that to talk of any other claimants having prior rights is an utter absurdity."

"Had not Hugh Mainwaring an elder brother?"

"He had; but you must be aware that he died a great many years ago."

"But had that elder brother no issue?"

"None living," Mr. Mainwaring replied, coldly. Then added, in the same tone, "Even had there been, that fact would have no bearing on this case, Mr. Whitney. The entire estate was transferred to Hugh Mainwaring by legal process before the death of his brother, he and his heirs having been forever disinherited, so that it is the same as though he had never existed."

While he was speaking, the secretary entered the library, his pallor and unusual expression attracting Mr. Whitney's attention. In response to a glance of inquiry from the latter, however, he merely said,-

"The copy is completed. You will find it on the desk," and passed from the library into the hall.

Still wondering at his appearance, Mr. Whitney proceeded to the tower-room, and a moment later both gentlemen were absorbed in the perusal of the duplicate of the lost will; but afterwards the attorney recalled that, on taking the document from the desk, he had noticed that the large blotter covering the top had been removed and replaced by a new one.

There was no perceptible change in Scott's appearance during the remainder of the day, except that he seemed more than usually thoughtful, sometimes to the verge of abstraction, but, in reality, his mind was so preoccupied with endless doubts and surmises regarding his recent discovery that he found it exceedingly difficult to concentrate his attention upon the work required of him. That afternoon, however, while engaged in looking through some important documents belonging to Hugh Mainwaring, kept at the city offices, a cablegram was handed him, addressed to himself personally, from Barton & Barton, a well-known legal firm in London. The despatch itself caused him little surprise, as he had been in correspondence with this firm for more than a year; but the contents of the message were altogether unexpected, and left him in a state of bewilderment. It read,-

"Have you met J. Henry Carruthers, of London, supposed to have sailed ten days since, or can you give us his whereabouts?"

Fortunately, Scott was alone, Ralph Mainwaring and the attorney being in the private offices, and he had plenty of opportunity to recover from his surprise. For half an hour he revolved the matter in his thoughts, wondering whether this had any bearing upon the question which for the last few hours he had been trying to solve. A little later he sent the following reply:

"Person mentioned seen on 7th instant. No trace since. You have my letter of 8th instant. Cable instructions."

As the Mainwaring carriage appeared at the offices at four o'clock, to convey the gentlemen to Fair Oaks, Mr. Whitney was surprised to find the secretary still engaged at his desk.

"If you will excuse me," the latter said, pleasantly, "I will not go out to Fair Oaks this evening. I have some unfinished work here, and I will remain in the city to-night."

Upon entering the offices the next day, however, the attorney found the following note addressed to himself:

"Mr. WHITNEY.

"DEAR SIR,-I regret to be compelled to inform you that you will have to look for another assistant, as important business calls me away for an indefinite period. Do not give yourself any trouble concerning the salary which you kindly offered me. I am not in need of it, and have only been too glad to render you the little assistance within my power, knowing, as I do, that you have no easy case on your hands.

"Trusting we shall meet in the future, I am, with great esteem, "Very truly yours, "H. SCOTT.

As Mr. Whitney read and reread this note, the words of the detective regarding the private secretary were recalled to his mind, and he muttered,-

"Yes, Merrick was right. It is very evident the young man is not 'looking for a job;' but I'll be blessed if I know what to think of him!"

Upon Mr. Whitney's return to Fair Oaks, he found the guests assembled on the veranda, overlooking the river, Mr. Merrick, who had just returned from a few days' absence, being also included in the company. There were many exclamations of surprise and considerable comment when Mr. Whitney told of the sudden disappearance of the secretary.

"Now, that is too bad!" cried Edith Thornton. "He was so interesting, and we were all beginning to like him so much."

"I don't know that any of us were so charmed with him as one might be led to suppose from your remark, Edith," said Isabel Mainwaring, with a disdainful glance towards the attorney, who had seated himself beside Miss Carleton; "but here, almost any one will answer for a diversion, and he was really quite entertaining."

"It is not to be expected that you would see or appreciate his good points," said her brother, with half a sneer; "but Scott is a fine fellow and a gentleman, and I shall miss him awfully."

Miss Carleton remained silent; but for some reason, unexplainable to herself, she was conscious of a vague sense of disappointment and injury. She would not admit to herself that she was troubled because Scott had gone, it was the manner of his departure. Surely, after the friendship and confidence she had shown him, he might at least have sent some word of farewell, instead of leaving as he had, apparently without a thought of her. However, she chatted graciously with Mr. Whitney, though, all the while, a proud, dark face with strangely beautiful eyes persistently forced itself before her mental vision, nearly obliterating the smiling face of the attorney.

Meanwhile, Ralph Mainwaring was giving the detective his views on the subject.

"I, for one, am not sorry that he has followed the example of the coachman and taken himself off. It is my opinion," he continued, in impressive tones, "that we will yet find he had reasons for leaving in this manner."

"Undoubtedly!" Merrick replied, with equal emphasis.

"Now, that's just where you're wrong, governor," said young Mainwaring. "Scott is as good as gold. There is no sneak about him, either; and if he had reasons for leaving as he has, they were nothing to his discredit; you can stake your last shilling on that!"

"Oh, I know he has pulled the wool over your eyes," said his father; "but he has never tried his smooth games on me; he knows I can see through him. I detest him. One of your typical American swells! Just what one would expect to find in a country where a common clerk is allowed to associate with gentlemen!"

"But, begging your pardon, Mr. Mainwaring," the detective interposed, quietly, "Mr. Scott is not an American. He has lived less than two years in this country."

A chorus of exclamations followed this statement.

"Not an American! Then he must be an Englishman," cried Miss Carleton, her sparkling eyes unconsciously betraying her pleasure at the discovery.

"Merrick, are you sure of that?" inquired Mr. Whitney, in astonishment.

"Certainly, or I would never have made the assertion I did."

Ralph Mainwaring suddenly turned the conversation. "How about that will business, Mr. Whitney? When will that come off?"

"The petition was filed this afternoon, and will be granted a hearing some time next week; I have not yet learned the day."

"And then will you gentlemen be ready to start for home?" Mrs. Mainwaring inquired, a touch of impatience in her voice.

"Well, by my soul! I should say not," laughed Mr. Thornton, before her husband could reply. "It will probably take a number of months, my dear madam, to settle up this estate, even if there should be no contest; and if the case is contested, it may drag on for years, eh, Mr. Whitney?"

"That will depend upon circumstances. A contest would, of course, delay the case, perhaps for several months; but I am not aware of any contestants with sufficient means for continuing it the length of time you mention."

"Mercy me!" exclaimed Mrs. Mainwaring, addressing her husband; "do you and Hugh intend to remain here all that time?"

"Our stay will probably be somewhat indefinite," he replied, evasively; "but that is no reason why you and the young ladies need remain against your will."

"Indeed! Why could you not have said as much before? Neither Isabel nor I care to remain here a day longer than is necessary; we have simply been awaiting your pleasure. Wilson, bring me the morning papers; I want to see what boats are expected. We will take the first steamer home. Mr. Thornton, will you and the young ladies accompany us, or do you prefer to remain in exile a while longer?"

"Well," replied that gentleman, smiling genially, "speaking for myself, I would more than half like to stay and see this thing through; but the ladies are in the majority, and I will abide by their decision. How is it, Edith? I suppose, as the novelists say, you will be 'torn by conflicting emotions.'"

"You horrid old papa! Of course, if auntie is going back, I shall go with her. What do you say, Winifred?"

"I have very little choice, one way or the other," Miss Carleton replied, more quietly than was usual for her; "whatever you and Uncle William decide, will suit me."

"Ab, here are the papers!" said Mrs. Mainwaring, adjusting her eye-glasses. "These dreadful American dailies!" she exclaimed, as she scanned the pages; "one never knows where to find anything. Ah, here it is, and just what we want! The 'Campania' sails Thursday, at three o'clock. That will suit us exactly."

"To-morrow! so soon!" exclaimed two or three voices.

"Certainly," she replied, rising. "I shall have the maids begin packing at once; and, Mr. Thornton, I shall instruct Wilson to attend directly to your luggage, for you would never think of it until within an hour of sailing."

Her departure seemed the signal for the breaking up of the little company. Mr. Whitney lingered a few moments at Miss Carleton's side, with a few murmured words of regret that she was to leave so soon, to which she listened courteously, though making little response. After he had gone she remained standing where he had left her, gazing dreamily out on the river and the distant bluffs. Merrick, slowly sauntering up and down the veranda, had observed the whole scene, and now watched the fair young face with a suggestion of a smile in his kindly eyes.

"H'm!" he soliloquized; "Whitney is a bigger fool than I've given him credit for if he thinks he stands any show in that direction. If I'm not mistaken, I know which way the wind blows, and it's dollars to doughnuts she'll lose that far-away expression of hers before she's been aboard the 'Campania' many hours. I'd like to be aboard myself and watch the transformation scene."

The attorney's voice here broke in upon his cogitations.

"I say, Merrick, that was a regular bomb you threw at Mainwaring with regard to young Scott! How did you discover he was an Englishman?"

"I very easily ascertained that he was not an American; that he was of English descent followed as a matter of course. I am not sure whether he is of English birth."

"You seem to be keeping an eye on him."

"It is my business just now to be posted regarding every one associated with this place. I've been keeping an eye on you for the last thirty minutes."

The attorney colored, and hastily reverted to the original topic of conversation. "Have you seen anything of him since he left us?"

"Since his resignation of the salary as well as the position of private 'secretary?'" queried the detective, half to himself, with a tone of amusement, which Mr. Whitney failed to comprehend. "Yes; I met him to-day at the Murray Hill."

"At the Murray Hill! Is he stopping there?"

"He evidently was this morning. So was I. Possibly we were both 'stopping' on the same business; I cannot say."

The detective's face was a study, as was also the attorney's.

"1 supposed," said the latter, after a short pause, "from the tenor of his note, that he intended to leave the city at once."

"Possibly he does," replied the other, enigmatically, and, having consulted his watch, turned abruptly in another direction.

"Say, what will you do about him? Shall you watch him?" Mr. Whitney called after the vanishing figure.

Merrick looked back over his shoulder with a peculiar smile. "I shall not lose track of him," he said, slowly; "he is too interesting."

CHAPTER XV

MUTUAL SURPRISE5

The Mainwaring party was among the latest arrivals at the pier on the following day, owing to the dilatoriness of Mr. Thornton, Mrs. Mainwaring's efforts to the contrary notwith-standing. At the last moment he appeared, serenely and smilingly unconscious of that lady's frowns of displeasure, to the infinite amusement of his daughter, who whispered to Miss Carleton,-

"Poor papa! See how auntie glares at him, and he does not even know it."

But even Mrs. Mainwaring's facial muscles relaxed slightly at the sight of the beautiful ocean greyhound lying in the harbor, her flags waving and streamers fluttering in the breeze, awaiting only the captain's orders to start on her homeward course.

The decks were crowded with humanity, for the most part laughing and chatting gayly and singing bits of song, though here and there were sad, tear-stained faces, where long farewells, some of them perhaps the last farewells, were being spoken.

"Thank heaven, there'll be no tears shed on this occasion!" said Isabel Mainwaring; "unless," she added, with a glance of scorn towards Miss Carleton's escort, "Mr. Whitney should contribute a few. I detest such vulgar demonstrations in public!"

The attorney certainly did not look very cheerful, and even Miss Carleton's sunny face was somewhat overcast, though why, it would seem difficult to determine, since she seemed to have no regrets at leaving America.

"Mercy me!" ejaculated Mrs. Mainwaring, "what a dreadful crowd! It is far worse than when we came over. Hugh, I wonder if your father examined the ship's list. I particularly requested him to do so. I wished to ascertain whether there would be any friends of ours on board. One does not care to make acquaintances promiscuously, you know."

"I don't think the governor investigated the subject very thoroughly," young Mainwaring replied, with a laugh. "I noticed when we registered there were three or four pages of names preceding ours, and I don't think he gave the matter much attention. If I had time I would look it up for you, mother, but we must go ashore in a few moments."

"If I am not mistaken, my dear lady," said Mr. Thornton, who had overheard the conversation, "you will have little time or inclination for looking up acquaintances on this trip."

"May I ask why?" Mrs. Mainwaring demanded.

"I think," he replied, maliciously, "that you and Isabel will be too much occupied in cultivating the acquaintance of mal de mer to care for your best friends."

"How's that, Thornton? Think it will be rough?" inquired Ralph Mainwaring.

"The captain tells me the wind is freshening every moment, and we'll have a decidedly choppy sea before night. I'm thinking we'll have a nasty trip."

"In that case, perhaps mamma and I will not be the only victims," said Isabel Mainwaring.

"I fear not," responded Mr. Thornton. "Were it not or my inherent chivalry, I should turn back; but I cannot leave you ladies to meet your fate alone."

Amid the general confusion of leave-taking, Mr. Whitney turned towards Miss Carleton, saying in a low tone, as he took her hand,-

"I have received cordial invitations both from yourself and Mr. Thornton to visit your home, and I feel assured of a welcome should I accept your courtesy; but, pardon me, Miss Carleton, if, after so brief an acquaintance as ours, I inquire whether I might ever hope for a welcome from you other than that of a friend?"

The beautiful brown eyes met his own frankly, but all the laughter and sunshine had gone out of them. They were serious and had almost a look of pain.

"I am sorry, Mr. Whitney," she said, simply; "but it would be very unjust if I led you to hope that I could ever regard you other than as an esteemed friend."

"Pardon me for troubling you," he said, gently. "Believe me always your friend, and forget that I ever asked for more than friendship," and, releasing her hand, he passed on to the others.

The final adieus were spoken; Ralph Mainwaring and his son, accompanied by the attorney, went ashore; and Miss Carleton, not caring just then to meet the curious glances of her companions, walked slowly towards the forward part of the deck. She had gone but a few steps, however, when she caught sight of the familiar figure of Mr. Merrick at a little distance, in conversation with a tall, slender man, with dark, piercing eyes. He was speaking rapidly in low tones, but his usually non-committal face wore an expression of unmistakable satisfaction. Suddenly he turned and walked swiftly in Miss Carleton's direction. Their eyes met, and in response to her glance of recognition he quickly crossed to where she was standing.

"I have but a few seconds left, Miss Carleton," he said, a genial smile lighting up his face; "but I am glad of an opportunity to wish you a pleasant trip. Are you a good sailor?"

"I hardly know," she answered. "I have had so little experience on the sea. Why? Shall we have a stormy passage, do you think?"

"Nothing dangerous; a little rough, perhaps; but with congenial company, such as I trust you will find," and his eyes gleamed with kindly merriment, "you will hardly mind that. Good-by, Miss Carleton; bon voyage; and if I can ever in any way serve you as a friend, do not fail to command me," and before she could reply he had vanished in the crowd. She looked in vain for any trace of him; then turning to glance at his companion of a moment before, discovered that he had disappeared also.

A moment later the great ocean liner glided majestically out from the harbor amid prolonged cheers and a final flutter of farewells; but she was well out upon the tossing waves ere Miss Carleton turned from watching the receding shore to join her friends, as yet having found no solution of the problem perplexing her, nor even the meaning which she felt must be concealed in the words of the detective.

They had not been out many hours before it became evident that Mr. Thornton's unfavorable predictions regarding their journey were likely to be fulfilled. The sea was decidedly "choppy" and the motion of the boat anything but exhilarating.

When the hour for dinner arrived, Mr. Thornton, his

daughter, and Miss Carleton were the only members of their party to venture forth to the dining-saloon, the others preferring to have a light repast served in their own apartments. The captain, having discovered in Mr. Thornton an old-time friend, had ordered seats for him and his party at his own table, and the young ladies, finding their appetites rather an uncertain quantity, had plenty of opportunity for observing their fellow-passengers, particularly an Anglomaniac of the most pronounced type, in the person of a callow youth seated opposite them, whose monocle, exaggerated collar, and affected drawl afforded them considerable amusement.

"Winifred," said Miss Thornton, as they were leaving the dining-saloon, "do you see that young Englishman at the farther table?"

Her cousin glanced carelessly in the direction indicated, noting the fine, athletic figure seated, back towards them, at some distance, attired in heavy English tweed.

"Yes. What of him?"

"Nothing in particular; only the sight of him is such a relief, you know, after that wretched caricature at our table."

"Poor little harmless dudelet!" mused Winifred, with a smile; his self-complacency will be short-lived whenever he meets Isabel. She will simply annihilate him with one of those glances of hers!"

At Miss Carleton's suggestion, they went on deck; but Edith grew so rapidly ill that her cousin assisted her below to their own elegant suite of apartments, which adjoined, on one side, those occupied by Mrs. Mainwaring and her daughter, while on the other was comfortable state-room belonging to Mrs. Hogarth.

Finding Mrs. Mainwaring and Isabel already reduced to a state of abject helplessness which required the attendance of both maids as well as of the stewardess, Miss Carleton left Edith in Mrs. Hogarth's care, and, wrapping herself warmly, again went on deck. The wind was increasing and she found the decks nearly deserted, but the solitude and the storm suited her mood just then, and, wrapping her rug closely about her, she seated herself in a comparatively sheltered place, alone with her own thoughts.

As she recalled the parting interview with Mr. Whitney, another face seemed to flash before her vision, and a half-formed query, which had been persistently haunting her for the last few hours, now took definite shape and demanded a reply. What would have been the result if that other, instead of leaving without one word of farewell, had asked for the hope of something better and deeper than friendship? What would her answer have been? Even in the friendly shadow of the deepening twilight she shrank from facing the truth gradually forcing itself upon her.

A solitary figure pacing the deck aroused her from her revery. As he approached she recognized the young Englishman of whom Edith had spoken. Dressed in warm jacket, with cap well pulled down over his eyes and hands clasped behind him, he strode the rolling deck with step as firm and free as though walking the streets of his native city. She watched him with admiration, till something in his carriage reminded her of the young secretary at Fair Oaks, and in the sudden thrill of pleasure produced by that reminder there was revealed to her inner consciousness a confirmation of the truth she sought to evade.

She watched the retreating figure with flashing eyes and burning cheeks. "It is not true!" she exclaimed, to herself, passionately. "I do not care for him! It was only a fancy, a foolish infatuation, of which, thank heaven, neither he nor any one else shall ever know."

But the monarch who had taken possession of her heart, call

him by what name she chose, was not to be so easily dethroned.

Meanwhile, the young English stranger passed and repassed, unconscious of the figure in the shadow, unconscious of the aversion with which one of his countrywomen regarded him because of his resemblance to another. He, too, was vainly seeking the solution of problems which baffled him at every turn, and waging an ineffectual warfare against the invisible but potent sovereign-Love.

All that night the storm raged with increasing fury, and morning found the entire Mainwaring party "on the retired list," as Miss Carleton expressed it. She herself was the last to succumb, but finally forced to an ignominious surrender, she submitted to the inevitable with as good grace as possible, only stipulating that she be left entirely to herself.

Towards night the storm abated slightly, and, weary of her own thoughts, which had been anything but agreeable, and bored by the society of her companions in misery, she wrapped her rug warmly about her and ventured out on deck. The air, laden with salt spray, seemed invigorating, and without much difficulty she found her way to her sheltered corner of the preceding evening. She had been seated but a few moments, however, when the young Englishman made his appearance, as preoccupied and unconscious of his surroundings and as free from any symptoms of discomfort as when she had last seen him. The sight of him was the signal for the return of the thoughts which had that day kept her company. She cast a wrathful glance upon the unconscious young stranger just then passing, his perfect health and evident good humor under existing circumstances adding to her sense of injury and exasperation. She grew ill, and determined to return at once to her apartments, but found her progress against the gale slower and more difficult than she had anticipated. Dizzy and faint, she had just reached the stairs when a sudden lurch threw her violently to one side; she staggered helplessly and would have fallen, but at that instant a strong arm was thrown about her and she felt herself lifted bodily. With a sigh of relief she turned her head towards her rescuer, supposing him one of the officers of the ship, only to discover, to her horror, that she was in the arms of the young Englishman. His face was in the shadow, but the light falling on her own face revealed her features, and at that instant she heard a smothered exclamation,-

"Great heavens! can it be possible?"

Something in the tone startled her and she listened, hoping he would speak again. He did not; but she noted the tenderness with which she was borne down the stairs and put in care of the stewardess. Again she listened eagerly for his voice, but his words were brief and in an altered tone.

During the succeeding twenty-four hours in which Miss Carleton tossed in misery, one thought was uppermost in her mind,-to discover, if possible, the identity of the stranger who had come to her assistance. The only information obtainable, however, was that he was evidently a gentleman of wealth, travelling alone, and apparently with no acquaintance on board with the exception of a young English officer. She determined, at the earliest possible moment, to meet her mysterious rescuer and thank him for his kindness, but was unable to carry her plan into immediate execution. Meantime, she learned that he had twice inquired for her.

On Sunday afternoon, their fourth day out, the storm had ceased and the weather was gradually clearing, and Miss Carleton, somewhat pale but quite herself again, came out for a promenade. She found quite a number of passengers on deck, but for some time she looked in vain for her unknown friend. At last, after several brisk turns, she saw him standing at a little distance, talking with the tall, dark-eyed man whom she had seen in conversation with Mr. Merrick. The younger man's cap was thrown back, revealing to Miss Carleton the fine profile, almost classical in its beauty, of the secretary at Fair Oaks. For a moment her pulse throbbed wildly. She felt a thrill of pleasure, not unmingled with a twinge of the resentment which she had been nursing for the last few days. Then she walked calmly in his direction, saying to herself, -

"At least, I will thank him for his kindness. I am no love-lorn peasant maid wearing my heart upon my sleeve!"

She had nearly reached his side, though he was unaware of her presence, when the young English officer approached from the other side and, slapping him familiarly upon the shoulder, exclaimed, -

"Well, Mainwaring, my boy, you've kept your sea-legs well on this trip."

The tall, dark-eyed man withdrew, and Miss Carleton, utterly bewildered, turned and slowly retraced her steps. Mainwaring! What did it mean? She heard the name distinctly, and he had taken it as a matter of course, replying pleasantly and quietly, as though he had known no other name. The mystery which she had thought to solve had only deepened tenfold. She was aroused by the cheery voice of the captain.

"Well, well, Miss Carleton, glad to see you out! I congratulate you on your speedy recovery. How are the ladies? and how is my old friend Thornton?"

They took a few turns up and down, chatting pleasantly, till Miss Carleton, looking into the face overflowing with kindliness and good humor, said,-

"Captain, I have a great favor to ask of you."

"Granted, my dear young lady, to the half of my kingdom!"

"May I have your permission to examine the list of cabin passengers?"

The captain elevated his shaggy eyebrows and his eyes twinkled with merriment. "Ah! anxious to learn if some particular friend is on board, I suppose. Some one was inquiring of me the other night regarding your identity."

"Indeed!" said Miss Carleton, a world of inquiry in her eyes.

"Yes; Mr. Mainwaring, the gentleman conversing with Lieutenant Cohen over there. He and I both went to your assistance the other evening, but, much to my regret, he was quicker than I. He remarked to me after he came back on deck that he had supposed you were a stranger, but that your face looked familiar. He asked your name, and whether you were with Mr. Thornton and his daughter, stating that he had met you. Correct, I presume?"

"Quite so," said Miss Carleton, quietly.

"And now about that passenger list, Miss Carleton; you have my permission to examine it, and I will accompany you myself."

She thanked him. "Are you acquainted with Mr. Mainwaring?" she inquired, carelessly.

"Never met him until this trip. On first learning his name, I supposed him to be a member of your party, as he is evidently a gentleman; but I soon learned that he was alone."

A few moments later the register was opened for Miss Carleton's inspection, but she did not have to search long. Half-way down the first page she found, in the familiar writing of the secretary, the name which she sought-"Harold Scott Mainwaring."

CHAPTER XVI

MUTUAL EXPLANATIONS

Thanking the captain for his courtesy, Miss Carleton returned to her accustomed seat on deck, and, since one is never more alone than when surrounded by a crowd of utter strangers, she felt at liberty to pursue her own thoughts without interruption.

She could scarcely credit what her own ears had heard or her eyes had seen. Harold Scott Mainwaring! What could it mean? Could it be possible that the secretary, having familiarized himself with the family history of the Mainwarings, was now masquerading under an assumed name for some object of his own? But she dismissed this idea at once. She had assured him at Fair Oaks that she believed him incapable of anything false or dishonorable, and she would abide by that belief until convinced otherwise. But if this were indeed his name, what had been his object in assuming the role of Scott, the secretary? Which was genuine and which assumed? Who could tell? As if in answer to her thoughts, she saw the subject of them approaching. He was alone and looking in her direction, and on reading the recognition in her glance, his own face lighted with a smile that banished the last shade of resentment and suspicion from her mind, albeit there was a question in her eyes which prepared him in a measure for her first words. With a smile as bright as those with which she had been accustomed to greet him at Fair Oaks, she extended her band, saying, slowly, -

Maynard Barbour

"Mr. Mainwaring, this is indeed a surprise!" She watched him closely, but there was not the quiver of an eyelash, only a slow, inscrutable smile, as he replied, -

"Miss Carleton, I will add to that, and say that this is the pleasantest surprise of my life."

She blushed at the implied meaning of his words, and he added, -

"I have not seen you on deck until to-day."

"Not last Friday evening?" she inquired, archly. His smile deepened. "I did not know that it was you at that time until after I had started below. Did you recognize me?"

"I thought I recognized your voice; and I have often wished to thank you for your kindness, but this is my first opportunity, as I have not been out since until to-day."

"Please do not mention it. Had I dreamed who it was thus braving the storm, I would have offered my assistance earlier. I have not yet recovered from my surprise on discovering the identity of my fellow-passenger that evening."

"Indeed!" laughed Miss Carleton; "my presence here is very easily explained. It is simply the result of one of Mrs. Mainwaring's numerous whims, as she suddenly decided upon an immediate return to England. I think, however, that the surprise was mutual."

"Accordingly, I suppose that mutual explanations should follow," he answered, lightly. Then added, more seriously, "Miss Carleton, I am aware that there is much in my conduct that must seem inexplicable to you. In a few weeks everything will have been made clear, in the natural course of events; but, if you would be at all interested to hear, I would greatly prefer that you should have a perfect understanding of the situation before the facts become generally known."

"I should greatly appreciate such a mark of confidence," she replied.

"If agreeable to you, Miss Carleton, let us pass around to the other side; it is less crowded there. My friend and I have two chairs, and, as he has gone to his state-room to do some writing, we shall be in no danger of interruption."

When comfortably seated, the young man said, "It is a strange story which I have to tell, but I will try not to tax your patience too severely. One week ago this afternoon, Miss Carleton, in passing through the hall at Fair Oaks, I accidentally overheard a portion of your conversation with Mr. Whitney, as you related to him the story of the unfortunate love and death of my father, Harold Scott Mainwaring."

Miss Carleton started violently, but said nothing, and, after a slight pause, the speaker continued,-

"My earliest recollections are of a home in Australia, with foster-parents, whose name it is unnecessary to mention, but whose care and love for me seem, as I now look back, to have equalled that bestowed by natural parents upon their own child. Not until I had reached the age of fifteen years did I ever hear of my own father. I then learned that he had given me, at birth, into the keeping of my foster-parents, with instructions that, unless he himself should call for me, I was not even to know of his existence until within five or six years of my majority. I learned, further, that his action in thus placing me in the hands of others had been solely on account of deep trouble and sorrow, of which he wished me to know nothing until I had reached the years of manhood. When giving me into their keeping he had also given them a small packet, containing a sealed letter, which was to be read by me on my twenty-first birthday, if he had not himself claimed me before that time. I was told that, while I was too young to retain any remembrance of him, he frequently visited me and manifested the greatest devotion to his child, but as I grew older he remained away, writing occasionally to my foster-father.

"In the last letter received from him, when I was about five years of age, he stated that he was going to Africa to make a fortune for his son. Nothing further was heard from him until there came tidings of his death at sea, in the manner which you recently related.

"Of all this I, of course, knew nothing until ten years later, but what was told me at that time made a deep impression upon me. Of my mother I could learn absolutely nothing; but for my father, of whom I had no personal knowledge, and concerning whom there seemed so much that was mysterious, I felt a love and reverence almost akin to adoration, and I longed for the day to come when I could read the letter he had left for me and learn the whole secret of that sad life.

"My twenty-first birthday arrived, and the mysterious little packet was placed in my hands. It contained a few valuable keepsakes and my father's letter, written out of the bitter anguish of a broken heart. He told the story of his disinheritance, with which you are familiar; but the loss of the property he cared little for in comparison with the loss of his father's love; but even that was as nothing to the sorrow which followed swiftly and which broke his heart. He stated that, because of this great sorrow, he had placed me in the hands of trusted friends that I should be banished from the false-hearted woman who had borne me and who believed me dead, as it was his wish that neither of us should ever know of the existence of the other."

Harold Mainwaring paused for a moment, and Miss Carleton, who had been listening with great interest, exclaimed, -

"And is it possible, Mr. Mainwaring, that, in all these years, you have had no knowledge concerning your mother?"

"It is a fact, Miss Carleton, that I do not even know her name, or whether or not she is living. I only hope and pray that I may never knowingly meet her, for her heart and life must be-pardon the expression-as false and as black as hell itself."

There was a look on his face which Miss Carleton had never seen. Gradually, however, his features softened, and he continued,-

"In accordance with my father's wish, expressed in the letter, that I should complete my studies in England, I sailed for that country within a few weeks of my twenty-first birthday; and while there I learned that part of my story which is of more especial interest to all parties concerned at the present time."

"I had been but a few months in England when I felt a great desire to visit, incognito, the old Mainwaring estate. Accordingly, under the name by which you have known me, I arrived at the estate, only to learn that the home of my father's boyhood, and of the Mainwarings for several generations, had passed into the hands of strangers. My grandfather had died within two years of my father's marriage, and the younger son had sold the estate and gone to America. Incidentally, I was directed to an old servant of my grandfather's, who yet remained on the place and who could give me its whole history. That servant, Miss Carleton, was old James Wilson, the father of John Wilson, Ralph Mainwaring's present valet."

"Ah!" ejaculated Miss Carleton, her face lighting with pleasure; "I have seen the trusty old fellow hundreds of times, you know. Indeed, he could give you the history of all the Mainwarings for the last three hundred years."

"He gave me one very important bit of history," Harold Mainwaring replied, with a smile. "He told me that old Ralph Mainwaring, after the departure of his son for Australia, failed rapidly. He was slowly but surely dying of a broken heart, and, though he never mentioned the name of his elder son, it was evident that he regretted his own harshness and severity towards him.

"On the night before his death he suddenly gave orders for an attorney to be summoned, and was so insistent in his demand, that, when it was ascertained that his old solicitor, Alfred

Barton, the father of the present firm of Barton & Barton, had been called out of the city, a young lawyer, Richard Hobson by name, who had formerly been an articled clerk in Barton's office, was called in in his stead. A little before the hour of midnight, in the presence of his son, Hugh Mainwaring, Richard Hobson, the attorney, and Alexander McPherson, an old and trusted Scotch friend, Ralph Mainwaring caused to be drawn and executed a will, completely revoking and setting aside the process of law by which Harold Scott Mainwaring had been disinherited, and restoring to him his full rights as the elder son, McPherson and the attorney signing the will as witnesses."

Miss Carleton's eyes dilated and her breath came and went swiftly, but she spoke no word save a single, quick exclamation.

"James Wilson, the servant, was also present, but in an obscure corner, and his presence seems to have been unnoticed. The next morning, at five o'clock, Ralph Mainwaring passed away, happy in the thought that he had at last made reparation for his injustice to his elder son. Within two months the old Scotchman died, and Richard Hobson was then the sole surviving witness of the last will and testament of Ralph Maxwell Mainwaring."

"This was all the direct information I could obtain from Wilson, but from other sources I learned that Hugh Mainwaring was never the same after his father's death. He grew stern and taciturn, and would allow no mention of his brother's name, and within two years he had disposed of the estate and left England forever; while a few years later tidings were received of the death of Harold Scott Mainwaring at sea. I also learned that about this time Richard Hobson suddenly rose from the position of a penniless pettifogger to that of an affluent attorney, though he was engaged in questionable speculations far more than in the practice of law."

"I visited the chambers of Barton & Barton, and learned

through them that everything had been adjusted in accordance with the terms of the will in their possession, which disinherited the elder son; but Hugh Mainwaring's action in disposing of the estate had excited considerable comment."

"Having pledged them to secrecy, I disclosed my identity and related to them the story of the old servant. To my surprise, they were inclined to give the story credence; and, acting upon their advice, I obtained all possible information regarding Hugh Mainwaring, and, when my studies were completed, sailed for America, with the express determination to secure proof in verification of the facts which I had already gathered, and to establish my claim as the legal heir of the Mainwaring estate. I was not without means to do this, as my father had accumulated considerable property during the few years he lived in Australia, and my foster-parents are people of wealth."

"You will understand now, Miss Carleton, why I took the position of private secretary to Hugh Mainwaring. You will realize how eagerly I studied the correspondence between him and Richard Hobson, from which I learned that the latter was extorting large sums of money as the price of his silence regarding some fraudulent transaction, presumably the destruction of the will; and perhaps you can imagine my feelings on discovering, one day, among Hugh Mainwaring's private papers, a memorandum to the effect that the will had never been destroyed, but was still in existence and in his possession. I knew that to make any demand upon him for the document would be worse than useless, as he would never admit my claim. I must find it for myself. I searched for that will as for hidden treasure, and, Miss Carleton, I found it!"

"Oh!" she exclaimed, unable to repress her emotion, "I am so glad! Do tell me how and when!"

"I found it on the last day of Hugh Mainwaring's life, within two hours after he had signed his own last will and testament."

"What a strange coincidence!"

"It was strange; and it was my discovery on that day which formed the subject of my thoughts on the following night, the night of the murder, and which kept me pacing my room until three o'clock in the morning."

"Did Mr. Mainwaring know of your discovery?"

"No; I had no opportunity to see him that evening until too late, even if I had chosen to broach the subject to him at that time."

"Might he not have discovered in some way that you had found the will?"

"I think not. Why do you inquire?"

"It only occurred to me if it might not be possible that he had reason to think his secret had at last been discovered, and, rather than face the consequences, committed suicide; but it seems improbable. But to think that you are the son of the one whom I have always considered the noblest of all the Mainwarings, and that you, and not Hugh, are the rightful heir to the old Mainwaring estate! I am more than glad, and Hugh will be glad also. He will not begrudge you one shilling or have one unkind thought towards you, though I cannot say the same for his father."

"Hugh is a noble-hearted fellow," said Harold, warmly. "He has promised me his friendship, and I believe he will stand by it."

He spoke briefly of his plans; of his business in London for a few days; and, when the will should have been probated in the English court, of his return to America to establish his claim there.

"Mr. Mainwaring," said Miss Carleton, after a pause, "I am inexpressibly glad to learn what you have told me, and you have my sincerest wishes for your immediate success. I appreciate, more than I can tell, your confidence in permitting me to be the first to know of your good fortune. May I be the first to congratulate you?"

He took the proffered hand; but, looking into the beautiful eyes sparkling with happiness, his own face grew serious, as he replied, -

"I thank you for your congratulations and your good wishes, Miss Carleton, but I sometimes question whether my discovery, on that particular day, of the will-the last link in the chain of evidence against Hugh Mainwaring-was a matter for congratulation."

"How is that?" she inquired, quickly.

"Do you not see that when all these facts become known, they may be used by my enemies to direct suspicion against me as the possible murderer of Hugh Mainwaring?"

"Who would think of such a thing?" she exclaimed, indignantly.

"Ralph Mainwaring will," was his prompt reply.

"He might try to incite the suspicions of others against you, but he would know in his own heart that his insinuations were unfounded."

"I have no fear of him," said Harold, with a smile; "I only mentioned it to show that I do not anticipate upon my return to America that my pathway will be strewn with roses."

He paused a moment, then added, "I had this in mind, Miss Carleton, when I asked you once whether your confidence in me were strong enough to stand a heavy strain, if necessary."

She blushed slightly at the reminder, and a look of quick comprehension flashed across her face, as, for an instant, she dropped her eyes before his earnest gaze. When she again looked up the luminous eyes met his own unwaveringly, as she replied, in firm, low tones,-

"I will believe in you and trust you to the fullest extent, whatever happens."

"I thank you more than I can express," he answered, gravely; "for, believe me, Miss Carleton, I value your confidence and friendship far above any and every other."

"I did not suppose you needed any assurance of my friendship; though, after your sudden departure from Fair Oaks, I felt somewhat doubtful whether you cared for it."

He did not reply at once, and when he did, it was evident he was repressing some strong emotion. "I feel that there is an explanation due you for my manner of leaving Fair Oaks. I am aware that it had the appearance of rudeness, but I can only say that it was from necessity and not from choice. There is something more which I hope some day to tell you, Miss Carleton, but, until I can speak as I wish to speak, it is best to remain silent; meanwhile, I will trust to your friendship to pardon whatever in my conduct may seem abrupt or inexplicable."

The conversation was terminated at this point by the appearance of Lieutenant Cohen, whom Harold Mainwaring introduced as an old classmate, and presently all three adjourned to the dining-saloon.

To Harold Mainwaring and Miss Carleton the remainder of the voyage passed swiftly and pleasantly, and the friendship begun at Fair Oaks deepened with each succeeding day. Though no word of love passed between them, and though Miss Carleton sometimes detected on the part of her companion a studied avoidance of personal subjects, yet, while wondering slightly at his self-imposed silence, she often read in his dark eyes a language more eloquent than words, and was content to wait.

It was his desire that the other members of her party should still remain in ignorance of his real identity; and, as the greater part of the voyage proved somewhat rough, he had little difficulty in preserving his secret. Mr. Thornton and daughter soon made their appearance and greeted the quondam secretary with unaffected cordiality, but Mr. Thornton was too deeply engrossed in renewing acquaintance with one or two old friends to pay much attention to the younger man, while Edith felt in duty bound to devote herself to the entertainment of Mrs. Mainwaring and Isabel, a task which Miss Carleton was not at all disposed to share. Not until the last few hours of the trip, when fair weather had become an established fact and land had been sighted, did Mrs. Mainwaring and her daughter appear on deck, and in the general excitement Harold Mainwaring escaped their observation.

The parting between himself and Miss Carleton was necessarily brief. She gave him her address, saying,-

"I would be delighted if you could consider yourself our guest while in London, and I hope at least that I may see you often before your return."

"I thank you, Miss Carleton," he replied. "If present circumstances would admit of it, nothing would give me greater pleasure than to accept your invitation, but under existing conditions it is, of course, impracticable. I cannot now say how long I will remain in London, but I wish to make my stay as brief as possible, and to that end shall devote almost my entire time to business; but," he added, with a peculiar smile, "I shall not repeat the offence committed at Fair Oaks. You may rest assured I shall not return to America without seeing you, and I hope at that time to be able to speak more definitely regarding my future."

There was that in his eyes as he spoke that suffused the fair English face with lovely color and caused a tender, wistful smile to linger about the sweet mouth long after he had left her side.

He was one of the first to land, and Miss Carleton, watching from the deck, saw, almost as soon as he had reached the pier, a fine-looking gentleman in the prime of life step quickly out from, the crowd, and, grasping him cordially by the hand, enter at once into earnest conversation. Harold Mainwaring turned towards the steamer for a parting salute, and, as both gentlemen raised their hats, she recognized in the new-comer, Alfred Barton, the junior member of the firm of Barton & Barton. She watched them until they disappeared in the crowd, then, turning to rejoin her companions, she noted, standing at a little distance, the slender, dark-eyed individual whom she had observed on previous occasions, also watching the scene with a smile of quiet satisfaction, much like that which Mr. Merrick's face had worn at the beginning of the Voyage.

CHAPTER XVII

LOVE FINDS A WAY

Less than three weeks later, Harold Mainwaring entered Miss Carleton's private drawing-room in Mr. Thornton's London home. Soon after her arrival in the city she had received from him a brief note of apology, stating that unexpected business of the greatest importance would render it impossible for him to call as early as he had anticipated; hence this was their first meeting since the leave-taking on board the "Campania."

As Miss Carleton stepped forward with cordial smile and hand extended to welcome her visitor, she was shocked at the change in his appearance. He was pale, almost haggard, and deep lines about the mouth and eyes told of some intense mental strain. She gave a low cry of astonishment, for it seemed as though years, instead of only a few weeks, had intervened since she had seen that face.

"Mr. Mainwaring, you have been ill!" she exclaimed.

"No, Miss Carleton," he replied, his face lighting with a rare smile; "I have been perfectly well, but loss of sleep and constant care and anxiety have told rather severely on me. Nothing more serious, I assure you."

"Anxiety!" she repeated, at the same time motioning him to a seat by her side. "Surely you do not anticipate any difficulty in establishing your claim?"

Maynard Barbour

"No difficulty so far as its validity is concerned. My attorneys assure me there can be no question as to that with such irrefutable proofs in my possession, but some unlooked-for complications have arisen, and we have had to prepare ourselves to meet them. But I did not call to burden you with my perplexities, Miss Carleton. Tell me of yourself. I trust you have been well since I last saw you."

Yes, I am usually well," said Miss Carleton, who thought she detected on the part of her visitor an avoidance of any details concerning himself; "but I have been rather bored of late." Then, in answer to his look of inquiry, she continued, "Of course, on account of Hugh Mainwaring's death, we have been living very quietly since our return, but, notwithstanding that fact, society has been paying due homage to the prospective increase of fortune and added social position of the Mainwarings. I am not particularly fond of society in the ordinary sense of the word, you know, and I have found it exceedingly tiresome."

"From reports, I should judge 'society' to be very fond of yourself," he remarked, with a smile.

"After its own fashion," she replied, smiling in return; "but it becomes very monotonous. It is the same old round, you know, only that just now it bows a little lower than formerly, while it mingles condolences and congratulations in the most absurd manner. One hears, 'Such a dreadful affair! so shocking, don't you know!' and 'Such delightful fortune! I quite envy you, my dear!' all in the same breath. I am only awaiting what society will say when the real facts become known."

Harold Mainwaring made no reply, but a strange pallor overspread his already pale face, at which Miss Carleton wondered.

"I have thought very often of you during these past weeks," she continued, "and felt quite impatient to learn how you were progressing, and your note was so brief, you know. It left so much unsaid. I fear you forget how interested I am in all that concerns yourself."

"No," he replied, slowly, "I do not forget; and I appreciate your interest in me even though I may not seem to, - even though I am forced, as you say, to leave so much unsaid which I had hoped to say."

Something in his manner, more than in what he said, thrilled her with a vague, undefinable sense of impending evil, and, during the slight pause which followed, she dreaded his next words, lest they should in some way confirm her apprehensions. He said nothing further, however, and when she spoke it was with an assumed lightness and cheerfulness which she was far from feeling.

"I hoped to have the pleasure of meeting you often ere this, and my uncle and cousin would have been so glad to welcome you to their home during your stay in London, but they have just gone out of town for a few days."

"Ordinarily, Miss Carleton," he replied, quietly, "I should be pleased to meet them, but on the present occasion, as I sail, to-morrow, I naturally care to see no one but yourself."

"To-morrow!" she exclaimed, while her own cheek suddenly paled. "Do you return so soon?"

"Yes," he replied, observing her emotion, and speaking rapidly to conceal his own feelings; "my business is at last completed. I have been detained longer than I expected, and I found the situation more complex than I anticipated, but I shall return well equipped for the battle."

"And you will win, I am sure. Tell me something regarding your plans," she added, with a wistful smile that touched her companion for more than he cared to betray.

"Mr. Alfred Barton goes with me to America," he said, speaking cheerfully; "and we have already cabled instructions to Mr. Sutherland, my New York attorney, regarding the initiatory steps. Mr. Barton and myself will be accompanied by James Wilson, the old servant who witnessed the execution of the will," - Miss Carleton's eyes brightened, - "and also by a thoroughly competent, first-class Scotland Yard officer."

She gave a low exclamation. "I see what a powerful witness old Wilson will make; but the detective, what will you do with him?"

"We are going to investigate the murder of Hugh Mainwaring," he said, calmly.

"Why, surely, you cannot mean-" she hesitated. "You do not think that suspicion will be directed against any of the guests at Fair Oaks, do you?"

"My dear Miss Carleton, I cannot say at present. Perhaps," he added, slowly, looking steadily into her eyes, "perhaps, when all is over, suspicion will be directed against myself so unmistakably that public opinion will pronounce me guilty."

"I cannot believe that," she cried; "and even were it so, - should the whole world pronounce you guilty, -I would still believe you innocent; and I think," she added, quickly, "that is your object in employing a detective: by finding the real murderer, you will establish your own entire innocence."

"May God grant it!" he replied, with a fervor she could not understand. "I thank you, Miss Carleton, for your kind words; I shall never forget them; and, however the battle goes, I can feel there is one, at least, whose friendship and confidence are mine, can I not?"

"Most assuredly, Mr. Mainwaring. But why do you speak as though there were a possibility of defeat or failure? I am so confident that you will win, after the story of your life that you have given me, that I am all impatience to learn the outcome of the contest, just as having read one chapter in some thrilling romance I am eager for the next."

He smiled at her comparison. "Real life, as well as romance, sometimes contains startling surprises, Miss Carleton. The next chapter might prove less pleasant."

She looked keenly into his face for a moment, and her manner became as serious as his own.

"There must be something," she said, "of which you have not told me; if so, I will not ask your confidence until you choose to bestow it, nor do I trust you, personally, any the less. It only seemed to me, with your prospects of success, and the great wealth and enviable position so soon to become yours, there could be no unpleasant anticipations for the future."

A bitter smile crossed his face, as he inquired in low, tense tones, "Of what avail are wealth and position to one who finds an insurmountable barrier placed between himself and all that he holds most precious on earth?"

"I fear I do not understand you," she replied. "I cannot imagine any barriers surrounding you; and did they exist, my judgment of you would be that you would find some way to surmount or destroy them."

"There are some barriers, some fetters," he said, gently, "against which humanity, even at its best, is powerless."

"Yes," she answered, a touch of sadness in her voice; "and there are sometimes sorrows and troubles in which even the closest and warmest friendship is powerless to aid or comfort."

"Don't allow yourself to think that of your friendship for me," he said, quickly. "Assured of your confidence and sympathy, I shall be ten times stronger to face whatever the future may bring. If I succeed in what I am about to undertake, I shall one day tell you all that your friendship has been worth to me. If I fail, the thought that you believe in me and trust me, while it will not be all that I could wish, may be all that I can ask."

"And if you should fail," she queried, slowly, "would you give me no opportunity to show you, and others, my confidence in you, even then?"

"My dear Miss Carleton," he replied, in tones tremulous with suppressed feeling, "much as I appreciate your kindness, I would never, now or at any future time, willingly mar your life or your happiness by asking you to share any burden which might be laid upon me. I would at least leave you to go your way in peace, while I went mine.

"And I?" she asked, reproachfully. "Would it contribute to my happiness, do you think, to remember the sorrow and suffering which I was not allowed to share?"

"Could you not forget?"

"Never!"

The young man sprang to his feet abruptly, his face working with emotion, and took two or three turns about the room. At last he paused, directly in front of her, and, folding his arms, stood looking down into the beautiful eyes that met his own so unflinchingly. He was outwardly calm, but the smouldering fire which seemed to gleam in his dark eyes told of intense mental excitement.

"Miss Carleton," he said, slowly, in low tones, but yet which vibrated through her whole being, "you are almost cruel in your kindness; you will yet make a coward of me!"

"I have no fear of that," she answered, quietly.

"Yes, a coward! Instead of remaining silent as I intended, and keeping my trouble within my own breast, you will compel me in self-defence to say that which will only give you pain to hear, thereby adding to my own suffering."

"Perhaps you misjudge," she replied, and her voice had a ring of pathos in it; "any word of explanation - no matter what- would be less hard for me to endure than this suspense."

"God knows I would make full explanation if I could, but I cannot, and I fear there is nothing I can say that will not add to your suspense. Miss Carleton, you must need no words from me to tell you that I love you. I have loved you almost from the first day of our meeting, and whatever life may have in store for me, you, and you alone, will have my love. But, loving you as I do, could I have looked forward to the present time, could I for one moment have foreseen what was awaiting me, believe me, you should never have known by word or look, or any other sign, of my love."

He paused a moment, then continued. "If that were all, I might have borne it; I could have locked my love forever within my own heart, and suffered in silence; but the fact that you have given me some reason to believe that you were not wholly indifferent to me, - the thought that I might in time have won your love, - makes the possibilities of the future a thousand times harder to bear. It is harder to forego the joys of Paradise when once you have had a glimpse within! It was to this I alluded when I spoke of the insurmountable barrier placed between myself and all that I hold holiest and best on earth!"

"But I do not understand!" she cried, her lovely color deepening and her eyes glowing with a new light, until Harold Mainwaring confessed to himself that never had he seen her so beautiful. "What barrier could ever exist between you and me?"

For an instant he looked at her in silence, an agony of love and longing in his eyes; then drawing himself up to his full height, he said, slowly, -

Maynard Barbour

"Not until I can stand before you free and clear from the faintest shadow of the murder of Hugh Mainwaring, will I ever ask for that most precious gift of your love!"

Her face blanched at the mere possibility suggested by his words. "But you are innocent!" she cried in swift protest, "and you could prove it, even were suspicion directed against you for a time."

"Even admitting that I were, the taint of suspicion is sometimes as lasting as the stain of crime itself."

She arose and stood proudly facing him. "Do you think I would fear suspicion? To hear from your own lips that you love me and that you are innocent would be enough for me; I would defy the whole world!"

He did not at once reply, and when he spoke it was slowly and reluctantly, as though each word were wrung from him by torture.

"My dear Miss Carleton, even to you I cannot say that I am innocent."

There was a moment's pause, during which she gazed at him, speechless with astonishment; a moment of intense agony to Harold Mainwaring, as he watched whether her faith in him would waver. But she gave no sign, though she scanned his face, as the condemned criminal scans the document handed him as the fateful day approaches, to ascertain whether it contains his pardon or his death sentence.

"Understand me," he said at last, gently, unable longer to endure the terrible silence, "I do not admit that I am in any way guilty, but until I am fully acquitted of any share in or knowledge of the death of Hugh Mainwaring, I can make neither denial nor admission, one way or the other."

"But you still love me?" she inquired, calmly.

"Miss Carleton, - Winifred, - how can you ask? You are, and always will be to me, the one, only woman upon earth."

"That is sufficient," she answered, with a strange, bright smile; "my faith in you is perfect, and faith and love can wait."

"Wait, my love! until when?" he cried.

"If needful, until Eternity's sunlight dispels Earth's shadows! Eternity holds ample compensation for all of Earth's waiting."

"But, my darling," he said, half protesting, while he folded her to his breast, "you know not the risk you may be running; I cannot accept the sacrifice that may be involved."

"My decision is taken, and it is irrevocable," she answered, with an arch smile; then added, "There can be no barriers between us, Harold, for Love will find a way!"

CHAPTER XVIII

AN UNFORESEEN FOE

Though nearly six weeks had elapsed since the death of the master of Fair Oaks, and as yet no light had been shed on that mysterious event, the interest of the public mind in the affair had in no wise abated during this brief interim. On the contrary, its curiosity had been so whetted by the partial revelations of the inquest, that it had eagerly followed each step of the legal proceedings leading towards the inevitable contest over the property, ready to hail with delight the appearance of the Mainwaring skeleton when it should step forth from its long hiding to disclose the secrets of the past.

As early as possible, a petition, setting forth the terms and conditions of the last will and testament of Hugh Mainwaring, and praying for letters of administration in accordance therewith to be issued to William H. Whitney, the executor named in said will, had been filed in the district court. A few days thereafter, the petition of Eleanor Houghton Mainwaring, for letters to be issued to Richard Hobson, was also filed. The hearing in the application for letters of administration occupied several days; very little evidence was adduced, however, which had not already been given at the inquest, and in due time an order was issued by the court, appointing Mr. Whitney administrator of the estate, with instructions that the same be adjusted according to the terms of the lost will. From this order, Eleanor Houghton Mainwaring, through her attorney, Hobson, had appealed , and the contest had at last begun.

For greater convenience during the legal proceedings, Ralph Mainwaring had closed the suburban residence, dismissing what servants were no longer needed, though still retaining the new coachman, and had removed to Hugh Mainwaring's city residence, where he and his son made themselves perfectly at home, dining with Mr. Whitney at his club. Mrs. LaGrange, having been compelled to resign her position at Fair Oaks, had also removed to the city and taken apartments in a convenient hotel until the termination of her suit.

The afternoon of the second day since the opening of the case was drawing to a close; the testimony on the appellant's side had been taken, and it was expected that the respondent would be heard on the following day, when an event transpired which completely overthrew all proceedings had thus far, and which promised the waiting public developments as startling as could be desired.

This event was none other than the filing in the district court of a document purporting to be the last will and testament of the father of the deceased Hugh Mainwaring, by the terms of which the Mainwaring estate, as it then existed, together with the bulk of his other property, passed to Harold Scott Mainwaring, an elder son who had been previously disinherited, but was by this will restored to his full rights. With this document, worn and yellow with age, was filed a petition, setting forth the claims of one Harold Scott Mainwaring, the lawful, living, and only son of the said Harold Scott Mainwaring named in the will, but since deceased, and sole heir of the Mainwaring estate, and praying for letters of administration to be issued to George D. Sutherland, attorney for the said lawful heir.

The court adjourned amid intense excitement, just as the newsboys were crying the headlines of the evening papers, -

"A New Heir to the Mainwaring Property! Discovery of Will secreted more than Twenty-five Years! Millions wrongfully withheld from the Rightful Owner!"

Strangely enough, the two most interested in this unexpected turn of affairs were among the latest to learn the surprising news. Ralph Mainwaring, having felt slightly indisposed, and knowing that his side would not come up for hearing until the following day, had made himself as comfortable as possible in the elegant apartments which he had appropriated to his own use, while his son had left the court-room at an early hour to devote the remainder of the afternoon to letter-writing.

The latter glanced up from his writing and nodded pleasantly, as Mr. Whitney, pale with excitement, was ushered by the butler into the library.

"Mr. Mainwaring, is your father in?" the attorney inquired, hastily.

"I believe so," replied the young man, smiling broadly; "the last I knew, the governor was luxuriating in his rooms up-stairs; I think you will find him there now. How's the case coming on, sir?" he added, as the attorney turned quickly towards the hall. "Anything new developed?"

"Yes; decidedly new!" Mr. Whitney answered, rather brusquely; "you had better join us up-stairs!" and he disappeared.

The young man's face grew suddenly serious, and, springing from his chair, he swiftly followed the retreating figure of the attorney, arriving just in time to hear the latter exclaim, in reply to some question from his father, -

"Well, sir, the storm has burst!"

Ralph Mainwaring was, as his son had said, "luxuriating" in a superb reclining chair, his eyes half closed, enjoying a fine Havana, but the attorney's words seemed to produce the effect of an electric shock.

"The deuce, sir! what do you mean?" he demanded, instantly assuming an upright position.

"I simply mean that what I have expected and dreaded all along has at last come to pass."

"Then, since it was not unexpected, it is to be presumed that you were at least prepared for it! That shyster and his designing client must, at the last moment, have exerted their inventive faculties to a remarkable degree!"

"On the contrary," said the attorney, quietly ignoring the other's sarcasm, and handing copies of the evening papers to father and son, "I am satisfied that neither Hobson nor his client has any part in the developments of this afternoon."

A brief silence followed, during which the attorney watched the two men before him, noting the strange contrast between them, never until that moment so apparent. Young Mainwaring's boyish face grew pale as he read, and he occasionally glanced at Mr. Whitney, as though seeking in his face either confirmation or contradiction of the report, but he remained calm and self-possessed, preserving his gentlemanly bearing to the close of the interview. The face of the elder man, however, rapidly assumed an almost apoplectic hue, the veins standing out from his temples like whip-cords, and when he spoke his voice trembled with rage. He was the first to break the silence, as, with an oath, he flung the papers upon the floor, exclaiming, -

"It is a lie from beginning to end! The most preposterous fabrication of falsehood that could be devised! The 'will,' as it is called, is nothing but a rank forgery, and the man who dares assert any claim to the estate is a damned impostor, and I'll tell him so to his face!"

"I examined the document very carefully, Mr. Mainwaring," said the attorney, "and I shall have to admit that it certainly had every appearance of genuineness; if it is a forgery, it is an exceedingly clever one."

"Do you mean to tell me that you believe, for one moment, in this balderdash?" demanded Ralph Mainwaring, at the same time rising and striding about the room in his wrath. "The utter absurdity of the thing, that such a will ever existed, in the first place, and then that it would be secreted all these years only to be 'discovered' just at this critical moment! It is the most transparent invention I ever heard of, and it is a disgrace to your American courts that the thing was not quashed at once!"

"That could not very well be done," said Mr. Whitney, with a quiet smile; "and as the matter now stands, the only course left open for us is to prepare ourselves for a thorough investigation of the case."

"Investigation be damned!" interrupted the other, but, before he could proceed further, he was in turn interrupted by young Mainwaring.

"I say, governor, you'd best cool down a bit and listen to what Mr. Whitney has to say; if this thing is a forgery, we surely can prove it so; and if it isn't, why, all the bluster in the world won't help it, you know."

His father faced him with a look of withering contempt. "If it is a forgery! I tell you there are no 'ifs' about it. I suppose, though, you are just fool enough that, if any man made a pretence of a claim to the estate, you would simply hand it over to him, and thank him for taking it off your hands!"

"That's just where you are wrong, governor. I would fight him, fair and square, and he would have to prove a better claim than mine before he could win. But the point is this, don't you know, you can fight better with your head cool and your plans well laid beforehand."

"The young man is right," said Mr. Whitney, quickly; "there is every indication that our opponent, whoever or whatever he may be, is well prepared for contesting the case. I understand he has plenty of evidence on his side and the best of legal counsel."

"Evidence, I suppose," interposed Ralph Mainwaring, with a sneer, "in support of a document that never existed, and a man that never lived on the face of the earth; for Harold Mainwaring never had a living son. Have you seen this remarkable individual?"

"I believe no one in this country has seen him as yet, sir. He is expected to arrive on the 'Umbria,' which I understand is due the early part of next week."

The face of the other showed slight surprise at this statement, but, before he could speak, the young man inquired, -

"I say, Mr. Whitney, what sort of a man is this attorney, Sutherland? Is he another Hobson?"

Mr. Whitney shook his head significantly. "Mr. Sutherland is one of the ablest men in his profession. I consider him a fine jurist, an eloquent pleader, and a perfect gentleman. I had some conversation with him after court adjourned, and while he, of course, stated no details, he gave me to understand that his client had a strong case. He also informed me that Barton & Barton, of London, had been retained in the case, and that his client would be accompanied to this country by the junior member of the firm, Alfred Barton."

"By Jove, that looks bad for us!" ejaculated young Mainwaring, while his father exclaimed, impatiently, -

"Barton & Barton? Impossible! that is mere bombast! Why, man, the Bartons, father and sons, have been the family solicitors of the Mainwarings for the past fifty years. The old firm of Barton & Sons had charge of the settlement of the estate when it passed into Hugh Mainwaring's possession at the death of his father."

"So I had understood," said the attorney; "I have heard Mr. Mainwaring himself speak of them."

"And," continued the other, "only a few days before sailing for America, I called at their chambers in London and told them of Hugh's intentions regarding my son and received their congratulations. Now, sir, do you mean to tell me, in the face of all this, that Barton & Barton are retained by this mushroom claimant, whoever he is? Pooh! preposterous!"

Mr. Whitney shook his head slowly. "Mr. Sutherland is not the man to make any misstatements or allow himself to be misinformed. All I have to say is, if those attorneys are retained in the case, it certainly looks as though our opponent must have some tenable ground in support of his claim. I am inclined to think they will make us a hard fight, but I am confident that we will win in the end. The main point is this: we must be prepared to meet them on whatever ground they may take, and, after hearing their side and the proof they set up, we can easily determine our line of defence."

"To the deuce with your line of defence! I tell you, Whitney, there is just one point to be maintained, and, by my soul, it shall be maintained at any cost!" and the speaker emphasized his words by bringing his clinched hand down upon a table beside him with terrific force "that point is this: Harold Scott Mainwaring never had a living, lawful son; no such person exists, or ever has existed on the face of the earth, and I can prove what I say."

"Have you absolute proof of that?" Mr. Whitney inquired, quickly.

"I have," replied Ralph Mainwaring, triumphantly, while his cold, calculating gray eyes glittered like burnished steel. "If any man thinks I have been asleep for the past twenty-one years, he is deucedly mistaken. Mr. Whitney, since the day of that boy's birth," pointing to his son, "I have had but one fixed resolve, which has been paramount to everything else, to which everything else has had to subserve,-the Mainwaring estate with its millions should one day be his. Not a day has passed in which this was not uppermost in my mind; not a day in which I have not scanned the horizon in every direction to detect the least shadow likely to intervene between me and the attainment of the dearest object of my life. When the news of Harold Mainwaring's death reached England, in order to guard against the possibility of a claim ever being asserted in that direction, I set myself at once to the task of finding for a certainty whether or not he had left any issue.

I never rested day or night until, after infinite labor and pains, I had secured the certificate of the attendant physician to the effect that the only child of Harold Mainwaring died within an hour from its birth."

"Have you that certificate now?" inquired the attorney.

"Not here; it is among my private papers at home."

"Cable for it at once; with the death of Harold Mainwaring's child fully established, the will would cut no figure, one way or another."

"That will," said Ralph Mainwaring, fiercely, turning upon Mr. Whitney with an expression which the latter had never seen, "let me tell you, will cut no figure one way or another in any event. That will, remember, is a forgery; and, if necessary, I will prove it so, if it takes my last shilling and the last drop of my heart's blood to do it; do you understand?"

The attorney understood, and was more than ever convinced in his ow mind that the old will filed that day was genuine.

Meanwhile, in another part of the city, Mrs. LaGrange sat alone in her apartments, awaiting the coming of Richard Hobson. It was considerably past the hour which he had set and daylight was slowly merging into dusk, yet enough light still remained to show the changes which the last few weeks had wrought in her face. Her features looked pinched and drawn, and a strange pallor had replaced the rich coloring of the olive skin, while her dark eyes, cold and brilliant as ever, had the look of some wild creature suddenly brought to bay. She shuddered now, as, from her window, she saw the cringing form of Hobson approaching the building.

" To think," she exclaimed to herself, passionately, "that that creature is the only one to whom I can go for counsel or advice! I loathe the very sight of him; fool that I was ever to place myself within his power! I thought I could use him as a tool like the rest; but it is like playing with edged tools; yet I dare not let him go."

A moment later, she heard a stealthy, cat-like tread in the corridor outside, followed by a low, peculiar tap at the door, and Hobson entered.

She crossed the room slowly, keeping her face in the shadow, and, motioning him to a chair, seated herself opposite, watching him narrowly.

"You are late," she said, coldly, in response to his greeting.

"Admitted, my lady," he replied, in his usual unctuous tones, "but I naturally wished to ascertain all the facts possible regarding this new deal, and, seeing Whitney nosing about on the trail, I decided to remain within ear-shot and pick up what information I could second-hand."

"What did you learn?"

"Nothing very definite, and yet enough, perhaps, to give us our cue until further developments. My dear lady, what do you think of this new turn of affairs?"

"The whole thing is simply preposterous; a piece of the most consummate audacity I ever dreamed of!"

"Ha! I thought it would strike you as particularly nervy. It is the most daring bit of invention I have seen for some time; and it must be a pretty cleverly concocted scheme and pretty well backed with the ducats also, for I learned to-night that the 'heir,'" laying special emphasis on the word, "has secured the services of Barton & Barton, and those birds are too old to be caught with chaff; besides, you know as well as I the part that firm has taken in the Mainwaring affairs."

"Barton & Barton? Incredible! The case is hopeless then for Ralph Mainwaring: he is a fool if he expects to win."

"Just what I was leading up to. Whitney is no match even for this man, Sutherland, and he will be a mere child in the hands of the Bartons. Now, the question is, where do we come in? As you say, Ralph Mainwaring's case is hopeless, unless -"and he looked significantly at his client.

"I do not think I quite catch the drift of your meaning," she answered, slowly.

"Has it not occurred to you that there are not two people in existence who can so quickly tear to shreds the scheme of this impostor as you and I? There is not a human being living outside of myself who knows the real facts concerning that will; and who could give such effective and convincing testimony regarding Harold Mainwaring's son as yourself?"

"Admitting all this, what do you propose?"

"When Ralph Mainwaring has staked his highest card and finds that the game is irrevocably lost, what will he not give at the last critical moment for assistance such as we can then furnish him?"

"And which course would you pursue in that event?" she asked, a tinge of irony in her tone. "Would you deny that such a will ever existed in face of whatever evidence may be brought forward in its support? or would you admit being a party to the destruction of the will?"

"My dear madam, I am perfectly capable of conducting this affair to our mutual satisfaction and without running my head into any trap, as you so pleasantly suggest. And right here allow me to say that it would be just as well for you not to make those insinuations which you are so fond of throwing out at random. As I said before, no living person outside of myself, including even yourself, knows the facts regarding that will. You have your own surmises, but they are only surmises, and you had best keep them to yourself as you know enough of me by this time to know it will be to your interest to accept my suggestions and fall in line with my plans."

Her face was in the shadow, and he did not see the scornful curl of her lip or her peculiar expression, as she remarked coldly,-

"You are only wasting words and time in your efforts to intimidate me. You have not yet made any suggestions or outlined any plans. I have asked you what you propose to do."

"I have not time to go into details, but, briefly stated, I propose, when the right opportunity presents itself, to prove, first, that this document filed to-day is a forgery. If I can show conclusively that the original will was accidentally lost, or intentionally destroyed, or if I happen to have the original in my possession, - under any of these conditions I gain my first point. Then, through your testimony, I shall demonstrate unequivocally a still more important point, that this so-called heir is a gross impostor, that no such individual exists."

"And for this, you expect-what?"

"For this I shall demand a handsome remuneration, to be divided, of course, between yourself and myself, and Ralph Mainwaring will only too gladly give the half of his kingdom for such services."

"And your testimony would have so much weight with Ralph Mainwaring and the Bartons, and with every one else who has any knowledge of your London history!"

Hobson winced visibly, but before he could reply she continued:

"You are talking the most arrant foolishness. You know that those men would not allow your testimony in court; they would very quickly procure evidence to show that your word, even under oath, is worthless; that you are a liar, a perjurer and a-"

"Not so fast, not so fast, my lady. If past histories are to be raked up, I know of one which embraces a much wider area than London alone; Melbourne, for instance, and Paris and Vienna, to say nothing of more recent events!"

"Do your worst, and I will do mine!" she replied, defiantly. "That is nothing to the point, however. What I have to say is this: You are a fool if you think that you or I can ever extort money from Ralph Mainwaring. He would give no credence whatever to anything that you might say, and if once my identity were revealed to him, he would go through fire and blood rather than that one shilling of his should ever become mine.

"And what do you propose to do?" he asked, sullenly. "Do you intend to give up the game?"

"Give up? Never! I would give my life first! I will yet have my revenge on the Mainwarings, one and all; and I will repay them double for all the insult and ignominy they have heaped upon me."

"That is to the point; but how will you accomplish it?" said Hobson, in a more conciliatory tone, for each feared the other, and he thoroughly understood the spirit of his client. "Let us be reasonable about this; you and I have too much at stake and too many interests in common for us to quarrel like children."

"If I were differently situated, I can assure you we would then have very few interests in common," she replied, bitterly.

"Well, supposing you were, what would you do in this case?" he inquired, softly, apparently taking no notice of her remark, but in reality making a mental note of it for future reckoning.

"Defeat Ralph Mainwaring, by all means; if necessary, produce testimony to show that this will is genuine. If he spends his last shilling to fight the case, so much the better. Then, when the case is settled and this so-called heir is master of the situation, or supposes himself so, bring suit to show that he is an impostor, and assert my own claim as the nearest living heir."

Hobson whistled softly. "A plan worthy of your ambition, my lady but hardly feasible. It is one thing to assert a claim, and another to be able to establish it. Through your over-ambition you would lose in the end, for, should you succeed in dispossessing this stranger, Ralph Mainwaring would surely come forward with his claim, and you would be beaten."

"When I lay down arms to a Mainwaring, I will lay down my life also," she answered, proudly.

"You think so, perhaps; but let me tell you the best course for you to pursue is to make terms, either with Ralph Mainwaring, as I first suggested, or else with this new-comer-should he prove victorious-by threatening to expose his whole scheme."

Mrs. LaGrange made no reply, and Hobson, rising to take leave, saw her face for the first time and paused, surprised at its strange expression.

"Well?" he said, with. a look of inquiry.

"My thoughts were wandering just then," she said, with a faint smile, and her tone was so changed the voice scarcely seemed her own. "I was wishing, just for the moment, that this stranger, whoever he may be, was in reality the one he claims to be. I would need no attorney to make terms with him then!"

"You forget; he would be a Mainwaring!"

"Yes; but he would be the only Mainwaring and the only human being I could ever have loved, and I would have loved him better than my own life."

"Love!" repeated Hobson, with a sneer. "Who would ever have thought to hear that word from your lips! But how about your son, Walter; do you not love him?"

"Him!" she exclaimed, passionately; "the price I paid hoping to win Hugh Mainwaring! I am proud of him as my own flesh and blood, but love him? Never!"

"But you have not yet told me what you think of my last suggestion," he said, tentatively, watching her closely. Her manner changed instantly; rising with all her accustomed hauteur and turning from him with a gesture of dismissal, she replied,-

"Come to me later, when I shall have measured lances with our new opponent, and you shall have your answer."

He would have spoken, but her dismissal was final, and with darkening face he left the room.

CHAPTER XIX

MUTUAL RECOGNITIONS

The sudden turn of affairs in the Mainwaring case excited no small amount of comment, and for the next ensuing days speculation was rife concerning the recently discovered will, but more particularly regarding the new and unknown claimant. At the clubs and elsewhere it formed the principal topic of conversation, and Ralph Mainwaring was loud in his denunciations of the one as a forgery, and of the other as an impostor. To all such remarks, however, as well as to the questions of the curious, Mr. Sutherland had but one reply, accompanied by a slow, quiet smile; that on the day set for the hearing, he would not only prove the validity of the will, but would also establish, beyond all doubt or question, the identity of the claimant.

As a result, public curiosity was so thoroughly aroused, that upon the arrival of the "Umbria," an unusual crowd of reporters was assembled at the pier, notwithstanding a pouring rain, and the gang-plank had no sooner been thrown down than a number of the more ambitious rushed on board, eager to be the first in gaining some bit of information or personal description. Their efforts, however, were unsuccessful, as the individuals whom they most desired to meet remained in their state-rooms and declined to be interviewed. Not until the crowd had about dispersed and the patience of a few of the more persistent was nearly exhausted, was their zeal rewarded by the sight of a party of four Englishmen, who hastily left the boat, completely enveloped in heavy mackintoshes, and, taking a closed carriage which was awaiting them, were driven rapidly to the Waldorf Hotel.

At the hotel the party still remained inaccessible to all visitors, with the exception of Mr. Sutherland, who spent much of his time in their apartments. It was ascertained that the party consisted of two gentlemen, one of whom was accompanied by a valet, the other-presumably the attorney-by a clerk, but all efforts towards gaining any more definite information prove absolutely futile. The arrival by the next steamer of another stranger, an elderly gentleman, who immediately joined the party at the Waldoff, after having registered under an evident alias, only served to deepen the mystery.

Upon the arrival of the day set for the hearing of the proof in support of the ancient will, the court-room was, at an early hour, packed to its utmost capacity. Occupying a prominent place were Ralph Mainwaring and his son, accompanied by Mr. Whitney, the sensitive face of the attorney more eager and alert than ever! At some distance from them, but seated rather conspicuously where she could command a good view of all that occurred, was Mrs. LaGrange, while in a remote corner of the court-room, partially concealed by the crowd, was Richard Hobson.

Within a few moments preceding the appointed hour, Mr. Sutherland appeared. His entrance caused a sudden hush of expectation throughout the crowd and all eyes were immediately turned in his direction. Accompanying him was a gentleman whose bearing commanded universal admiration, and whom the Mainwarings instantly recognized as the English barrister whose connection with the case they had deemed so incredible. But a still deeper surprise awaited them. Immediately following the attorneys was a young man whose features and carriage were familiar, not only to the Mainwarings, but to scores of spectators as well, as those of the private secretary of the deceased Hugh Mainwaring, whose testimony at the inquest had created so much of a sensation, and whose sudden disappearance thereafter had caused considerable comment. There was a ripple of excitement through the court-room, and the Mainwarings, father, and son, watched the young man with strangely varying emotions, neither as yet fully comprehending the real significance of his presence there.

"The secretary!" exclaimed Mr. Whitney, in a low tone. "Can it be possible that he is concerned in this?"

"He is probably the hired tool by means of which this has been brought about. I might have known as much!" replied the elder man, his old hatred and wrath reviving with greater intensity than ever, but before he could proceed further his glance fell on the secretary's companion.

He was a tall, elderly gentleman, with snow-white hair and beard, but with form erect and vigorous, and with piercing eyes which met those of Ralph Mainwaring with a flash, not of recognition alone, but of disdain and defiance that seemed to challenge him to do his utmost.

With a muttered oath, the latter half rose from his chair, but at that instant his attention was arrested by the two men bringing up the rear; one, small and of uncertain age, the other, older even than he appeared, and bearing the unmistakable air of an English servant. As Ralph Mainwaring recognized James Wilson, the last relic of the old Mainwaring household, he suddenly grew pale and sank back into his chair, silent, watchful, and determined; while his son and the attorney, quick to note the change in his appearance, made neither inquiries nor comments, but each drew his own conclusion.

There was one other to whom the white-haired gentleman did not seem an utter stranger. Mrs. LaGrange from her post of observation had watched the entering party with visible signs of excitement. Her lips curled in a mocking smile as she caught sight of the secretary, but glancing from him to his companion, she involuntarily recoiled in terror, yet gazed like one fascinated, unable to remove her eyes from his face. Suddenly the piercing eyes met her own, their look of astonishment quickly changing to scorn. She flushed, then paled, but her eyes never faltered, flashing back mocking defiance to his anger and scorn for scorn.

Meanwhile, the quondam secretary, seated between the attorneys on the one hand and his elderly companion on the other, seemed alike unconscious of the many curious glances cast in his direction and of the dark looks of Ralph Mainwaring now fastened on him. At a little distance was the old servant, his immovable features expressing the utmost indifference to his surroundings, looking neither to the right hand nor to the left.

Not so with the remaining member of the party, the so-called "clerk!" Seated beside the English barrister, his eye seemed to sweep the entire court-room with a glance that omitted no details, not even the cringing form of Hobson, who quailed and seemed to be trying to shrink still further into conceal-ment as he felt himself included in the search-light of that gaze. But no one saw the slip of paper which, a moment later, was handed to Alfred Barton, and by him passed to Mr. Sutherland. There was a hurried filling out of blanks lying among the papers on the table, a messenger was despatched, two or three men edged themselves into the crowd in Hobson's vicinity,-and that was all!

Promptly at the time appointed the case was called. There was perfect silence throughout the court-room as Mr. Sutherland arose, holding in one hand the ancient will, and with breath-less attention the crowd listened for the opening words of what was to prove one of the fiercest and most bitter contests on record, and of whose final termination even the participants themselves little dreamed.

After a few preliminaries, Mr. Sutherland said, addressing the court, -

"Before proceeding farther, your honor, I will give orders for the subpoena, as a witness in this case, of one Richard Hobson, alias Dick Carroll."

Then turning towards the crowd in the rear of the courtroom, he added, "Let the papers be served at once."

There was a stir of excitement and a sudden craning of necks in the direction indicated by the attorney's glance, where three men had sprung forward in obedience to his orders.

Hobson, at the first mention of his name, had glanced quickly about him as though seeking some means of escape, but on hearing the alias-the name he had supposed unknown in America-he paused for an instant, seemingly half paralyzed with terror. But the sight of the approaching sheriff broke the spell, and he made a sudden lunge through the crowd in the direction of an open window. His progress was speedily checked by one of the deputies, however, and after a short, ineffectual struggle he sullenly submitted.

"Bring the witness forward," said Mr. Sutherland, with his calm, slow smile; "we may call upon him before long, and he would probably prefer a seat convenient to the witness stand."

As he was seated opposite and facing the English party, it was noted that the face of the old servant lighted up with a look of recognition, and he watched the new-comer with evident interest. Hobson, having carefully avoided the eyes of both Alfred Barton and the private secretary, soon became aware of Wilson's scrutiny, and after regarding him fixedly for a moment seemed suddenly to recognize him in turn, and also to realize at the same time the import of his presence there, which, apparently, did not tend to lessen his agitation.

Slowly Mr. Sutherland unfolded the document he held, yellow with age, the edges of its folds so frayed and tattered as to render the writing in some places almost illegible. Slowly, in deep, resonant tones, he read the opening words of the old will; words of unusual solemnity, which caused a hush to fall over the crowded court-room:

"In the name of God; Amen. Know all men, that I, Ralph Maxwell Mainwaring, being of sound and disposing mind and memory, but now upon my death-bed, soon to appear in the presence of my Maker, do make and publish this, my last will and testament; hereby revoking and setting aside any and every will at any time heretofore made by me."

Then followed, in quaint phraseology, the terms of the will; by which the full right and title of the first-born son, under the English law, were conveyed to Harold Scott Mainwaring, and all legal processes theretofore entered into, depriving him of such rights, were forever annulled; restoring to the said Harold Scott Mainwaring, as his rightful inheritance, the entire family estate, including other valuable property; the said property at his death to pass to his eldest living son, or in case of his dying without issue, to revert to his brother Hugh, were the latter living, if not, to the nearest living heirs of the Mainwarings; but on no account was any portion of the estate or property to pass to the wife of Harold Scott Mainwaring, should she survive him.

As the reading of the will progressed, Hobson's feelings, too deep and genuine at that moment for disguise, were plainly mirrored in his face. Having for years believed the old will destroyed, as he now listened to the words dictated to himself upon that memorable night, so long ago, it was little wonder that to his cowardly soul it seemed like a voice from the dead, and that astonishment, fear, and dread were depicted on his features, merging into actual terror as the attorney at last pronounced the names of the witnesses, Alexander McPherson and Richard Hobson.

For a few seconds his brain reeled, and he saw only the face of the dying man as it looked that night, - stern and pale, but with dark, piercing eyes, deep-set, within whose depths still gleamed the embers of a smouldering fire which now seemed burning into his inmost soul. Trembling from head to foot, Hobson, with a mighty effort, regained his scattered faculties and again became conscious of his surroundings, only to find the eyes of the secretary fixed upon his face, and, as he shrank from their burning gaze, the truth flashed suddenly upon him.

"The face of old Mainwaring himself!" he muttered in horror; then added, with an oath, "Fool that I was not to have known it sooner! That woman lied!"

CHAPTER XX

OPENING FIRE

The first witness called to the stand by Mr. Sutherland was James Wilson. There were many present who noted the resemblance between him and his son, John Wilson, who had given testimony at the inquest, though unaware of the relationship between them.

"Mr. Wilson," said the attorney, after the usual preliminaries, "I understand you were for a number of years in the employ of Ralph Maxwell Mainwaring, the testator whose name is affixed to this will; is that so?"

"Yes, sir," was the reply, while the attention of the crowd was at once riveted upon the witness.

"Will you state how long you were in his employ, and in what capacity?"

"I was his valet, sir, from his twenty-fifth year until the day of his death, a little above thirty-five years, sir; and during his last illness, of about three months, I was with him constantly, you might say, sir."

"Do you recognize the document just read in your hearing as anything which you have heard before?"

"That I do, sir."

"State when and under what circumstances you have previously heard it."

"At the death-bed of Mr. Ralph Mainwaring, sir, twenty-five years ago the seventeenth of last November. I was present at the making of that will, sir, the night before Mr. Mainwaring died. I heard him give those words to the lawyer, and then heard them read to him before the will was signed."

"By whom was it drawn?"

"By Richard Hobson, sir; the man sitting there," pointing to the shrinking figure of Hobson.

"Do you positively identify that man as the writer of this will?"

"That I do, sir," with marked emphasis; "when one once sets eyes on the likes o' him, he's not likely to forget him soon."

"Was Richard Hobson the attorney of Mr. Mainwaring?"

"Ah, no, sir," with evident scorn; "his attorney was Mr. Alfred Barton, the father, sir, of this gentleman," indicating the English barrister, while the interest of the crowd deepened.

"How, then, was this man employed to draw the will?"

"Mr. Barton was out of town, sir; and as Mr. Mainwaring was dying and naught would satisfy him but to have a lawyer, they brought Mr. Barton's clerk."

"State the circumstances under which this will was drawn; was Mr. Mainwaring influenced by any one to make it?"

"He was influenced by none but his own conscience, sir. You see, sir, three or four years before, he was very angry with his elder son, and cut him off without a shilling and gave everything to Mr. Hugh. But it broke his heart to do it, for Mr. Harold was his favorite, as indeed he was everybody's, though he never mentioned his name again until the night he made the will. Well, sir, all that day we knew he was dying, and he knew it, and he was restless till late at night, when of a sudden he tells us to get his lawyer. Mr. Hugh tried to put him off, and told us his mind was wandering; but 'twas no use; and the carriage was sent for Mr. Barton, and when word was brought back that he was out of town, it was sent again and brought back his clerk. Everything was all ready, and he propped up in bed by pillows, his eyes burning as though there was fire in them. He repeated those words while the lawyer wrote them down, and then had them read to him, and at fifteen minutes of twelve o'clock the will was signed and sealed."

"You were present during the drawing up of the will?"

"Yes, sir, I was present through it all, but not where the others saw me. When the lawyer came, Mr. Hugh told me to leave the room; but as I was going his father called me back and bade me stay, and I was standing at the foot of the bed, hidden by the curtains of the canopy, so none but the old gentleman saw me."

"Who else was present?"

"Mr. Mainwaring's old friend, Sandy McPherson, Mr. Hugh, and the lawyer."

"No one else?" Were there no physicians present?"

"There were physicians in the house, sir, but not in the room."

"How long did Mr. Mainwaring live afterwards?"

"He died at five o'clock the next morning, sir; his strength went fast after that was done, but he rested easy and seemed satisfied."

"What was done with the will?"

"Mr. Hobson took it away with him that night."

"Have you ever seen it since?"

"No, sir."

"Mr. Wilson," said the attorney, showing the witness the will, "can you swear to these signatures as being the same which you saw affixed to the will upon that night?"

Wilson studied the document attentively for a moment. "Yes, sir, that is Mr. Mainwaring's writing, only a bit unsteady, for his hand trembled. McPherson's writing I know, and you mark that blot after his name?" I remember his fussing that night because he had blotted the paper."

"And the third name, is that the signature of this man, Richard Hobson?"

"I know naught about that man's writing," the old fellow replied, with a shrewd look; "but you will mind that the name is the same writing as the will itself, and he wrote that and signed his name to it, for I saw him."

"And you have neither seen that will, nor heard it read until this morning?"

"No, sir."

"You have remembered it all these years?"

"Maybe not word for word, sir, but I have kept the sense of it in my mind."

"Are you positive that this is the will drawn up on the night of which you speak?"

"That I am, sir."

"Did you ever speak to any one of this will?"

"To none but my son, sir. Mr. Hugh Mainwaring was that sort of a man, I could not speak to him about it, or ask about his brother. I asked to be allowed to stay about the old place in hopes that some day Mr. Harold would come back to have a look at his old home, and I could tell him of it, for I thought things had not gone right altogether. Then we heard of his death, and I thought it was too late; I could do no good by speaking, and I held my tongue until the young gentleman came."

Wilson was then dismissed and Hobson was next called to the stand. More even than the reading of the old will, the truth which had dawned upon Hobson's mind as he met the piercing gaze of the secretary, had convinced him that the position which he had intended to assume, adverse to the new claimant and as an ally of Ralph Mainwaring's, was neither politic nor safe. His views on that subject had undergone a decided change, and, with his usual weathervane proclivities, he was now preparing to take a totally different stand and strive to ingratiate himself into the favor of the new heir, at the same time leaving, if possible, a few loop-holes through which he could retreat, should some veering wind change his course in another direction.

"Mr. Hobson," said the attorney, somewhat abruptly, when the necessary preliminaries were over, "did you on the night of November 17, 18-, act as attorney for Ralph Maxwell Mainwaring, in the drawing up, at his request, of his last will and testament?"

"I believe so, sir," was the guarded answer.

"Did you or did you not?" Mr. Sutherland persisted.

"I did, sir."

"Have you, during all these years, had any knowledge that the will you drew under the circumstances already mentioned was still in existence?"

After a slight pause, the witness replied, "I had no positive knowledge to that effect."

"Did you believe the will to be in existence?"

Hobson reflected a moment, then replied, cautiously, "I was led to suppose that the will did not exist."

"You remember the form, terms, and conditions of the document drawn by yourself on that occasion?"

"I do, perfectly," he replied, with more assurance.

"State whether the will read in your hearing this morning is identical with the one drawn by yourself."

Hobson now saw the drift of the attorney's questions, but it was too late.

"As near as I can recollect," he stammered, but a word from Mr. Sutherland recalled him.

"You just said you remembered perfectly."

"I believe they are identical in form."

"Mr. Hobson," said the attorney, spreading out the document before the witness, but still retaining his hold upon it, "will you state to the court whether that is your writing, and whether the last name, that of the second witness, is your signature."

With great precision, Hobson adjusted a pair of eyeglasses and proceeded to scrutinize the writing closely. "Well," he remarked, at length, very deliberately, "I do not deny that to be my writing, nor am I prepared to positively affirm that it is such. The fact is, my chirography varies so much from time to time that I often find it difficult for me to verify my own signatures."

"Here are some papers which may assist the gentleman, and may be of some use to the court," said a deep voice with rich, musical inflections, but slightly tinged with sarcasm, and the English attorney handed a small package to Mr. Sutherland. "They contain," he added, "some specimens of the witness's chirography of about the same date as the will."

"The writing in both cases is identical," said Mr. Sutherland, as, having examined the papers, he showed them to Hobson, but a glance at their contents seemed rather to confuse the witness than otherwise, for he remained silent.

"Do you acknowledge these letters to be of your writing?" inquired the attorney.

"I do, sir; and I have no doubt but that the other is my writing also."

"You acknowledge this, then, as the will which you wrote at the dictation of Ralph Maxwell Mainwaring the night before his death?"

"I believe it is, sir."

"Mr. Hobson, why was this will not make public following Mr. Mainwaring's death and burial?"

"On the day after his death, I gave it into the keeping of his son, Hugh Mainwaring, at his own request, and he afterwards gave me to understand that it was lost."

"And you were paid for keeping silent as to the existence of such a will, were you not?"

"I may have been," the witness replied, with a calmness born of desperation.

"That is sufficient for the present."

A few moments followed in which the attorneys consulted together, while comments in tones of subdued excitement and expectancy were exchanged among the crowd. Ralph Mainwaring had sat with darkening face throughout the testimony thus far; now he remarked to Mr. Whitney, with a bitter sneer,-

"Fine witnesses! A beggarly shyster whose oath is worthless, and an imbecile old servant, who could be bought for a half-crown!"

Young Mainwaring turned upon his father a look of indignant surprise. "Governor," he said, "it would not be well for you if either old James Wilson or his son heard that remark of yours!"

"It will be well for you to attend to your own business and keep your mouth shut!" responded his father, angrily.

Beneath the calm exterior which the young man preserved, the old Mainwaring blood was now fast rising, but he made no reply, for at that instant Mr. Sutherland announced the name of the next witness:

"Harold Scott Mainwaring!"

There was a sudden hush throughout the court-room, broken an instant later by a low murmur of mingled astonishment, incredulity, and wonder as the private secretary rose and walked towards the witness stand. A few comments reached his ears, but he seemed unconscious of them, and, having taken his place, turned towards the audience a face cold and impassive, inscrutable to his enemies, who could read nothing of the conflicting emotions beneath that calm, immobile surface.

He saw the crowd of upturned faces-incredulous, wondering, curious; he caught the mocking smile of Mrs. LaGrange and Ralph Mainwaring's dark, sinister sneer; but he took little note of these. Like an arrow speeding to the mark, his glance sought the face of young Hugh Mainwaring. Their eyes met, and in that brief moment there was recalled to each a starlit night on one of the balconies at Fair Oaks, and the parting words of young Mainwaring to the secretary, "I'm your friend, Scott, and whatever happens, I'll stand by you."

With swift intuition each read the other's thought, and, although there was no outward sign, Harold Mainwaring knew from that instant that there would be no retraction of that pledge.

The slight ripple of excitement died away while the witness was sworn, and the crowd listened with interest even to the preliminary interrogatories.

"Where were you born?" asked the attorney.

"In Melbourne, Australia," was the reply, while deep silence awaited Mr. Sutherland's next question.

"Mr. Mainwaring, I believe you are familiar with the will just read, are you not?"

"I am."

"Please state when, and under what conditions, you gained your knowledge of this will."

"I first learned that such a will had existed and knew its general terms, between five and six years since, through information given me by James Wilson. From data found a little over a year ago among the personal letters of the deceased Hugh Mainwaring, I ascertained that the will was still in existence, and on the 7th of July last I discovered the document itself and became personally familiar with its contents."

At the mention of the name of Hugh Mainwaring and of the date so eventful in the recent history of Fair Oaks, the interest of the crowd deepened.

"Did you discover the document accidentally, or after special search for it?"

"As the result of a systematic search for more than a year."

"Please state whether you took any steps leading to the discovery of this will during the four or five years immediately following your first knowledge of it; and if so, what?"

"As I first learned of the will soon after entering Oxford, my studies necessarily occupied the greater part of my time for the next three or four years; but I lost no opportunity for gaining all possible information relating not only to the Mainwaring estate, but more particularly to Hugh Mainwaring and his coadjutor, Richard Hobson. Among other facts, I learned that immediately after the settlement of the estate, Hugh Mainwaring had disposed of the same and left England for America, while about the same time Richard Hobson suddenly rose from a penniless pettifogger to a position of affluence."

"As soon as my studies were completed, I sailed for America, with the avowed determination of securing further evidence regarding the will, and of establishing my claim to the property fraudulently withheld from my father and from myself. In the securing of the necessary evidence I succeeded beyond my expectations. As Hugh Mainwaring's private secretary, I gained access to the files of his personal letters, and soon was familiar with the entire correspondence between himself and Richard Hobson, from which I learned that the latter demanding and receiving large sums of money as the price of his silence regarding some past fraudulent transaction. The nature of that transaction, I ascertained in this marginal note, in Hugh Mainwaring's handwriting, upon one of Hobson's letters which happened to be more insolent in its tone than the rest. With the permission of the court I will read it:"

"He insinuates that I destroyed the will; I only gave him to understand that it was lost." Little he dreams it is still in my possession and will be, until such time as I, too, have to make final disposition of my estate! Why I did not destroy it, or why I do not, now that the property is rightfully mine, I cannot say, except that I dare not! "Thus conscience does make cowards of us all?"

"With the discovery of these words," concluded the witness, "began my search for the will itself."

"From the discovery of this letter which led you to believe the will was still in existence, you prosecuted your search for the document until the 7th of last July?"

"Yes, sir, whenever an opportunity for search was offered."

"Where did you finally find the will?"

"In the safe, in Mr. Mainwaring's private apartments at Fair Oaks."

"On July 7 last?"

"Yes, sir."

"That was the day on which you, acting as Hugh Mainwaring's secretary, had drawn, at his dictation, his last will and testament, was it not?"

"It was."

"Mr. Mainwaring," said the attorney, deliberately, his eye quick to read the faces about him, "is there in your mind any connection between that event and your discovery of this will?"

"Only the most indirect," was the reply, given with equal deliberation. "The fact that Hugh Mainwaring was making final disposition of his property naturally spurred me on to increased action, since, in making final adjustment of his papers, he would be more than likely to destroy the old will. This incentive, together with the fact that opportunity was given me for a more thorough search than I had been able to make prior to that time, combined to bring about the discovery of the will."

"Please state the time and circumstances of your finding it."

"I found it late in the afternoon, while Mr. Mainwaring and his guests had gone for a long drive. I determined to leave no place unexplored where it could possibly be concealed; after about an hour's search I found it."

"What did you then do with it?"

"I retained it in my possession, and at the earliest opportunity secreted it within my own room."

"It was in your possession during the following evening and night?"

"It was."

"Mr. Mainwaring," said Mr. Sutherland, with marked emphasis, "please state whether you mentioned to Hugh Mainwaring the discovery of the will, or had any conversation with him relating thereto."

"I made no mention of the matter to him whatever. Except for a few moments, immediately upon his return, I did not see him alone until about midnight, when he appeared fatigued, and I would not introduce the subject at a time so inopportune."

After a slight pause, Mr. Sutherland continued. "You claim to be the lawful son of the Harold Scott Mainwaring mentioned in this will, and as such the lawful heir, under its terms and conditions, of the Mainwaring property?"

"I do."

"Has it not been generally understood among those supposed to have knowledge of the facts in the case that Harold Scott Mainwaring, at the time of his death, had no living child?"

"That has been the general understanding."

"Will you explain how the fact of your existence has been kept concealed all these years?"

The silence following the attorney's question was so deep as to be oppressive until broken by the answer of the witness, clear, cold, and penetrating to the remotest corner of the crowded room.

"Within an hour from my birth, a dead child was substituted in my place, and I was secretly given by my father into the keeping of trusted friends, with instructions that until I had nearly attained my majority I was not even to know of his existence, or of the relationship existing between us."

"Mr. Mainwaring," said the attorney, "are you willing to state the reasons for such an extraordinary proceeding on his part?"

For the first time the impassive bearing and the calm, even tones of the witness gave way; the smouldering fire in his dark eyes burst forth, as with impassioned utterance and voice vibrating with emotion, he replied, -

"It was done because of sorrow, more bitter than death, in his own heart and home, of which he wished me to know nothing until I had reached the years of manhood and could understand the nature of his wrongs; it was done that I should be forever barred from all association with, or knowledge of, the base, false-hearted woman who bore his name only to dishonor it, - who, though she had given me; birth, yet believed me dead, - that I might live as ignorant of her existence as she of mine; it was done because of his love for his only child, a love for which I would to-day gladly suffer dishonor and even death, if I could but avenge his wrongs!"

Only Harold Mainwaring's attorneys understood the spirit which prompted his words, but they carried his audience with him in a sudden wave of sympathy, and as he paused, men applauded and women sobbed, while the judge vainly rapped for order.

One figure alone remained motionless, spellbound. Amid the general excitement, Mrs. LaGrange sat as though turned to stone, her hands clasped so tightly that the jewels cut deeply into the delicate flesh, every vestige of color fled from her face, her lips ashen, her eyes fixed upon the witness, yet seemingly seeing nothing. Gradually, as she became conscious of her surroundings and of the curious glances cast in her direction, she partially recovered herself, though her eyes never left the face of the witness.

"Mr. Mainwaring," continued the attorney, when order had been restored, "when and how did you first learn that you were the son of Harold Scott Mainwaring?"

"My first knowledge regarding my own father I received at the age of fifteen from my foster-parents, who told me of the manner in which I had been given to them and of the death of my father a few years later; but the full particulars I did not learn until my twenty-first birthday, when I received a letter written by my father soon after my birth, and intrusted to the keeping of my foster-parents until I should have attained my majority. In that letter he gave me the story of his life, of his marriage and consequent disinheritance, and of the yet greater sorrow which followed shortly, which led him to voluntarily exile himself from his beloved England, and which finally led to his sacrifice of the love and companionship of his only child."

As Harold Mainwaring paused, Mr. Sutherland remarked, "I, myself, have seen the letter to which the witness refers, but I consider it of too personal a nature and too private in character to submit for examination. I will say, however, that both my honored colleague, Mr. Barton, and myself have compared it with other letters and documents known to have been written by Harold Scott Mainwaring, the elder son of Ralph Maxwell Mainwaring, and have found the writing in all cases identically the same. There is yet one more question which may have a bearing later upon this case, which I will ask the witness. Mr. Mainwaring, have you, during this time, received any clue regarding the identity of your mother, or is that still unknown to you?"

With great deliberation, the witness replied, "Until within the past three or four days, I have known absolutely nothing regarding even the name of the woman whom my father made his wife, or whether she were still in existence. I have recently learned, however, that she is living, and," he added, more slowly, "I know that she is present in this court-room."

It was afterwards recalled that, as the witness resumed his seat, a curious sound, something between a gasp and a sob was heard, but amid the tremendous sensation produced by his last statement it passed unnoticed.

With very little delay, Mr. Sutherland announced the name of the last witness, -

"Frederick Mainwaring Scott!"

Again the silence deepened as the white-haired gentleman, with great dignity, took his place upon the stand. His heavy, sonorous tones rang out over the court-room, while from time to time the piercing eyes beneath the beetling, snow-white brows sought the face of Ralph Mainwaring with their silent but unmistakable challenge. At the first sound of his voice, Mrs. LaGrange's agitation increased perceptibly; her expression changed to abject terror, yet she seemed unable to move or to withdraw her gaze from his face.

To the question, "Where were you born?" the witness replied, "I was born in London, but for the past forty-five years have been a resident of Melbourne, Australia."

"Are you not connected with the Mainwaring family?"

"Distantly. The Scott and Mainwaring families have inter-married for many years, but I have waived all claims of relationship for nearly half a century."

"Were you acquainted with the Harold Scott Mainwaring mentioned in this will?"

"Intimately acquainted with him, as we were associated together in business during his entire stay in Australia."

"In what business were you engaged?"

"In the sheep business, principally; we were also interested in the mines."

"For how long a time were you associated together?"

"Six years, or thereabouts."

"Mr. Scott, you are the foster-father of Harold Scott Main-waring who has just preceded you upon the witness stand, are you not?"

"I am, and have been from the day of his birth."

"Will you state the circumstances under which you became his foster-parent?"

"Harold Scott Mainwaring, the elder son of Ralph Maxwell Mainwaring, came to Australia within a year after the marriage for which he was disinherited. His reason for leaving England was not, as many have supposed, on account of his father's severity, but because of the discovery of his wife's infidelity after all that he had sacrificed for her. He brought her to Australia in the vain hope that, removed from other influences - the influence of his own brother, in particular, - she would yet prove true to him. Within the following year, his son was born; but before that event he had fully learned the character of the woman he had married, and he determined that no child of his should be disgraced by any knowledge of its mother, or contaminated by association with her. To my wife and myself he confided his plans, and, as we had no children of our own, he pledged us to the adoption of his child while yet unborn. An old and trusted nurse in our family was also taken into the secret, but not the physician employed on that occasion, as he was a man of no principle and already in league with the false wife against her husband. When the child was born, Mrs. Mainwaring was very ill and the babe received comparatively little notice from the attendant physician. A dead child, born but a few hours earlier, was therefore easily substituted for the living child of Harold Mainwaring, while the latter was secretly conveyed to my own home.

"A few weeks later, the child was privately christened in a small church on the outskirts of Melbourne and the event duly recorded upon the church records. He was given his father's name in full, Harold Scott Mainwaring, but until his twenty-first birthday was known among our acquaintances as Harry Scott, the same name by which he has been known in your city while acting as private secretary to Hugh Mainwaring."

"Are you familiar with the letter written by Harold Main-waring to his son?"

"Perfectly so; he gave it into my keeping on the day of the christening, to be given to his son when he should have reached his majority, if he himself had not, before that time, claimed him as his child."

"You can then vouch for its genuineness?"

"I can."

"How long a time elapsed between the birth of this child and the death of Harold Mainwaring, the father?"

"About five years. He left his wife soon after the birth of this child and spent the greater part of his time at the mines. He finally decided to go to the gold fields of Africa, and a few months after his departure, we received tidings of the wreck of the vessel in which he sailed, with the particulars of his death at sea."

"Mr. Scott, did you ever hear of the existence of this will?"

"Not until the boy, Harold, learned of it, soon after he entered Oxford."

"Do you know how he first heard of it?"

"He heard of it from Wilson, one of the old servants on the Mainwaring estate, who recognized in him a resemblance to Ralph Maxwell Mainwaring, and, learning of his identity, told him the history of the will."

"You have been kept informed of his search for the will and of its final discovery?"

"From the first; and though the boy has a good bit of money in his own name, I will back him in getting his rights to the very last pound in my possession, and that," he added, while his dark eyes flashed ominously, "will outlast the bank-roll of any that can go against him."

"Have you any further direct evidence which you can produce in support of the identity of the claimant?"

"I have," the witness replied, and having taken from his pocket a large memorandum book and extracted therefrom a paper, he continued, with great deliberation, -

"I have here a certified copy of the record of the christening, at the church of St. Bartholomew, on June 24, 18 -, of Harold Scott Mainwaring, the first-born son of Harold Scott and Eleanor Houghton Mainwaring."

A piercing shriek suddenly rang out through the hushed court-room, and the crowd, turning involuntarily at the familiar name of Eleanor Houghton Mainwaring towards the seat occupied by Mrs. LaGrange, saw that wretched woman sink, with a low, despairing moan, unconscious to the floor. As several sprang to the assistance of the unfortunate woman, Mr. Scott, turning swiftly towards the judge, exclaimed,-

"There, your honor, is a most unwilling witness, but one who has very effectively confirmed my testimony!"

The greatest confusion followed, several women having fainted from nervous excitement, and, as it was then nearly noon, the court adjourned until the afternoon session.

CHAPTER XXI

THE LAST THROW

There being no further testimony in the case, but little time was occupied by Mr. Sutherland at the afternoon session. Briefly and forcibly he summarized the evidence already adduced, emphasizing the strongest points and closing with numerous citations bearing upon the case taken from recent decisions of the highest legal authorities.

Several days would be required for consideration of the case pending the decision of the court, and as the crowd surged out into the corridors and diffused itself through the various exits, there was much speculation as to what that decision would be and what would be the action taken by the opponents. Among the clubmen who had made the acquaintance of Ralph Mainwaring, heavy bets were offered that he would contest the case before the will was even admitted to probate.

"He is a fool if he does," said one; "the young fellow has the best show."

"He'll not give up, however," was the reply; "he's got too much of the bull-dog about him; nothing will make him break his hold till he has spent his last shilling."

"Well, he'll spend it for nothing, that's all!" said another. "I'll wager you a dinner for the whole club that the young fellow will beat him. Anybody that knows Sutherland, knows he hasn't played his trump card yet; and you may rest assured that English lawyer isn't over here as a figure-head!"

Ralph Mainwaring, passing hastily from the court-room, accompanied by Mr. Whitney, overheard the last remark. His only reply, however, was a look of scorn flashed at the speaker, but the sardonic smile which lingered about his closely compressed lips betokened on his part no anticipations of defeat, but rather the reverse. Even Mr. Whitney wondered at his silence, but young Mainwaring, leisurely following in the rear, knew it to be only the calm which presages the coming storm.

His father, followed by the attorney, stepped quickly into the Mainwaring carriage and beckoned impatiently for him to follow, but the younger man coolly declined the invitation.

"No, thank you, governor. I'm going for a bit of a stroll; I'll join you and Mr. Whitney at dinner."

As the carriage rolled away he stood for a few moments lost in thought. His father's words to him that morning had stung his pride and aroused in him a spirit of independence altogether new, which had made him the more keen in observing his father's expressions and movements, and in drawing his own deductions therefrom. He had formed some theories of his own, and as he now stood in the soft, autumnal sunshine, he resolved to put them to the test.

Turning suddenly in an opposite direction from that which he had at first taken, he found himself confronted by Harold Mainwaring and his party as they descended the court-house steps to the carriages in waiting.

Instantly the young men clasped hands, and the frank, blue eyes gazed into the piercing dark ones, with a friendliness of whose sincerity there could be no doubt.

"Egad, old fellow!" he exclaimed, in low tones, "I'm glad to see you, though you have taken us rather by surprise. I'll not take back a word of the promise I made you, nor of what I've said about you, either."

"I did not think you would, Hugh," Harold replied, grasping the proffered hand heartily; "I had a great deal of faith in you and in your word. I only regretted that I could not explain matters at the time; it seemed like taking advantage of you and your friendship, though I warned you that the future might make some unexpected revelations."

"Well, I don't regret anything. I always said you had good blood in you, don't you know," Hugh continued, with a boyish laugh, then added, a little huskily, "I'll say this much, and I mean it. I would rather give up what I supposed was mine to you than to anybody else that know of."

"Thank you, Hugh; I appreciate that, I assure you. Come around to the Waldorf, I would like to have a talk with you."

"Indeed I will. Of course, I suppose it would be of no use to ask you up to the house; I couldn't expect you to come, but I'll see you as soon as I can," and with another handclasp the young men parted.

On arriving at the Waldorf, a note was handed to Harold Mainwaring, with the information that the bearer had been waiting nearly an hour, as there was an answer expected. He well knew the writing; it was the same as that of the little missive given him on the first day of the inquest, and with darkening face he opened it and read the following lines:

"I must see you at once, and I beg of you to come to my apartments this afternoon at five o'clock, without fail. In the name of mercy, do not deny me this one favor. I can tell you something important for you to know, of which you little dream.

   "ELEANOR HOUGHTON MAINWARING."

After brief consultation with his attorneys, an answer was sent to the effect that he would call in compliance with the request, and a little later he started upon his strange errand.

With what wildly conflicting emotions Mrs. LaGrange in her apartments awaited his coming may perhaps be more easily imagined than portrayed. She had not recovered from the morning's shock, but was nerving herself for the coming ordeal; preparing to make her final, desperate throw in the game of life. Success now, in this last venture, would mean everything to her, while failure would leave her nothing, only blank despair. Pride, the dominant passion of her life, struggled with a newly awakened love; doubt and dread and fear battled with hope, but even in the unequal contest, hope would not be vanquished.

Shortly before the hour appointed, Richard Hobson's card was handed her with the information that he must see her without delay. She understood the nature of his errand; she knew his coming was inevitable; her only desire was to postpone the meeting with him until after the interview with Harold Mainwaring, but on no account would she have him know of her appointment with the latter. She tore the bit of pasteboard in two.

"Tell him to call to-morrow," she said to the messenger; but he soon returned, with another card on which was written,-

"Important! must see you to-day."

It was nearly five. Quickly, with fingers trembling from her anxiety lest he delay too long, she wrote,-

"Call at eight o'clock this evening; I can see no one earlier."

As she gave the card to the messenger, she glanced again at the little French clock on the mantel.

"Three hours," she murmured; "three hours in which to decide

Maynard Barbour

my fate! If I succeed, I can bid defiance to that craven when he shall come to-night; if not-" she shuddered and walked over to the window, where she watched eagerly till she saw the cringing figure going hastily down the street.

He had but just disappeared around the corner of the block when a closed carriage was driven rapidly to the hotel, and a moment later Harold Scott Mainwaring was announced.

Her heart throbbed wildly as she turned to meet him, then suddenly stopped, seeming a dead weight in her breast, as her eyes met his.

For a moment neither spoke; once her lips moved, but no sound came from them. Before that face, hard and impassive as granite, and as cold, the impulse which she had felt to throw herself at his feet and plead for mercy and for love died within her; her tongue seemed paralyzed, powerless to utter a word, and the words she would have spoken fled from her brain.

With swift observation he noted the terrible change which the last weeks, and especially the last few hours, had wrought in the wretched woman before him, and the suffering, evidenced by her deathly pallor, her trembling agitation, and the look of dumb, almost hopeless pleading in her eyes, appealed to him far more than any words could have done.

He was the first to speak, and though there was no softening of the stern features, yet his tones were gentle, almost pitying, as he said,-

"I have come as you requested. Why did you send for me? What have you to say?"

At the sound of his voice she seemed somewhat reassured, and advancing a few steps towards him, she repeated his words,-

"Why did I send for you?" Why should I not send for you?"Think you a mother would have no desire to see her own son after long years of cruel separation from him?"

"There is no need to call up the past," he said, more coldly; "the separation to which you refer was, under existing circumstances, the best for all concerned. It undoubtedly caused suffering, but you were not the sufferer; there could be no great depth of maternal love where there was neither love nor loyalty as a wife."

Her dark eyes grew tender and luminous as she fixed them upon his face, while she beckoned him to a seat and seated herself near and facing him.

"You forget," she replied, in the low, rich tones he had so often heard at Fair Oaks; "you forget that a mother's love is instinctive, born within her with the birth of her child, while a wife's love must be won. I must recall the past to you, and you must listen; 'twas for this I sent for you, that you, knowing the past, might know that, however deeply I may have sinned, I have been far more deeply sinned against."

"Not as regards my father," he interposed, quickly, as she paused to note the effect of her words; "he sacrificed fortune, home, friends, everything for you, and you rewarded his love and devotion only with the basest infidelity."

"That your father loved me, I admit," she continued, in the same low, musical tones, scarcely heeding his words; "but, as I said a moment ago, a wife's love must be won, and he failed to win my love."

"Was his treacherous brother so much more successful then in that direction than he?" Harold questioned, sternly. "Within six months after your marriage to my father, you admitted that you married him only that you might have Hugh Mainwaring for your lover."

She neither flushed nor quailed under the burning indignation of his gaze, but her eyes were fastened upon him intently as the

Maynard Barbour

eyes of the charmer upon his victim.

"Half truths are ever harder to refute than falsehood," she replied, softly. "I said that once under great provocation, but if I sought to make Hugh Mainwaring my lover, it was not that I loved him, but through revenge for his having trifled with me only to deceive and desert me. Before I married your father, both he and his brother were among my most ardent admirers. The younger brother seemed to me far more congenial, and had he possessed one-half the chivalry and devotion which the elder brother afterwards manifested, he would have completely won my love. The rivalry between the two brothers led to bitter estrangement, which soon became known to their father, who lost no time in ascertaining its cause. His anger on learning the facts in the case was extreme; he wrote me an insulting letter, and threatened to disown either or both of his sons unless they discontinued their attentions to a 'disreputable adventuress,' as he chose to style me. Hugh Mainwaring at once deserted me, without even a word of explanation or of farewell, and, as if that were not enough, on more than one occasion he openly insulted me in the presence of his father, on the streets of London. I realized then for the first time that I cared for him, coward that he was, though I did not love him as he thought, - had I loved him, I would have killed him, then and there. Mad with chagrin and rage, I married your father, partly for the position he could give me - for I did not believe that he, the elder son and his father's favorite, would be disowned - and partly to show his brother and their father that I still held, as I supposed, the winning hand. On my wedding-day I vowed that I would yet bring Hugh Mainwaring to my feet as my lover, and when, shortly afterwards, your father was disinherited in his favor, my desire for revenge was only intensified. I redoubled my efforts to win him, and I found it no difficult task; he was even more willing to play the lover to his brother's wife than to the penniless girl whom he had known, with no possessions but her beauty and wit. At first, our meetings were clandestine; but we soon grew reckless, and in one or two instances I openly boasted of my conquest, hoping thereby to arouse his father's displeasure against him also. But in that I reckoned wrong. He disinherited and disowned his son for having honorably married a woman whom he considered below him in station, but for an open affaire d'amour with that son's wife, he had not even a word of censure.

"Your father discovered the situation and decided upon a life in Australia. If he had then shown me some consideration, the future might have been vastly different; but he grew morose and taciturn, and I, accustomed to gay society and the admiration of crowds, was left to mope alone in a strange country, with no companionship whatever. What wonder that I hungered for the old life, or that a casual admiring glance, or a few words even of flattery, were like cold water to one perishing with thirst! Then new hope came into my lonely life, and I spent months in dreamy, happy anticipations of the future love and companionship of my child. But even that boon was denied me. It was hard enough, believing, as I did, that my child had died, but to find that I was robbed of that which would have been not only my joy and happiness, but my salvation from the life which followed!" She paused, apparently unable to proceed, and buried her eyes in a dainty handkerchief, while Harold Mainwaring watched her, the hard lines deepening about his mouth.

"After that," she resumed, in trembling tones, "all hope was gone. Your father deserted me soon afterwards, leaving me nearly penniless, and a flew years later I returned to England."

"To find Hugh Mainwaring?" he queried.

"Not at the first," she answered, but her eyes fell before the cynicism of his glance. "I had no thought of him then, but I learned through Richard Hobson, whom I met in London at that time, of the will which had been made in my husband's favor, but which he told me had been destroyed by Hugh Mainwaring. He said nothing of the clause forbidding that any of the property should pass to me, and I immediately sailed for America in search of Hugh Mainwaring, believing that, with my knowledge of the will, I, as his brother's widow, could get some hold upon him by which I could compel him either to share the property with me or to marry me."

"Then you were not married to Hugh Mainwaring in England, as you testified at the inquest?"

"No," she replied, passionately; "I was never married to him. I have made many men my dupes and slaves, but he was the one man who made a dupe of me, and I hating him all the time!"

"And Walter!" he exclaimed, "you stated that he was the son of Hugh Mainwaring."

"He is Hugh Mainwaring's son and mine," she answered, with bitter emphasis; "that was another of my schemes which failed. I found I had little hold upon Hugh Mainwaring, while he had the same power over me as in the days before I had learned to despise him. When Walter was born, I hoped he would then fulfil his promises of marriage; but instead, he would have turned me adrift had I not threatened that I would then disclose everything which I knew concerning the will. He sneered at me, but offered me a place as servant in his home, and support and education for his child on condition that the relationship should never be known, and that I would remain silent regarding the will. I could do nothing then but accept his conditions, but they were galling,-too galling at last to be longer endured!"

"How is it that you and Walter bear the name of LaGrange?" he asked.

She hesitated a moment, then replied: "I married a man by that name soon after leaving Australia."

"Before or after the tidings of my father's death?" he questioned, sternly.

"We heard the news of his death soon after our marriage, but he had deserted me years before, so it made little difference. I met Captain LaGrange in Sydney, and we sailed together for Paris and were married there, but we soon grew tired of each other. I left him in about two years and went to Vienna, and from there returned to England. In some way, Hugh Mainwaring learned of the marriage, and when I came to Fair Oaks, he insisted on my taking that name for myself and child."

She spoke wearily and with an air of dejection, for it was plainly evident that Harold Mainwaring was not to be deceived by misstatements, however plausible, nor were his sympathies to be aroused by simulated grief. A few moments of silence followed, while she watched him intently, her face again falling into the pinched and haggard outlines which he had observed on entering the room.

When he at last spoke, his voice was calm, without a trace of anger or bitterness.

"Mrs. LaGrange, I have been informed that in the days before you ruined my father's life you were an actress in a second-class London playhouse, and I see you have not yet lost some little tricks of the stage; but we are not now before the footlights, and it will be much better to lay aside everything pertaining to them. Nothing that you have said has awakened my pity or touched my sympathies for you; in fact, what you have told me has only steeled my heart against you because of its utter falsity. It is unnecessary to go over the ground again, but if you could not reciprocate the love and devotion bestowed upon you by my father, you should never have accepted it; but accepting it as you did, you were bound by every consideration to be true and loyal to that love and to him. Instead, from beginning to end, you have been false to him, false to his memory, false to your own wifehood and motherhood, false to yourself! I have not come here to reproach you, however. I will only say that I do not believe the capacity - the capability even - of love exists, or has ever existed, within you. But," he continued, in gentler tones, "the capacity for suffering does exist, and I can see without any simulation on your part that you have suffered."

Before the look of pity which now for the first time softened the stern features, she broke down, and genuine tears coursed down her pallid cheeks as she cried, "Suffered! what have I not suffered! I am homeless, penniless, degraded, an outcast! There is no hope, no help for me unless you will help me. I know what you must think of me, how even you, my son, must despise me, but as a drowning man catches at a straw, I sent for you, hoping that you would in mercy pity me and help me."

"Do you wish me to help you pecuniarily?" I will willingly do that."

"Pecuniarily!" she exclaimed, almost in scorn. "Cannot you understand what I need most?" It is pity, sympathy, love! I want the love and support of my first-born son, and I am willing to beg for it," and, rising from her chair, she threw herself upon her knees beside him, "only be my son, forget the past and let me be to you, as I am, your mother! No, let me be!" she exclaimed, as he would have raised her from her kneeling posture. "I have no son but you, for Walter, like his father, has deserted me, with taunts and sneers. I can help you, too," she added, eagerly, but in low tones, "help you in a way of which you little dream. Do you know what Ralph Mainwaring will attempt next?" He will try to implicate you in the murder of Hugh Mainwaring!"

"That will be no more than you yourself attempted at the inquest," he answered.

"Ah, but his motive is different; in my case it was but the resort of a weak woman to divert suspicion from herself; but he will seek to fasten this crime upon you to defeat you, to crush and ruin you, because he fears you as his opponent, and it is within my power to clear you from any charges he may bring against you."

Her voice sank nearly to a whisper, her eyes were dilated, and she was trembling with excitement.

He watched her intently for a moment, then spoke in a tone of calm command. "Tell me how you could help me. What do you know of that affair?"

"Listen, and I will tell you," and leaning towards him, she whispered a few words in his ears.

Only a few words, but Harold Mainwaring started as from a shock, while his face grew as pale as her own, and it was with difficulty he could control his voice, as he demanded in quick, excited tones, -

"Do you know what you are saying?" Are you speaking the truth?"

"Yes, before Heaven, it is the truth, and the horror of it has haunted me day and night; the thought of it has driven me nearly mad, but I dared not breathe it to any living human being."

"You have told no one else what you have just told me?"

"No, I dared not."

He asked a few more questions which she answered, and from her manner he was convinced that she spoke the truth. Then he sat for a moment silent, his head bowed, his eyes covered, lost in thought, while strangely commingled emotions surged within his breast.

At last she broke the silence. "It will help you-what I have told you-will it not?"

"It is of inestimable value to me," he answered, but instead of exultation, there was a strange sadness in his voice.

"You will let me help you, and you will be a son to me, will you not?"

He looked at her with an expression of mingled pity and bitterness, and then, without replying, lifted her gently but firmly and reseated her, while he himself remained standing at a little distance. She watched him anxiously.

"Harold," at last she ventured, "think what I have suffered, and do not refuse my one prayer."

"I can see that you have suffered," he answered, gently; "and, as I have told you, I will help you pecuniarily and will befriend you, only do not ask me that which I cannot give."

"I ask nothing more," she exclaimed, passionately, rising to her feet, "than that you be a son to me, and I will accept nothing less."

"I am sorry to hear you say that," he replied, "for you are only unnecessarily depriving yourself of many benefits that might be yours. I would provide a home for you where you would be unknown, and means that you could spend the remainder of your life in comfort."

"What would I care for any home or wealth that you might provide for me," she demanded, angrily, "if you yourself would not acknowledge me as your mother! I will accept nothing from you under such conditions."

"Then we may as well end this conference," he replied, calmly, "for I hold my father in too deep love and reverence ever to permit of my applying to you the sacred name of 'Mother.'"

Her eyes flashed at the mention of his father, and she was about to speak, but he lifted his hand warningly. "Hush!" he commanded; "not one word shall you speak against him in my presence! Before I go, I will give you an opportunity to reconsider your declaration of a moment ago."

"I will not reconsider it. You are like every Mainwaring that I have ever known, in that you think money and shelter, such as you might fling at some superannuated servant, will take the place of the true position and honor that are my due."

"Do you then, finally and once for all, refuse any and all offers of assistance from me?" he asked.

"I do," she replied, proudly; "I will not accept charity from a Mainwaring,-not even from you!"

"Very well; if that is your decision, I bid you adieu," and before she could reply, he was gone.

He passed swiftly down the corridor, his head bowed slightly, looking neither to the right hand nor to the left, but his step had an elasticity it had not possessed in weeks, and any one passing near him would have heard the single exclamation, "Thank God!"

Upon reaching his carriage, he spoke quickly to the driver, "To the Waldorf at once!" and was borne away by the impatient steeds even more swiftly than he had come.

Meanwhile, within the room which he had just left, the wretched woman, whose falseness and pride had wrought her own undoing, stood listening to the retreating footsteps; she heard them die away in the distance, heard the carriage-wheels roll rapidly down the avenue, then sank upon a low couch with a cry of despair.

"All is over," she moaned, "and I have failed. I could not force him to my terms, and I would never yield to his. I will take charity from no one, least of all from him. I will be first, or nothing!" and she shivered faintly.

After a tune she arose, and ringing for her maid, ordered a light repast brought to her room, as she would not go down to dinner; "And," she concluded, "you can have the evening to yourself: I expect callers, and will not need you."

An hour later, Richard Hobson crept along the corridor and tapped for admittance. There was no answer, and cautiously pushing open the door, he entered unbidden, but started back in horror at the sight which met his eyes. The electric lights had not been turned on, but a few tall wax tapers, in a pair of candelabra upon the mantel, were burning, and in the dim, weird light, Mrs. LaGrange, still elegantly attired for her interview with Harold Mainwaring, lay upon the low couch near the grate, her features scarcely paler than a few hours before, but now rigid in death. Upon the table beside her, the supper ordered by the maid stood untasted, while on the same table a small vial bearing the label of one of the deadliest of poisons, but empty, told the story. Underneath the vial was a slip of paper, on which was written,-

"I have staked my highest card-and lost! The game is done."

Terror-stricken, Hobson glanced about him, then pausing only long enough to clutch some of the gleaming jewels from the inanimate form, he stealthily withdrew, and, skulking unobserved along the corridors, passed out into the darkness and was gone.

CHAPTER XXII

SECESSION IN THE RANKS

When Ralph Mainwaring and Mr. Whitney arrived at the club they found young Mainwaring already awaiting them at their private table, but it was far from a social group which sat down to dinner that evening. The elder Mainwaring still preserved an ominous silence, and in his dark, glowering face few would have recognized the urbane guest whom Hugh Mainwaring had introduced to his small coterie of friends less than three months before. The younger man, though holding a desultory conversation with the attorney, yet looked decidedly bored, while from time to time he regarded his father with a cynical expression entirely new to his hitherto ingenuous face. Mr. Whitney, always keenly alert to his surroundings, became quickly conscious of a sudden lack of harmony between father and son, and feeling himself in rather a delicate position, carefully refrained in his remarks from touching upon any but the most neutral ground.

A couple of hours later, as the three with a box of cigars were gathered around an open fire in Ralph Mainwaring's apartments, it was noticeable that young Mainwaring was unusually silent. In a few moments, however, his father's long pent-up wrath burst forth.

Addressing the attorney in no very pleasant tone, he demanded, "Well, sir, what do you now propose to do about this matter?"

"It is to be a fight, then, is it?" Mr. Whitney asked with a smile, knocking the ashes from his cigar.

"Yes, by my soul, and a fight to the finish. Understand, I will have no time lost. This farce has got to be quashed at once, and the sooner the better, so you may enter protest and file an application for hearing, or whatever your mode of procedure is in this country, at the earliest possible moment. Meanwhile, I'll secure the best legal talent that money can get to help you. I've a longer purse than that old Australian sheep-herder thinks, and when the time for contest comes, I'll meet him on his own ground."

"If you are going to employ additional counsel," interposed Mr. Whitney, "allow me to suggest the name of P. B. Hunnewell, of this city; he is one of the ablest attorneys in the United States, particularly in matters of this kind. His fees are somewhat exorbitant, but money is no object with you in this case."

"None whatever," the other interrupted, impatiently; "we will retain this Hunnewell upon your recommendation, but in the morning I shall cable for Upham & Blackwell, of London. They rank right in the same line with Barton & Barton; they have conducted considerable business for me, and I am satisfied," he added, with peculiar emphasis, "they could not be tampered with or bought at any price. I shall also cable for Graham, the expert on chirography and on all kinds of forgeries, and we will have his decision upon that will. I am going, first of all, understand, to have that document proven a forgery. That done, the whole fabrication of this cunning impostor falls to the ground, and then, when I have him completely floored in that direction, he will find that I have only just begun with him."

"How is that?" questioned the attorney. "You surely do not intend to dispute his identity after the unmistakable proofs submitted?"

"I care nothing about his identity," Mainwaring retorted, with a sneer. "Whether he is the son of Harold Mainwaring or of Frederick Scott, matters little; both were renegades and outcasts from their homes. No, sir," and there was a ring of exultation in his tone, while his steel-gray eyes glittered, "I have a surprise in store for the young man; when he gets through with this contest, he will find himself under arrest as the murderer of Hugh Mainwaring.'

Young Mainwaring rose suddenly and began pacing the room, while Mr. Whitney exclaimed, -

"Mr. Mainwaring, you astonish me! I certainly fail to see how you can connect the young man with that terrible affair."

"What else could be expected of a man who acknowledges that for years he has been dogging the steps of Hugh Mainwaring and acting the part of a spy, not only in his private offices, but even in his own home, stooping to any means, no matter how contemptible, to further his nefarious designs?" Would such a man, when his schemes were finally matured, have any scruples about taking the life of the one who stood in the way of their fulfilment?"

"But, sir," protested the attorney, "such a deed would be wholly unnecessary. Admitting all that you have said regarding the means employed by him, would it not be much more reasonable to suppose that he would attempt to bring his man to terms either through a personal interview or by bringing suit against him, rather than by resorting to brutal crime?"

"And supposing he did have a personal interview for the purpose of setting forth his claims, do you think that Hugh Mainwaring would be bamboozled by any of his cheap trickery?" No, sir, not for one moment. He would simply pronounce the whole thing a sham. Well, sir, if you will recall some of the testimony at the inquest, you will see that is precisely what occurred. Hugh Mainwaring, within twenty or thirty minutes preceding his death, was heard to denounce some one as a 'liar' and an 'impostor.' An 'impostor,' mark you! Very applicable to the case we are now supposing. And in the altercation which followed, the other party called him a 'thief,' and made some allusion - I do not recall the exact words-to his being 'transported to the wilds of Australia.' Now, sir, there is no doubt in the mind of any sane man that those words were spoken by the murderer of Hugh Mainwaring, and I think now we have a pretty good clue to his identity."

"But the young man stated emphatically this morning that he made no mention of the will to Hugh Mainwaring."

"To the devil with his statements! There is evidence enough against him that he will be ruined when I get through with him. He has dared to try to thwart me in the plans of a lifetime, and I'll make it the worst piece of business he ever undertook. Understand, I want you to institute proceedings against him at once!"

"Governor," said young Mainwaring, quietly, before Mr. Whitney could respond to this tirade, "in whose name will these proceedings be instituted, yours or mine?"

"Well," replied his father, with a sneer, "I don't know that it makes any particular difference to you in whose name it is done, so long as it is for your benefit."

"Begging your pardon, sir, I believe it does make considerable difference. And I will say right here that I will have no proceedings entered, either in my name or for my benefit, for two reasons: first, Harold Scott Mainwaring is no impostor; we had abundant proof to-day that, under the terms of that will, he is the sole claimant to the property; and second, you know, sir, as well as I, that years ago, your own servant, John Wilson, told you that such a will had existed, and there is every ground for believing that this document is genuine. I just begin to understand your little game, governor, and, by Jove! I will not be a party to it."

Up to this point, astonishment at his son's audacity seemed to have bereft Ralph Mainwaring of the power of speech, but now he demanded in thunderous tones, while his face grew purple with rage, "What do you mean, sir, by daring to address such language to me?" You impudent upstart! let me tell you that you had best attend to your own business!"

"This is the second time you have told me that today," said the young man, calmly, though the hot blood was fast rising; "allow me to inform you, governor, with all due respect, that henceforth I will attend to my own business, and will not trouble you to attend to it for me. If you had any just or tenable grounds for the proceedings you are about to institute, I would have nothing to say; but, begging your pardon, you have none whatever; it is simply a piece of dirty work with which I will have nothing to do."

"You ungrateful dog! This is your return for my care and forethought for you, is it?" Do you retract every word which you have said, or I'll cut you off without a penny," and with a fearful oath he swung himself around in his chair with such violence as to overturn the small onyx table upon which the cigars were standing, shattering it to fragments.

The young man paused directly in front of his father. "I retract nothing," he said, quietly but firmly. "You are at liberty to follow the example of old Ralph Maxwell Mainwaring if you wish, but you may regret it later, as he did."

"And do you think Edith Thornton will marry a penniless beggar, a pauper?" Or do you propose to live upon her fortune?"

"No; I will not touch a penny of her fortune," he replied, his cheek flushing; "and I am not quite a pauper, for I have the money left me by Uncle Tom years ago; and if Edith is the girl to be turned from me under the circumstances, why, the sooner I find it out the better."

Maynard Barbour

"A paltry twenty thousand pounds! a fine fortune!" sneered his father, ignoring his last remark.

"Many a fortune has been made from a much smaller start; but it is useless to waste words further. You understand my position, and that is enough. Mr. Whitney," he continued, addressing the attorney, "according to the terms of Hugh Mainwaring's will, I, and not my father, am heir to the property, and therefore the one to contest the claim of Harold Mainwaring if it is contested at all. I wish to state to you here and now, distinctly, that I will not contest the case, nor will I authorize any one to do so for me; and now, gentlemen, I bid you both good-evening!" and he quietly left the room.

"Zounds!" exclaimed the elder man, as the door closed upon his son, "I didn't suppose the boy had so much spirit! I've often wished he and Isabel could change places, because she was so much more like myself and what I would like a son to be."

"He has the Mainwaring blood all right," replied the attorney, with more inward admiration for the young man than he dared to express.

"Not if he will throw away a fortune in this manner; it is probably some boyish whim, however and the young fool will look at it in a different light to-morrow."

"I think not, Mr. Mainwaring," said the attorney, quietly; "he is enough like Hugh Mainwaring, and like yourself, that when he decides upon a certain line of action, he will not be easily turned aside. You may rest assured that he will have nothing whatever to do with this contest, and that if you wish to carry on the fight, you will have to do so under your own colors."

"I'll do it, too," he replied, fiercely; "I'll enter proceedings in my own name, as the nearest heir after Hugh Mainwaring."

"In that case, your brother must be notified, as he will be

entitled to share the estate with you; that may cause us some little delay, but -"

"Curse it all!" the other interrupted, angrily; "I had not thought of that; he will have to come in for a share; confound that boy's foolishness! I'll get hold of him tomorrow morning and see if I cannot talk some reason into him," and Ralph Mainwaring relapsed into sullen silence. It was a new experience for him to meet with opposition in his own family, least of all from his son, and he felt the first step must be to quell it, though decidedly at loss just how to proceed.

A little later, Mr. Whitney, finding his client disinclined to further conversation, after making an appointment for the next morning, excused himself and took his departure for his own apartments at the club.

As he passed down the stairway into the spacious hall, what was his surprise to see Mr. Merrick comfortably ensconced in a large leather chair, reading the evening papers.

The two men shook hands warmly, and together passed out into the cool, starlit night.

"When did you arrive, Merrick?" and from what point of the compass?" inquired the attorney.

"Got in on the 9.30 train," the detective replied, seeming not to have heard the second question; "learned you were at Mainwaring's, so I stopped in, but told the butler not to disturb you, as I was in no hurry."

"I noticed you were looking over the evening papers, did you read the account of this morning's proceedings in court?"

"I did."

"What do you think of them?"

"I am not in the least surprised."

"Not surprised!" echoed the attorney. "Do you mean to say that the reappearance of the missing secretary as the heir to the Mainwaring estate is no surprise to you?"

"None whatever," Merrick replied, with the most exasperating coolness, adding, as he noted the other's incredulous smile, "you may recall a hint given you at Fair Oaks, one evening, of the possible existence of claimants, perhaps not far distant, whose rights superseded those of Hugh Mainwaring himself."

Mr. Whitney started involuntarily as the detective's words of a few weeks before were thus recalled, then looking his companion squarely in the face, he exclaimed, half playfully, half indignantly, "I don't suppose you will go so far as to claim any familiarity with that old will which has just been resurrected."

"Well," said Merrick, deliberately stopping to relight his cigar, "I was aware that there was such a will in existence, or at least that it had existed up to the time of Hugh Mainwaring's death, and I supposed all along that it was in the possession of Harold Scott Mainwaring, otherwise known as Harry Scott, secretary."

"By George! when and how did you get hold of all this?" questioned the attorney, in a tone of bewilderment.

"I was pretty well conversant with the facts in the case a few days before the young man took passage for England, in the 'Campania.'"

"The 'Campania !' Heavens and earth, man! Do you mean to say that he went over on the same boat with Miss-with the ladies from Fair Oaks?"

"Certainly; and I don't think," Merrick continued, watching the attorney shrewdly, "that Miss - the ladies from Fair Oaks-objected to him as a fellow-traveller, either."

Mr. Whitney changed the subject. "Then you know that will to be genuine, do you?"

"H'm! am I on the witness stand?"

"No; but I think I ought to subpoena you to keep the other side from getting your testimony; you might make a troublesome witness against us."

"My testimony might be worth much or little; I am not giving it to either side at present."

"Well, I would not have it go out, of course; but for my part, I am inclined, to believe not only that the will is genuine, but also that Ralph Mainwaring knows that it is."

"He will fight it all the same."

"Yes, but on rather different grounds from what he first anticipated," and Mr. Whitney gave Merrick an account of young Mainwaring's defection. "In my private opinion," concluded the attorney, "Ralph Mainwaring is a fool, for he has got a pretty hard combination to go against; they've evidently got a strong case, splendid legal talent, and plenty of money to back it all. However, I'm making a good thing out of it."

"Yes," said Merrick, enigmatically, "Barton & Barton are undoubtedly men of great ability in their professions but that 'clerk' of theirs who has come over with the party," with peculiar emphasis, "is the smartest man in the whole crowd!"

"The clerk! why I thought he seemed rather an insignificant sort of a fellow; what do you know about him?"

For reply the detective only gave a short, unpleasant laugh, and, touching his cap, turned abruptly down another street.

"Hold on!" cried the attorney; "you haven't told me anything about yourself yet. What have you been doing? and how long are you going to be in town?"

"A day or two, perhaps, possibly a week; I cannot say."

"How are you getting on?"

But the detective was lost in thought and apparently did not hear the question. "I suppose you read of the arrest of Brown, the coachman?" he remarked, abstractedly, after a moment's silence.

"The coachman?" No! you don't say that he was really concerned in that affair?" the attorney exclaimed, excitedly.

"What affair, the Mainwaring murder?" I don't know that I have said that he was concerned in that," Merrick answered, suddenly coming to himself and evidently enjoying the attorney's expression of blank perplexity; "he was mixed up in a shooting affair, however, which occurred about that time, and by holding him in custody we hope to get on to the principals. Oh," he added, carelessly, anticipating another inquiry from Mr. Whitney, "I'm getting there all right, if that is what you want to know; but I won't have somebody else dogging my tracks and then claiming the game by and by."

"Man alive! what in the dickens are you driving at? You are in one of your moods to-night."

"Perhaps so," Merrick replied, indifferently, then added quickly, "There is a sensation of some sort in there; see the crowd of reporters!"

They were standing on a street corner, near a large hotel, and glancing through the windows in the direction indicated by the detective, Mr. Whitney saw, as he had said, a crowd of reporters in the office and lobbies, some writing, some talking excitedly, and others coming and going. Just then one who was leaving the building passed them, and Merrick stopped him.

"What is going on?" What's the excitement?"

"Suicide!" the young man replied, hastily. "That woman who was mixed up in the Mainwaring case has suicided by poison."

The attorney and the detective exchanged startled glances, then both entered the hotel.

CHAPTER XII

FLOTSAM AND JETSAM

An hour later, the attorney and the detective reappeared, and, threading their way through the crowd still lingering about the hotel, walked rapidly down the street, arm in arm, conversing in low tones.

"A case of suicide, undoubtedly," said the attorney "and scarcely to be wondered at, taking all the circumstances into consideration. Do you know, I am now more than ever inclined to the belief that she was in some way connected with Hugh Mainwaring's death, and that, after such a revelation of her character as was made in court this morning, she feared further disclosures."

Mr. Whitney glanced at his companion, but the latter seemed engrossed with his own thoughts and made no reply.

"I never was so completely floored in my life," the attorney continued, "as when it came out that Harold Mainwaring was her son; and I yet fail to see the necessity for introducing that feature into the testimony. I should have thought that would have been passed over in silence."

"As near as I can judge from reading of the case," Merrick replied, "it seems to have been done with a purpose. His attorneys were leading up to that very point in such a manner that, when the climax was reached, she would involuntarily betray herself - as she did - thus confirming in the strongest manner the testimony already given."

"I believe you may be right," said the attorney, musingly, "though it had not occurred to me."

After a short pause, Merrick continued: "When I was first called to Fair Oaks, I suspected some relationship between that woman and the secretary, as he was then called; there was a marked resemblance between them; both had the same peculiar olive skin, while their features and carriage were almost identical."

"Yes, I recall your mentioning the likeness to me, and at the same time I was puzzled by the resemblance between him and Hugh Mainwaring. Well, I always said he was a mystery, and no wonder!"

They had reached the club-house by this time, and, as Merrick declined Mr. Whitney's invitation to enter, both men remained outside for a few moments. Once again, the attorney endeavored to sound the detective regarding his work and the progress he was making, but the latter suddenly became strangely uncommunicative.

"My client is going to charge Harold Mainwaring with the murder," said the attorney at last.

Merrick laughed scornfully, and for the second time that evening wheeled abruptly and turned down a side street, leaving Mr. Whitney standing upon the club-house steps, watching the rapidly retreating figure with mingled vexation and amusement.

"Something has upset Merrick," he soliloquized, as he finally turned towards the entrance; "who can he imagine is 'dogging' his tracks, as he terms it?" These detectives seem about as jealous of their reputation as we lawyers are supposed to be. Ralph Mainwaring is going to engage 'the best legal talent that money can get!' H'm! when he comes to settle, he may find that my 'legal talent' will come just as high as the best of them."

Could Mr. Whitney have been present at a conference held that evening in one of the private parlors of the Waldorf, he might have had a better understanding of the cause of Merrick's perturbation.

Immediately upon returning to the hotel, Harold Mainwaring had communicated to the English attorney and to Mr. Scott the particulars of his interview with Mrs. LaGrange. Mr. Scott at once expressed his satisfaction at the outcome, in that she had rejected all offers of assistance except upon her own terms.

"That is best, that is best just as it is," he said, emphatically; "you do not want to be hampered with any obligations she might impose upon you, and as for ever recognizing or acknowledging any relationship, it is not to be thought of for one moment. Your course was right, perfectly right. But what was the statement of such importance which she was to make?"

"That is just what I am coming to," the young man replied; and drawing his chair closer to those of his companions, he repeated in low tones the secret intrusted to him by Mrs. LaGrange. The faces of the two men were a study as he ended his recital.

"Are you confident that she spoke the truth?" questioned Mr. Barton eagerly.

"I am positive that she did; she seemed like one terror-stricken, and said that the horror of it had haunted her day and night."

"There could be no reason in this instance for doubting her," commented Mr. Scott, thoughtfully; "she would have no motive for making such a statement if it were not true."

"My dear Mainwaring!" exclaimed the attorney, "it is what I

have suspected ever since you gave me the details of the affair; you remember what I told you before we left London!"

"Certainly; but it seemed to me then too improbable."

"The improbable is, sometimes, what we must look for in cases like this," he replied; "McCabe should be put on to this immediately, and we must call Sutherland. I will summon him, myself, at once," and he left the room.

The foster-father and son, left for a few moments to themselves, had little to say, but sat looking into each other's faces with eyes full of meaning, each understanding what was in the other's heart. At last, as they heard returning footsteps, the elder man spoke, -

"It was a good thing you went there, my boy; come what may, you will never regret it."

"Never!" the other replied with emphasis.

It seemed but a few moments ere hurried steps were heard along the corridor, followed by a light, familiar knock, and Mr. Sutherland entered.

"I recognized your voice at the 'phone, Mr. Barton," said the attorney, after greetings had been exchanged, "and something in its tone, aside from the general import of your message, led me to believe that the call was of special importance, therefore I lost no time in coming here."

"You were correct," replied the English barrister; "we have made a most important discovery, bearing not only upon the case in hand, but also upon the Mainwaring murder case."

"Ah-h!" responded the attorney with evident interest; then drawing his chair near the group seated about the open fire, he asked, with a swift glance about the room, "But where is your 'clerk,' Mr. Barton?" Should he not be present?"

"My 'clerk!'" replied Mr. Barton, with peculiar emphasis, and plainly appreciating the humor of the inquiry; "my 'clerk' is, I believe, at present engaged in most assiduously cultivating the acquaintance of Ralph Mainwaring's coachman."

Then, as Mr. Sutherland elevated his eyebrows in mute inquiry, he continued, -

"The coachman, I have understood, is a recent acquisition, taken, I believe, upon the recommendation of this Merrick; and while he seems eminently satisfactory as a coachman, I have my doubts as to whether he will prove quite so satisfactory to his superior officer upon his return."

"Ah, I see!" ejaculated the other; "he is what might be denominated a 'sub.'"

"Yes; and so exceedingly verdant that McCabe thought it worth while to make his acquaintance. But now to present business!"

Again the strange story was repeated, Mr. Sutherland listening with grave attention, which deepened as the recital proceeded, until, at its completion, he could scarcely restrain his enthusiasm; exultation was plainly written on his face, but there was a peculiar gentleness in his manner as he first approached his young client, saying in a low tone, as he cordially grasped his hand, -

"I realize, Mr. Mainwaring, all that this means to you, and I am sure you will understand me when I say that I congratulate you."

Harold Mainwaring bowed silently, and Mr. Sutherland, turning towards the English barrister, exclaimed, "This explains everything! This will make our case absolutely incontrovertible; but, first, we must secure that man at all hazards and at any cost just as quickly as possible; think what a witness he will make!"

"Just what I had in mind" was the response, "and McCabe is the man to locate him if he is upon the face of the earth. But we must decide immediately upon our own course of action, for this will necessitate certain changes in our plans, and we must act at once, and, at the same time, with the utmost caution and secrecy."

Dinner was ordered and served in the privacy of their own apartments that they might be entirely free from intrusion or interruptions during their deliberations, and it was at a late hour when, their consultation ended, they gathered about the open fire with their cigars, awaiting, with much self-congratulation and cheerful talk, the return of the absent McCabe.

"Confound it!" exclaimed Mr. Barton, presently, glancing at his watch; "what in the deuce is keeping that fellow so late?" If we had not especially wanted him, he would have been here two hours ago."

"Perhaps," suggested Mr. Sutherland, "he may have found the coachman more communicative than he anticipated."

"He has doubtless struck some clue which be is following," was the reply; but at that instant there was a light tap at the door, and the man generally known as the English barrister's "clerk" entered.

"Well, Mac," said Mr. Barton, cheerfully, "'speak of the devil' - you know what follows! What luck to-night?"

"Very fair, sir," said the man, quietly taking in the situation at a glance, as he noted the eager, expectant faces of the four men, and, dropping into a chair near the group, he instantly assumed an attitude of close attention.

Ordinarily, McCabe was, as Mr. Whitney had remarked, rather an insignificant looking man. He was below medium stature and somewhat dull in appearance, owing to the fact that he seemed to take little interest in his surroundings, while his face, when his eyes were concealed, as was generally the case, by the heavily drooping lids and long eyelashes, was absolutely expressionless. When, however, he raised his eyes and fixed them upon any one, the effect was much the same as though a search-light suddenly flashed in one's face; but this was only upon rare occasions, and few casual observers would dream of the keen perceptive faculties hidden beneath that quiet exterior.

"Tell us your story first, Mac," said Mr. Barton, after a moment's silence, thoroughly understanding his man, "ours will keep for a little bit."

"There's not much to tell, sir."

"How are you and the coachman coming on?"

"We'll not be very intimate after to-night, I'm thinking."

"How is that?" questioned the attorney, at the same time smiling broadly at his companions.

"Well, sir, there'll be no call for it, for one thing, as I've got all the points in the case I wanted; and for another, his chief returned this evening, and, from the few words I overheard upon his arrival, I don't think the coachman will feel over-confidential the next time he sees me," and McCabe smiled grimly to himself.

"So Merrick is back!" interposed Mr. Sutherland, laughing. "Did you and he meet?"

"Meet, sir?" Ah, no, not much o' that! I heard a step coming up the stairs, and as I thought the room was hardly big enough for three, I excused myself to Mr. Jim Matheson-alias Matthews, the coachman-and made for the hall. We passed each other at the head of the stairs, and I cluttered down, making as much racket as I could; then at the foot of the stairs I took off my boots and crept upstairs again, more to hear the fellow's voice than anything else, so I could recognize him afterwards."

"What did you hear?" inquired Mr. Barton, as McCabe paused to light a cigar which Mr. Sutherland had handed him.

"I heard him say, 'Who was that I passed outside, Jim?' 'Only a cross-country friend of mine,' says Jim. 'What friends are you entertaining here in these quarters?' says he, kind o' sharp like. 'An' sure,' says Jim, 'it was only Dan McCoy, the clerk of the big London lawyer who has come over with the young Mr. Mainwaring I've heard you speak of, and a right clever fellow he is, too!' 'Clerk!' he roars out, 'clerk, you blithering idiot! he's no more clerk than you are coachman, nor half so much, for you're fit for nothing but to take care of horses all your days! Do you want to know,' says he, 'who you've been entertaining?" That's no more nor less than Dan McCabe, a Scotland Yard man they've brought over, nobody knows what for, but whatever his game, he's made you play into his hand!' I didn't stay to hear more," McCabe concluded, "I got out."

"But how does this Merrick know you?" Mr. Barton inquired, as the laughter caused by McCabe's recital subsided.

"He doesn't know me, he only knows of me," the man replied. "I found that out an hour or two later, when I met him in a crowd at the Wellington Hotel ;"the speaker glanced curiously in the direction of Harold Mainwaring for an instant, and then continued, "I knew him by his voice, but I spoke with him, and he had no idea who I was."

"But how has he heard of you?" persisted Mr. Barton.

"There was an American detective-a friend of his-who came over on the 'Campania' on the same trip with Mr. Mainwaring. He was following up a case in London, but he managed to keep his eye on Mr. Mainwaring and kept this Merrick posted of all that he was doing. It was because of some remarks of his that I got wind of, that I determined from the first to get onto his game."

"Well, Mac," said Mr. Barton, tentatively, "are you ready to go to work now?"

The keen eyes flashed for an instant in the attorney's face, then the man answered quietly, "If you've nothing to tell me, I'm ready to go to work on my own hook and in my own way; if you've anything to say, I'll hear it."

Mr. Barton glanced at the others. "We had better tell McCabe what we have learned, and also just what our plans are."

The others bowed in assent, and the chairs were drawn closer together while Mr. Barton, in low tones, told, as briefly and clearly as possible, the discovery which they had made. McCabe listened to the attorney's story, but whether or not the secret were already guessed by him, his face gave no sign. When it was ended he glanced curiously at Harold Mainwaring.

"Mrs. LaGrange told you this?"

"She did."

"At what time, if you please, sir?"

"At about half-past five."

"Are you aware, sir, that, with the exception of her maid, you are probably the last person who saw Mrs. LaGrange living?"

"Saw her living!" Harold Mainwaring repeated, astonished, while Mr. Barton demanded, "What do you mean, Mac?"

"I mean, sir," said McCabe, slowly, "that Mrs. LaGrange committed suicide at about seven o'clock this evening, less than two hours after Mr. Mainwaring saw her."

"When did you learn of this?" "What do you know of the affair?" questioned the attorneys quickly, while Harold Mainwaring, more deeply shocked than he would have thought possible, listened to the man's reply.

"I happened along by the Wellington about two hours ago, and saw considerable stir around there. I learned 'twas a case of suicide, but thought nothing of it till I heard the woman's name, then I dropped in and picked up the facts in the case," and he proceeded to relate the details of the affair.

As Harold Mainwaring listened, he recalled the looks and words of the wretched woman, her genuine misery, her falsehood and deceit, her piteous pleadings, and the final rage and scorn with which she had rejected his assistance even in the face of such desperation and despair; and a sickening sense of horror stole over him, rendering him almost oblivious to the conversation around him.

"'Twas there I saw this man Merrick," McCabe was saying in conclusion. "I heard him questioning the maid about Mr. Mainwaring's interview with the woman; he evidently was onto that. I saw the girl myself shortly afterwards and gave her a hint and a bit of money to keep her mouth shut about Mr. Mainwaring. She seemed pretty bright, and I think she will understand her business."

"Confound that meddlesome Yankee! what was he prowling around there for?" interrupted Mr. Scott, angrily. "He has no business prying into Harold Scott Mainwaring's affairs, and I'll have him understand it; let him attend to his own duties, and I think, from all reports, he will have his hands more than full then. Mr. Sutherland," he continued, addressing the attorney, "there's no knowing what that beastly bungler who calls himself a detective will do next; this thing is likely to be out in the morning papers with the boy's name mixed up in it, and it must be stopped right here. His name must be kept out of this at any price, and you probably can reach the New York press better than any one of us."

"You are right," said Mr. Sutherland, rising hastily and preparing to leave; "our client wants no notoriety of that sort; and I will make sure that nothing of the kind occurs. I have a friend who has unlimited influence with the newspaper men, and I will have him attend to the matter at once, and see to it that everything of that nature is suppressed."

"That is best," said Harold Mainwaring gravely, coming forward. "I would have rendered the woman any necessary assistance; I am willing to do whatever is needful now, but, living or dead, her name shall never be coupled with my father's name and mine."

"You understand, of course, that money is no object in this matter," added Mr. Scott.

"I understand perfectly, sir," said the attorney, courteously; "everything will be attended to; and, Mr. Barton, you will kindly confer with Mr. McCabe, and I will see you in the morning regarding your final decision. Good-night, gentlemen."

An hour later, McCabe took his departure. Of his own theories or plans he had said little more than that he was to leave the Waldorf that night for another part of the city, but all details for communication with him in case of necessity had been carefully arranged.

"Your 'clerk' has been suddenly called to London on important business," he said to Mr. Barton, with a quiet smile, adding, "You may meet me occasionally, but it's not likely or best that you recognize me, and when I have anything to report you will hear from me," and with these words he was gone.

When at last Harold Mainwaring and his foster-father were again by themselves, the latter, noting the younger man's abstraction, said,-

"This is naturally a great shock to you, my boy, but it is only what might be expected after such a life as hers. You have done nothing for which to censure yourself; you have done all that could be done under existing conditions, and more than was actually required of you; so you need have no regrets over the affair."

"I understand that, sir; but the thought that I cannot banish from my mind is, knowing so well her treachery and deceit, is it possible that she herself had a hand in the murder, and finding at last that there was no hope of gaining my friendship, did she fear the developments which might follow from what she had told?"

The elder man shook his head thoughtfully. "We cannot say, my boy; the thought occurred to me almost instantaneously, for, without doubt, she both hated and feared him; but time alone will tell."

CHAPTER XXIV

BETWEEN THE ACTS

For the ten days next ensuing the public craving for sensational developments in the Mainwaring case seemed likely to be gratified to an unusual degree. To the exciting scenes of the court-room was added the suicide of Mrs. LaGrange, immediately followed by news of the discovery that Richard Hobson, the unwilling witness in the previous day's proceedings, had absconded, leaving not the slightest indication of even the direction in which he had vanished. By many the suicide of the one and the sudden disappearance of the other, occurring simultaneously, were considered as prima facie evidence that the two, so closely associated with each other, had been in some way connected with the Fair Oaks tragedy.

From this phase of the affair, however, public attention was speedily diverted by the report that proceedings to contest the old will had been instituted, but in the name of Ralph Mainwaring and his brother, Harold W. Mainwaring; his son, the sole heir under the will of Hugh Mainwaring, having altogether withdrawn from the contest. This had caused an open rupture between father and son, and the latter had established himself in a suite of apartments at the Murray Hill.

Young Mainwaring's course occasioned great surprise; many commended his wisdom, but few gave him credit for the genuine sense of honor which had actuated him.

"A neat little stroke of diplomacy," said one club-man to another, "and worthy of Hugh Mainwaring himself! There is no show for him, anyway, and it's much better policy to yield the point now, don't you see, than to fight it out along with that pig-headed father of his."

"He understands on which side his bread is buttered, and don't you forget it, my dear boy," was the laughing rejoinder. "It's always best to stand in with the winning side; he won't lose anything in the long run, and he knows it."

Such remarks occasionally reached young Mainwaring, making him exceedingly indignant.

"You may say, once and for all," he said to a reporter who was interviewing him in his apartments at the Murray Hill, "that in withdrawing from this contest I am not currying favor with Harold Scott Mainwaring. He and I are the best of friends, but that fact would not hinder me from giving him a fair and square fight if there were the slightest doubt as to the validity of his claim. But there isn't; he has proved his right, legally and morally, to the property, and that's enough for me."

"But Mr. Ralph Mainwaring must have some tenable ground for contesting his claim," said the reporter, tentatively, hoping to get some of the inside facts of the case.

Young Mainwaring froze instantly. "I have nothing whatever to say, sir, regarding the governor's action in this matter; any information you desire on that point you will have to obtain from him."

The next development in the Mainwaring case was a report to the effect that the whereabouts of Harold W. Mainwaring could not be ascertained, and it was generally supposed among his London associates that he had followed his brother to America by the next steamer. As this report was supplemented by the further facts that he was a man of no principle, heavily involved in debt, and deeply incensed at Ralph Mainwaring's success in securing for his son the American estate in which he himself had expected to share, public speculation was immediately aroused in a new direction, and "that Mainwaring affair" became the absorbing topic, not alone at the clubs and other places of masculine rendezvous, but at all social gatherings as well.

Regarding the principal actors in this drama, however, around whom public interest really centred, little could be definitely ascertained. To many, who, on the following morning, read the details of the suicide at the Wellington, it was a matter of no small wonder that the name of Harold Scott Mainwaring was not once mentioned in connection with that of the woman shown by the preceding day's testimony to have been so closely related to him. Perhaps no one was more surprised at this omission than Merrick himself but if so, his only comment was made mentally.

"He's got the cinch on them all around, and he'll win, hands down!"

The inquest, held at an early hour, was merely a matter of form, the evidence of intentional suicide being conclusive, and the interment, a few hours later, was strictly private. Excepting the clergyman who read the burial service, there were present only the two sons of the wretched woman.

It was their first meeting since learning of the strange relationship existing between them, and Walter LaGrange, as he entered the presence of the dead, cast a curious glance, half shrinking, half defiant, at the calm, stern face of Harold Mainwaring, who had preceded him. His own face was haggard and drawn, and the hard, rigid lines deepened as his glance fell for an instant on the casket between them. Then his eyes looked straight into those of Harold Mainwaring with an expression almost imploring.

"Tell me," he demanded in low, hoarse tones, "is it true that I am - what she once said and what report is now saying -

the son of Hugh Mainwaring?"

"It is true, "the other replied, gravely.

"Then curse them both!" he exclaimed, while his hands
clinched involuntarily. "What right had they to blight and ruin
my life? What right had they to live as they did, and let the
stigma, the shame, the curse of it all fall on me?" A few months
since I had the honor and respect of my classmates and
associates; to-day, not one will recognize me, and for no fault
of mine!"

"Hush!" interposed Harold Mainwaring; "I know the wrong
which has been done you, - they have wronged me, also, far
more deeply than you know, - but this is no time or place to
recall it!"

The calmness and kindness of his tones seemed to soothe and
control his excited companion.

"I know they have wronged you," the latter replied; "but they
have not ruined you! You have not only friends and wealth,
but, more than all, your father's name. I," he added bitterly,
"am a pauper, and worse than a pauper, for I have not even a
name!"

For a few moments Harold Mainwaring silently studied the
haggard young face confronting him, in which anger was
slowly giving place to dull, sullen despair; and his own heart
was suddenly moved with pity for the boy

"Robbed of his birthright before he was born," reared in an
atmosphere of treachery and deceit calculated to foster and
develop the evil tendencies already inherited; yet, notwithstanding all, so closely akin to himself.

"Walter," he said, gravely, at the same time extending his hand
across the casket, "I realize the truth of much that you have
said, but you need not allow this to ruin or blight your life.

Mark my words, your future from this time forth is, to a great extent, in your own hands; your life will be what you make it, and you alone. See to it that it is not blighted by your own wrong-doing! Be yourself a man of honor, and I will assure you, you can depend upon me to stand by you and to help you." Walter LaGrange raised his eyes in astonishment at these words, containing a pledge of probably the first genuine friendship he had ever known in his young life. He gave a look, searching, almost cynical, into Harold Mainwaring's face; then reading nothing but sincerity, he took the proffered hand, saying brokenly, -

"Do you really mean it? I supposed that you, of all others, would despise me; and it would be no great wonder if you did!"

"It will depend entirely upon yourself, Walter, whether or not I despise you. If I ever do, it will be the result of your own unworthiness, not because of the wrong-doing of others."

There were signs in the boy's face of a brief struggle between the old pride, inherited from his mother, and the self-respect which Harold Mainwaring's words had but just awakened.

"If it were the other fellow," he said, slowly, "the one the old man intended to make his heir, had made me such a proposition, I would tell him to go to the devil; but, by George! if you will stand by me, it's all right, and I'll be man enough anyway that you'll never regret it."

A few days later, Walter LaGrange, penniless and friendless, had disappeared, whither his former associates neither knew nor cared. In a large banking establishment in one of the principal western cities, - a branch of the firm of Mainwaring & Co., - a young man, known as the ward of Harold Scott Mainwaring, was entered as an employee, with prospect of advancement should he prove himself worthy of responsibility and trust. But of this, as of many other events just then quietly transpiring behind the scenes, little or nothing was known.

Meanwhile, as the days slipped rapidly away, the party at the Waldorf was not idle. There were conferences, numerous and protracted, behind dosed doors, telegrams and cablegrams in cipher flashed hither and thither in multitudinous directions, while Mr. Sutherland seemed fairly ubiquitous. Much of his time, however, was spent in the private parlors of the English party, with frequent journeys to the court-house to ascertain the status of the case. >From one of these trips he returned one evening jubilant.

"Well," said he, settling himself comfortably, with a sigh of relief, "the first point in the case is decided in our favor."

"That is a good omen," Mr. Barton replied cheerfully; "but may I inquire to what you refer?"

"I have succeeded in getting the date for the hearing set for the next term of court, which opens early in December."

"I am glad to hear it; a little time just now is of the utmost importance to our interests. Did you have any difficulty in securing a postponement until the next term?"

"Whitney, of course, opposed it strongly. He said his client wanted the matter settled at the earliest possible moment; but I told him that so long as Ralph Mainwaring persisted in butting against a stone wall, just so long a speedy settlement was out of the question; it was bound to be a hard fight, and would be carried over into the next term in any event. Then I had a private interview with Judge Bingham, and, without giving particulars, told him that new developments had arisen, and, with a little time in which to procure certain evidence, we would have our opponents completely floored, - they would not even have an inch of room left to stand upon, - while under present conditions, Mainwaring, so long as he had a shilling, would, if beaten, move for a new trial, or appeal to a higher court, - anything to keep up the fight. So he will grant us till December, which, I am inclined to think, will be ample time."

"It looks now," said Mr. Barton, producing a telegram, "as though we might succeed in securing that evidence much sooner than we have anticipated. What do you think of that?" and he handed the despatch to Mr. Sutherland.

The face of the latter brightened as he glanced rapidly over the yellow sheet.

"The dickens! McCabe has left the city!" he exclaimed.

Mr. Barton bowed. "Which means," he said in reply, "that he has evidently struck the scent; and when he once starts on the trail, it is only a question of time - and usually not any great length of time, either - before he runs his game to cover."

"Well," ejaculated Mr. Sutherland, rubbing his hands together enthusiastically, "I, for one, want to be 'in at the death' on this, for it will simply be the finest piece of work, the grandest denouement, of any case that has ever come within my twenty years of legal experience!"

Mr. Barton smiled. "My brother is evidently of the same opinion with yourself," he said. " I received a cablegram from him to-day, requesting me to inform him at once of the date set for the hearing, as he stated he would not, for a kingdom, fail of being present at the trial."

With the announcement that the case of Mainwaring versus Mainwaring had been set for the opening of the December term of court, the public paused to take breath and to wonder at this unlooked - for delay, but preparations for the coming contest were continued with unabated vigor on both sides. Contrary to all expectations, Ralph Mainwaring, so far from objecting to the postponement of the case, took special pains to express his entire satisfaction with this turn of affairs.

"It is an indication of conscious weakness on their part," he remarked with great complacency, as he and Mr. Whitney were dining at the club on the following day. "They have evidently discovered some flaw in their defence which it will take some time to repair. I can afford to wait, however; my attorneys and experts will soon be here, and while our side could easily have been in readiness in a much shorter time, this, of course, will give us an opportunity for still more elaborate preparation, so that we will gain an immense advantage over them."

"I suppose, Mr. Mainwaring," said one of his listeners, giving a quick side-glance at his companions, "I suppose that during this interim a truce will be declared, and for the time being there will be a cessation of hostilities between the parties in interest, will there not?"

"Sir!" roared Ralph Mainwaring, transfixing the speaker with a stare calculated to annihilate him.

"I beg pardon, sir, I intended no offence," continued the irrepressible young American, ignoring the warning signals from his associates; "it only occurred to me that with such an immense advantage on your side you could afford to be magnanimous and treat your opponent with some consideration."

"I am not accustomed to showing magnanimity or consideration to any but my own equals," the other rejoined, with freezing dignity; "and the fact that my 'opponent,' as you are pleased to designate him, is, for the present, allowed liberty to go and come at his pleasure, although under strict surveillance, is, in this instance, sufficient consideration."

"Harold Scott Mainwaring under surveillance? Incredible!" exclaimed one of the party in a low tone, while the first speaker remarked, "I certainly was unaware that the gentleman in question was to be regarded in the light of a suspected criminal!"

"It is to be presumed," said Ralph Mainwaring, haughtily, stung by the tinge of irony in the other's tone, "that there are a number of points in this case of which people in general are as yet unaware, but upon which they are likely to become enlightened in the near future, when this person who has assumed such a variety of roles will be disclosed in his true light, - not that of a suspected criminal merely, but of a condemned criminal, convicted by a chain of evidence every link of which has been forged by himself."

There was an ominous silence as Ralph Mainwaring rose from the table, broken at last by an elderly gentleman seated at a little distance, who, while apparently an interested listener, had taken no part in the conversation.

"Begging your pardon, Mr. Mainwaring, I would judge the charges which you would prefer against this young man to be unusually serious; may I inquire their nature?"

The words were spoken with the utmost deliberation, but in the calm, even tones there was an implied challenge, which was all that was needed at that instant to fan Ralph Mainwaring's wrath into a flame. Utterly disregarding a cautionary glance from Mr. Whitney, he turned his monocle upon the speaker, glaring at him in contemptuous silence for a moment.

"You have decidedly the advantage of me, sir, but allow me to say that the person under discussion has not only, with unheard of effrontery, publicly and unblushingly proclaimed himself as a blackmailer and knave, capable of descending to any perfidy or treachery for the purpose of favoring his own base schemes, but he has also, in his inordinate greed and ambition, unwittingly proved himself by his own statements and conduct to be a villain of the deepest dye; and I will say, furthermore, that if Harold Scott Mainwaring, as he styles himself, ends his days upon the gallows in expiation of the foul murder of Hugh Mainwaring, he will have only himself to thank, for his own words and deeds will have put the noose about his neck."

Having thus expressed himself:, Ralph Mainwaring, without waiting for reply, left the room accompanied by Mr. Whitney.

The latter made no comment until they were seated in the carriage and rolling down the avenue; then he remarked, casually, -

"I was surprised, Mr. Mainwaring, that you failed to recognize the gentleman who addressed you as you were leaving the table."

"His face was somewhat familiar; I have met him, but I cannot recall when or where. I considered his tone decidedly offensive, however, and I proposed, whoever he might be, to give him to understand that I would brook no interference. Do you know him?"

"I have never met him, but I know of him," the attorney replied, watching his client closely. "He is the Honorable J. Ponsonby Roget, Q. C., of London. I supposed of course that you knew him."

"J. Ponsonby Roget, Queen's Counsel? Egad! I have met him, but it was years ago, and he has aged so that I did not recognize him. Strange!" he added, visibly annoyed. "What the deuce is he doing in this country?"

"That is just what no one is able to say," replied the attorney, slowly. "He is stopping at the Waldorf, with our friends, the English party, but whether as a guest or in a professional capacity, no one has been able to ascertain."

"Zounds, man! why did you not give me this information earlier?"

"For the good and sufficient reason, Mr. Mainwaring, that I did not learn of the facts myself until within the last two hours. My attention was called to the gentleman as I entered the club. I assumed, of course, that you knew him, at least by sight, and when he addressed you I supposed for the instant that you were acquaintances."

"But how came he at the club? None of the party from the Waldorf were with him."

"He was there as the especial guest of Chief-Justice Parmalee, of the Supreme Court, the gentleman on his left. Judge Parmalee spent much of his life in London, and the two are particular friends."

"Well, it's done, and can't be undone, and I don't know that I regret it," Ralph Mainwaring remarked, sullenly. "If he chooses to identify himself with that side of the case he is at liberty to do so, but he has my opinion of his client gratis."

Mr. Whitney made no reply, and the drive was concluded in silence.

Meanwhile, Ralph Mainwaring had no sooner left the club than a chorus of exclamations, protests, and running comments arose on all sides.

"Harold Scott Mainwaring the murderer of Hugh Mainwaring! That is carrying this farce beyond all bounds!"

"If he cannot get possession of the property in any other way, he will send the new heir to the gallows, eh?"

"He will attempt it, too; he is desperate," said one.

"He may make it pretty serious for the young fellow," said another, thoughtfully. "You remember, by his own statements he was the last person who saw Hugh Mainwaring alive; in fact, he was in his library within a few moments preceding his death; and after all that has been brought to light, it's not to be supposed that he had any great affection for his uncle."

"What is this, gentlemen?" said a reporter, briskly, appearing on the scene, note-book in hand. "Any new developments in the Mainwaring case?"

"Yes, a genuine sensation!" shouted two or three voices.

"Gentlemen, attention a moment!" said a commanding voice outside, and an instant later a tall, well-known form entered.

"The ubiquitous Mr. Sutherland!" laughingly announced a jovial young fellow, standing near the entrance.

"Sutherland, how is this?" demanded one of the elder gentlemen. "Have you a private battery concealed about your person with invisible wires distributed throughout the city, that you seem to arrive at any and every spot just on the nick of time?"

"That is one of the secrets of the profession, Mr. Norton, not to be revealed to the uninitiated," replied the attorney, while a quick glance flashed between himself and the Queen's Counsel.

"There is one thing, gentlemen," he continued, with great dignity, "to which I wish to call your attention, particularly you gentlemen of the press. I am aware of the nature of the 'sensation' of which you made mention a moment ago, but I wish it distinctly understood that it is to be given no publicity whatever. The name of my client is not to be bandied about before the public in connection with any of Ralph Mainwaring's imputations or vilifications, for the reason that they are wholly without foundation. We are thoroughly cognizant of that gentleman's intentions regarding our client, and we will meet him on his own ground. In the coming contest we will not only establish beyond all shadow of doubt our client's sole right and title to the Mainwaring estate, but we will, at the same time, forever refute and silence any and every aspersion which Ralph Mainwaring may seek to cast upon him. Even were there any truth in these insinuations, it would be time enough, when the charges should be preferred against our client, to brazen them before the public, but since they are only the product of spleen and malignity, simply consign them to the odium and obloquy to which they are entitled."

"That is right!" responded two or three voices, while the reporter replied, courteously,-

"We will certainly respect your wishes, sir; but you see the public is on the qui vive, so to speak, over this case, and it is our business to get hold of every item which we can to add to the interest. You have checked us off on some rather interesting matter already, I believe."

"Perhaps so," said Mr. Sutherland, quietly, "but I can promise you that before long there will be developments in the case which will give you boys all the interesting matter you will need for some time, and they will be fact, not fabrication."

As the result of Mr. Sutherland's prompt action, the newspapers contained no allusion to that evening's scene at the club; but even his energy and caution were powerless to prevent the spread of the affair from lip to lip. Mentioned scarcely above a whisper, the report rippled onward, the waves widening in all directions, with various alterations and additions, till it was regarded as an open secret in all circles of society. It reached young Mainwaring in his rather secluded bachelor quarters at the Murray Hill, and he bowed his head in shame that a Mainwaring should stoop to so disgraceful an exhibition of his venomous rage and hatred. It reached Harold Scott Mainwaring, and the smouldering fire in the dark eyes gleamed afresh and the proud face grew rigid and stern. Donning overcoat and hat, he left his apartments at the Waldorf; and started forth in the direction of the club most frequented by Ralph Mainwaring and Mr. Whitney.

He had gone but a short distance when he met young Mainwaring. The young men exchanged cordial greetings, and, at Harold's request, his cousin retraced his steps to accompany him.

"Why are you making such a stranger of yourself; Hugh? I

have scarcely seen you of late," said Harold, after a little general conversation.

"Well, to be frank with you, old boy, I haven't been around so often as I would like for two reasons; for one thing, I find people generally are not inclined to regard our friendship in the same light that we do. You and I understand one another, and you don't suspect me of any flunkeyism, or any ulterior motive, don't you know, -"

"I understand perfectly," said Harold, as his cousin paused, seeming to find some difficulty in conveying his exact meaning; "and so long as you and I do understand each other, what is the use of paying any attention to outsiders? Whether we were friends, or refused to recognize one another, their small talk and gossip would flow on forever, so why attempt to check it?"

"I believe you are right; but that isn't all of it, don't you know. What I care most about is the governor's losing his head in the way he has lately. It is simply outrageous, the reports he has started in circulation!"

Hugh paused and glanced anxiously into his cousin's face, but the frank, brotherly kindness which he read there reassured him.

"My dear cousin," said Harold, warmly, "nothing that Ralph Mainwaring can ever say or do shall make any difference between us. There are but two contingencies in this connection that I regret."

"And those are what?" the younger man questioned eagerly.

"That he bears the name of Mainwaring, and that he is your father!"

"By Jove! I'm with you on that," the other exclaimed heartily, and I hope you'll win every point in the game; but I've been awfully cut up over what he has said and done recently. I know that he intends to carry his threats into execution, and I'm afraid he'll make it deucedly unpleasant for you, don't you know."

They had reached the club-house, and Harold Mainwaring, as he paused on the lowest step, smiled brightly into the boyish face, regarding him with such solicitude.

"I understand his intentions as well as you, and know that it would give him great delight to carry them into execution; but, my dear boy, he will never have the opportunity to even make the attempt."

Young Mainwaring's face brightened. "Why, are you prepared to head him off in that direction? By Jove! I'm right glad to know it. Well, I'll be around to the Waldorf in the course of a day or two No, much obliged, but I don't care to go into the club-rooms to-night; in fact, I haven't been in there since the governor made that after-dinner speech of his. Good-night!"

As Harold Mainwaring sauntered carelessly through the club-rooms, returning the greetings of the select circle of friends which he had made, he was conscious of glances of interest and undisguised curiosity from the many with whom he had no acquaintance. No allusion was made to the subject which he well knew was in their minds, however, until, meeting Mr. Chittenden, the latter drew him aside into an alcove.

"I say, my dear Mainwaring, are you aware that your esteemed kinsman has you under strict surveillance?"

Mainwaring smiled, though his eyes flashed. "I am aware that he has made statements to that effect, although, thus far, his 'surveillance' has interfered in no way either with my duties or pleasures, nor do I apprehend that it will."

"My dear fellow, it is simply preposterous! The man must be insane."

"Is he here this evening?" Mainwaring inquired.

"No; to tell the truth, he has not found it so very congenial here since that outbreak of his; he seldom is here now, excepting, of course, at meals. Mr. Whitney is here, however."

"I came here," Harold Mainwaring replied, "with the express purpose of meeting one or the other, or both; on the whole, it will be rather better to meet Mr. Whitney."

"No trouble, no unpleasant words, I hope?" said the elder man, anxiously.

"Mr. Chittenden, when you knew me as Hugh Mainwaring's private secretary, you knew me as a gentleman; I trust I shall never be less."

"You are right, you are right, my boy, and I beg your pardon; but young blood is apt to be hasty, you know."

A little later Harold Mainwaring strolled leisurely across the large reading-room to a table where Mr. Whitney was seated. The latter, seeing him, rose to greet him, while his sensitive face flushed with momentary excitement.

"Mr. Mainwaring, I am delighted to meet you. I had hoped from the friendly tone of that rather mysterious note of yours, upon your somewhat abrupt departure, that we might meet again soon, and, though it is under greatly altered circumstances, I am proud to have the opportunity of congratulating you."

The younger man responded courteously, and for a few moments the two chatted pleasantly upon subjects of general interest, while many pairs of eyes looked on in silent astonishment, wondering what this peculiar interview might portend.

At last, after a slight pause, Harold Mainwaring remarked,

calmly, "Mr. Whitney, I understand that, when the coming litigation is terminated, your client intends to institute proceedings against me of a far different nature, - criminal proceedings, in fact."

The attorney colored and started nervously, then replied in a low tone, "Mr. Mainwaring, let us withdraw to one of the side rooms; this is rather a public place for any conversation regarding those matters."

"It is none too public for me, Mr. Whitney, as I have nothing unpleasant to say towards yourself personally, and nothing which I am not perfectly willing should be heard by any and every individual in these rooms to-night. You have not yet answered my inquiry, Mr. Whitney."

The attorney paused for a moment, as though laboring under great excitement, then he spoke in a tone vibrating with strong emotion, -

"Mr. Mainwaring, regarding my client's intentions, you have, in all probability, been correctly informed. I believe that he has made statements at various times to that effect, and I am now so well acquainted with him that I know there is no doubt but that he will attempt to carry out what he has threatened. But, Mr. Mainwaring, I wish to say a word or two for myself. In the coming litigation over the estate, I, as Ralph Mainwaring's counsel, am bound to do my part without any reference to my own personal opinions or prejudices, and I expect to meet you and your counsel in an open fight,-perhaps a bitter one. But this much I have to say: Should Ralph Mainwaring undertake to bring against you any action of the character which he has threatened," here Mr. Whitney rose to his feet and brought his hand down with a ringing blow upon the table at his side, "he will have to employ other counsel than myself, for I will have nothing whatever to do with such a case."

He paused a moment, then continued: "I do not claim to understand you perfectly, Mr. Mainwaring. I will confess you have always been a mystery to me, and you are still. There are depths about you that I cannot fathom. But I do believe in your honor, your integrity, and your probity, and as for taking part in any action reflecting upon your character, or incriminating you in any respect, I never will!"

A roar of applause resounded through the club-rooms as he concluded. When it had subsided, Harold Mainwaring replied,-

"Mr. Whitney, I thank you for this public expression of your confidence in me. The relations between us in the past have been pleasant, and I trust they will continue so in the future. As I stated, however, I came here to-night with no unfriendly feeling towards yourself, but to ask you to be the bearer of a message from me to your client. Ralph Mainwaring, not content with trying by every means within his power to deprive me of my right and title to the estate for years wrongfully withheld from my father and from myself, now accuses me of being the murderer of Hugh Mainwaring I Say to Ralph Mainwaring, for me, that, not through what he terms my 'inordinate greed and ambition,' but through God-given rights which no man can take from me, I will have my own, and he is powerless to prevent it or to stand in my way. But say to him that I will never touch one farthing of this property until I stand before the world free and acquitted of the most remote shadow of the murder of Hugh Mainwaring; nor until the foul and dastardly crime that stains Fair Oaks shall have been avenged!"

Amid the prolonged applause that followed, Harold Mainwaring left the building.

CHAPTER XXV

RUN TO COVER

A dull, cheerless day in the early part of December was merging into a stormy night as the west-bound express over one of the transcontinental railways, swiftly winding its way along the tortuous course of a Rocky Mountain canyon, suddenly paused before the long, low depot of a typical western mining city. The arc lights swinging to and fro shed only a ghastly radiance through the dense fog, and grotesque shadows, dancing hither and thither to the vibratory motion of the lights, seemed trying to contest supremacy with the feeble rays.

The train had not come to a full stop when a man sprang lightly from one of the car platforms, and, passing swiftly through the waiting crowd, concealed himself in the friendly shelter of the shadows, where he remained oblivious to the rain falling in spiteful dashes, while he scanned the hurrying crowd surging in various directions. Not one of the crowd observed him; not none escaped his observation. Soon his attention was riveted upon a tall man, closely muffled in fur coat and cap, who descended from one of the rear coaches, and, after a quick, cautious glance about him, passed the silent, motionless figure in the shadow and hastily entered a carriage standing near. The other, listening intently for the instructions given the driver, caught the words, "545 Jefferson Street."

As the carriage rolled away, he emerged from the shadow and

jotted down the address in a small note-book, soliloquizing as he did so,-

"I have tracked him to his lair at last, and now, unless that infernal hoodoo looms upon the scene, I can get in my work in good shape. I would have had my game weeks ago, but for his appearance, confound him!"

He looked at his watch. "Dinner first," he muttered, "the next thing in order is to find the alias under which my gentleman is at present travelling. No one seems to know much about him in these parts."

The dim light revealed a man below medium height, his form enveloped in a heavy English mackintosh thrown carelessly about his shoulders, which, as he made his notes, blew partially open, revealing an immaculate shirt front and a brilliant diamond which scintillated and sparkled in open defiance of the surrounding gloom. A soft felt hat well pulled down concealed his eyes and the upper part of his face, leaving visible only a slightly aquiline nose and heavy, black mustache, which gave his face something of a Jewish cast. Replacing his note-book in his pocket, he called a belated carriage, and hastily gave orders to be taken to the Clifton House.

Arriving at the hotel, the stranger registered as " A. Rosen-baum, Berlin,' and, having secured one of the best rooms the house afforded, repaired to the dining-room. Dinner over, Mr. Rosenbaum betook himself to a quiet corner of the office, which served also as a reading-room, and soon was apparently absorbed in a number of Eastern papers, both English and German, though a keen observer would have noted that the papers were occasionally lowered sufficiently to give the eyes-again concealed beneath the hat-brim-an opportunity for reconnoitering the situation. He was attired in a black suit of faultless fit, and a superb ruby on his left hand gleamed and glowed like living fire, rivalling in beauty the flashing diamond. He speedily became the subject of considerable speculation among the various classes of men congregating in the hotel office, most of them for an evening of social enjoyment, though a few seemed to have gathered there for the purpose of conducting business negotiations. Among the latter, after a time, was the tall man in fur coat and cap, who appeared to be waiting for some one with whom he had an appointment, as he shunned the crowd, selecting a seat near Mr. Rosenbaum as the most quiet place available. Having removed his cap and thrown back the high collar of his fur coat, he appeared to be a man of about fifty years of age, with iron-gray hair and a full, heavy beard of the same shade. He wore dark glasses, and, having seated himself with his back towards the light, drew forth from his pocket a number of voluminous type-written documents, and became absorbed in a perusal of their contents.

Meanwhile, the proprietor of the Clifton House, feeling considerable curiosity regarding his new guest, sauntered over in his direction.

"Well, Mr. Rosenbaum," he remarked, genially, "you have hit on rather a stormy night for your introduction to our city, for I take it you are a stranger here, are you not?"

The soft hat was raised slightly, revealing a rather stolid, expressionless face, with dark eyes nearly concealed by long lashes.

"Not the most agreeable, certainly," he answered, with an expressive shrug and a marked German accent, at the same time ignoring the other's question.

"Your first impressions are not likely to be very pleasant, but if you stop over a few days you will see we have a fine city. Do you remain here long?"

"I cannot say at present; depends entirely upon business, you understand."

"I see. What's your line?"

For reply the stranger handed the other a small card, on which was engraved, "Rosenbaum Brothers, Diamond Brokers, Berlin," and bearing on one corner his own name, "A. Rosenbaum."

"Diamond brokers, eh?" You don't say!" exclaimed the proprietor, regarding the bit of pasteboard with visible respect. "Must be quite a business. You represent this firm, I suppose; you are their salesman?"

The stranger shook his head with a smile. "We have no salesmen," he answered, quietly. "We have branch houses in Paris, London, and New York, but we employ no travelling salesmen. Any one can sell diamonds; my business is to buy them," with marked emphasis on the last words.

"Well," said his interlocutor, "you're not looking for 'em out here, are you?"

"Why not here as well as anywhere?" So far as my experience goes, it is nothing uncommon in this part of the country to run across owners of fine stones who, for one reason or another, are very glad to exchange the same for cash."

"Yes, I suppose so. When a fellow gets down to bedrock, he'll put up most anything to make a raise."

"There are many besides those who are down to bedrock, as you call it, who are glad to make an exchange of that kind," said Mr. Rosenbaum, speaking with deliberation and keeping an eye upon his neighbor in the fur coat; "but their reasons, whatever they may be, do not concern us; our business is simply to buy the gems wherever we can find them and ask no questions."

By this time a fourth man was approaching in their direction, evidently the individual for whom the man in the fur coat was waiting, and Mr. Rosenbaum, thinking it time to put an end to the conversation, rose and began to don his mackintosh.

Maynard Barbour

"Surely you are not going out to-night!" said the proprietor; "better stay indoors, and I'll make you acquainted with some of the boys."

"Much obliged, but an important engagement compels me to forego that pleasure," said Mr. Rosenbaum, and, bidding his host good-evening, he sallied forth, well aware that every word of their conversation had been overheard by their silent neighbor, notwithstanding the voluminous documents which seemed to engross his attention.

Passing out into the night, he found the storm fast abating. Stopping at a news-stand, he inquired for a directory, which he carefully studied for a few moments, then walked down the principal thoroughfare until, coming to a side street, he turned and for a number of blocks passed up one street and down another, plunging at last into a dark alley.

Upon emerging therefrom a block away, the soft felt hat had given place to a jaunty cap, while a pair of gold-rimmed eye-glasses perched upon the aquiline nose gave the wearer a decidedly youthful and debonnaire appearance. Approaching a secluded house in a dimly lighted location, he glanced sharply at the number, as though to reassure himself, then running swiftly up the front steps, he pulled the door-bell vigorously and awaited developments. After considerable delay the door was unlocked and partially opened by a hatchet-faced woman, who peered cautiously out, her features lighted by the uncertain rays of a candle which the draught momentarily threatened to extinguish.

"Good-evening, madam," said the stranger, airily. "Pardon such an unseasonable call, but I wish to see Mr. Lovering, who, I understand, has rooms here."

"There's no such person rooming here," she replied, sharply, her manner indicating that this bit of information ended the interview, but her interlocutor was not to be so easily dismissed.

"No such person!" he exclaimed, at the same time scrutinizing in apparent perplexity a small card which he had produced. "J. D. Lovering, 545 Jefferson Street; isn't this 545, madam?"

"Yes," she answered, testily, "this is 545; but there's nobody here by the name of Lovering."

The young man turned as if to go. "Have you any roomers at present?" he inquired, doubtfully.

"I have one, but his name is Mannering."

"Mannering," he repeated, thoughtfully, once more facing her; "I wonder if I am not mistaken in the name? Will you kindly describe Mr. Mannering?"

The woman hesitated, eying him suspiciously. "He ain't likely to be the man you want," she said, slowly, "for he don't have no callers, and he never goes anywhere, except out of the city once in a while on business. He's an oldish man, with dark hair and beard streaked with gray, and he wears dark glasses."

"Ah, no," the young man interrupted hastily, "that is not the man at all; the man I am looking for is rather young and a decided blond. I am sorry to have troubled you, madam; I beg a thousand pardons," and with profuse apologies he bowed himself down the steps, to the evident relief of the landlady.

As the door closed behind him, Mr. Rosenbaum paused a moment to reconnoitre. The house he had just left was the only habitable building visible in the immediate vicinity, but a few rods farther down the street was a small cabin, whose dilapidated appearance indicated that it was unoccupied. Approaching the cabin cautiously, Mr. Rosenbaum tried the door; it offered but slight resistance, and, entering, he found it, as he had surmised, empty and deserted. Stationing himself near a window which overlooked No. 545, he regarded the isolated dwelling with considerable interest. It was a two-story structure with a long extension in the rear, only one story in height. With the exception of a dim light in this rear portion, the house was entirely dark, which led Mr. Rosenbaum to the conclusion that the landlady's private apartments were in this part of the building and remote from the room occupied by her lodger, which he surmised to be the front room on the second floor, a side window of which faced the cabin.

For more than an hour Mr. Rosenbaum remained at his post, and at last had the satisfaction of seeing the tall figure in the fur coat approaching down the dimly lighted street. He ascended the steps of 545, let himself in with a night-key, and a moment later the gas in the upper front room was turned on, showing Mr. Rosenbaum's surmise to be correct. For an instant the flaring flame revealed a pale face without the dark glasses, and with a full, dark beard tinged with gray; then it was lowered and the window blinds were closely drawn, precluding the possibility of further observation. The face was like and yet unlike what Mr. Rosenbaum had expected to see; he determined upon a nearer and better view, without the dark glasses, before making any decisive move.

The following evening, as soon as it was dusk, found Mr. Rosenbaum again at the window of the deserted cabin, keenly observant of No. 545. A faint light burned in the rear of the lower floor, while in the front room upstairs a fire was evidently burning in an open grate, the rest of the house being in darkness. Presently a man's figure, tall and well formed, could be seen pacing up and down the room, appearing, vanishing, and reappearing in the wavering firelight. For nearly an hour he continued his perambulation, his hands clasped behind him as though absorbed in deep thought. At last, arousing himself from his revery, the man looked at his watch and vanished, reappearing ten minutes later at the front door, in the usual fur coat and cap, and, descending the steps, turned towards town and proceeded leisurely down the street, Mr. Rosenbaum following at some distance, but always keeping him in view and gradually diminishing the distance between them as the thoroughfare became more crowded, till they were nearly opposite each other.

Finally, the man paused before a restaurant and, turning, looked carefully up and down the street. For the first time he observed Mr. Rosenbaum and seemed to regard him with close attention, but the latter gentleman was absorbed in the contemplation of an assortment of diamonds and various gems displayed in a jeweller's window, directly opposite the restaurant. In the mirrored back of the show-case the restaurant was plainly visible, and Mr. Rosenbaum noted with satisfaction the other's evident interest in himself, and continued to study the contents of the show-case till the man had entered the restaurant, seating himself at one of the unoccupied tables. Having observed his man well started on the first course of dinner, Mr. Rosenbaum crossed the street slowly, entered the restaurant and with a pre-occupied air seated himself at the same table with Mr. Mannering. After giving his order, he proceeded to unfold the evening paper laid beside his plate, without even a glance at his vis-a-vis. His thoughts, however, were not on the printed page, but upon the man opposite, whom he had followed from city to city, hearing of him by various names and under various guises; hitherto unable to obtain more than a fleeting glimpse of him, but now brought face to face.

"Alias Henry J. Mannering at last!" he commented mentally, as he refolded his paper; "you have led me a long chase, my man, but you and I will now have our little game, and I will force you to show your hand before it is over!"

Glancing casually across at his neighbor, he found the dark glasses focused upon himself with such fixity that he responded with a friendly nod, and, making some trivial remark, found Mr. Mannering not at all averse to conversation. A few commonplaces were exchanged until the arrival of Mr. Rosenbaum's order, when the other remarked, -

"Evidently you do not find the cuisine of the Clifton House entirely satisfactory."

"It is very good," Mr. Rosenbaum answered, indifferently, "but

Maynard Barbour

an occasional change is agreeable. By the way, sir, have I met you at the Clifton? I do not remember to have had that pleasure."

"We have not met," replied the other. "I saw you there last evening, however, as I happened in soon after your arrival."

"Ah, so? I am very deficient in remembering faces."

Mr. Mannering hesitated a moment, then remarked with a smile, "I, on the contrary, am quite observant of faces, and yours seems somewhat familiar; have I not seen you elsewhere than here?"

Mr. Rosenbaum raised his eyebrows in amusement. "It is very possible you have, my dear sir; I travel constantly, and for aught that I know you may have seen me in nearly every city on the globe. May I inquire your business, sir? Do you also travel?"

"No," said Mr. Mannering, slowly, but apparently relieved by Mr. Rosenbaum's answer, "I am not engaged in any particular line of business at present. I am interested in mining to a considerable extent, and am out here just now looking after my properties. How do you find business in your line?"

Mr. Rosenbaum shook his head with a slight shrug.

"Nothing so far to make it worth my while to stay. You see, sir, for such a trade as ours we want only the finest gems that can be bought; we have no use for ordinary stones, and that is all I have seen here so far;" and, having thrown out his bait, he awaited results.

A long pause followed, while Mr. Mannering toyed with his fork, drawing numerous diagrams on the table-cloth.

I think," he said at last, slowly, "that I could get you one or two fine diamonds if you cared to buy and would give anything like their true valuation."

"That would depend, of course, upon the quality of the diamonds; really fine gems we are always ready to buy and to pay a good price for."

"If I am any judge of diamonds, these are valuable stones," said Mr. Mannering, "and the owner of them, who is a friend of mine, being himself a connoisseur in that line, would not be likely to entertain any false ideas regarding their value."

"And your friend wishes to sell them?"

"I am inclined to think that he might dispose of one or two for a sufficient consideration, subject, however, to one condition,- that no questions will be asked."

"That goes without saying, my dear sir; asking questions is not our business. We are simply looking for the finest stones that money can buy, without regard to anything else. Perhaps," added Mr. Rosenbaum, tentatively, "we might arrange with your friend for a meeting between the three of us."

"That would be impracticable," Mr. Mannering replied; "he is out of the city; and furthermore I know he would not care to appear in the transaction, but would prefer to have me conduct the negotiations. I was going to suggest that if you were to remain here a few days, I shall see my friend in a day or so, as I am going out to look over some mining properties in which we are both interested, and I could bring in some of the gems with me, and we might then see what terms we could make."

"I can remain over, sir, if you can make it an object for me, and if the stones prove satisfactory I have no doubt we can make terms. Why, sir," Mr. Rosenbaum leaned across the table and his voice assumed a confidential tone, "money would be no object with me if I could get one or two particular gems that I want. For instance, I have one diamond that I would go to the ends of the earth and pay a small fortune when I got there, if I could only find a perfect match for it!" and he launched forth upon an enthusiastic description of the stone, expatiating upon its enormous size, its wonderful brilliancy and perfection, adding in conclusion, "and its workmanship shows it to be at least two hundred years old! Think of that, sir! What would I not give to be able to match it!"

A peculiar expression flitted over his listener's face, not unobserved by Mr. Rosenbaum. He made no immediate response, however, but when at last the two men separated, it was with the agreement that they should dine together at the same caf, three days later, when Mr. Mannering would have returned from his conference with his friend, at which time, if the latter cared to dispose of his jewels, they would be submitted for inspection.

Upon retiring to his room that night, Mr. Rosenbaum sat for some time in deep abstraction, and when he finally turned off the gas, he murmured, -

"He will produce the jewels all right, and may heaven preserve us both from the hoodoo!"

For the two days next ensuing, Mr. Rosenbaum watched closely the arrivals in the city, but, notwithstanding his vigilance, there slipped in unaware, on the evening of the second day, a quiet, unassuming man, who went to the Windsor Hotel, registering there as "A. J. Johnson, Chicago." At a late hour, while Mr. Rosenbaum, in the solitude of his own room, was perfecting his plans for the following day, Mr. Johnson, who was making a tour of inspection among the leading hotels, sauntered carelessly into the office of the Clifton. He seemed rather socially inclined, and soon was engaged in conversation with the proprietor and a dozen of the "boys," all of whom were informed that he was travelling through the West on the lookout for "snaps" in the way of mining investments. This announcement produced general good feeling, and there were not wanting plenty who offered to take Mr. Johnson around the city on the following day and introduce him to the leading mining men and promoters.

"Much obliged, boys," said Mr. Johnson, "but there's no rush. I expect to meet some friends here in a few days, and till they come I shall simply look around on the q. t., you understand, and make some observations for myself. And that reminds me, gentlemen," he added, "do any of you happen to know a man by the name of Mannering, who is interested in mines out here?"

"Mannering?" answered one of the group; "there's a man by that name has been around here off and on for the last two or three months; but I didn't know he was interested in mines to any extent, though he seems to have plenty of money."

"I think that is the man I have in mind; will you describe him?"

"Well, he's tall, about middle age, rather gray, wears blue glasses, and never has anything to say to anybody; a queer sort of fellow."

Mr. Johnson nodded, but before he could reply, another in the group remarked, "Oh, that's the fellow you mean, is it? I've seen him at the Royal Caf, for the last six weeks, and in all that time he's never exchanged a dozen words with anybody, till here, the other night, that diamond Dutchman of yours," addressing the proprietor of the Clifton, "came waltzing in there, and I'll be hanged if the two didn't get as confidential over their dinner as two old women over a cup of tea."

Mr. Johnson turned towards the proprietor with a quiet smile. "The 'diamond Dutchman!' Is he a guest of your house?"

"Mr. Rosenbaum?" Yes; do you know him?"

"Not by name, but I think I have seen the gentleman on my travels; engaged in the jewelry business, isn't he, and carries his advertisements on his shirt-front and fingers?"

"That's the man," the proprietor replied, amid a general laugh. "Why?" He's all right, isn't he?"

"All right for aught that I know, sir; I haven't the pleasure of the gentleman's acquaintance, though possibly I may have if we both remain here long enough," and he carelessly turned the subject of conversation.

A little later, as Mr. Johnson left the Clifton, he soliloquized, "Well, if I haven't exactly killed two birds with one stone, I think I've snared two birds in one trap. Since coming West I haven't located one without seeing or hearing of the other; it's my belief they're 'pals,' and if I can pull in the pair, so much the better."

The following evening found Mr. Johnson in the vicinity of the Royal Caf,; having discovered a small newsstand opposite, he strolled in thither, and, buying a couple of papers, seated himself in a quiet corner, prepared to take observations. He had not waited long when Mr. Mannering made his appearance, and, after pausing a moment to look up and down the street, entered the restaurant. He had been seated but a moment when Mr. Rosenbaum appeared, crossing the street, having evidently left the jeweller's store, and also entered the caf,. The two men shook hands and immediately withdrew to one of the private boxes. Mr. Johnson had visited the Royal Caf, earlier in the day and made himself familiar with its interior arrangement. Knowing the box just taken to be No. 3, and that No. 4 directly opposite was unoccupied, he at once proceeded across the street to the restaurant. Stopping at the cashier's desk, he said in a low tone, "I expect some friends later, and don't wish to be disturbed till they come; understand?"

The man nodded, and Mr. Johnson passed on noiselessly into No. 4. Meanwhile, the occupants of No. 3 having received their orders, dismissed the waiter, with the information that when they needed his services they would ring for him. Mr. Mannering was visibly excited, so much so that his dinner remained almost untasted, and the other, observing his evident agitation, pushed aside his own plate and, folding his arms upon the table, inquired indifferently, -

"Well, my dear sir, what was your friend's decision?"

For reply, the other drew from his pocket a small case, which he silently handed across the table. Mr. Rosenbaum opened it, disclosing, as he did so, a pair of diamonds of moderate size, but of unusual brilliancy and perfectly matched. He examined them silently, scrutinizing them closely, while his face indicated considerable dissatisfaction.

"What does your friend expect for these?" he asked at length.

"What will you give for them?" was the counter-question.

"I do not care to set a price on them, for I do not want them," he replied, rather shortly.

"I think," said Mr. Mannering, "that my friend would dispose of them at a reasonable figure, as he is at present in need of ready cash with which to consummate an important mining negotiation."

After considerable fencing and parrying, Mr. Rosenbaum made an offer for the gems, to which Mr. Mannering demurred.

"Show me a higher class of gems and I will offer you a better price," said Mr. Rosenbaum, finally seeming to grow impatient. "Show me one like this, for instance, and I will offer you a small fortune," and opening a case which he had quickly drawn from his pocket, he took from it an enormous diamond, beside whose dazzling brilliancy the pair of gems under consideration seemed suddenly to grow dim and lustreless. He held it up and a thousand rays of prismatic light flashed in as many different directions.

Maynard Barbour

"What do you think of that, my dear sir? When I can find a match for that magnificent stone, we can fill an order which we have held for more than twelve months from the royal house in Germany. But where will I find it?"

Twirling the gem carelessly between his thumb and finger, he watched the face of his companion and saw it change to a deathly pallor.

"May I see that for one moment?" he asked, and his voice sounded unnatural and constrained, while the hand which he extended across the table trembled visibly.

"Most certainly, sir," Mr. Rosenbaum replied, and, in compliance with the request, handed to Mr. Mannering the gem which the latter had himself disposed of less than three months before in one of the large Western cities. Nothing could escape the piercing eyes now fastened upon that face with its strange pallor, its swiftly changing expression. Unconscious of this scrutiny, Mr. Mannering regarded the gem silently, then removed his glasses for a closer inspection. Having satisfied his curiosity, he returned the stone to Mr. Rosenbaum, and as he did so, found the eyes of the latter fixed not upon the gem, but upon his own face. Something in their glance seemed to disconcert him for an instant, but he quickly recovered himself, and, replacing the colored glasses, remarked with a forced composure,-

"That is a magnificent stone. May I ask when and where you found it?"

"I picked it up in one of your cities some three months ago, maybe, more or less."

"You bought it in this country, then? Why may you not expect to match it here?"

"Simply on the theory, my dear sir, that the lightning never strikes twice in the same place."

"Well, sir," said Mr. Mannering, calmly, "I will show you a stone so perfect a match for that, you yourself could not distinguish between the two."

"You have such a diamond!" Mr. Rosenbaum exclaimed; "why then are you wasting time with these?" and he pushed the smaller diamonds from him with a gesture of contempt. "Why did you not produce it in the first place?"

"Because," replied Mr. Mannering, his composure now fully restored, "I do not propose to produce it until I know somewhere near what you will give for it."

"My dear sir," Mr. Rosenbaum's tones became eager, "as I have already told you, if I can match this stone," placing it on the table between them, "I will pay you a small fortune; money would be no object; you could have your own price."

Without further words, Mr. Mannering drew forth a small package, which he carefully opened, and, taking therefrom an exact duplicate of the wonderful gem, placed it upon the table beside the latter.

With a smile which the other did not see, Mr. Rosenbaum bent his head to examine the stones; he had recognized his man in the brief instant that their eyes had met, and now, within his grasp, lay, as he well knew from the description which he carried, two of the finest diamonds in the famous Mainwaring collection of jewels, stolen less than six months before; his triumph was almost complete.

Meanwhile, Mr. Johnson, who had overheard much of their conversation, was congratulating himself upon the near success of his own schemes, when the officiousness of a waiter overthrew the plans of all parties and produced the greatest confusion. Catching sight of the gentleman waiting in No. 4, he ignored the cashier's instructions and entered the box to take his order. Mr. Johnson's reply, low and brief though it was, caught the quick ear of Mr. Rosenbaum, who muttered under his breath, -

"The hoodoo! confound him!"

At the same instant a draught lifted the curtain to NO. 3, revealing to the astonished Mannering a view of Mr. Johnson's profile in the opposite box. His own face grew white as the table-cloth before him; he reached wildly for the diamond, but both gems were gone, and Rosenbaum confronted him with a most sinister expression.

"My diamond!" he gasped.

"The diamonds are safe," replied the other in a low tone, "and you," addressing Mannering by his true name, "the more quiet you are just now the better."

The elder man's face grew livid with rage and fear, and, rising suddenly to his feet, his tall form towered far above Rosenbaum.

"Wretch!" he hissed, with an oath, "you have betrayed me, curse you!" and, dealing the smaller man a blow which floored him, he rushed from the box.

In an instant Rosenbaum staggered to his feet, and, pausing only long enough to make sure of the safety of the jewels, rushed from the caf,, reaching the street just in time to see his man jump into a cab, which whirled swiftly and started down the street at break-neck speed. Two cabmen, talking at a short distance, hurried to the scene, and, calling one of them, Mr. Rosenbaum hastily took a second cab and started in pursuit of the first, but not before he had caught a glimpse of Mr. Johnson making active preparations to follow them both.

"Hang that fellow!" he muttered, as he heard wheels behind him. "This is the third time he has spoiled the game; but I've got the winning hand, and he'll not beat me out of it!"

By this time the first cab, having turned a corner a short distance ahead, was out of sight, but Rosenbaum, convinced from the direction taken of its destination, and knowing a more direct route, shouted to the driver what streets to follow, and to come out upon the alley near No. 545 Jefferson Street.

"The old fellow will think I've lost the trail when he finds he's not followed," he soliloquized, amid the joltings of the vehicle, "and maybe it will throw the hoodoo off the track."

But Mr. Johnson had no intention of being thrown off. He had seen cab No. 2 a take a different course, and, having lost sight of No. 1, decided that a bird in the hand would be worth two in the bush, and that he would follow up the "pal."

As cab No. 2 approached Jefferson Street, Rosenbaum called to the driver to slacken and drive on the dark side of the alley. He jumped out to reconnoitre; a cab was just stopping at No. 545, a tall figure got out and hastily disappeared up the steps, while the cab whirled rapidly away.

"Turn about, drive back quietly, and answer no questions," Rosenbaum said, slipping a bill into the driver's hand, and then glided swiftly through the shadow to No. 545. His maneuvers were seen, however, by Mr. Johnson, who immediately proceeded to follow his example.

Running quickly up the steps to No. 545, Rosenbaum produced a bunch of skeleton keys, which he proceeded to try. The first was useless, the second ditto; he heard steps approaching; the third fitted the lock, but, as it turned, a hand was laid upon his shoulder, a dark lantern flashed in his face, and a voice said, -

"Your game is up, my man; you had better come with me as peaceably as possible!"

For answer, the other turned quickly, and, without a word, lifted the lapel of his coat, where a star gleamed brightly in the rays of the lantern.

The band holding the lantern dropped suddenly, and its owner ejaculated, "Heavens and earth! what does this mean? Who are you?"

"I am Dan McCabe, at your service," was the cool reply; then, as the other remained speechless with astonishment, McCabe continued: "I've no time to waste with you, Mr. Merrick; we may have a desperate piece of work on hand; but if you'll come with me, I give you my word for it that before this job is over you'll meet the biggest surprise of your life."

Pushing open the door, McCabe noiselessly climbed the stairs, beckoning Merrick to follow. By the light of the dark lantern he selected the door leading to the room occupied by Mann-ering, and, after listening a moment, nodded signifi-cantly to Merrick.

"Is he there?" the latter whispered.

"He is there," said McCabe, grimly, "but not the man you are looking for. I'll tell you who is there," and he whispered in his ear.

Merrick staggered as if from a blow. "Great God!" he exclaimed aloud.

There was a sudden sound within as of some one frightened and moving hastily. McCabe again called the man by name, and demanded admittance. There was a moment's silence, and then McCabe, with Merrick's aid, forced in the door, and as it yielded there came from within the sharp report of a revolver, followed by a heavy groan.

CHAPTER XXVI

MAINWARING VS. MAINWARING

The case of Mainwaring versus Mainwaring had been set for the opening of the December term of court, being the first case on the docket. The intervening weeks, crowded with preparation for the coming litigation, had passed, and now, on the eve of the contest, each side having marshalled its forces, awaited the beginning of the fray, each alike confident of victory and each alike little dreaming of the end. >From near and far was gathered an array of legal talent as well as of expert testimony seldom equalled, all for the purpose of determining the validity or invalidity of a bit of paper-yellow with age, time-worn and musty which stood as an insurmountable barrier between Ralph Mainwaring and the fulfilment of his long cherished project.

The Fair Oaks tragedy still remained as deep a mystery as on the morning when, in all its horror of sickening detail, it had startled and shocked the entire community. No trace of the murderer had been as yet reported, and even Mr. Whitney had been forced to acknowledge in reply to numerous inquiries that he had of late received no tidings whatever from Merrick, either of success or failure.

Since the announcement of Harold Mainwaring at the club that he would not touch a farthing of the Mainwaring estate until not only his own name should be cleared of the slightest imputation of murder, but until the murder itself should be avenged, it had been rumored that the party at the Waldorf was in possession of facts containing the clue to the whole mystery. Though this was mere conjecture, it was plainly evident that whatever secrets that party held in its possession were not likely to be divulged before their time. The party had been augmented by the arrival of the senior member of the firm of Barton & Barton, while the register of the Waldorf showed at that time numerous other arrivals from London, all of whom proved to be individuals of a severely judicial appearance and on extremely intimate terms with the original Waldorf party. Of the business of the former, however, or the movements of the latter, nothing definite could be learned. Despatches in cipher still flashed daily over the wires, but their import remained a matter of the merest surmise to the curious world outside.

Ralph Mainwaring, on the contrary, since the arrival of his London attorneys, Upham and Blackwell, with Graham, the well-known chirographical expert, had seized every opportunity for rendering himself and them as conspicuous as possible, while his boasts of their well-laid plans, the strong points in their case, and their ultimate triumph, formed his theme on all occasions. Mr. Whitney's position at this time was not an enviable one, for Ralph Mainwaring, having of late become dimly conscious of a lack of harmony between himself and his New York attorney, took special delight in frequently flouting his opinions and advice in the presence of the English solicitors; but that gentleman, mindful of a rapidly growing account, wisely pocketed his pride, and continued to serve his client with the most urbane courtesy, soothing his wounded sensibilities with an extra fee for every snub.

On the day prior to that set for the opening of the trial, among the numerous equipages drawn up at one of the piers, awaiting an incoming ocean-liner, was the Mainwaring carriage, containing, as usual, Ralph Mainwaring, Upham and Blackwell, and Mr. Whitney. The carriage and its occupants formed the centre of attraction to a considerable portion of the crowd, until attention was suddenly diverted by the sight of a stylish turnout in the shape of an elegant trap and a pair of superb bays driven tandem, which passed the Mainwaring carriage and took its position at some distance nearer the pier. Seated in the trap were Harold Mainwaring and Hugh Mainwaring, junior. Their appearance together at that particular time and place excited no little wonder and comment, especially when, the gangplank having been thrown down, the young men left the turnout in care of a policeman and walked rapidly towards the hurrying stream of passengers, followed more slowly by Ralph Mainwaring and his party.

All was explained a few moments later, as that embodiment of geniality, William Mainwaring Thornton, loomed up in the crowd, his daughter upon one arm, upon the other Miss Carleton, and accompanied by Mrs. Hogarth and the usual retinue of attendants.

"Looks like a family reunion, by George!" exclaimed one of the on-lookers, as a general exchange of greetings ensued, but to a close observer it was evident that between some members of the different parties the relations were decidedly strained. No so with Mr. Thornton, however; his first greetings were for the young men.

"Well, well, Hugh, you contumacious young rascal! how are you?. I hear you've kicked over the traces and set the governor and his sovereigns at defiance! Well, you've shown yourself a Mainwaring, that's all I have to say! Here is a young lady, however, who is waiting to give you a piece of her mind; you'll have to settle with her."

"Papa!" exclaimed Edith Thornton in faint protest, her fair face suffused with blushes as she came forward to meet her lover, while her father turned towards Harold Mainwaring.

"Well, my dear sir," he said, extending his hand with the utmost cordiality, "I am glad to meet you in your own proper sphere at last; I always thought you were far too good looking for a secretary! But, joking aside, my dear boy, let me assure you that as the son of Harold Scott Mainwaring, one of the most royal fellows I ever knew, I congratulate you and wish you success."

Deeply touched by Mr. Thornton's kindness and his allusion to his father, the young man thanked him with considerable emotion.

"That is all right," the elder man responded heartily; "I was very sorry not to have met you in London, but I heard the particulars of your story from Winifred, and-well, I consider her a very level-headed young woman, and I think you are to be congratulated on that score also."

"No one is better aware of that fact than I," said the young man, warmly, and passed on to meet the young ladies, while Mr. Thornton turned to confront the frowning face of Ralph Mainwaring.

"Hello, Mainwaring! what's the matter?" you look black as a thunder-cloud! Did you have something indigestible for luncheon?"

"Matter enough I should say," growled the other, unsuccessfully trying to ignore Mr. Thornton's outstretched hand, "to find you hobnobbing with that blackguard!"

Mr. Thornton glanced over his shoulder at the young people with a comical look of perplexity. "Well, you see how it is yourself, Mainwaring: what is a fellow to do? This is a house divided against itself, as it were, and no matter what my personal sentiments towards you might be, I find myself forced to maintain a position of strict neutrality."

"Neutrality be damned! you had better maintain better parental government in your own family!"

"As you do in yours, for instance."

"You know very well," continued Ralph Mainwaring, flushing angrily, "that if you had forbidden Edith marrying Hugh under present conditions, he would have got down off his high horse very quickly."

"That is something I would never do," Mr. Thornton replied, calmly, "for two reasons; first, I have never governed my daughter by direct commands and prohibitions, and, second, I think just as much of Hugh Mainwaring without his father's money as with it; more, if it is to be accompanied with the conditions which you imposed."

"Then am I to understand," demanded the other, angrily, "that you intend to go against me in this matter?"

"My dear Mainwaring," said Mr. Thornton, much as he would address a petulant child, "this is all the merest nonsense. I am not going against you, for I have no part in this contest; my position is necessarily neutral; but if you want my opinion of the whole matter, I will tell you frankly that I think, for once in your life, you have bitten off more than you can swallow, and you will find it so before long."

"Perhaps it might be just as well to reserve your opinion till it is called for," the other answered, shortly.

"All right," returned Mr. Thornton, with imperturbable good humor; "but any time that you want to wager a thousand or so on the outcome of this affair, remember the money is ready for you!"

The conversation changed, but Ralph Mainwaring was far more chagrined and annoyed than he would have acknowledged. Mr. Thornton's words rang in his ears till they seemed an augury of defeat, and, though outwardly as dogged and defiant as ever, he was unable to banish them, or to throw off the strange sense of depression which followed.

Meanwhile, amid the discordant elements surrounding them,

Harold Mainwaring and Winifred Carleton found little opportunity for any but the most desultory conversation, but happily there was little need for words between them. Heart can speak to heart through the subtle magnetism of a hand-clasp, or the swift flash from eye to eye, conveying meanings for which words often prove inadequate.

"You wrote that you were confident of victory, and your looks bear it out," she said, 'with a radiant smile; "but I would have come just the same, even had there been no hope of success for you."

"I need no assurance of your faith and loyalty," he replied, gazing tenderly into her luminous eyes, "but your coming will make my triumph ten times sweeter."

"Of course you will spend the evening with, us at our hotel,-uncle cabled for apartments at the Savoy,-and I am all impatience to learn whatever you are at liberty to tell me concerning your case, for there must have been some wonderful developments in your favor soon after your arrival in this country, you have seemed so much more hopeful; and do not let me forget, I have something to show you which will interest you. It is a written statement by Hugh Mainwaring himself regarding this identical will that is causing all this controversy."

"A statement of Hugh Mainwaring's!" Harold repeated in astonishment; "how did it come into your possession?"

"That is the strangest part of it," she replied, hurriedly, for they had now reached the carriages in waiting for them. "I received it through the mail, from America, a few days before I left London, and from-you cannot imagine whom-Mr. Merrick, the detective. How he ever knew my address, or how he should surmise that I was particularly interested in you," she blushed very prettily with these words, "is more than I can understand, however."

"I think I can explain that part of it," said Harold, with a smile; "but how such a statement ever came into his hands is a mystery to me. I will see you this evening without fail," and, assisting Miss Carleton into the carriage, he bade her au revoir, and hastened to rejoin young Mainwaring.

That evening witnessed rather a novel reception in the private parlors of the Savoy; both parties to the coming contest being entertained by their mutual friends. When Harold Mainwaring finally succeeded in securing a tete-a-tete conversation with Miss Carleton, she placed in his hands a small packet, saying,-

"You will find in this the statement of which I spoke to you, and I wish you would also read the accompanying note, and explain how the writer came to have so good an understanding of the situation."

With eager haste he drew forth a sheet of paper little less time-worn and yellowed than the ancient will itself, upon which was written, in the methodical business hand with which he was so familiar, a brief statement to the effect that a certain accom-panying document described as the last will and testament of Ralph Maxwell Mainwaring had been drawn and executed as such on the night preceding his death, its intent and purpose being to reconvey to an elder son the family estate, to which he had previously forfeited all right and title; that efforts made to communicate with the beneficiary had proved unavailing, as he had left the country and his place of residence was unknown. Then followed Hugh Mainwaring's signature. At the bottom of the page, however, was a foot-note of much later date, which put a different complexion on the foregoing, and which read as follows:

"It has now been ascertained for a certainty that the beneficiary mentioned in the accompanying will is no longer living. I have, therefore, a clear title to the estate, as it would revert to me at his death. The document itself is worthless, except as a possible means of silencing that scoundrel, Hobson, should he attempt to reveal anything of the past, as he has threatened to do, and for this purpose I shall retain it in my possession until such time as I make final adjustment of my affairs.

"HUGH MAINWARING."

"Ah," said Harold Mainwaring, thoughtfully, as he suddenly recalled the morning when he had discovered Merrick and his assistant dragging the lake at Fair Oaks, "I think I understand how this paper came into Merrick's possession. It was evidently kept in the same receptacle which held the will, but in my haste and excitement at the discovery of the will I must have overlooked it. The box in which these papers were kept afterwards fell into Merrick's hands, and he must have found this."

"That solves one riddle, here is the other," and Miss Carleton handed her lover a small note, covered with a fine, delicate chirography whose perfectly formed characters revealed a mind accustomed to the study of minute details and appreciative of their significance. He opened it and read the following:

"MY DEAR MISS CARLETON:

"Pardon the liberty I take, but, thinking the enclosed bit of paper might be of some possible assistance to one in whose success I believe you are deeply interested, I send it herewith, as, for obvious reasons, I deem this circuitous method of transmission better than one more direct.

"As when taking leave of you on board the 'Campania,' so now, permit me to assure you that if I can ever serve you as a friend, you have but to command me. "Most sincerely yours,

"C. D. MERRICK."

A smile of amusement lighted Harold Mainwaring's face as, glancing up from the note, his eyes met those of Miss Carleton's with their expression of perplexed inquiry.

"This is easily explained," he said; "do you remember the tall, slender man whom we observed on board the 'Campania' as being rather unsocial and taciturn?"

"Yes, I remember he rather annoyed me, for I fancied he concentrated considerably more thought and attention upon us than the circumstances called for.

"Which shows you were more observing than I. Such a thought never entered my mind till 1 had been about ten days in London, when it occurred to me that, considering the size of the town and the fact that he and I were strangers, we met with astonishing frequency. I have since learned that he was a detective sent over to London on an important case, and being an intimate friend of Merrick's, the latter, who, I am informed, was shadowing me pretty closely at the time, requested him to follow my movements and report to him, which he evidently did, as I have since heard that Merrick had expressed to one or two that he was not at all surprised by the developments which followed my return to this country. Consequently, it is not to be wondered at if he has an inkling that you may be somewhat interested in this case."

"But what could have been Mr. Merrick's object in shadowing you?"

"I cannot say. It may have been only part of his professional vigilance in letting nothing escape his observation; but from the first I was conscious of his close espionage of my movements. Now, however, I am satisfied that he had none but friendly intentions, and I appreciate his kindness, not only towards myself, but more especially towards you."

"Will that statement be of any assistance to you, do you think?"

"I hardly think so under our present plans," he replied, after a moment's reflection; "under recent developments our plans differ so radically from what we first intended, that we will probably have little use for any of the testimony which we had originally prepared."

"But these recent developments which have so changed your plans must certainly have been in your favor and have rendered your success the more assured, have they not?"

"Not only more assured, but more speedy and complete. To me, the coming trial means far more than the settlement of the controversy over the estate; it means the complete and final vindication of my character, so that I can stand before you and before the world acquitted of every charge which my enemies would have sought to bring against me."

Her face grew radiant with sympathy. "I well know what that means to you, and I would be first to congratulate you on such a victory, for your own sake; but I needed no public acquittal to convince me of your innocence,-not even," she added, slowly, "when you yourself for some reason, which I hope one day to understand, were unable to assure me of it."

His dark eyes, glowing with suppressed feeling, met hers, the intensity of their gaze thrilling her heart to its inmost depths.

"Do not think that I can ever forget that," he said in low tones which seemed to vibrate through her whole being; "do not think that through any triumphs or joys which the future may bring, I can ever forget, for one moment, the faith and love which stood loyally by me in my darkest hour,-the hour when the shadow of the crime, which has forever darkened Fair Oaks, was closing about my very soul!"

Startled at the sudden solemnity of his words and manner, she remained silent, her eyes meeting his without a shade of doubt or distrust, but full of wondering, tender inquiry, to which he replied, while for an instant he laid his hand lightly and caressingly on hers, "Only a few days longer, love, and I will tell you all!"

On the morning of the following day a dense crowd awaited,

at an early hour, the opening of the December term of court; a crowd which was steadily augmented till, when the case of Mainwaring versus Mainwaring was called, every available seat was filled. All parties to the suit were promptly on hand, and amid a silence almost oppressive, proponent and contestant, with their counsel and witnesses, passed down the long aisle to their respective places.

Seldom had the, old court-room, in its long and varied history, held so imposing an array of legal talent as was assemble that morning within its walls. The principal attorneys for the contestant were Hunnewell & Whitney of New York, and the London firm of Upham & Blackwell, while grouped about these were a number of lesser luminaries, whose milder rays would sufficiently illumine the minor points in the case. But at a glance it was clearly evident that the galaxy of legal lights opposing them contained only stars of the first magnitude. Most prominent among the latter were Barton & Barton, of London, with Mr. Sutherland and his life-long friend and coadjutor, M. D. Montague, with whom he had never failed to take counsel in cases of special importance, all men of superb physique and magnificent brains; while slightly in the rear, as reinforcements, were the Hon. I. Ponsonby Roget, Q.C., another Q.C. whose name had not yet reached the public ear, and a Boston jurist whose brilliant career had made his name famous throughout the United States.

Prominent among the spectators were Mr. Scott and Mr. Thornton, apparently on the best of terms, and watching proceedings with demonstrations of the liveliest interest, while seated at a little distance, less demonstrative, but no less interested, was young Mainwaring, accompanied by Miss Thornton and Miss Carleton.

The first day was devoted to preliminaries, the greater part of the time being consumed in the selection of a jury. One after another of those impaneled was examined, challenged by one ide or the other, and dismissed; not until the entire panel had been exhausted and several special venires issued, was there found the requisite number sufficiently unprejudiced to meet the requirements of the situation.

The remainder of the day was occupied by counsel for contestant in making the opening statement. A review of the grounds upon which the contest was based was first read by one of the assistant attorneys, after which Mr. Whitney followed with a lengthy statement which occupied nearly an hour. He reviewed in detail the circumstances of the case, beginning with the death of Hugh Mainwaring, and laying special stress upon his irreproachable reputation. He stated that it would be shown to the jury that the life of Hugh Mainwaring had been above suspicion, an irrefutable argument against the charges of fraud and dishonesty which had been brought against him by those who sought to establish the will in contest. It would also be shown that the said document was a forgery, the result of a prearranged plan, devised by those who had been lifelong enemies of Hugh Mainwaring and the contestant, to defraud the latter of his rights, and to obtain possession of the Mainwaring estate; and that the transparency of the device in bringing the so-called will to light at that particular time and under those particular circumstances was only too plainly evident.

Mr. Whitney was warming with his subject, but at this juncture he was peremptorily called to order by Mr. Sutherland, who stated that he objected to counsel making an argument to the jury, when he should confine himself simply to an opening statement. Mr. Whitney's face flushed as a ripple of amusement ran through the courtroom, but the objection was sustained, and, after a brief summary of what the contestant proposed to show, he resumed his seat, and the court then adjourned until the following morning.

The first testimony introduced on the following day was to establish the unimpeachable honesty and integrity of the deceased Hugh Mainwaring. Both Mr. Elliot and Mr. Chittenden were called to the stand, and their examination-particularly the cross-examination, in which a number of damaging admissions were made-occupied nearly the entire forenoon; the remainder of the day being devoted to the testimony of witnesses from abroad, introduced to show that for years a bitter estrangement had existed between Frederick Mainwaring Scott, the alleged foster-father of the proponent, and the members of the Mainwaring family,-the deceased Hugh Mainwaring and the contestant in particular; and also to show the implacable anger of Ralph Maxwell Mainwaring against his elder son and the extreme improbability of his ever relenting in his favor.

Day after day dragged slowly on, still taken up with the examination of witnesses for contestant; examinations too tedious and monotonous for repetition, but full of interest to the crowds which came and went, increasing daily, till, on the days devoted to the expert testimony, galleries and aisles were packed to overflowing, while throngs of eager listeners gathered in the corridors about the various exits.

It soon became evident that Ralph Mainwaring's oft repeated assertions concerning the elaborate preparation he had made for the coming contest were no idle boast. Nothing that human ingenuity could devise had been left undone which could help to turn the scale in his own favor. The original will of Ralph Maxwell Mainwaring, by which his elder son was disinherited, was produced and read in court. Both wills were photographed, and numerous copies, minute in every detail, made, in order to show by comparison the differences in their respective signatures. Under powerful microscopes it was discovered that several pauses had been made in the signature of the later will. Electric batteries were introduced to show that the document had been steeped in coffee and tobacco juice to give it the appearance of great age. Interesting chemical experiments were performed, by which a piece of new paper was made to look stained and spotted as if mildewed and musty, while by the use of tiny files and needles, the edges, having first been slightly scalloped, were grated and the paper punctured, till it presented a very similar aspect to the will itself as though worn through at the creases and frayed and tattered with age.

But the accumulation of this overwhelming mass of expert testimony failed to make the impression upon counsel for proponent which had been anticipated by the other side. Mr. Sutherland varied the monotony of the direct examinations by frequent and pertinent objections, while Barton & Barton took occasional notes, which were afterwards passed to Sutherland and Montague, and by them used with telling effect in the cross-examinations, but the faces of one and all wore an expression inscrutable as that of the sphinx.

Only once was their equanimity disturbed by any ripple of agitation, and then the incident was so little understood as to be soon forgotten. As the third day of the trial was drawing to a close, a despatch in cipher was handed Mr. Sutherland, which when translated seemed to produce a startling effect upon its readers. Barton & Barton exchanged glances and frowned heavily; Mr. Sutherland's face for one brief moment showed genuine alarm, and Harold Mainwaring, upon reading the slip of paper passed to him, grew pale. A hurried consultation followed and Mr. Montague left the court-room.

On the following morning the papers announced that at 11 P.M. the preceding night, the Victoria, the private car of the president of one of the principal railway lines, with special engine attached, had left for the West, evidently on business of great importance, as everything on the road had been ordered side-tracked. It was stated that no particulars could be ascertained, however, regarding either her passengers or her destination, the utmost secrecy being maintained by those on board, including even the trainmen. This item, though attracting some attention, caused less comment than did the fact that for the three days next ensuing, neither the senior Mr. Barton nor Mr. Montague was present in court; but no one suspected any connection between the two events, or dreamed that the above gentlemen, with two of New York's most skilled surgeons, were the occupants of the president's private car, then hastening westward at almost lightning speed.

On the afternoon of the sixth day of the trial, as it became apparent that the seemingly interminable evidence submitted by contestant was nearly at an end, the eager impatience of the waiting crowd could scarcely be restrained within the limits of order. A change was noticeable also in the demeanor of proponent and his counsel. For the two days preceding they had appeared as though under some tension or suspense; now they seemed to exhibit almost an indifference to the proceedings, as though the outcome of the contest were already a settled fact, while a marked gravity accompanied each word and gesture.

At last the contestant rested, and all eyes were fixed upon Mr. Sutherland, as, after a brief pause, he rose to make, as was supposed, his opening statement. Instead of addressing the jury, however, he turned towards Judge Bingham.

"Your honor," he began, in slow, measured tones, "it now lacks but little more than an hour of the usual time for adjournment, and after the constant strain which has been put upon our nerves for the past six days, I feel that none of us, including yourself, your honor, are in a sufficiently receptive mood to listen to the testimony which the proponent has to offer. In addition to this is the fact that our most important witness is not present this afternoon. I would therefore ask for an adjournment to be taken until ten o'clock next Monday morning, at which time I will guarantee your honor and the gentlemen of the jury that the intricate and elaborate web of fine-spun theories which has been presented will be swept away in fewer hours than the days which have been required for its construction."

There was an attempt at applause, which was speedily checked, and without further delay the court adjourned.

As judge, jury, and counsel took their respective places on the following Monday at the hour appointed, the scene presented by the old court-room was one never before witnessed in its history. Every available inch of standing room, both on the main floor and in the galleries, was taken; throngs were congregated about the doorways, those in the rear standing on chairs and benches that they might obtain a view over the heads of their more fortunate neighbors, while even the recesses formed by the enormous windows were packed with humanity, two rows deep, the outer row embracing the inner one in its desperate efforts to maintain its equilibrium.

The opposing sides presented a marked contrast in their appearance that morning. Ralph Mainwaring betrayed a nervous excitement very unusual in one of his phlegmatic temperament; his face alternately flushed and paled, and though much of the old defiant bravado remained, yet he awaited the opening of proceedings with visible impatience. Nor was Mr. Whitney less excited, his manner revealing both agitation and anxiety. On the part of Harold Mainwaring and his counsel, however, there was no agitation, no haste; every movement was characterized by composure and deliberation, yet something in their bearing-something subtle and indefinable but nevertheless irresistible-impressed the sensibilities of the vast audience much as the oppressive calm which precedes an electric storm. All felt that some great crisis was at hand, and it was amid almost breathless silence that Mr. Sutherland arose to make his opening statement.

"Gentlemen of the jury," he began, and the slow, resonant tones penetrated to the farthest corner and out into the corridors where hundreds were eagerly listening, "as a defence to the charges sought to be established in your hearing, we propose to show, not by fine-spun theories based upon electrical and chemical experiments, nor brilliant sophistries deduced from microscopic observations, but by the citation of stubborn and incontrovertible facts, that this document (holding up the will), copies of which you now have in your possession, is the last will and testament of Ralph Maxwell Mainwaring, executed by him on the night preceding his death, and as such entitled to stand; that this will, from the date of its execution to the day of its discovery on the seventh of July last, was wilfully and fraudulently withheld from publication, and its existence kept secret by the deceased Hugh Mainwaring. That the proponent, Harold Scott Mainwaring, is the lawful and only son of the beneficiary named therein, and as such the sole rightful and lawful heir to and owner of the Mainwaring estate. More than this, we propose at the same time and by the same evidence to forever disprove, confute, and silence any and every aspersion and insinuation which has been brought against the character of the proponent, Harold Scott Mainwaring; and in doing this, we shall at last lift the veil which, for the past five months, has hung over the Fair Oaks tragedy."

Mr. Sutherland paused to allow the tremendous excitement produced by his words to subside; then turning, he addressed himself to the judge.

"Your honor, I have to request permission of the court to depart in a slight degree from the usual custom. The witness for the defence is in an adjoining room, ready to give testimony when summoned to do so, but in this instance I have to ask that the name be withheld, and that the witness himself be identified by the contestant and his counsel."

The judge bowed in assent, and amid a silence so rigid and intense as to be almost painful, at a signal from Mr. Sutherland, the doors of an anteroom were swung noiselessly open and approaching footsteps were heard.

CHAPTER XXVII

THE SILENT WITNESS

Approaching footsteps were heard, but they were the steps of men moving slowly and unsteadily, as though carrying some heavy burden. An instant later, six men, bearing a casket beneath whose weight they staggered, entered the court-room and, making their way through the spell-bound crowd, deposited their burden near the witness stand. Immediately following were two men, one of whom was instantly recognized as Merrick, the detective; the other as the man who, a few months before, had been known as the English barrister's clerk, now wearing the full uniform of a Scotland Yard official. Bringing up the rear was an undertaker, who, amid the breathless silence which ensued, proceeded to open the casket. This done, Mr. Sutherland rose and addressed the judge, his low tones for the first time vibrating with suppressed feeling.

"Your honor, I request that William H. Whitney be first called upon to identify the witness."

Controlling his agitation by a visible effort, Mr. Whitney approached the casket, but his eyes no sooner rested on the form and features within than his forced composure gave way. With a groan he exclaimed,

"My God, it is Hugh Mainwaring!" and bending over the casket, he covered his face with his hands while he strove in vain to conceal his emotion.

His words, ringing through the hushed court-room, seemed to break the spell, and the over-wrought nerves of the people began to yield under the tremendous pressure. Mr. Sutherland raised a warning hand to check the tide of nervous excitement which threatened to sweep over the entire crowd, but it was of little avail. Piercing screams followed; women fainted and were borne from the room, and the faces of strong men blanched to a deathly pallor as they gazed at one another in mute consternation and bewilderment. For a few moments the greatest confusion reigned, but when at last order was restored and Mr. Whitney had regained his composure, Mr. Sutherland inquired, -

"Mr. Whitney, do you identify the dead man as Hugh Mainwaring?"

"I do."

"But did you not identify as Hugh Mainwaring the man who, at Fair Oaks, on or about the eighth of July last, came to his death from the effect of a gunshot wound?"

"I supposed then, and up until the present time, that it was he; there certainly was a most wonderful resemblance which I am unable to explain or account for, but this, beyond all question, is Hugh Mainwaring."

"Will you state what proof of identification you can give in this instance that was not present in the other?"

"Hugh Mainwaring had over the right temple a slight birth-mark, a red line extending upward into the hair, not always equally distinct, but always visible to one who had once observed it, and in this instance quite noticeable. I saw no trace of this mark on the face of the murdered man; but as the face was somewhat blackened by powder about the right temple, I attributed its absence to that fact, and in the excitement which followed I thought little of it. On the day of the funeral I also noted certain lines in the face which seemed unfamiliar, but

Maynard Barbour

realizing that death often makes the features of those whom we know best to seem strange to us, I thought no further of the matter. Now, however, looking upon this face, I am able to recall several differences, unnoticed then, but all of which go to prove that this is Hugh Mainwaring."

Ralph Mainwaring was the next one summoned for identification. During Mr. Whitney's examination his manner had betrayed intense agitation, and he now came forward with an expression of mingled incredulity and dread, but upon reaching the casket, he stood like one petrified, unable to move or speak, while no one who saw him could ever forget the look of horror which overspread his features.

"Mr. Mainwaring," said Mr. Sutherland at length, "do you know the dead man?"

"It is he," answered Ralph Mainwaring in a low tone, apparently speaking more to himself than to the attorney; "it is Hugh Mainwaring; that was the distinguishing mark between them."

"Do you refer to the mark of which Mr. Whitney has just spoken?"

"Yes."

"What do you mean by designating it as 'the distinguishing mark between them'?"

Ralph Mainwaring turned from the casket and faced Mr. Sutherland, but his eyes had the strained, far - away look of one gazing into the distance, unconscious of objects near him.

"It was the mark," he said, speaking with an effort, "by which, when we were boys, he was distinguished from his twin brother."

"His twin brother, Harold Scott Mainwaring?" queried

the attorney.

"Yes," the other answered, mechanically.

"Do you then identify this as Hugh Mainwaring?"

"Yes; and the other-he must have been-no, no, it could not be-great God!" Ralph Mainwaring suddenly reeled and raised his hand to his head. Mr. Whitney sprang to his assistance and led him to his chair, but in those few moments he had aged twenty years.

A number of those most intimately acquainted with Hugh Mainwaring were then called upon, all of whom identified the dead man as their late friend and associate. These preliminaries over, Mr. Sutherland arose.

"Your honor and gentlemen of the jury, before proceeding with the testimony to be introduced, I have a brief statement to make. Soon after the commencement of this action, we came into possession of indisputable evidence that Hugh Mainwaring, the supposed victim of the Fair Oaks tragedy, was still living, and that of whatever crime, if crime there were associated with that fearful event, he was not the victim but the perpetrator. We determined at all hazards to secure him, first as a witness in this case, our subsequent action to be decided by later developments. Through our special detective we succeeded in locating him, but he, upon finding himself cornered, supposing he was to be arrested for the murder of his brother, attempted suicide by shooting. The combined skill of the best surgeons obtainable, though unable to save him, yet prolonged life for three days, long enough to enable two of our number, Mr. Barton and Mr. Montague, to reach him in season to take his dying statement; a statement not only setting forth the facts relating to the will in question, but embracing also the details of the Fair Oaks tragedy and mystery. This statement, made by Hugh Mainwaring and attested by numerous witnesses present, will now be read by Mr. ontague."

Amid an impressive silence, Mr. Montague stepped to the side of the casket and, unfolding a document which he held, read the following:

"I, Hugh Mainwaring, freely and voluntarily and under no duress or compulsion, make this, my dying statement, not only as a relief to the mental anguish I have endured for the past few months, but also in the hope that I may thereby, in my last hours, help in some degree to right the wrong which my life of treachery and cowardice has wrought. To do this, I must go back over twenty-five years of crime, and beyond that to the inordinate greed and ambition that led to crime.

"My brother, Harold Scott Mainwaring, and I were twins, so marvelously alike in form and feature that our parents often had difficulty to distinguish between us, but utterly unlike in disposition, except that we both possessed a fiery temper and an indomitable will. He was the soul of honor, generous to a fault, loyal-hearted and brave, and he exacted honor and loyalty from others. He had no petty ambitions; he cared little for wealth for its own sake, still less for its votaries. I was ambitious; I loved wealth for the power which it bestowed; I would sacrifice anything for the attainment of that power, and even my boyish years were tainted with secret envy of my brother, an envy that grew with my growth, till, as we reached years of maturity, the consciousness that he, my senior by only a few hours, was yet to take precedence over me - to possess all that I coveted-became a thorn in my side whose rankling presence I never for a single waking hour forgot; it embittered my enjoyment of the present, my hopes and plans for the future.

"But of this deadly undercurrent flowing far beneath the surface neither he nor others dreamed, till, one day, a woman's face-cold, cruel, false, but beautiful, bewitchingly, entrancingly beautiful, - came between us, and from that hour all semblance of friendship was at an end. With me it was an infatuation; with him it was love, a love ready to make any sacrifice for its idol. So when our father threatened to disinherit and disown either or both of us, and the false, fickle heart of a woman was laid in the balances against the ancestral estates, I saw my opportunity for seizing the long coveted prize. We each made his choice; my brother sold his birthright for a mess of pottage; his rights were transferred to me, and my ambition was at last gratified.

"Between three and four years later, on the night of November seventeenth, within a few hours preceding his death, my father made a will, revoking the will by which he had disinherited his elder son, and restoring him again to his full right and title to the estate. This was not unexpected to me. Though no words on the subject had passed between us and my brother's name was never mentioned, I had realized for more than a year that my father was gradually relenting towards the son who had ever been his favorite, and on the last day that he was able to leave his room, I had come upon him unaware in the old picture gallery, standing before the portrait of his elder son, silent and stern, but with the tears coursing down his pallid cheeks. When, therefore, on the night preceding his death, my father demanded that an attorney be summoned, my feelings can be imagined. Just as the prize which I had so long regarded as mine was almost within my grasp, should I permit it to elude me for the gratification of a dying man's whim? Never! In my rage I could have throttled him then and there without a qualm; fear of the law alone held me back. I tried to dissuade him, but it was useless. I then bribed the servant sent to bring the attorney to report that he was out of town, and when that proved of no avail, I sent for Richard Hobson, a penniless shyster, whose lack of means and lack of principle I believed would render him an easy tool in my hands. He came; I was waiting to receive him, and we entered into compact, I little dreaming I was setting loose on my track a veritable hell-hound! The will was drawn and executed, Hobson and one Alexander McPherson, an old friend of my father's, signing as witnesses. Within twenty-four hours of its execution, Richard Hobson was richer by several hundred pounds, and the will was in my possession. Two days later, I had a false telegram sent to our place, summoning McPherson to his home in

Scotland. He left at once, before my father's burial, and his death, which occurred a few weeks later, removed the last obstacle in the way of carrying my plans into execution. My brother at that time was in Australia, but in what part of the country I did not know, nor did I try to ascertain. My constant fear was that he might in some way-though by what means I could not imagine-get some knowledge of the will and return to set up a claim to the estate. As soon as possible, therefore, notwithstanding the protests of my attorneys, I sold the estate and came to America.

"Concerning the years that followed, it is needless to go into detail; they brought me wealth, influence, power, all that I had craved, but little of happiness. Even when there came tidings of my brother's death at sea, and I felt that at last my title to the estate was secure, I had little enjoyment in its possession. Richard Hobson had already begun his black-mailing schemes, his demands growing more frequent and exorbitant with each succeeding year. Through him, also, the woman who had wrecked my brother's life received some inkling of my secret, and through this knowledge, slight as it was, gained enough of a hold over me that life was becoming an intolerable burden. Through all these years, however, I kept the will in my possession. Even after hearing of the death of my brother, a cowardly, half-superstitious dread kept me from destroying it, though doubtless I would have done so soon after making my own will had I not been prevented by circumstances unforeseen, which I will now state.

"The events which I am about to relate are stamped upon my brain as though by fire; they have haunted me day and night for the past five months. On the seventh of July last, I made and executed my will in favor of my namesake, Hugh Mainwaring, and on the following day-his birthday and mine-he was to be declared my heir. It was past eleven o'clock on the night of that day when I retired to my private library, and it was fully an hour later when, having dismissed my secretary, I finally found myself alone, as I supposed, for the night. My thoughts were far from pleasant. I had just had a stormy interview with my housekeeper, Mrs. LaGrange, who had tried, as on previous occasions, to coerce me by threats into a private marriage and a public recognition of her as my wife and of her child and mine; and, in addition, the occurrences of the day had been of a nature to recall the past, and events which I usually sought to bury in oblivion were passing before my mental vision despite my efforts to banish them. Suddenly a voice which seemed like an echo of the past recalled me to the present. Somewhat startled, I turned quickly, confronting a man who had entered unperceived from the tower-room. He was my own height and size, with curling black hair and heavy mustache, but I was unable to distinguish his features as he remained standing partly in the shadow. Before I could recover from my surprise, he again spoke, his voice still vaguely familiar.

"'The master of Fair Oaks'-the words were spoken with stinging emphasis-'seems depressed on the eve of his festal day, the day on which he is to name the heir and successor to his vast estates!'"

"I remembered that a stranger had called that day during my absence, who, my secretary had informed me, bad shown a surprising familiarity with my private plans.

"'I think,' I replied, coldly, 'that you favored me with a call this afternoon, but whatever your business then or now, you will have to defer it for a few days. I do not know how you gained admittance to these apartments at this hour, but I will see that you are escorted from them without delay,' and as I spoke I rose to ring for a servant."

"He anticipated my intention, however, and with the agility of a panther sprang noiselessly across the room, intercepting me, at the same time raising a large, English bull-dog revolver, which he levelled at me."

"'Not so fast, not so fast,' he said, softly; 'you can afford to wait a little; I have waited for years!'"

"I stood as though rooted to the spot, gazing at him with a sort of fascination. As he emerged into the light there was something almost familiar in his features, and yet something horribly incongruous and unreal. His eyes glowed like living fire; his soft, low tones reminded me of nothing so much as the purring of a tiger; while the smile that played about his lips was more terrible than anything I had ever seen on human face. It was ten times more fearful than the muzzle of the revolver confronting me, and seemed to freeze the very blood in my veins."

"You take a base advantage; I am unarmed," I sneered.

"'I knew too well with whom I had to deal to come unarmed,' he replied; 'though this,' and he lowered the revolver, 'this is not the sort of weapon you would employ,-a thrust in the dark, a stab in the back, that is your style, coward!"

"'I demand an explanation of this,' I said."

"He folded his arms, still retaining his hold upon the weapon, as he answered, 'Explanations will follow in due time; but surely, on the eve of the fiftieth anniversary of such a life as yours, congratulations are first in order. Allow me to congratulate you, Hugh Mainwaring, upon the success which has attended and crowned the past twenty-five years of your life! upon the rich harvest you have reaped during all these years; the amassed wealth, the gratified ambitions, the almost illimitable power, the adulation and homage,-all so precious to your sordid soul, and for which you have bartered honor, happiness, character, all, in short, that life is worth. Standing, as you do to-night, at the fiftieth milestone on life's journey, I congratulate you upon your recollections of the past, and upon your anticipations for the future, as you descend to an unhonored and unloved old age!'"

"Every word was heaped with scorn, and, as I looked into the burning eyes fixed upon mine and watched the sardonic smile hovering about his lips, I wondered whether he were some

Mephistopheles-some fiend incarnate-sent to torture me, or whether he were really flesh and blood."

"The mocking smile now left his face, but his eyes held me speechless as he continued,-"

"No wonder that memories of bygone years haunted your thoughts to-night! Memories, perhaps, of a father whose dying will you disregarded; of a brother whom you twice defrauded,-once of the honor and sanctity of his home, then, as if that were not enough, of his birthright,-his heritage from generations of our race -"

"'Stop!' I cried, stung to anger by his accusations and startled by the strange words, 'our race,' which seemed to fall so familiarly from his lips. 'Stop! are you mad?' Do you know what you are saying? Once more I demand that you state who or what you are, and your business here!"

"'That is quickly stated, Hugh Mainwaring,' he answered, in tones which made my heart beat with a strange dread; 'I am Harold Scott Mainwaring! I am here to claim no brotherhood or kinship with you, but to claim and to have my own, the birthright restored to me by the last will and testament of a dying father, of which you have defrauded me for twenty-five years!"

"'You are a liar and an impostor!' I cried, enraged at the sound of my brother's name, and for the instant believing the man to be some emissary of Hobson's who had used it to work upon my feelings."

"Drawing himself up to his full height, his eyes blazing, he answered in low tones, 'Dare you apply those epithets to me, usurper that you are? You are a liar and a thief, and if you had your deserts you would be in a felon's cell to-night, or transported to the wilds of Australia! I an impostor? See and judge for yourself!' and with a sudden, swift movement the black curling hair and mustache were dashed to the floor, and he stood before me the exact counterpart of myself. Stunned by the transformation, I gazed at him speechless; it was like looking in a mirror, feature for feature identically the same! For a few seconds my brain seemed to reel from the shock, but his tones recalled me to myself."

"'Ah!' he said, with mocking emphasis, 'who is the impostor now?'"

"My first thought was of self-vindication, and to effect, if possible, a compromise with him. 'I am no impostor or usurper,' I said, 'because, believing you dead, I have used that to which in the event of your death I would be legally entitled even had you any claim, and I am willing, not as an acknowledgment of any valid claim on your part, but as a concession on my own part, to give you a liberal share in the estate, or to pay you any reasonable sum which you may require -'"

"He stopped me with an intolerant gesture. 'Do not attempt any palliation of the past with me,' he said, sternly; 'it is worse than useless; and do not think that you can make any compromises with me or purchase my silence with your ill gotten wealth. That may have served your purpose in the past with your associate and coadjutor, Richard Hobson, the man who holds in his mercenary grasp the flimsy reputation which is all that is left to you, or with the woman-cruel as the grave and false as hell-who once wrecked my life, and now, with the son that you dare not acknowledge, rules your home, but you cannot buy my silence. I come to you as no beggar! I am a richer man to-day than you, but for the sake of generations past, as well as of generations yet to come, I will have my own. The estate which was once my forefathers shall be my son's, and his sons' after him!'"

"As I listened, my whole soul rose against him in bitter hatred, the old hatred of my youth. 'I defy you,' I' cried, hotly, 'to produce one atom of proof in support of your claim or of your charges against me! The estate is mine, and I will make you rue the day that you dare dispute my right and title to it!'"

"His eyes flashed with scorn as he replied, 'You lie, Hugh Mainwaring! Your life for the past twenty-five years has been nothing but a lie, and the day just closed has witnessed the final act in this farce of yours. That I have already undone, and just as surely I will undo the work of the past years. And let me assure you I have no lack of proof with which to verify either my own claim or any assertion I have made, or may yet make, against you. I have proof that on the night preceding my father's death he made a will restoring to me my full rights, which you have fraudulently withheld all these years; and through my son, whom you have known for the past eighteen months as your private secretary, I have proof that that will is still in existence, of itself an irrefutable witness against you!'"

"With the mention of my secretary the truth flashed upon me. I realized I was completely in his power, and with a sense of my own impotency my rage and hatred increased. Forgetful of the weapon in his hand and almost blind with fury, I sprang towards him, intending to throttle him-to strangle him-until he should plead for mercy. Instantly he raised the revolver in warning, but not before I had seized his wrist, turning the weapon from myself. A brief struggle followed, in which I soon found my strength was no match for his. Growing desperate, I summoned all my strength for one tremendous effort, at the same time holding his wrist in a vice-like grip, forcing his hand higher and turning the revolver more and more in his direction. Suddenly there was a flash, - a sharp report, - and he fell heavily to the floor, dragging me down upon him."

"For an instant I was too much stunned and bewildered to realize what had happened, but a glance at my opponent revealed the situation. He lay motionless where he had fallen, and a ghastly wound over the right eye told the terrible story. Dazed with horror, I placed my hand over his heart, but there was no motion, no life, - he was dead! The awful truth forced itself upon me. Mad and blind with rage, I had turned the weapon upon him and it had discharged,-whether by some sudden movement of his hand, or by the accidental pressure of my own fingers upon the trigger, God alone knows, I do not!

Maynard Barbour

One fact I could not then, nor ever can, forget; it was my hand that gave the weapon its deadly aim, however blindly or unwittingly, and the blood of my brother whom I had wronged and defrauded now lay at my door."

"The agony of remorse that followed was something beyond description, beyond any suffering of which I had ever dreamed; but suddenly a thought flashed upon me which added new horror, causing me to spring to my feet cold with terror, while great beads of perspiration gathered on my brow. When that terrible scene should be revealed, not alone in the approaching morning light, but in the light of past events which, if the last words spoken by those lips now sealed in death were true, could no longer be kept secret, what would be the world's verdict?" Murder! fratricide! and I? Great God! of what avail would be any plea of mine in the face of such damning evidence?

"I rushed to the tower-room, and hastily opening my safe, took from a private drawer therein a key and with trembling fingers fitted it into the lock of a large metallic box which contained the family jewels, and which for more than twenty-five years had held the old will executed by my father on his death-bed. I had seen it there less than forty-eight hours before, and in my desperation I now determined to destroy it. My very haste and eagerness delayed me, but at last the cover flew back, revealing the gleaming jewels, but-the will was not there! Unable to believe my own eyes, I drew my fingers carefully back and forth through the narrow receptacle where it had lain, and among the satin linings of the various compartments, but in vain; the will was gone! My brother had spoken the truth, and the will was doubtless in the possession of his son, who, under its terms, was now himself heir to the estate. The room grew dim and the walls themselves seemed to whirl swiftly about me as, with great difficulty, I groped my way back to the library, where I stood gazing at that strange counterpart of myself, till, under the growing horror of the situation, it seemed to my benumbed senses as though I were some disembodied spirit hovering above his own corpse. The horrible illusion was like a nightmare; I could not throw it off, and I would then and there have gone stark, staring mad, but that there came to me out of that awful chaos of fancies a suggestion which seemed like an inspiration. 'It is Hugh Mainwaring,' I said to myself, 'Hugh Mainwaring died to-night!'"

"My fevered brain grew cool, my pulse steady, and my nerves firm as I proceeded at once to act upon the idea. Kneeling beside the dead man, I examined the wound. The bullet had entered above the right eye and passed downward, coming out at the base of the brain; from both wounds the blood was flowing in a slow, sluggish stream. Drawing a large hand-kerchief from my pocket, I bound it tightly about the head over both wounds, knotting it firmly; then carrying the body into the tower-room, I made sure that all doors were locked, and proceeded to put into execution the plan so suddenly formed. By this time I was myself, and, though the task before me was neither easy nor pleasant to perform, I went about it as calmly and methodically as though it were some ordinary business transaction. As expeditiously as possible I removed the dead man's clothing and my own, which I then exchanged, dressing the lifeless form in the clothes I had worn on the preceding day, even to the dressing-gown which I had put on upon retiring to my apartments, while I donned his somewhat travel-worn suit of tweed. Having completed this gruesome task, I left the body in much the same position in which it had originally fallen, lying slightly upon the right side, the right arm extended on the floor, and, to give the appearance of suicide, I placed my own revolver-first emptying one of the chambers-near his right hand. On going to my desk for the revolver, I discovered the explanation of my brother's words when he said that he had already undone my work of the preceding day, the final act of the farce I had carried out. In the terrible excitement of those moments his meaning escaped my mind; now it was clear. My own will, executed with such care, and which early in the evening I had left upon my desk, was gone. That he had destroyed it in his wrath and scorn I had abundant proof a little later, upon incidentally finding in the small grate in that room the partially burned fragments of the document, which I left to tell their own tale."

"Having satisfactorily disposed of Hugh Mainwaring (as the dead man now seemed to my over-wrought imagination), I made preparation for my immediate departure. This occupied little time. There was fortunately some cash in the safe, which I took; all drafts and papers of that nature I left,-they were of value only to Hugh Mainwaring, and he was dead! As the cash would be inadequate, however, for my needs, I decided after considerable deliberation to take the family jewels, though not without apprehension that they might lead to my detection, as they finally did. These I put in a small box covered with ordinary wrapping-paper to attract as little attention as possible,' and, having completed my preparations, I removed the bandage from the dead man's head and threw it with the private keys to my library into the metallic box which had held the jewels. Then donning the black wig and mustache which my visitor had thrown aside on disclosing his identity, together with a long ulster which he had left in the tower-room, I took one farewell look at the familiar apartments and their silent occupant and stole noiselessly out into the night. I remained on the premises only long enough to visit the small lake in the rear of the house, into which I threw the metallic box and its contents, then, following the walk through the grove to the side street, I left Fair Oaks, as I well knew, forever. While yet on the grounds I met my own coachman, but he failed to recognize me in my disguise. My plans were already formed. I had come to the conclusion that my late visitor and the caller of the preceding afternoon, whose card bore the name of J. Henry Carruthers, were one and the same. My secretary had stated that Carruthers had come out from the city that day, so my appearance at the depot, dressed in his own disguise, would probably attract no attention. I was fortunate enough to reach the depot just as two trains were about to pull out; the suburban train which would leave in three minutes for the city, and the north-bound express, due to leave five minutes later. I bought a ticket for New York, then passing around the rear of the suburban train, quietly boarded the express, and before the discovery of that night's fearful tragedy I was speeding towards the great West."

"But go where I might, from that hour to this, I have never been free from agonizing remorse, nor have I been able for one moment to banish from my memory the sight of that face, - the face of my brother, killed by my own hand, and a discovery which I made within the first few hours of my flight made my remorse ten times deeper. In going through the pockets of the suit I wore I found a letter from my brother, addressed to his son, written in my own library and at my own desk while he awaited my coming. He seemed to have had a sort of presentiment that his interview with me might end in some such tragedy as it did, and took that opportunity to inform his son regarding both his past work and his plans for the future. What was my astonishment to find that his son was, at that time, as totally unaware of his father's existence as was I a few hours before of the existence of a brother!"

"From this letter I learned that the son had been given away at birth, and was to know nothing of his true parentage until he had reached years of maturity; that he himself had been shipwrecked, as reported years ago, but had escaped in some miraculous manner; that reaching Africa at last, he disclosed his identity to no one, but devoted all his energies to acquiring a fortune for his son. He succeeded even beyond his anticipations, and when nearly twenty years had elapsed, sailed for his old Australian home, to find his son. Arriving there, he learned that his son, while pursuing his studies in England, had obtained information of the will made in his father's favor, and learning facts which led him to believe that the will was still in existence and in the possession of his father's younger brother, had, with the advice of his London attorneys, gone to America, and was then in his uncle's employ for the purpose of securing proof regarding the will, and, if possible, possession of the will itself. Upon learning these facts, my brother had immediately proceeded to London and to Barton & Barton, his son's attorneys, who, upon his arrival there, informed him of his son's success up to that time, and also notified him that his brother was about to celebrate his approaching fiftieth birthday by naming the son of Ralph Mainwaring as his heir, Ralph Mainwaring and family having just sailed to America for that purpose. My brother then took the first steamer for America, arriving only two days later than Ralph Mainwaring. Though unable to obtain an interview with me at once, as he had intended, he had succeeded in catching sight of me, in order to assure himself that the marked resemblance between us still existed, and, to emphasize that resemblance, he then shaved and had his hair cut in the same style in which I wore mine, so as to render the likeness the more striking and indisputable when he should announce himself to me."

"His existence and return he wished kept secret from his son until the successful consummation of his plans, but he wrote the letter as an explanation in case there should be any unforeseen termination. The letter was overflowing with a father's love and pride; his allusion to the difficulty with which he had restrained his feelings when he found himself face to face with his son on the afternoon of his call, being especially touching. The perusal of that letter added a hundred-fold to my own grief and remorse. I dared not run the risk of disclosing myself by sending it to my brother's son, but I have preserved it carefully for him, and desire it to be given him as quickly as possible."

"Through New York papers I learned from time to time of the murder of Hugh Mainwaring, the lost will, the discovery of the old will, and the appearance of the rightful heir. From that source, also, I learned that Merrick, the detective, was shadowing the murderer, who was generally supposed to be a man by the name of Carruthers. I had one advantage of Merrick. I knew him-my old friend Whitney having often pointed him out to me-while he did not know the man he sought. Many a time in my wanderings I have seen him, and, knowing well the game he was after, eluded him, only to fall at last into the snare of one whom I did not know. The man searching for the murderer of Hugh Mainwaring encountered another, trailing the murderer of Harold Scott Mainwaring, and I suddenly ound my time had come! A coward then, as always, I tried to shoot myself. In the darkness I held the muzzle of my brother's revolver to my own temple; instantly there flashed before me his face when I had killed him! I grew sick, my hand trembled and dropped; then, as my pursuers came nearer, I aimed for my heart and fired! This is the result. Death was not instantaneous, as I had hoped; instead, I was given this opportunity to make some slight reparation for my sin; to aid, as I said before, in righting the wrong wrought by my past life."

"And now, in these my last moments, I do solemnly affirm and aver that on the night preceding his death, my father executed a will restoring to my elder brother his full right and title, which will I have for more than twenty-five years last past wrongfully and fraudulently withheld and concealed; and that my brother being now dead, killed by my own hand, though unwittingly and unintentionally, his son, Harold Scott Mainwaring, is the rightful and sole heir to the entire Mainwaring estate."

"Signed by Hugh Mainwaring in the presence of the following witnesses: William J. Barton, M. D. Montague, Joseph P. Sturgiss, M.D., M. J. Wheating, M.D., Daniel McCabe and C. D. Merrick."

At the conclusion of this statement, there was shown in evidence the rusty metallic box-dragged from the lake-with the keys and the knotted, blood-stained handkerchief found therein. This was followed by brief testimony by Harold Scott Mainwaring and the old servant, James Wilson, but the proceedings following the reading of the statement were little more than mere form. There was little attempt at cross-examination, and when the time came for the argument by counsel for contestant, Mr. Whitney, who had been deeply affected by the confession of his old friend, declined to speak.

All eyes were fastened upon Mr. Sutherland as he arose, as was supposed, for the closing argument. For a moment his eyes scanned the faces of the jurors, man by man, then addressing the judge, he said slowly, in clear, resonant tones,-

"Your honor, I submit the case without argument."

In less than forty-five minutes from the conclusion of the statement the jury retired, but no one moved from his place in the crowded court-room, for all felt that little time would be required for their decision. In ten minutes they returned, and, amid the silence that followed, the foreman announced the verdict, "for the proponent, Harold Scott Mainwaring."

Cheers burst forth from all parts of the room, and the walls rang with applause, which was only checked by a sudden, simultaneous movement of several men towards the contestant. With the announcement of the verdict, Ralph Mainwaring had risen to his feet, as though in protest. For an instant he stood gasping helplessly, but unable to utter a word; then, with a loud groan, he sank backward and would have fallen to the floor but for his attorneys, who had rushed to the assistance of the stricken man.

A few moments later the lifeless remains of Hugh Mainwaring were carried from the court-room, while, in another direction, the unconscious form of Ralph Mainwaring was borne by tender, pitying hands, among them those of the victor himself, and the contest of Mainwaring versus Mainwaring was ended.

* * * * * * * *

The bright sunlight of a December afternoon, ten days after the close of the trial, crowned with a shining halo the heads of Harold Scott Mainwaring and his wife as they stood together in the tower-room at Fair Oaks. But a few hours had elapsed since they had repeated the words of the beautiful marriage service which had made them husband and wife. Their wedding had been, of necessity, a quiet one, only their own party and a few of their American friends being present, for the ocean-liner, then lying in the harbor, but which in a few hours was to bear them homeward, would carry also the bodies of the Mainwaring brothers and of Ralph Mainwaring to their last resting place.

Here, amid the very surroundings where it was written, Harold Mainwaring had just read to his wife his father's letter, penned a few hours before his death. For a few moments neither spoke, then Winifred said brokenly, through fast falling tears,-

"How he loved you, Harold!"

"Yes," he replied, sadly; "and what would I not give for one hour in which to assure him of my love! I would gladly have endured any suffering for his sake, but in the few moments that we stood face to face we met as strangers, and I have had no opportunity to show him my appreciation of his love or my love for him in return."

"Don't think he does not know it," she said, earnestly. "I believe that he now knows your love for him far more perfectly than you know his."

He kissed her tenderly, then drawing from his pocket a memorandum-book, took therefrom a piece of blotter having upon it the impress of some writing. Placing it upon the desk beside the letter, he held a small mirror against it, and Winifred, looking in the mirror, read, "Your affectionate father,

"HAROLD SCOTT MAINWARING."

Then glancing at the signature to the letter, she saw they were identical. In answer to her look of inquiry, Harold said,-

"I discovered that impress on the blotter on this desk one morning about ten days after the tragedy, and at once recognized it as my father's writing. In a flash I understood the situation; my father himself had returned, had been in these rooms, and had had an interview with his brother! I knew of the marked resemblance between them, and at once questioned, How had that interview ended? Who was the murdered man? Who was the murderer? That was the cause of my trip to England to try to find some light on this subject. I need no words to tell you the agony of suspense that I endured for the next few weeks, and you will understand now why I would not-even to yourself-declare my innocence of the murder of Hugh Mainwaring. I would have bourne any ignominy and dishonor, even death itself, rather than that a breath of suspicion should have been directed against my father's name."

"My hero!" she exclaimed, smiling through her tears; then asked, "When and how did you learn the real facts?"

"Almost immediately upon my return to this country, and from Mrs. LaGrange," and he told her briefly of his last interview with that unhappy woman. "Up to the day of the funeral, she was ignorant of the truth, but on that day she detected the difference, which none of the others saw. She knew and recognized my father."

Standing at last on the western veranda, they took their farewell of Fair Oaks.

"Beautiful Fair Oaks!" Winifred murmured; "once I loved you; but you could never be our home; you hold memories far too bitter!"

"Yes," Harold replied, gravely, "it is darkened by crime and stained with innocent blood. The only bright feature to redeem it," he added with a smile, "is the memory of the love I found there, but that," and he drew her arm closely within his own, "I take with me to England, to my father's home and mine."

Together they left the majestic arched portals, and going down the oak-lined avenue, through the dim twilight of the great boughs interlocked above their heads, passed on, out into the sunlight, with never a fear for shadows that might come; each strong and confident in the love that united them "for better for worse, for richer for poorer, in sickness and in health, . . . till death us do part."

Choose from Thousands of 1stWorldLibrary Classics By

A. M. Barnard
Ada Leverson
Adolphus William Ward
Aesop
Agatha Christie
Alexander Aaronsohn
Alexander Kielland
Alexandre Dumas
Alfred Gatty
Alfred Ollivant
Alice Duer Miller
Alice Turner Curtis
Alice Dunbar
Allen Chapman
Alleyne Ireland
Ambrose Bierce
Amelia E. Barr
Amory H. Bradford
Andrew Lang
Andrew McFarland Davis
Andy Adams
Angela Brazil
Anna Alice Chapin
Anna Sewell
Annie Besant
Annie Hamilton Donnell
Annie Payson Call
Annie Roe Carr
Annonaymous
Anton Chekhov
Archibald Lee Fletcher
Arnold Bennett
Arthur C. Benson
Arthur Conan Doyle
Arthur M. Winfield
Arthur Ransome
Arthur Schnitzler
Arthur Train
Atticus
B.H. Baden-Powell
B. M. Bower
B. C. Chatterjee
Baroness Emmuska Orczy
Baroness Orczy
Basil King
Bayard Taylor
Ben Macomber
Bertha Muzzy Bower
Bjornstjerne Bjornson

Booth Tarkington
Boyd Cable
Bram Stoker
C. Collodi
C. E. Orr
C. M. Ingleby
Carolyn Wells
Catherine Parr Traill
Charles A. Eastman
Charles Amory Beach
Charles Dickens
Charles Dudley Warner
Charles Farrar Browne
Charles Ives
Charles Kingsley
Charles Klein
Charles Hanson Towne
Charles Lathrop Pack
Charles Romyn Dake
Charles Whibley
Charles Willing Beale
Charlotte M. Braeme
Charlotte M. Yonge
Charlotte Perkins Stetson
Clair W. Hayes
Clarence Day Jr.
Clarence E. Mulford
Clemence Housman
Confucius
Coningsby Dawson
Cornelis DeWitt Wilcox
Cyril Burleigh
D. H. Lawrence
Daniel Defoe
David Garnett
Dinah Craik
Don Carlos Janes
Donald Keyhoe
Dorothy Kilner
Dougan Clark
Douglas Fairbanks
E. Nesbit
E. P. Roe
E. Phillips Oppenheim
E. S. Brooks
Earl Barnes
Edgar Rice Burroughs
Edith Van Dyne
Edith Wharton

Edward Everett Hale
Edward J. O'Biren
Edward S. Ellis
Edwin L. Arnold
Eleanor Atkins
Eleanor Hallowell Abbott
Eliot Gregory
Elizabeth Gaskell
Elizabeth McCracken
Elizabeth Von Arnim
Ellem Key
Emerson Hough
Emilie F. Carlen
Emily Bronte
Emily Dickinson
Enid Bagnold
Enilor Macartney Lane
Erasmus W. Jones
Ernie Howard Pie
Ethel May Dell
Ethel Turner
Ethel Watts Mumford
Eugene Sue
Eugenie Foa
Eugene Wood
Eustace Hale Ball
Evelyn Everett-green
Everard Cotes
F. H. Cheley
F. J. Cross
F. Marion Crawford
Fannie E. Newberry
Federick Austin Ogg
Ferdinand Ossendowski
Fergus Hume
Florence A. Kilpatrick
Fremont B. Deering
Francis Bacon
Francis Darwin
Frances Hodgson Burnett
Frances Parkinson Keyes
Frank Gee Patchin
Frank Harris
Frank Jewett Mather
Frank L. Packard
Frank V. Webster
Frederic Stewart Isham
Frederick Trevor Hill
Frederick Winslow Taylor

Friedrich Kerst
Friedrich Nietzsche
Fyodor Dostoyevsky
G.A. Henty
G.K. Chesterton
Gabrielle E. Jackson
Garrett P. Serviss
Gaston Leroux
George A. Warren
George Ade
Geroge Bernard Shaw
George Cary Eggleston
George Durston
George Ebers
George Eliot
George Gissing
George MacDonald
George Meredith
George Orwell
George Sylvester Viereck
George Tucker
George W. Cable
George Wharton James
Gertrude Atherton
Gordon Casserly
Grace E. King
Grace Gallatin
Grace Greenwood
Grant Allen
Guillermo A. Sherwell
Gulielma Zollinger
Gustav Flaubert
H. A. Cody
H. B. Irving
H.C. Bailey
H. G. Wells
H. H. Munro
H. Irving Hancock
H. R. Naylor
H. Rider Haggard
H. W. C. Davis
Haldeman Julius
Hall Caine
Hamilton Wright Mabie
Hans Christian Andersen
Harold Avery
Harold McGrath
Harriet Beecher Stowe
Harry Castlemon
Harry Coghill
Harry Houidini

Hayden Carruth
Helent Hunt Jackson
Helen Nicolay
Hendrik Conscience
Hendy David Thoreau
Henri Barbusse
Henrik Ibsen
Henry Adams
Henry Ford
Henry Frost
Henry James
Henry Jones Ford
Henry Seton Merriman
Henry W Longfellow
Herbert A. Giles
Herbert Carter
Herbert N. Casson
Herman Hesse
Hildegard G. Frey
Homer
Honore De Balzac
Horace B. Day
Horace Walpole
Horatio Alger Jr.
Howard Pyle
Howard R. Garis
Hugh Lofting
Hugh Walpole
Humphry Ward
Ian Maclaren
Inez Haynes Gillmore
Irving Bacheller
Isabel Cecilia Williams
Isabel Hornibrook
Israel Abrahams
Ivan Turgenev
J.G.Austin
J. Henri Fabre
J. M. Barrie
J. M. Walsh
J. Macdonald Oxley
J. R. Miller
J. S. Fletcher
J. S. Knowles
J. Storer Clouston
J. W. Duffield
Jack London
Jacob Abbott
James Allen
James Andrews
James Baldwin

James Branch Cabell
James DeMille
James Joyce
James Lane Allen
James Lane Allen
James Oliver Curwood
James Oppenheim
James Otis
James R. Driscoll
Jane Abbott
Jane Austen
Jane L. Stewart
Janet Aldridge
Jens Peter Jacobsen
Jerome K. Jerome
Jessie Graham Flower
John Buchan
John Burroughs
John Cournos
John F. Kennedy
John Gay
John Glasworthy
John Habberton
John Joy Bell
John Kendrick Bangs
John Milton
John Philip Sousa
John Taintor Foote
Jonas Lauritz Idemil Lie
Jonathan Swift
Joseph A. Altsheler
Joseph Carey
Joseph Conrad
Joseph E. Badger Jr
Joseph Hergesheimer
Joseph Jacobs
Jules Vernes
Julian Hawthrone
Julie A Lippmann
Justin Huntly McCarthy
Kakuzo Okakura
Karle Wilson Baker
Kate Chopin
Kenneth Grahame
Kenneth McGaffey
Kate Langley Bosher
Kate Langley Bosher
Katherine Cecil Thurston
Katherine Stokes
L. A. Abbot
L. T. Meade

L. Frank Baum
Latta Griswold
Laura Dent Crane
Laura Lee Hope
Laurence Housman
Lawrence Beasley
Leo Tolstoy
Leonid Andreyev
Lewis Carroll
Lewis Sperry Chafer
Lilian Bell
Lloyd Osbourne
Louis Hughes
Louis Joseph Vance
Louis Tracy
Louisa May Alcott
Lucy Fitch Perkins
Lucy Maud Montgomery
Luther Benson
Lydia Miller Middleton
Lyndon Orr
M. Corvus
M. H. Adams
Margaret E. Sangster
Margret Howth
Margaret Vandercook
Margaret W. Hungerford
Margret Penrose
Maria Edgeworth
Maria Thompson Daviess
Mariano Azuela
Marion Polk Angellotti
Mark Overton
Mark Twain
Mary Austin
Mary Catherine Crowley
Mary Cole
Mary Hastings Bradley
Mary Roberts Rinehart
Mary Rowlandson
M. Wollstonecraft Shelley
Maud Lindsay
Max Beerbohm
Myra Kelly
Nathaniel Hawthrone
Nicolo Machiavelli
O. F. Walton
Oscar Wilde

Owen Johnson
P.G. Wodehouse
Paul and Mabel Thorne
Paul G. Tomlinson
Paul Severing
Percy Brebner
Percy Keese Fitzhugh
Peter B. Kyne
Plato
Quincy Allen
R. Derby Holmes
R. L. Stevenson
R. S. Ball
Rabindranath Tagore
Rahul Alvares
Ralph Bonehill
Ralph Henry Barbour
Ralph Victor
Ralph Waldo Emmerson
Rene Descartes
Ray Cummings
Rex Beach
Rex E. Beach
Richard Harding Davis
Richard Jefferies
Richard Le Gallienne
Robert Barr
Robert Frost
Robert Gordon Anderson
Robert L. Drake
Robert Lansing
Robert Lynd
Robert Michael Ballantyne
Robert W. Chambers
Rosa Nouchette Carey
Rudyard Kipling
Saint Augustine
Samuel B. Allison
Samuel Hopkins Adams
Sarah Bernhardt
Sarah C. Hallowell
Selma Lagerlof
Sherwood Anderson
Sigmund Freud
Standish O'Grady
Stanley Weyman
Stella Benson
Stella M. Francis

Stephen Crane
Stewart Edward White
Stijn Streuvels
Swami Abhedananda
Swami Parmananda
T. S. Ackland
T. S. Arthur
The Princess Der Ling
Thomas A. Janvier
Thomas A Kempis
Thomas Anderton
Thomas Bailey Aldrich
Thomas Bulfinch
Thomas De Quincey
Thomas Dixon
Thomas H. Huxley
Thomas Hardy
Thomas More
Thornton W. Burgess
U. S. Grant
Upton Sinclair
Valentine Williams
Various Authors
Vaughan Kester
Victor Appleton
Victor G. Durham
Victoria Cross
Virginia Woolf
Wadsworth Camp
Walter Camp
Walter Scott
Washington Irving
Wilbur Lawton
Wilkie Collins
Willa Cather
Willard F. Baker
William Dean Howells
William le Queux
W. Makepeace Thackeray
William W. Walter
William Shakespeare
Winston Churchill
Yei Theodora Ozaki
Yogi Ramacharaka
Young E. Allison
Zane Grey